The Man from Tegner

The Man from Tegner

Ruth Stockhouse

VANTAGE PRESS
New York/Los Angeles/Chicago

FIRST EDITION

Published by Vantage Press, Inc.
516 West 34th Street, New York, New York 10001

Manufactured in the United States of America
ISBN: 0-533-08303-6
Library of Congress Catalog Card No.: 88-90461

Contents

The Man from Tegner

Part One

The Stranger

Chapter One

Early one evening during the supper hour, a middle-aged man called Spenner stepped into a Greek cafe in a rather rundown area of the city of Tegner. He was dressed too lightly for the coolness of the weather and, astonishingly, his clothes and his head were soaking wet though it had not rained. Yet the man seemed oblivious of his appearance; his face showed no concern or anxiety. Instead, he looked angry and frustrated and his countenance was serious and grim.

His shoulders slouched over but he walked with gritty determination to a table near the front window and along the wall so he could see all who entered and he, too, could be seen from the outside of the cafe. He was watching for the man who was following him.

Spenner had just come from the city park, several blocks away, where he was seen and followed by a man who had been watching him for the past week. Today, the man had followed him to the outdoor cage of the polar bears in the park zoo. Yesterday, the man had seated himself on a bench and peered at Spenner from behind a newspaper. Earlier, when Spenner first became aware of him, the man had circled the drinking fountain many times, lowered his head, pretending to drink, but raising his eyes to look directly at Spenner. The man remained in the park as long as Spenner, looking at him from a distance and trying, like a boil, to be unnoticed.

The man was plainly not a professional hireling of any sort; he was too obvious and clumsy and possessed no stealth or slyness. Spenner had caught on to him immediately. The man was like a stray dog, afraid, circling around some human he had attached himself to but not daring to come near. He did use camouflage in dress for his clothes were drab and inconspicuous, always the same dark trousers and jacket and a knit cap on his head. Spenner had grunted and laughed to himself when he first observed the man and thought him a simpleton, but Spenner was annoyed and irritated also and he had to be suspicious for *whatever* did this fool want of him?

3

Now Spenner was not a steady worker and he had no skills in any craft. He took whatever odd jobs he could get at a multitude of chores. When he was not working, as now, he became a park loafer, taking a daily stroll to the city park, passing time away sitting on a bench doing nothing. His isolation and existence had been entirely his own decision; he preferred to live in obscurity and he believed his life could continue to be thus, that is, until the past week when he had been vexed by the appearance of this strange man.

Spenner's first response was to keep this man-dog on a string and make him believe that he was unaware of him. Spenner just continued his present habits. He selected the same park bench which now received most of the diluted warmth of the sun for an unusual chillness had come with the early days of autumn. Soon the man would appear and go through his curious behavior of spying. For a week Spenner had the patience to bear this stiff exhibition of himself while the idiot-stray ogled him over drinking fountains and from behind newspapers.

It was enough!

Spenner decided to test and confront the man directly. He changed his place, moving to a bench near the zoo. If the man was not another park loafer, which Spenner doubted, he would follow after and find him. The bench Spenner selected was in the shade and his thin jacket was not heavy enough to keep him from becoming chilled and uncomfortable. He waited a long while. The cold was becoming more penetrating and Spenner's limbs began to ache and he shivered. "Ah!" he said aloud in disgust and silently he cursed the man for provoking him to change his habits and bring this wretchedness upon him. He was thinking of returning to the bench in the sun when he saw the man turn the corner at the animal house. The man seemed flustered and exhausted and he was breathing heavily. He had been walking so rapidly that when he slowed his pace, he almost stumbled to the side. He stopped abruptly when he saw Spenner but it was too late to look away for Spenner gave him a look of recognition, staring directly at him. The man stared back for a moment, with a quick, satisfying look, then he sighed and tried to relax and appear nonchalant as he turned his face away toward the polar bear cage.

"Ah!" Spenner muttered again. "It is absurd. *It is absurd!*" Physically cold and aching and filled with resentment, Spenner pushed himself to his feet and straightened his body. He walked directly

4

toward the zoo, but away from the man, to the last cage which housed black bears. His idea was to be completely visual, then walk back toward the man, advancing on him very slowly. The man would have the choice to move away if he chose; otherwise Spenner intended to challenge him directly.

The man stood with his head down and his hands in his pockets. He did not move but he had braced himself for his thick, sturdy body looked tense and rigid. Spenner moved gradually along before the cages. He drew close and stopped. He waited only a moment, then turned quickly and looked straight at the man. The man was surprised but reacted in kind, his look was drawn to Spenner and the two of them stared at each other. Strange, but at this close proximity, the man looked funny, almost silly. His face was circular with comic proportions but covered with coarse, reddish-brown, burned-looking skin. His eyes were large and round with glint of amicability, reminding Spenner again of the dog but one which wishes to be friendly.

Nevertheless, Spenner's gaze was stern and challenging, full of the anger he felt and, if there could be violent action in a look, the man would have been whipped. The man was startled by this aversion and he stepped back. His gaze flickered instinctively and his lips parted as if to utter a cry, or had he intended to smile?

"What is it, you fool?" Spenner asked aloud. "What do you want of me? I have seen you watching me for the past week. What are you up to? I refuse to put up with this . . ."

At that moment, an unexpected, almost ridiculous incident occurred. Without warning, a large polar bear dived into the pool and sent water spraying about like a geyser. Spenner was caught unawares and the water doused over him as if he were under a fountain. He was shocked and stunned and jerked himself about. The bear surfaced and shook himself; his mouth opened and he looked as if he were laughing. Spenner turned back to the man who was also startled and he looked no better than the animal for his face became quizzical and humorous as his lips turned upward in a smirk. Spenner suspected that an incredulous mirth was coming over the man. The man's body lost its rigidity, he relaxed and seemed to sag. His eyes glistened and his lips parted again, wider than before, but, lo, he did not laugh.

Spenner remained stunned and he could not move or react. The cold water added numbness to his already chilled and aching body. His anger deepened but it could only smolder within him and now

5

he was mortified. He had planned to be fearless and indignant, he wanted to intimidate this man he thought a fool. Instead, his domineering pose was broken. He could not utter a word. His determination had disappeared and he had the comic appearance of being fully dressed and wet with the water running down his face and dripping from his nose. He could only glare at the man leaning against the fence and trying to restrain his amusement. Spenner's anger turned inward and he told himself, "Get away. Get away from this fool. Leave him and get away!" He backed away but now he was the one who stumbled as he turned around, trying to hurry.

Spenner followed a path to leave the park and not once did he look back, not caring whether or not the man came after him. When he arrived at the park exit, he found that the gate was closed. The street outside was being repaired. It was now a gaping hole and he could not cross. Cement dust swirled like a low fog amongst a potpourri of machine noises and stress sounds of commands and directions from the working men. At times, the sounds would halt, then resume like a burst of gunfire. Spenner had to walk another block to the next exit. The road was clear and he crossed over and then headed back to the other side of the street. His route enabled Spenner to see the park and the path he had taken directly across the street and he saw the man, following him, moving along in the same, stray-dog manner. Now Spenner noticed that the stumbling gait of the man was due to a decided limp in his right leg, a defect made more obvious as the man was trying to walk rapidly. He kept his eyes on Spenner, all pretext and pretense gone, as he stumbled along beside the clouds of cement dust.

Spenner headed for the Greek cafe. He had to turn from the street into an area of small shops and stores. The cement dust had drifted over them and brought dirt and an added stench to the area. Spenner walked fast, not unaware of the squalid surroundings, but goaded by the bad mood still upon him and the presence of the man trailing him. He stepped inside the cafe and was smothered by the pungent aroma of spicy cooking and the heat of the room. He shivered once, without control, as the warm atmosphere collided with his cold, aching body. He dropped into the chair and his shoulders pressed back against the wall, but his head was erect and he was staring at the window.

At the moment, the cafe was half filled with patrons but there

6

was such a general commotion of talk and rattling of dishes that the place seemed more crowded than it actually was. Slowly, Spenner became tantalized by the warmth and the food odors in the cafe. He was also heartened, for he knew that today the restaurant would serve potato soup. Between jobs, he ate mostly soup because he could not afford more and the potato soup, thick and creamy, was the most to his liking. The waitress, Maria Lundee, was coming toward him and she knew his eating habits. When he began to order only soup, he was admitting to her that he was out of work and, at those times, without a word, she served him extra portions of bread and crackers with the soup.

"Just soup," he said, but Maria Lundee looked at him longer and more closely than usual.

"You have stayed in the park too long, James," she said. "You look like you have been freezing."

He nodded, not surprised by her perception. "It is getting colder," he answered. He looked at her and frowned, repulsed by her looks. Her hair was disorderly and flat so he knew she had spent the previous day at the hospital with her son. She had painted her lips too red, apparently to distract from her hair, but it gave a brazen appearance to her usual rosy face. Maria Lundee was not a large woman but she had a sturdy beauty, large eyes and full lips and a round face with puffed cheeks. Most of the time she looked neat with her bright blond hair arranged in a bird's nest of perfect curls all over her head and around her neck. Spenner thought it took much time to form such a style with all those ringlets and that she had to neglect her coiffure on visitation days at the children's hospital. Always, the day after such visits, she looked as she did now—with no style to her hair and excessive lip color.

She told him once about her sick boy, mentioning "support systems" and "intravenous tubes," "sometime prolonged therapy" and concluding with an unbelievable diagnosis that "it takes time" and "he may grow out of it." Spenner did not understand and he was not interested in asking for more detailed explanations of the boy's illness. She sensed his indifference and she did not speak of the boy on her own again. Sometimes, when Spenner looked at her and saw that she had been at the hospital, he asked simply, "How is the boy?" but her answers had been repetitious. "He is the same," she would reply and say no more. Her eyes would soften and glisten with tears but she never cried. She was solemn most of the time and concealed her concern; but occasionally Spenner saw her smile if a customer joked or laughed but the smile was sad and made her gentle and sweet looking.

"Just dress a little warmer, James," she paused, leaned forward and looked closer at him. Her eyes opened wider with surprise. "Why you are wet too. Whatever . . .?"

"Don't ask," Spenner replied sharply.

"You'll catch your death," she went on. "Let me take your jacket to the kitchen to dry." She helped him remove the jacket although Spenner started to protest but then said nothing. Her face became worried and troubled but, though trying to reproach him, her voice remained soft and unabrasive. "I have an old sweater of Carl's that I will bring you. You should have an extra sweater if it is getting colder. It may not fit too well but it will be warm."

Spenner wanted to decline but she seemed to sense his refusal and moved quickly away so she would not hear him. Tomorrow, he knew, she would have the sweater for him, as she had done before with shirts and trousers and even socks after her late husband.

Spenner looked at the front of the cafe and at the windows but the man had not appeared. He continued to look until Maria Lundee returned with the soup and a plate with a heap of thick slices of dark rye bread. She tried to smile, as if in reconciliation, but Spenner, absorbed in thoughts of the strange man, did not smile or say anything but he frowned again at her outward appearance and turned away.

He began eating for the soup was hot and delicious and he ate ravenously, pricked by hunger pangs. His intense appetite and the good food engrossed him momentarily so when he paused and looked up, he saw the man outside the window gazing in upon him. The man's round face, with the dark eyes glittering and blinking, was looking directly upon Spenner. Perhaps it was the warm surroundings or the concern of Maria Lundee or the hot, good food, but Spenner felt some of the agitation toward the man diminish. He was upset at the sight of him but now Spenner felt more curious than angry. Soon he would have another chance at the man and Spenner sensed that confidence and self-control had returned to him. Spenner looked down and resumed eating but his senses sharpened as he heard the cafe door open and close and felt the breath of cold air that entered.

8

He was aware of the man's presence, coming directly upon him. Spenner did not look up until the man stopped before his table.

They stared at each other as they had done in the park but the man's expression had changed to a suggested friendliness. His dark eyes were glistening as before but from a projected smile upon his face. He glanced over Spenner, at his thin shirt and matted hair, and his smiled deepened but without mockery. "Bears," he said lightly. "That bear . . . never mind that. It was a natural thing for it to do. Do not be annoyed."

Spenner glared at him but the vehemence he tried to show was subdued.

"My presence offends you?" the man asked in a surprisingly soft voice.

Spenner looked down and shook his head and tried to be discourteous by not replying.

"May I sit here?" the man went on, tapping the chair opposite Spenner. Spenner nodded and the man began a sliding ordeal into the chair. His limp leg would not bend and he had to turn himself to one side and then swing his body into the chair. "Oh!" he cried in pain. "My leg is very bad today. The cold and the walking. Too much of either does it no good." He paused and then said evenly, "War injury." He glanced quickly at Spenner as he spoke, then he removed his cap and thrust it into the pocket of his jacket which he unbuttoned and flung back over the chair. Spenner looked at him again and saw that his hair was short and grey and stiff as broom bristles. The reddish-brown color looked as if it had been painted over his face and was so imbued in his skin that it could not possibly change or fade with a season.

Spenner returned to eating and made no attempt at conversation, but he was spared from talking as Maria Lundee approached. Spenner had always eaten alone and she eyed the man curiously, then looked questioningly at Spenner. He shook his head at her and was grateful that she understood he did not wish to talk. The man was studying the menu, but he inquired, "Oh, corned beef and cabbage. I haven't had that for a long time. You are not out of it?"

Maria shook her head.

The man smiled. "I suppose it is good? You will say so, of course."

But Maria did not say, her lips parted but she was mute, almost dumbfounded. She glanced quickly again at Spenner and at the bowl of soup before him. She turned to the man as he continued speaking. "I will take it then, and extra corned beef, if you don't mind. I will pay for it. I see you have dark rye bread. Good. I will have that, too, and a pot of coffee. No dessert," he said quickly, "whether you serve it or not."

As Maria wrote the order, she cast a sympathetic glance at Spenner. She still was curious and slightly angered but he shook his head again. She understood and said nothing as she turned away.

The man leaned down and rubbed his leg and another expression of pain crossed his face. "It will be real cold soon. My leg tells me that. All these years, it has been like a barometer." He continued to rub his leg for a while, then he rubbed his hands together and placed both elbows on the table. Finally, he looked squarely at Spenner and said, "Oh, I know you resent me. Perhaps you prefer to eat alone? Understandable, completely understandable. Strangers can be a curse, that is for certain. Privacy is a blessing and that is for certain, too, but when an opportunity arrives, a chance, a dream come true . . . Oh, that is a double blessing. It is a miracle." He paused to rub his hands again. "Allow me to say that I am Alec Thurston, retired from military service and, to use a phrase, getting along. May I ask, are you also retired?"

"Yes," Spenner replied curtly, not wishing to say anything about his work situation.

"So I thought," Thurston said softly, "and your name, my friend?"

Disgust for the man was building within Spenner once more, especially since his attitude and words were becoming more familiar and personal. "It is none of your business," Spenner replied.

"I understand. I understand," Thurston said quickly, "but as I said. . . ."

Spenner interrupted. "What is your purpose in hounding me? Why did you come here? You said you were getting along. Well, do it . . . get along!"

Thurston's eyes brightened and he laughed. "My friend, we use the same words yet how clearly we misunderstand each other. You say 'get along' for an action, a clever use of words, but I say 'get along' as my state of being, my situation . . ."

"Ah!" Spenner grunted. The man was becoming a boring nuisance.

"Never mind, never mind," Thurston leaned forward and said in his soft voice. "I know your meaning, friend."

"I am not your friend. I do not know you."

Thurston went on cheerfully. "My imposing upon you and your privacy has great significance for I offer you a chance, a glorious chance."

He was talking funny, Spenner thought, trying to appear intelligent with a sense that the intelligence was not there. His expression of privacy and blessings and state of being sounded more like rehearsed speeches and opinions heard elsewhere and he merely repeated them. "A chance!" Thurston said again like a salesman.

"What do you mean a chance?" Spenner asked.

"A chance that I will explain." He hesitated and once more leaned over the table. "But you did not say your name."

Spenner frowned in exasperation, but he declined to argue. "James Spenner," he answered reluctantly.

'Oh, James Spenner. It is my pleasure to make your acquaintance. Now we know each other's name, but we are still strangers and you cannot trust me. But I see that I have chosen correctly. I see on your face a look that I understand. You are stern and now you are resentful, but you have a look of resignation that your present lot will not be any better and you would be thankful to hang on to that. My friend, Mr. Spenner, it need not be so. The chance. *The chance* will change it all for both of us. When I tell you, I know you will understand what I am talking about. You have little time to wait but I—I have waited twenty years."

Spenner stopped eating and looked directly at Thurston. "Twenty years," he repeated in a whisper.

"Since the end of the war. Do you remember the war?"

Spenner nodded.

"Were you *in* the war?"

Spenner shook his head. "Not in the fighting."

"Fortunately for you."

At that moment, Maria returned to the table with arms laden with food. Thurston leaned back in his chair as she set the food before him. She glanced at Thurston with a resentful flicker in her eyes as she set down the overflowing plates of steaming food. Spenner noted that she brought no bread plate for Thurston but, instead, placed the bread on his plate, indicating they share and, thus, Spenner could

11

eat more. Her face was pale, probably with subdued anger, which made her bright mouth more red and firm. Spenner thought her look was helpless, though defiant, and she went away without smiling.

The pungent aroma of the cabbage and meat came over Spenner with an impressive force. His stomach seemed to tighten as he gazed at the huge limp wedge of light-green cabbage with steam still rising from its sections. Alongside were double slices of thick rose-colored meat and halves of white potatoes floated with tiny circlets of fat in the amber juice. Spenner's stomach tightened again and he closed his eyes and looked down.

"Oh!" and "Umm!" Thurston said several times with delight as he began to eat heartily. After chewing a measure of each vegetable and the meat along with a side of dark bread, he spoke again. "Now I will tell you about the chance."

"I don't want to hear it," Spenner interrupted angrily. "I don't know you and I don't want any part of you or your chance, whatever that is."

"I understand," Thurston replied. "I am the untrustworthy stranger again. You don't know me—yet. I must insist that you hear me. I must tell you about *the chance*. Oh, I shall be happy to tell you." He leaned over the table. "I shall begin when *the chance* itself began, during the war."

"The war?"

"I was entirely unaware of it then. After all, it was twenty years ago. I was first mate on the ship *Bellmann* which was anchored at Valiterra. One of the biggest battles of the war was fought over Valiterra. It was under siege when I was transferred there with orders to help evacuate the population. Let me say anyone was lucky to get out of that place alive and it was an ordeal the likes of which I will never forget. I remember. Oh, I remember that night when the city was abandoned and everyone tried to escape. My friend, I am a compassionate man and to see and experience such terror cannot be believed."

He paused to eat more, his cheeks puffed out as he chewed. He became thoughtful after he had spoken but after a moment he grunted with the "Oh" and "Umm" delight sounds as he consumed the food. Finally, he continued.

"It was cold, really cold. The middle of January at its worst—that kind of cold. The winds were whipping across the base and the buildings were covered with ice and frost. Such a harsh winter added to all the suffering. Valiterra was lost, the city could not be defended and the concern was to try to get out. Defeat and humiliation were another addition to the suffering." Thurston raised his shoulders and asked, "Can you understand, my friend, that for a compassionate man like me, it was the lowest, the end?"

His shoulders sagged and he returned to eating. He still was chewing when he said, "We received military orders to evacuate as many people as possible on the *Bellmann*. Such orders would have been comical if they were not so tragic. This ship, the *Bellmann*, was the only ship secured in port at that time and she had not been used for three years. Imagine, an unused relic? An emergency, so anything was being used, anything that was available. I went on as first mate and, can you believe, when I boarded, they were still working on the ship to try to get her going? Oh, rotten! Such orders, but that is what we had—a vessel that had not been used for three years to try to escape and haul out as many people as possible.

"The wind seemed twice as cold when I got on deck. It was blowing furiously and I took a whiplash beating. In the distance, I could hear the boom of the enemy artillery. They had broken through the mountain ridge along the western flank of Valiterra. The sound of the gunfire was ceaseless, pounding away all the time, and the enemy soldiers were sweeping down to encircle the city.

"The population was crowding the streets and into the naval base and pushing toward the docks, trying to get to the *Bellmann*. Oh, such a ragged group, in all manner of dress and some carrying a few possessions, driven from their homes like animals. The end of a city, everything was a wreck at that time—the city, the ship, the people. They were stopped at the gate by an infantry battalion and the colonel was directing the loading. The soldiers kept it orderly. They got the wounded on board first and then allowed the civilians on. People were jammed into every space on the ship, the cabins, lounges, salons, empty swimming pools. They even hung on lifelines and masts for support.

"And it got colder. Oh, I could not believe! The wind became stronger and picked up sleet and the temperature fell. My friend, I had such heart for all those people, freezing and suffering and pushing and shoving to get aboard and find a space. I went to the bridge and I was surprised to see armed guards there, soldiers, standing at at-

13

tention. I spoke to the captain about them and he said they were there to keep people off the bridge. I was shocked, but I was more shocked by what he told me next. My friend, you would not believe. *You would not believe* what he told me. There was no accurate count, but the captain believed there were over eighty-five hundred people aboard the *Bellmann*—almost five times the capacity of the ship. I was astounded and shocked and I protested. It was an emergency situation but *I did protest*. His reaction was to tell me to take no more aboard. Can you believe that? When the ship already was bursting, he says no more aboard. Then the captain said, as if to calm me down, that two other vessels were headed for Valiterra to pick up the remaining horde. 'Tell them, Thurston,' he shouted at me, 'tell those people that two more ships are coming.' I had to give those orders."

Thurston's voice became low. "My friend, I did not believe him, but it was my duty to call out the orders. 'No more! No more can be taken! Clear the decks!' It was such a shock that there was a moment of complete, stunned silence and every movement halted as though the world itself had stopped spinning. The colonel of the infantry broke the spell. 'What of the rest of these people?!' he screamed. 'What of my men?'

"I shouted back, 'Captain's orders!'

"Now the crowd became hysterical and began to fight to reach the ship. They pushed and shoved and tore at each other like wild beasts. I screamed at them. 'Two more ships are coming! Other ships are coming! You must wait!' They could not hear, of course, because they were so frenzied. The colonel recovered and ordered his men to advance on them. The soldiers formed a line and tried to hold them back. I saw eerie things happen. I saw a man and a woman holding hands break from the crowd and make a run for the ship as the gang plank was going up. They were running hard and fast, pulling each other, but the soldiers opened fire and both were gunned down. They lay together in a heap and no one dared move to help them. Many of the others, hundreds of them, broke away and jumped into the water to try to swim for the ship. They avoided gunfire but they were just as pitiful for they were caught in the ship's undertow and drowned. Then, my friend, an odd thing happened. The crowd was stopped, stunned, I think, by the shooting and the drownings and not knowing any way to turn. They huddled together, then one person cried aloud and soon the entire horde began to wail. It was low and mournful and, mixed with the cold, fierce wind, sounded like the sobs of the dying.

"I went back to the pilothouse as quickly as I could. The *Bellmann* was trying to get under way. She groaned and sputtered but finally the engines began to grind evenly and we pushed away from the dock. I felt the greatest sense of relief, sick relief, when we finally headed out to sea. Now the *Bellmann* was not an old ship, really, although she had not been used for several years. About ten years old, I guessed, but she was twenty-five thousand tons and had been used for pleasure cruises. The ship was warm, at least, and had sufficient food for a short voyage as we were to head for the first open port. We felt better when we were under way and everyone seemed to calm down a bit.

"We were making our way rather well when suddenly the captain approached me. He was angry and shouted, 'Thurston, who ordered the running lights out?' I said that I did as there were reports of submarines. The captain was tense and worried and he shouted again, 'There is a greater danger of collison! The two other ships are in this area, heading for Valiterra. Have the lights put on!' I was stunned and shocked. Another order that was disagreeable to me, but, oh, I had to obey. I had to obey. The lights were put on and we sailed, looking like a beacon.

"The weather became worse. A storm blew up and snow and sleet hit hard. The *Bellmann* had to struggle against sea and storm. She lost speed and churned about in all that turbulence. I kept hearing screams and cries from those who lost their grip or their footing and fell overboard. Other passengers became ill and their sickness was spilled all over the passageways and decks which became unbearable with stench and filth. But, my friend, that was nothing compared to the horror which was to come. I can repeat it like a book because I can never forget it. We were in open sea about four hours out when the torpedo hit us. It struck right behind the bridge on the starboard side. That *boom—boom* was repeated two or three times and then the ship began to tilt at an awkward angle. It took a little time for the dazed and sick people to become aware of what happened. When they did, you can guess there was panic. I went on deck to try to get them to stay calm, to shout to them that we would be safe if they remained calm. It did no good. They were so filled with fear and desperate and ill, that they could not be disciplined. They became a stampede and could not be stopped. They headed for the lifeboats, slipping everywhere in the ice and the sickness. I screamed into the speaker system that there was no danger, that no order had come to abandon ship, but they paid no heed. I was screaming into the wind, all for nothing. Then the disaster began. The people became crazed. First, lifeboats could not be launched; the davits were frozen. Yet, the people crowded and piled into those boats. They kicked and pounded at the davits which was of no use. One boat did become loose and it fell on the deck, killing people in and out of the boat, then sliding across the slimy deck and knocking others out like ten-pins.

"I tried to get back to the pilothouse to get orders from the captain but the horde was out of control, running all over and fighting each other. The structure of the *Bellmann* began to tear apart, injuring and burying people with each crash. The stairways were blocked. There was no way to get to the lockers where the life preservers were kept. Many were trapped in cabins. The soldiers were trying to drive the people into control by firing guns into the air, but the gunfire frightened and confused them and they turned on the soldiers, taking the guns and killing themselves and their families. One man got a gun and ran wildly about, firing and screaming, 'Punishment! Punishment for war! Punishment for killing!' The wounded soldiers we had taken aboard were trampled to death and I saw people setting fire to themselves and going into a crazy dance of burning flesh and hair. I can still see the woman with a child in her arms running toward me. 'What shall I do?' she screamed. 'What shall I do?' I could not stop her and she continued running to the side of the ship and threw the baby over. I saw people trapped on other side of portholes, looking like they were in fish bowls. I grabbed an ax and tried to break the glass but a man wrenched the ax from me and slammed it into the head of a woman beside him as he shouted, 'Dear one! My dear one!'

"Horrors. Oh, such horrors!"

Spenner sat stiff and silent as he listened to Thurston's story. He had not looked at Thurston all the time he spoke. His soup bowl was empty and he had tried to scrape the bowl with a piece of bread, but he stopped and pushed the dish aside. The food on Thurston's plate was half gone so that fat circlets had gathered together and formed a large, thick greasy membrane that wobbled around in the juice.

16

Spenner closed his eyes and shook his head and looked downward toward the floor.

Thurston coughed and his throat became tight. He drank coffee and took a bite of bread but he seemed to have difficulty in swallowing. After a while, he spoke again but his voice was lower and softer than before. "I notice you are listening carefully. You are an interesting man." He hesitated and then went on. "About this time, there came an abrasive, scratching noise from deep within the ship. The sound was repeated and became louder and louder as it hit every part of the ship. I knew tons of water were pouring in and the ship was almost on her side. The pressure cracked everything and the bodies came out like bloated balloons. Equipment was flying like paper in a windstorm and that was when something hit my leg. I became a cripple but I was too numb to realize it then. I knew I was hurt but I just wanted to keep moving. At last, I got back to the pilothouse. One soldier was with the captain. The captain had a gun on him and I heard the captain demanding the soldier to tell him if the running lights should have been put out. The soldier was crazy and confused and could not answer. The captain turned his back and an odd feeling struck me. I lunged toward the captain but not in time to save him. The pistol went off in his mouth and his head exploded. The body was writhing as it fell to the floor, but then the waves came and dragged all of us away.

"I was in open water and bodies were floating all about me. I thought I had only one leg for it was all I could feel so I had to tread water. A pair of hands grabbed my throat and I would have gone under but I doubled up and punched the man with all my strength and broke free. The people around me were fighting for pieces of wreckage or equipment, anything to cling to. I saw many pulled down by the suction of the ship and many became paralyzed by the freezing water and drowned. Cries of despair and grief were everywhere.

"I was trying to swim away when something hit me. I turned to defend myself but it was a crowded rubber raft. I grabbed two children floating by with their arms locked. I hung on to the children with one arm and threw the other over the side of the raft and held on. I was frozen, my hands were numb, my face was stiff and cut and the sleet and wind were beating us in a rage. There were too many people on the raft and they were trying to push each other off. Someone began pounding on me and the children. My grip broke and I had

17

to let go. One child sank but I quickly grabbed the other and reached for the raft again. At that time, a woman screamed, struggling against a man, but she was pushed over and went down immediately and out of sight.

"Well, we drifted until a lifeboat saved us. A rescue ship had come. The captain had been right about that. The lifeboat followed the rubber raft and took us to a safe port. There we got food and treatment and later we were loaded into railroad coaches and taken to other places. For me, it was a hospital where, fortunately, after a long while, my leg was saved."

There was silence. Spenner sat back, bewildered and amazed by Thurston's story. "Ghastly," he said softly under his breath.

"Hmph?" Thurston asked. "Oh, yes, ghastly it was and you know, my friend, it took only fifty-five minutes for the ship to sink after the torpedo hit. Think of it, all that suffering and death and destruction in fifty-five minutes, not even an hour." Thurston paused and emitted a sigh as if exhausted.

Spenner stared at him. For a full minute he examined Thurston's face. He saw the dark eyes glisten again but the big eyes and the moon-shaped face did not look silly any more. The comic appearance was there but something else seemed preserved also. Thurston called himself a "compassionate man" and perhaps that is what he was. His pity for the unfortunate was apparent so there could be no subterfuge. Spenner could not doubt his story and he could envision this sturdy clump of a man tearing about the ship in a frenzy trying to help others.

"Were there many?" Spenner asked. "I mean were there many left?"

Thurston's eyes flickered. "Maybe four hundred or so, I heard later. No one knows for certain."

Spenner straightened his body. "But you said over eight thousand were aboard!"

Thurston nodded. "Which means about eight thousand . . ." Thurston paused and gestured with an upraised hand, "died."

Thurston went back to eating. He would raise the fork with a bit of food on it then drop it again. He had to raise the fork a second time before he could eat, but then he pushed the plate aside and did not try again to finish the meal. He said nothing more for a while. When he spoke again, his voice was low and almost quiet. "That was

18

war, Mr. Spenner. That was war. Did it do us any good? I mean, we have not realized any value out of it, have we?"

Spenner was staring at Thurston. "Why did you tell me all of this?"

"So you can understand *the chance* and why it is so important."

"What do you mean?" Spenner asked.

"What was it for us, the likes of you and me, except injuries for me and a crumbum life for you?" Thurston paused. "There is an opportunity *now* to make a bit of money and I think you might be interested." He leaned over the table and whispered softly but distinctly to Spenner. "You *are* interested, aren't you, Mr. Spenner?"

Spenner remained silent as he stared at Thurston.

"Let me show you something," Thurston said as he fumbled into his jacket pocket and withdrew a newspaper picture which he thrust directly in front of Spenner.

Spenner gasped.

"Surprised you, eh?" Thurston laughed. "Could be a picture of yourself, could it not? Oh, not completely. You may not have looked just like that twenty years ago. Your nose is too crooked and you could walk a little straighter. The hair—ah, but that can change in twenty years, become thinner and more grey. Otherwise, your build, your stature—a good resemblance. Agree?"

Still, Spenner did not utter a word.

Thurston continued. "Do you know who that is? That is Collis Whitmore, mayor of Valiterra. Oh, not the present one, to be sure, but twenty years ago." Thurston leaned back and paused while he put the picture back in his pocket. "The likeness astounded you, did it not?"

Spenner shifted himself but he nodded slightly.

"Oh, that man does not interest me," Thurston continued, "except for someone who resembles him and that, my friend, is you. When I first saw you, I could not believe such an image. Good fortune for me, like a thunderbolt from the blessed God. I have seen *the chance!*"

Finally, Spenner spoke. "The chance. The chance. What are you talking about?"

"I am talking about money." Thurston leaned across the table once more. "And all that means is that you must be the mayor of Valiterra."

19

Spenner's body stiffened.

"Not Collis Whitmore. He is dead, but an impostor."

At first, Spenner did not understand the statement. "What?" he asked in a soft voice.

"Well, I should have said that the old mayor is assumed to be dead. It is believed that Collis Whitmore died in the war but no body, no trace of him has been found. But who is to say that he *may* have been one of the survivors of the *Bellmann*?"

"The mayor?" Spenner asked incredulously.

"Why not? All those people, you know," Thurston gestured again with an upraised hand. "I am bringing him back, through you. Don't you see that? Some of the survivors of the *Bellmann* were brought here to Tegner, so I came here to find someone—you—to be the mayor. It makes the plan, the *chance*, plausible."

Spenner shook his head, still disbelieving.

"If the man has never been traced, it does not mean that he does not exist and that makes it possible to bring him back."

Spenner looked at Thurston with a steady gaze. "Why?"

Thurston replied hastily. "Now just a minute and hear me through. I said there is money in this and it can be made now. The Whitmore estate is being disposed of in three weeks at Valiterra and if there are no other claimants, everything will go the mayor's sons. *You* are going to come forth as the father and get your share."

Spenner's eyes blinked and he fell back against his chair. He shook his head vigorously. "No," he answered and his voice was firm.

"You do not *see* it yet, my friend," Thurston went on. His dark eyes had softened but they glittered with enthusiasm. "Of course, no one can become another person, but you can pretend, assume, that you are someone else. Not forever. That is the important point of this whole idea. Only until the estate is settled and you have your share which," Thurston paused and smiled, "you share with me for doing all of this."

Spenner did not reply.

"You can pass for that man in the picture, even allowing for twenty years. I, too, when I first saw you believed you could be him."

"Crazy," Spenner interrupted. "People know each other. They would know I was pretending, or assuming, as you say."

Thurston shook his head. His voice was becoming steady and confident. "There is no one to know, Mr. Spenner. No one. That is why I know this thing will work. I have thought it out and I know it can be done."

"You mentioned his sons. How about them?"

'They are twins. They will be twenty-one in three weeks and that is when they come into the money. Think, Mr. Spenner, twenty years ago they were babies. What could they know about their father?"

Spenner was silent for a moment, then he said, "But their mother, she would know."

Thurston shook his head again. "Gessie Whitmore? No. She died about sixteen years ago and there is no other family."

Spenner looked downward and once again he was silent. Then he said, "No, it is too risky and it is still—crazy."

"It is not risky or crazy, believe me. I have checked this whole scheme out and I know it can be pulled off. I tell you there would be no one to challenge you. I have checked out all the physical facts, too, about the mayor's estate, the house and the people working there. Now I know there are some old timers who go back twenty years . . ."

"There you are," Spenner interrupted. "They would know right away."

Thurston continued as if he had not been interrupted. "They could not prove anything. It has been twenty years since the mayor lived in that house. That is in your favor. As for anyone unexpected, look at your odds. You have to do this—pretend, assume—for only three weeks. What is the margin for upsetting anything in that time?"

'It will not work."

"All right then, you blame the war. Mr. Spenner, you have the best alibi possible, just blame the blasted war for everything—amnesia, injuries, forgetfulness—just use that as an excuse for anything! No one can argue about that."

"Where did you get all this information and the picture about the mayor?"

"Accidentally. I overheard a conversation in a tavern about the estate and the missing mayor. I went to the library for the picture. I asked discreet questions about the situation of the trust and the household in general and then I began to formulate my scheme. Oh, it was the turning point of my life!"

"I do not like it," Spenner replied.

Thurston's lips tightened. "Hmph," he grunted and he looked

Spenner over carefully. "Mr. Spenner, has it been easy for you? Your life, I mean. How old are you, may I ask?"

"Fifty-five."

"Fifty-five," Thurston repeated. "And a job? Do you have one?"

"Not steady."

"Then why are you playing satisfied with such a life? And look at me? What have I got? A no-good leg, second-rate jobs, a meager pension. I have had too much pain. Can you understand pain so great that your entire body feels weakened? I have felt that way. Pain so overwhelming that I could not support myself and if, somehow, someone would brush me, I would topple over and collapse. I have dreamed of a *chance* like this. Only three weeks, then take the money and blow. It is a chance, one chance, for both of us." He paused and a smile came upon his lips. "I would go someplace where it was hot and just lie on a beach all day, taking in the sun, and live it out like a God. This old leg, well, I would dig it deep into the hot sand and just let it cook all that pain away. I would not care if it boiled the leg to pieces or ripped it into shreds. That kind of pain I could take. After dragging with this leg all these years, I could revel in pain like that. Can you believe?"

Thurston paused but Spenner did not answer.

"You could do the same, my friend. Go any place you wish, live as you dream. Isn't it worth a try?"

Still, Spenner said nothing. Thurston shrugged and patted his stomach. "Can I buy something? You're not finished eating, are you?"

"I don't want anything more."

"You have been a revelation to me, Mr. Spenner. Oh, believe me. When I saw you and your resemblance to the mayor, I thought for certain that my life might change. I could wish, I could dream. You appeared so perfect, you were alone, a man with no ties. At least, I observed that you never met anyone, never spoke to anyone," he hesitated. "If you change your mind about the deal, come see me. I am down the street at the Atlas Hotel, room 303. I will be there for another day." He reached over and patted Spenner on the shoulder. "Think of it." He rose, making a deliberate, awkward movement and a clumsy shift of weight. He sighed, as if in pain, shook his head, turned and went away limping.

Spenner remained in the cafe for a long time afterward. He was absorbed in thought, he stared ahead and his eyes were glazed and large and several times he frowned for he was agitated and disturbed. In the time to himself after Thurston had left, he had changed. He had become harsh and angry and all his feelings of isolation had become artificial. The attitude remained with him when he left the cafe and returned to his room. He threw himself across the bed without removing his clothes. He lay very quiet although inwardly he felt restless and something like terror pulsed through his body. He began to perspire and his clothes became clammy and he felt very cold.

The room was getting darker but an outside street light cast a dim reflection into the room. Spenner could see the large crack in the plaster that ran across the ceiling and began descending along the far wall. Through the years he had watched that crack make its way across the top of the room. Sometimes the building shook and rattled and it was almost as if he could see and hear the plaster splitting above him. Once, a chunk had fallen away from the ceiling and it frightened him for it occurred at night. He reacted by sitting up straight in bed and staring ahead of him into the darkness. Nothing moved so no one was there. He rose, turned on the light, and saw the large plaster piece lying next to his bed. It had fallen inches from his head. After that, he continually moved his bed as far as possible from the cracks that were breaking around him.

Spenner closed his eyes and his mind was recounting, almost word for word, the conversation with Thurston. He remembered the words vividly and they came back verbatim in the way and tone Thurston had spoken them. The things Thurston talked about overcame him and his body convulsed as he thought about the night of horror and suffering when the *Bellmann* sank. All of a sudden, the chills in his body gave way to a curious warmth. It felt like the sickness he had had once when his body was actually hot and cold and he had suffered pain between the two extremes. He had been very sick that time. His body would tremble with cold, then suddenly a fire seemed to burn within his body, especially in his throat, and he perspired profusely, then pain shots, like arrows from the fire, shot through all parts of his body. He became dizzy, his eyes blurred, and every muscle was so weak that he could not raise himself. He lay in a cloud, floating, hitting the shoals of ice and fire in a pained journey to nowhere.

"I cannot be sick now," he said to himself. "Perhaps Maria Lundee was right. I was in the park too long, cold and wet." Now he felt hot. He removed his shoes and his shirt and lay back again, thinking of Thurston. Thurston's proposition went over and over in his mind and what had seemed unthinkable was becoming plausible. He was getting into Thurston's perspective, *the chance* began to seem logical and capable of accomplishment. All—but it was everything—he had to be was appear as this Collis Whitmore, the mayor—former mayor of Valiterra for three weeks? The war, as Thurston said, could be the perfect alibi for any question or explanation. He began to form answers in his mind and he was saying mentally, "The war . . . injured in the war. Can't remember really . . . the war, you know. Lost my memory." He did not know what kind of an actor he could be but surely he could repeat those lines for three weeks. Then he thought of the epilogue, the ending of it all, after those weeks. He saw himself, as Thurston had, far away in a sunny climate, basking in warmth and relaxation with money enough for anything he wished.

Spenner opened his eyes, then sat straight up on the bed. He had been dreaming but he was not aware that he had even slept. How could he have been asleep? Yet, he must have slept, dozed off for a minute or two perhaps. He sighed heavily, filled with relief, for the thoughts and the words were receding, becoming fainter. How good, he said to himself, that he was only dreaming for he could never do it, never pretend to be another person.

Another thought came to him and he was shocked for he was awake now, but the dream was continuing and he was thinking, what if he were discovered and pursued? Could he get a year, even six months in a sunny paradise, before he was caught? Maybe he could go someplace where they could not bring him back. Or what if he were revealed in the middle of the masquerade? He would implicate Thurston, of course. Thurston had put him up to it. It was all his idea, his scheme. That might make it easier for me, letting Thurston take the blame. Was it worth it? Again, he found himself thinking like Thurston. What had he now? No steady or even a good job. A disagreeable life of carrying his aching body through cold winters and hot summers, accepting handouts like clothes from Maria's late husband, practically begging for food, living in a small, uncomfortable room with the plaster falling down around him.

Spenner fell back on the bed and closed his eyes. He slept once more for he became conscious as if something surprised him and his body was twitching. The outside light was off and his room was dark and much colder. He rose and put on his shirt and went to the window. All the street lights were off and the scene outside was quiet and looked dismal and void. He returned to bed and tried to relax himself into more sleep but his body would not respond. He was not sick as before; he was thankful for that. Yet, his heavy eyes would open, then close, he was resting, but he would not sleep and, of course, then he could not dream.

It was barely light when Spenner was in the street on his way to the Atlas Hotel. The hotel was an old brick building, constructed narrow and tall, but a new glass door had been put in the entrance and was the only mark of modernization. Spenner pushed the door open and stepped into the lobby. At this early hour, the interior was shadowy and still and there was only a small light over the vacant desk. Spenner crossed the grey floor toward the elevator, which was between two enormous shaggy plants that must have grown old with the hotel. Spenner took the elevator to the third floor and stepped out into a dingy corridor. Before him stretched a narrow hallway of closed doors, each identified with an overhead light bulb. Spenner walked along past the gazing lamps to room 303. He heard movement behind the door after he knocked. Thurston opened the door, smiled with a winning frankness, and let him enter. The room was small and cramped and Thurston quickly sat down on the bed, allowing Spenner to take the only chair. Thurston's eyes were very bright and there was a glow to the reddish color in his skin which was flushed and looked warm. He looked happy, though slightly silly, as if he had been drinking.

There was silence between the two men as they settled down. Spenner sensed that he was expected to talk first as Thurston looked at him, smiling and expectant.

"I'm early," Spenner said awkwardly.

Thurston shrugged his shoulders. "I have been waiting for you."

Small, introductory talk was not necessary, Spenner was certain, so he said outright, "I have decided to give your plan a try."

Thurston half rose and leaned over to Spenner. He slapped his shoulder and exclaimed, "Oh, my friend, I knew you would! Oh, you don't know, *you don't know*, what this means to me!"

He was upright on the floor now and the upper part of his body bounced up and down. He was so jovial he might have danced if

25

there had been room. "Oh," he slapped his hands together, "I will coach you. I will coach you on all the information I have on Collis Whitmore." He paused. "Collis Whitmore," he repeated and then slapped Spenner's shoulder again. "Think of that as your name from now on."

"Three weeks only," Spenner said hurriedly.

Thurston laughed. "You are sharp and you are right. Three weeks only. Yet, now you must begin to think of that as your name . . . please?"

Spenner nodded.

"I also have the layout of the estate," Thurston went on, trying to sound serious, "and the floor plan of the house so you will have no hesitation about the rooms or the grounds. It is a good size place."

"Thurston, where did you get this information?" Spenner asked.

Thurston answered quickly. "Never mind, never mind that. Ah, but I see it disturbs you. Well, I got it . . . overheard it, as I said before, but I must keep that as my secret. Do not let that disturb you, do not worry; but I can say that everything is truthful." He looked over Spenner. His face changed to a certain commanding bravado and he evaluated Spenner closely. "I will stake you to some new clothes," he said.

Spenner winced, which Thurston noticed so he went hastily on, "Do not worry about that either, my friend, I am not buying the best, only what is presentable. After all, you do not want to reappear as a long lost well-to-do. Not when you are supposed to be a roamer with amnesia and war phobias and the like. However, if you come as a bum, you will be thrown out, eh?"

Spenner winced again.

"I am not giving you the clothes, you understand," Thurston said and chuckled. "You can pay me back when you come into the money. Just say I am charging it to your account. But it will not be expensive, as I said, not expensive."

Spenner looked sternly at Thurston and asked, "Thurston, why did you come here to Tegner?"

Thurston tried to become serious at the unexpected change of subject. He thought for a moment and then replied. "Easy. The plan of mine—ours—must have some logic. It has got to be believable. I will be honest and tell you that there might be some checking on you. In fact, I am certain there will be a check made. You, as Collis

Whitmore, have been gone for twenty years, do not forget. Now some survivors from the *Bellmann* got here to Tegner. It makes sense that the mayor could have been one of them. It makes the plan acceptable. Understand, Mr. Spenner?" He hesitated and laughed. "Ah, my mistake—Whitmore. See, I have to adapt also. I am going to call you Whitmore while I am instructing you. You are Collis Whitmore."

"What if I cannot do it?" Spenner asked.

"But you can. Everything is in your favor. You look like the man, except for the nose, but that could be an injury. You are from here, a logical place, and I will tell you everything else you need to know."

Spenner looked away and his face became tense. Thurston studied him for a moment and then said, "And you cannot run out in the middle of the plan or try to double cross me. I can always expose you as an impostor. Sounds sort of brutal, doesn't it?" His expression brightened and he smiled. "But I would not do that. Oh, no. Never. But it is best to be completely frank and honest. That is what we have, a frank and honest understanding between us. I trust you and you know you can trust me."

Spenner turned and looked at him. "Thurston, you presented yourself as a man of compassion. Your own words, you know, and now I see you, the man of compassion . . ."

"Become the man of chance," Thurston interrupted. "I am still compassionate, believe me, but I have added to that the *chance* and, perhaps, now I am more the man of chance."

"What is the money involved? How much is the estate?"

"It must be many thousands. Not only money, but property and investments."

"What is your share," Spenner asked and now he smiled sardonically, "of my share?"

Thurston answered with determination. "I am entitled to sixty percent, forty for you."

"But I am doing the job."

"But it is my plan." Thurston thought again and then said, "You think I am no longer a man of compassion? Well, I will tell you. We make the plan strictly fifty-fifty. How is that for an equal bargain? That will buy me all the sunny places I want."

Spenner nodded. "All right."

Without a thought of the small space of the room, Thurston jumped around in an erratic dance step. "Ah!" he exclaimed. He hit the bed post and almost staggered over Spenner. "Shall we shake hands? As partners?" He put forward his hand and Spenner shook it.

"Now, let us have something more to seal our pact." Thurston went to the bureau and took out an amber bottle of whiskey. The bottle was not full and Spenner was certain that Thurston had celebrated earlier. Thurston poured two glasses and handed one to Spenner.

A kind of comical, harmonious celebration followed. They clicked the glasses together and smiled at each other.

"To Collis Whitmore," Thurston said.

"To *the chance*," Spenner responded.

They clicked the glasses together again and drank. The whiskey seemed to go right to Spenners' toes as if his body was empty. He coughed and gasped for breath and had a queer thought that there was nothing inside of him—he was empty. He tried to laugh but he still was short of breath and made only whimpering, wheezing sounds.

"You need more," Thurston said and filled Spenner's glass. Responding to Spenner, Thurston began to laugh too. His eyes were sparkling with excitement and his face flushed a deeper red. He tried again to dance and he increased his pace when he jumped which made him weave around on his bad leg and he fell onto the bed.

"*You* need more," Spenner said but his head shook and his mouth felt as though it could not open and his words were gurgling inside.

"Ah, yes." said Thurston, trying to rise from the bed. He hoisted the bottle and tried to steady it over his glass but the whiskey spilled over his hand as he poured. "Ah," he said again and put his hand to his mouth to lap up the overflow. He weaved on his feet and held the bottle high. "Just enough left for you," he said and he swung toward Spenner.

Spenner tried to rise to meet him but he fell back into the chair as if the drink had settled in his feet like an anchor. "I am not used to this," he thought, "I cannot drink this. You take it," he said aloud to Thurston.

Thurston laughed and then put the bottle to his mouth and emptied it. "I will make it! We will make it!" Thurston exclaimed. "Say so, Whitmore, say so!"

Spenner tried to laugh at him. His voice was rasping and he hooted like a soaked whistle. "Oh whee! Yes!" was all he could sputter.

The daylight came but the two men did not see it. One was prone on the bed; the other in the chair. The empty bottle was on the floor between them.

Chapter Two

The train ride to Valiterra was long and monotonous to Spenner. He started from Tegner in the early evening and rode all night, going eastward through endless night.

Spenner secluded himself in the back seat of one of the coaches and ignored the other passengers. He leaned back in the thickly covered seat and closed his eyes so he would not see or catch the glances of other travelers. Sitting still, he appeared calm and relaxed, but he was alert and impatience stirred within him along with an intense anxiety and uneasiness. He could not sleep during the night and several times a nervous twitch shook his body and he would sit upright and stare into the rumbling darkness.

His mind throbbed over the four-day education he received under Alec Thurston. He had become exasperated also with Thurston who, fortunately, did not drink during those days, but he might have been for he acted just as ecstatic and wild as he had the first night. He was excited and buoyant because of the beginning of his plan, *the chance*, as he would sing under his breath, but he took no drink because he wanted to be certain that his teaching to Spenner would be exact and accurate. The experience had been like memorizing a book and knowing what page to turn up, to confront the correct information and respond accordingly. "Ah!" Thurston would exclaim when Spenner answered correctly. "Ah!" he would say again and then murmur softly, *"The chance."* Then he would laugh or smile and spin around in jubilation.

He would groan and shake his head if Spenner hesitated or erred. "Whitmore!" he cried. "No! Try again!" He would stand before Spenner, bending over with clenched fists, urging Spenner to remember, to get things right. Thurston had discovered the physical features of the estate, the layout of the house and grounds, and he spoke of a few of the personalities involved, but it was like an outline sketch of a plot for some play. Now I am going for the performance, Spenner thought, his performance as Collis Whitmore, who once had been mayor of Valiterra.

Spenner opened his eyes and looked out but could see nothing in the darkness. The night was black and shivering as the train sped onward. Once, he looked up and there saw the faintest light in a moment of a twinkling star. It is too far away to make any difference, he thought. He pushed himself back into the soft cushion of the seat. "I am Collis Whitmore," he said to himself, "coming home after twenty years." What defense would the man have, what would he do? Then Spenner's eyes closed once more. Alec Thurston had supplied it all. It was the war—the war—the answer to it all.

These thoughts made Spenner uneasy and then his body would twitch. He tried to believe that he was uncomfortable because of his new garments. Thurston had purchased them as well as the train ticket. The clothes were subdued and presentable, not expensive as Thurston promised; but Spenner felt overdressed and stifled from head to toe. The trousers were dark grey and the shoes black, the short overcoat and hat were brown. The stiff, new clothes fit him fairly well but he was not used to such restrictions after the seconds, all ill-fitting, that he received from Maria Lundee. The shoes squeezed his feet and the collar was tight around his neck so he constantly pulled at his collar and wriggled his feet in the shoes. Alec Thurston had even included a small cardboard valise with a change of socks and undergarments. Yet, Spenner had packed his own things too. He took the ill-fitting, second-hand clothes that he had received from Maria Lundee. Why, he did not know, but he just did not want to leave them—he sensed that they were a part of him as James Spenner that he did not wish to cast aside.

The late morning was misty as the train began to ascent into a low mountain range that was on the western side of Valiterra. The flatlands were disappearing as the train eased upward between the high crevices of the thick mountains. Valiterra was like a fortress situated on high ground between the mountains and the sea on the east. It took a while for the train to pull through the mountains, descend, and head overland toward the sea. During the descent, the blue sea could be seen in the distance and even the waves were noticeable as they leaped high and arching toward the shoreline.

The train entered Valiterra through a small industrial area, weaving like a slow snake around box-like, brick buildings. The structures were unattractive for they had no yard enclosures or landscaping and the dirt from the fumes of manufacturing clung to the structures and the streets. Just beyond the crude site was the railroad station and the train came to an easy halt in one of the gloomy interior tunnels.

Spenner left the train quickly, looking nowhere but ahead as he hurriedly crossed the station lobby and stepped outside into a fine drizzle of rain. It was colder by the sea and the rain drops were icy as they hit against Spenner's face while he waited for a taxicab. Carefully, he gave the driver an address he had memorized. The taxicab sped away and entered the busy section of the city where there were shops and stores but had to slow down, for even in the rain, the weaving traffic of vehicles and pedestrians was light but steady. The taxicab left the bothersome area and turned into the business section of tall, communal palaces of identical burnt-orange brick with steel trim. This area had no adornments of yard, enclosures or landscaping either, but nevertheless its atmosphere was imposing and majestic. The taxicab stopped before one of the older buildings and Spenner got out. He stood still for a moment and looked up at the lean, darkened tower before him. He entered the building and went immediately to the lobby directory. He noted that the law firm of Norman, Benchley and Sundahl was located on the top floor. He moved with a crowd into the elevator and was the only one remaining when the elevator reached the top. When Spenner stepped out, he stood in front of the glass doors with the firm's name emblazoned across them in large, gold block letters.

Spenner glanced around at the inside but there was no one in the waiting room. At the side, a young girl with spectacles and brown hair, cut even and straight at her shoulders, sat at a desk, looking downward at some papers. Spenner twisted the door knob. It turned easily and he pushed the door open. The girl looked up immediately and gazed intently at Spenner as he approached her desk. Her eyes looked large and deep brown behind the spectacles and their steadiness reflected a concentrated intelligence and confidence. Spenner stopped before he was too near and was about to speak when a rear door opened and an elderly man stepped out.

"Miss Martin," the man said, "are the papers . . ." He halted and stared at Spenner. His lower lip dropped and his mouth remained open for few seconds before he exclaimed, "Mayor Whitmore!" He stopped instantly as if astounded by his own words. A stunned look came over his face and his mouth dropped open again. He stepped closer to Spenner and whispered breathlessly, "It *is* Mayor Whitmore, isn't it?"

Spenner stood still, looking at the man. He did not say a word, but he nodded his head.

The man stepped back as if hit but he continued to stare at Spenner. "Well, bless my soul!" he said, still in a whisper. Trying to gain his aplomb, he came around to the front of the desk and stretched forth his hand. Yet, Spenner remained rigid and did not say anything or raise his hand for the handclasp.

The man was too flustered to notice. "You remember me?" he asked. "Grant Deakins?"

Spenner gazed at the small man. He had thin white hair and grey eyes and, though short, there was a stately appearance about him, perhaps because of his immaculate dress and very straight posture. His dark blue suit was cut and fitted to perfection and the matching vest folded neatly over his rotund chest. A gold pin, not too discernible, shone from his lapel.

"Grant Deakins," the man repeated.

Finally, Spenner blinked his eyes and nodded again. "Oh, yes, I remember. Grant Deakins. You have been with the firm for many years." He stepped forward. "You must forgive me. I am still a little confused."

"Certainly, certainly," Grant Deakins replied quickly. "I cannot believe . . ." He hesitated and then went on, "I think we should go to my office." He gestured toward the room he had just left. "Miss Martin," he said, turning toward the girl, "no interruptions, please." The girl had stared at them with such wide, unbelieving eyes that she looked alarmed. Her glance had shifted questioningly from one to the other and she gazed after them as they went toward Grant Deakins' office.

Spenner held back until Deakins moved and then he followed into a room with thick red carpet and shiny mahogany furniture. Deakins indicated a wide leather chair for Spenner. Spenner obeyed and the chair cushion was so soft that he sank deep toward the floor. Grant Deakins took his chair behind the desk but directly across from Spenner. His familiar place seemed to give him an anchor and he regained his composure quickly. His spirits perked up and good humor appeared across his face as he smiled. Spenner thought that,

33

despite this geniality, Grant Deakins was trying to suppress his uneasiness and embarrassment.

"Well," Deakins began, the breathlessness gone from his voice, "this is certainly a surprise. The story—the explanation," he hesitated, "it has been many years. Whatever happened?"

Spenner sighed heavily and looked at him and thought a moment, as if trying to remember his lines, then he began his rehearsed speech. "I know I have shocked you and I will probably shock others, but I have been gone . . ." he pretended to stumble on his words, "I have been gone, I mean my mind has been gone for all these years."

"Amnesia?" Deakins asked, looking directly at him.

"Yes," replied Spenner and he nodded his head. "I have come from Tegner."

"Tegner?" Deakins asked again.

"Yes," Spenner repeated. "You have heard of it?"

"Oh, yes," answered Deakins carefully. "I have heard of Tegner. Yes."

Spenner continued slowly so Deakins could absorb each word. "I had a strange experience about a week ago. I was in a Greek cafe near the city park when a man approached me and called me Collis Whitmore. I thought he was daft, had mistaken me for someone else. My name is—was—James Spenner."

Deakins' eyes flickered but his calm mood did not change and he did not interrupt.

"This man talked to me and continued to call me Collis Whitmore. I could not convince him otherwise, but that night I had a seizure."

"A seizure?" Deakins said softly. "Oh."

Spenner shook his head and grasped the arms of the chair tightly and stiffened his entire body. "I never had a seizure before, not that I could recall, and may I never go through such an experience again. My head ached so badly that it felt as though it would blow right off my body. I had dreams, bad dreams, like hallucinations, and people and places from the past were dredged up in all sorts of vibrations, like ghosts dancing and running about in a wild frenzy. It was horrendous. I could not explain this awful nightmare. I felt completely helpless. When I woke, my body was hot and then cold and I was shaking like a leaf on the wind and I was shouting, 'Let me die!' "

Spenner stopped and his head hung down toward his chest.

34

"Do you need something, Mr. Whitmore?" Deakins asked, a little anxious. "Water or . . ."

"No, no," Spenner replied hurriedly. "I am all right." But he raised his head and sighed heavily, then he sat back in the big chair. He looked directly at Grant Deakins as he continued, "The next morning, I felt altogether different. I cannot describe it to you, except that I was just different. I was not ill but I felt I had overcome an illness, as if I had been trapped in a strange nightmare and now I was released. Everything seemed odd except for one revelation: I sensed I was in my correct mind. *I knew I was Collis Whitmore.*"

Deakins had been listening attentively, he sat still and very straight in his chair; but Spenner had noted that several times there was a slight lift of his eyebrows and his eyes were steady as he heard each word.

Suddenly, he smiled briefly. "Well, it sounds very unusual and I am certain it was difficult for you, but you say you never had a seizure like this previously, not even in your recollection?"

"Never. I cannot explain what brought it on except that man saying my name and making me aware of my real identity," Spenner said in a monotone. "It triggered something in my subconscious."

'Yes, yes. This man. Did he tell you his name? Did you know him?"

"I said he was a stranger. I did not know him and I never saw him again."

Now Deakins moved, just an uneasy shift, to lean back in his chair. "So long ago," he whispered and his grey eyes stared ahead but not at Spenner. Then he shifted again and leaned forward. He looked at Spenner and smiled. "Could you, perhaps, describe this man?"

Spenner shook his head. "Hardly. I was put off by him. I said I thought he was daft and I tried to disregard him and shrug him off. He wore dark clothes, as I recall, but I paid little attention to his looks. If I had seen him after the seizure, I would have taken more note of him."

"Yes, yes," Deakins said softly. "You said he called you Collis Whitmore. How did he know you were Mr. Whitmore? Did he tell you anything else about yourself?"

"Nothing more," Spenner answered, "except that he mentioned the war and that was how he knew me as Collis Whitmore."

35

"The war? I see," answered Deakins and his grey eyes became reflective, but he answered with his own question. "You remember that, too?"

Spenner shifted in the deep cushions and closed his eyes to appear to be concentrating. "I recollect the war. I was mayor then and I know the time was bad, desperate, a turmoil I should say. But I do not remember much. The amnesia must have set in."

"Sad indeed, Mr. Whitmore, sad indeed for you. The war was going badly," Deakins paused. "There was no trace of you, it seems no one knew what happened to you. But it was a bad time, as you say, a bad time."

Spenner noted that Deakins had not written anything down. He had talked in a calm, encouraging voice, never seeming doubtful or resentful. Perhaps he did not want Spenner to be inhibited in any way, yet Spenner was certain that Deakin's legal mind was totaling facts for a future "check" as Thurston had predicted.

"When you were James Spenner did you have any recollection of the past?" Deakins asked.

"No," replied Spenner.

"You say you came from Tegner. Can you remember how you got there?"

Spenner shook his head. "Sometimes I had pains about my head." He swept his hand across his face to accentuate his nose which Thurston said was not quite right for Collis Whitmore. "I must have been hit on my head or my face in some way. I cannot say how I got to Tegner. I was there, but I never knew about my past. I believe that is why I lived there as a recluse. You have no idea what it is to know nothing about your past." Spenner hesitated and leaned forward. He covered his face with his hands. "But I cannot be wrong now. I am certain I am Collis Whitmore." He moved his head swiftly and looked up at Deakins. "Even *you* called me by that name."

Deakins' face flushed and, for the first time, Spenner saw color in his face. His eyebrows had arched and his grey eyes flared with a look of astonishment.

"Then I must be," Spenner said hurriedly and he smiled at Deakins. "You saw me. You knew. Now I am more certain of who I am. Unless—" he stopped and then went on in a firm voice, "You know something about me? Is there anything?"

Deakins' face still was flustered and pink but his voice was even,

36

almost sharp. "Only what I said, that there was no trace." He moved in his chair so that he sat very straight and looked keenly at Spenner. "Do you have any illnesses or ailments now?"

Spenner was surprised and his body became tense. "Not that I am aware of," he replied. "Do you wish me to be examined?" He gasped after he said the words and wondered if that was the right thing to say. He was certain he had answered too quickly.

But Deakins was shaking his head. "No, no not now. You have come through quite an ordeal. We must be sensible. I cannot see that there will be any question." He glanced quickly at Spenner as though now his words had been too hasty. The "any question" did not sound quite judicial and seemed a little too revealing.

Spenner pretended not to notice and said, "I am most willing."

"Later, perhaps," Deakins replied. "Now let us clarify, if you will, the situation. At this time you remember that you were the mayor. You recall the war, and you have been living since that time in Tegner as a victim of amnesia." Along with his rigid posture, Deakins spoke forcibly and he seemed like a lawyer challenging a witness.

"As James Spenner," Spenner said and his voice failed. "In Tegner I was James Spenner. I lived in a boarding house on Ten Street."

"Of course, as James Spenner. And such you were, all these years, at the boarding house, until a week go when you were approached by a stranger who recognized you as Collis Whitmore."

Spenner did not reply but he began to moan. "Oh!" he uttered and his voice was low like a murmur. "Oh!" He relaxed and sank back in the easy chair. His head lowered and he closed his eyes. He did not moan again; he was quiet as if in sleep.

Deakins, too, became quiet and soon he leaned forward and called out, "Mr. Whitmore."

Spenner remained silent but his head stirred slightly when Deakins called out again, "Mr. Whitmore."

"Oh," Spenner cried out in another moan. He swung his head from side to side, gazed upward, and rolled his eyes. "Oh!" he repeated. "H'mm?" he added, then dropped his head again.

Grant Deakins half rose from his chair. "Mr. Whitmore, are you all right?"

Slowly Spenner looked up but his head was steady and his look intent. "What?" he asked quietly. "What? You called me Mr. Whitmore? Am I dreaming when I hear someone call me Mr. Whitmore?"

Deakins was standing over his desk but he had grabbed the edge as though to support himself. He stared at Spenner and his eyes were shining like brilliant stones. He began to sit down but he did not say anything. Spenner leaned as close to the desk as possible and made certain Deakins was looking at him as he said, "I want to see Gessie and my boys."

Deakins slumped into his chair. His mouth opened and closed like a fish and the embarrassing pink flush came over his face once more. His voice wavered when he spoke. "Why Mrs. Whitmore died many years ago."

Spenner acted surprised. "Gessie is dead?"

"Yes, I am sorry to tell you, but Mrs. Whitmore passed away not long after the war. She was ailing. She had consumption, as I remember."

"Oh, Gessie!" Spenner covered his face and slumped back into the chair. "So much I do not know. So many years. I knew it had to be different but . . . Gessie . . . gone?"

"I am sorry," Deakins repeated, "but your sons are fine. Lee and Lester are grown, soon they will be twenty-one. They still live at the estate but they are planning their futures." Deakins stopped and then he spoke another thought. "Are you planning to go directly to the estate?"

Spenner thought for a moment. "I had not thought about that, but should I go? Perhaps I shall find that it would be better that I not come back."

"No, no," Deakins insisted. "I only suggested what must be done eventually. You understand, of course?"

Spenner nodded. "I should like to return to my home."

"Fine," replied Deakins. "I would be happy to escort you there if you wish."

Spenner tried to protest. "I take so much of your time. You are a busy man and I am grateful that you have been considerate and understanding of me."

"I, and the firm, are still at your service, as we always have been. It is no trouble whatsoever. I will call for my car." As he picked up the telephone, he had another thought. "Would you like me to call

ahead and let them know you are coming? Under the circumstances—"

"Yes," Spenner answered quickly. "Most considerate of you and
a very good idea."

"I will call Anton Dyer."

"Anton!" Spenner exclaimed. "He is still there?"

Deakins paused but only for a moment. "All these years, Mr.
Whitmore. He took care of the boys and the estate and managed
everything."

"How good, how good it will be to see him again." Spenner rose.
He shook his body and caught the edge of the chair. "Perhaps I can
wait in the outer room until we are ready to leave?"

"Absolutely. I will have Miss Martin . . ."

"Do not impose on her," Spenner interrupted. "I will be all
right. I assure you." He made his way toward the door. He turned
there with a brief nod to Deakins and left the room.

Miss Martin studied him with the same intent as when he entered
the office. Spenner merely glanced at her as he went to the window
and stood with his back to her. Now, he relaxed and smiled. It was
good, he thought, that he not be an audience but let Grant Deakins
explain and announce his arrival at the estate. Let Deakins answer
the questions of shock and surprise and prepare the meeting with the
old butler, Anton Dyer, who was still at the estate as Thurston had
said.

As he relaxed, Spenner felt surprised and exhilarated. The first
step had been accomplished and it had been easier than he had
thought. He had been nervous but he was amazed at how quickly he
had overcome it. The smart lawyer Grant Deakins had believed and
received him as Collis Whitmore. Such a buffoon! Spenner had told
lies and Grant Deakins believed him. Well, so what? He had agreed
to lying and deception when he accepted Thurston's offer. He overcame the feeling just as easily as he had overcome his nervousness.
Once again, he smiled to himself. He felt assured and knew there
was courage within him. He could do this. He could carry out *the
chance* and see it through.

Chapter Three

Deakins and Spenner took an elevator to the lower concourse of the building and waited until Deakins' car was brought around. There was a strained, tense feeling between the two men and they were silent except for the time when Spenner asked, "How was Anton Dyer and what did he say?"

"Oh, he was surprised, very surprised. Naturally," Deakins replied and there was a calm upon his face. "Yet he said he was overjoyed to know that you are alive and back and he cannot wait to see you." Deakins smiled slightly but nothing else was spoken.

Deakins drove and he headed his car up a ramp and out onto the street. The mist of the morning had turned into a light rain which was sprinkling over the pavements. As Deakins drove, he returned to the commercial area of shops and stores where he slowly circled and wove through traffic, then he drove through a small park in what seemed endless, curving paths and out again on another avenue to the other side of the city. He traveled a short distance and made another turn on to a narrow street lined with a rubble of buildings. He turned yet another time into a second park and suddenly an acrid odor infiltrated the air. It came from the sea and became more pungent as they headed toward the open shore. They cruised around the shore line then headed in the direction of a large, bronze statue. "War memorial," Deakins said as they passed and Spenner glanced quickly upward at the stilted, strong looking soldier whose face was blank. They left the seaside park and drove inland past areas of vacant lots or half constructed building projects.

The route had been unusual, Spenner thought. Grant Deakins was driving as though he were lost. The drive was not a sightseeing pleasure trip, there was little beauty to behold and the rain made everything desolate and deserted. No one was in the streets and certainly not in the parks, and the buildings were either demolished or half-finished with no one attending their wet frames. Spenner wondered if Deakins was doing this deliberately, perhaps to test him. He did not feel uneasy but he vowed to be alert and make no comment on anything.

Then Deakins spoke. "It is different, is it not?"

Spenner did not reply but merely nodded his head in agreement.

"It is expected, of course," Deakins continued. "Much had to be rebuilt and there are things still to be rebuilt. A good part of the city was destroyed in the war and it takes time, one might say, to grow again." He paused and glanced at Spenner. Again, he smiled lightly and then said, "I drove around a bit so you could see."

And perhaps remember, Spenner thought, as he nodded once more but said nothing.

They drove back into another section of the city where they approached the river which ran an erratic course through Valiterra. Deakins turned onto the bridge which was expansive and solid and new looking. As they crossed, the river below was high and looked dark and cold but the fine rain made the water jump in a rhythmical beat. Once over the bridge, Deakins made a quick turn along the river front and drove through an area of large, expensive-looking new homes surrounded by wide acres. He passed through and along a highway until he came to a lonesome road which led them to a wooded section enclosed by a tall, iron fence. Deakins sped along the narrow road, following the fence for several miles until an open gate appeared before them. He drove through it into a paved road lined with trees toward a white stone building, streaked with rain water, set ahead in the center of a curved driveway.

Spenner leaned forward as if to appear excited. "It is the same!" he exclaimed, recalling the picture of the estate which Thurston had shown him. "It is the same!"

Deakins glanced quickly at Spenner. "Yes, there have not been many changes here."

Spenner continued to lean forward, staring ahead of him. Deakins stopped under the covered entrance and stepped out of the car, but Spenner did not follow. Without looking back, Deakins moved up the stairs and toward the door, but the door opened before he reached it and a stocky, partially bald man stepped out. Before he greeted Deakins, he cast a rapid glance at Spenner. Then he started down the stairs but Deakins reached out his hand and stopped him.

This is Anton Dyer, the butler, Spenner identified the man to himself. He stared at them and thought how much the two of them looked alike—short men, old men, bald, but they were the ones who knew and were close to Collis Whitmore. The butler spoke quickly to Deakins but continued to look at Spenner. The two men talked together. They huddled close, they nodded their heads, they cast hurried looks at Spenner and then they turned away. The stout old men looked like a silly, entertainment mime team, acting like a couple of guilty cronies, whispering, looking slyly at him, curious, preparing for what? Whatever are they talking and acting about, Spenner wondered? Did not Deakins explain previously? Had he not telephoned Anton Dyer for that reason?

Spenner sat back for he felt as though a sudden paralysis had come over him and he could not move or direct his body. He continued to stare ahead and he tried to breathe deeply to calm himself. It seemed as if a hidden restraint had taken hold of him and a chilling uneasiness spread over him. Am I to have a real seizure, he thought wildly. But breathing heavily and deeply he sensed that he was only afraid. He was at the estate now, the home of the mayor, and the devil's own game of deception he had entered into was now open before him. This was the brink, the precipice. Once he moved into that house, he moved directly into Thurston's plan, and he would become the center of the whole scheme and the success or failure would be entirely upon him.

Why did he feel this foreboding? Not long ago, after he met Grant Deakins, he was confident and assured; told himself that the plan would be easy to complete. Why did he lose that feeling now? He had sensed a bit of the challenge just in driving here with Grant Deakins. Maybe this moment was the true reality of the plan. Each challenge could test him in this way. Each confrontation and question could frighten him and make him cautious and wary about discovery, but he had to believe all the while that he could master any situation. For three weeks, he told himself, just for three weeks! There will be times of crisis and times of confidence and it would be fatal to allow one to overcome the other. He had to be careful but he had to try to be assured and bold.

Grant Deakins and Anton Dyer had ended their comic play and turned and walked down the stairs to the car. Spenner touched his forehead and it was moist with perspiration. He wiped it and began to breathe heavily again. He wished he could control his breathing.

"Go on," he coaxed himself, "go ahead and meet them." His hand was trembling but he opened the door and tried to make make a slow, easy attempt to get out of the car.

Anton Dyer was upon him. "Mr. Whitmore! Oh, sir!" he called out and his look was steady but with complete astonishment on his face. Yet, Spenner was not prepared for the tears which came to Anton Dyer's eyes. Dyer's eyelids were slightly drooped so the tears filled his eyes though he seemed to try to hold them back. However, the tears crept out of the corners of his eyes and went down over his cheeks. "Forgive me, sir," he said, "but I cannot believe this is true! Can you make it, sir? Let me help you."

"Anton." Spenner said softly and took the butler's hand, grasping it tightly. "Anton," he repeated, "how good to see you again." Spenner could feel Dyer's hand shaking within his but his grip was strong enough to help Spenner from the car. They stood together, looking at each other. "I know I have shocked you," Spenner said.

"Yes," Dyer answered. "It is unexpected. It has been a long time, sir, a very long time." His voice lowered and he said in a reverent whisper, "Oh, Mr. Whitmore, to see you again!"

"I have been away a long time, Anton. I did not know . . . my mind . . ." Spenner's voice faltered. Why must Dyer cry, Spenner thought uneasily, for an old man to cry . . .

Grant Deakins moved between them. "We should go inside," he said and took an arm of each and pushed them toward the door. They stepped into a large, cool hallway with a corridor extending from it. There were several doors along the corridor and all were closed. Spenner's look darted about, noting the doors and a stairway at the end of the corridor. Long, lancet windows were behind the stairway which had a landing in the center and forked into two other staircases leading upward to the left and to the right. Spenner smiled to himself for the plan of the ground floor, the entrance, the corridor and the staircases, was as Thurston had said.

A door slammed upstairs and when he heard the sound, Spenner's head jerked toward the staircase. He looked up and waited. Then a young man came along the balustrade, descended from the right staircase and stopped in the landing. He paused and looked at Spenner. Anton Dyer stepped beside Spenner and said, "Mister Lester, sir. I called him from school." The lad was tall and thin. He bent over so the thinness of his body made him look weak but, in youth, such slimness usually means, if not strength, a wiriness of the kind that bends but does not break. The lad was blond and, standing before the windows, the light shone around his head, making him look dazzling. He did not smile but the expression on his face was quizzical and expectant. He descended the long staircase in rapid and agile movements and came toward Spenner.

"I saw you come," the lad said. His voice choked but his eyes were full of surprise and curiosity. Then he smiled and grabbed Spenner by the upper arms and uttered, hesitatingly, "Dad!"

Spenner was unprepared for the gesture and the greeting and his body stiffened. The thin hands held him tightly with a pressure of affection but Spenner sensed their strength. His arms were pinned against his body and Spenner was grateful that he did not have to touch the boy. Spenner had to look up to him, however, and, surprisingly, a gasp emerged from his throat and without control, he said softly, "Lester, Lester."

Lester slapped his hands again on Spenner's arms and shook him gently. He smiled with warmth and affection and his light blue eyes were glistening. "Dad," he said again. "We are glad you're home. I could not believe it when Anton phoned the school and they had to get me out of class to tell me about you. I just could not believe."

Spenner stared at the boy and he swayed slightly for he was shaking. Another gasp surged in his throat but he suppressed it. *Dad*. The boy was calling him *Dad*. The gasp Spenner suppressed was one of dismay for he wondered, am I father to this? A nice boy, no doubt, those eyes are light and soft but he is tall and all bones and has poor posture. He leans over like he has no strength to hold himself erect, yet there is a vitality about him, a certain vigor. What is he saying—college student? Oh, my son, you look so inexperienced and naive. Can you know anything? What can you cope with, let alone solve. Spenner paused as the thought came to him. But soon you will be rich, not as you think, because I am here; but you are one of the heirs. Spenner paused again—but there were two.

"Where is Lee?" Spenner found himself asking.

Lester still was smiling but he replied, "He is out with Karin."

Oh, thought Spenner immediately, Karin, *a new name*.

"His fiancée," Lester went on. "We could not reach him so we left a message at her home."

Anton Dyer stepped forward once more. His eyes still were misty

44

as he looked at Spenner and Lester. "We have prepared a light supper, sir, as you may be hungry. Mr. Deakins will also stay."

"Oh," Spenner said with surprise. "How thoughtful, Anton. Very thoughtful." He was bobbing his head with thanks and he turned to see Anton and Grant Deakins both smiling at him. Anton's smile was warm but made sad by the tears that still filled his eyes; while Deakins' smile was just a thin line of his lips that turned upward at the corners. Spenner beamed a smile at the two men but he took Lester's hand so he would lead the way to one of the closed doors. Lester went down the corridor and pushed open a door and they entered a dining room. A long table was set in the middle of the room and Lester took Spenner to a high-backed chair at the front of the table. Lester sat to the right and Grant Deakins took the place at the opposite end.

Spenner stared at the bleak table. The cloth spread before them was startingly white but there was no food. They sat at an empty table. Suddenly, like a stage performance, a side door opened and Dyer entered followed by a woman and both were carrying trays of food. The woman seemed harried but she followed Dyer's lead in placing large platters of food on the table. Spenner was transfixed by the heavy-scented aroma of the food. His eyes were staring and wide and he swayed in his chair as the fragrance and sight of the food mixed together and taunted his senses. He realized he was very hungry. There was a plate of beef, cut in thick slices with crisp, pink edges, and a plate of three different breads—one wheat, one dark and a white bread. There was butter and a vegetable and also pickles and preserves. Dyer set a pitcher of milk and one of coffee in front of him.

"If you will forgive me, sir," Dyer said, noting Spenner's surprise, "the meal is quite simple. Naturally, the cook had no idea. We will order and supply tomorrow."

"The cook," Spenner murmured, still gazing at the table before him.

"Mrs. Roland, sir. She came to us three years ago."

Well, I don't have to remember her, Spenner thought and reached for the dark bread and several slices of beef. He was unable to calm himself and he let out a moan of pleasure as he made a sandwich. "H'mm," he said and then repeated it in a louder voice, "H'mm!"

Lester, along with Grant Deakins and Dyer, stared at him. Spenner looked around at the three of them as he reached for pickles, a heaping tablespoon of preserves and then the coffee which went steaming hot into his cup. He did not care about their stares and he cried out more as he began to eat, "H'mm!"

"Dad," Lester said quickly, leaning toward him, "It is all right. Everything is all right."

"Oh, certainly," Spenner mumbled as he was eating. "Everything is all right."

"Be careful, Dad," Lester went on, "just take it slow."

Spenner bit off another chunk of the sandwich but he nodded toward Lester. "It is good to be here . . . so good to be here."

Lester smiled and said, "Sure, Dad. We understand."

Spenner did not look at them again but he sensed that they did not eat much. The plates were not passed and the coffee pitcher went only once to Grant Deakins.

Soon Deakins rose and stood straight and stiff by his place for a moment, then he came forward. "Mr. Whitmore," he said, "I know you and Lester want this time together so I will excuse myself."

Spenner stood up and took Deakins' outstretched hand. "Sorry," he mumbled, "that there has been no conversation. I am just . . . I cannot yet express myself."

"I know, Mr. Whitmore. Do not be concerned. I understand." He turned toward Lester and bid him goodbye. "Take care, Lester," and then he added, "let me know if you need any help."

Spenner smiled at that but he said, "I thank you for everything, Grant. You have been most helpful and I, too, may have to call on you for a while."

"I will be available at any time," Deakins answered and then stepped out into the corridor where Dyer met him with his overcoat and hat.

He was alone with the boy. Spenner noted that Lester had hardly eaten and only stared at him with a candid look in his eyes. He smiled every time Spenner looked at him, as though he was trying hard to be liked. He said little except to encourage Spenner to eat more. "It is only leftovers, anyway," he said as he pushed the plates toward Spenner. Spenner ate because the food tasted good and it took time so he did not have to talk. At last, Spenner sat back in his chair. He felt contented and puffed with delight. Now he looked directly at the boy. "Lester," he began, "we can talk now. There is much to say, I know."

46

Lester nodded. "We can go to the library, Dad."

"Good," Spenner replied and rose slowly to his feet. Again, he allowed Lester to lead and he followed him to a room at the end of the corridor and to the right of the stairway. Lester pushed open the double doors to a cozy room lined with shelves and books. Spenner stopped at the doorway. Directly across the room was a fireplace and above it was a large painting of a woman. The painting was formal and full length and the woman's gaze was straightforward and compelling with only a touch of a smile upon her lips. She was young looking and quite beautiful. Her auburn hair was arranged on the top of her head and her shimmering yellow dress was without straps or sleeves so a line of bare flesh extended from beneath her ears and down the neck and small shoulders and arms to tiny hands clasped in front of her. The painter had no jewelry to contend with and, even if he had, they could not diminish the piercing eyes, painted blue, which fixed solidly on anyone who looked upon her.

Lester noted Spenner's hesitation at the doorway and his absorption in the painting. "That is Mom," he said. "We never took it down."

"It is . . ." Spenner groped for words, "a good likeness."

Lester shrugged. "I guess so. I was small at the time it was painted." He paused and then said, "I was small when Mom died."

Spenner entered the room. "Grant Deakins told me that she had passed away."

Again, Lester shrugged. "I was about five years old."

"Five years old? Then it would be sixteen years ago that she died?"

Lester nodded.

Spenner had looked at the painting almost from the first he saw it, but he noted that Lester never once looked up at the portrait of his mother. "Deakins also told me that she had been ill."

"Yes," Lester replied. "Mom was sick so much."

"I am sorry about all of it, Lester. That I was not here."

"We buried her in the family plot beyond the woods," Lester answered as he turned to the fireplace to shake the logs. A quick blaze flared and the fire spread bright and warm before the grate. Lester took to one of two black leather chairs before the fire and Spenner made his way to the other. There was a smoking stand beside the chair and Spenner reached out and grabbed a pipe but he caught himself immediately. He wondered if he should smoke. He hesitated and, at that moment, he sensed that someone was in the doorway. He had not closed the doors. Slowly, he glanced around and saw Anton Dyer looking straight at him. They stared at each other and Spenner began to feel uneasy. But then Dyer smiled and said, "I am sorry to stare, sir, but I just cannot believe you are back with us. It is like the old days when you enjoyed your smoke after dinner by the fire."

Spenner relaxed. He breathed heavily and sat back in the chair.

"Are you comfortable, sir?" Dyer went on. "I just came around to check the fire."

"I've got it, Anton," Lester said.

Dyer smiled again as he gazed at Spenner. "Sir, do you wish to meet the staff in the morning?"

Staff! Yes, of course, there was the *staff*. Spenner blinked his eyes and answered in a faltering tone, "Why, yes. Yes, Anton."

"I will arrange it," Dyer spoke again. "I have prepared your room, sir. You may wish to retire early."

Spenner nodded. "Thank you, Anton." He lit the pipe to purposely allow time to lapse, then he asked cheerfully. "I assume I have the same room?" To himself he said, the upper floor, on the right, and at the end of the passageway.

"Yes, sir. It is unchanged but it has been cleaned and fresh linen has been brought in."

Spenner thanked him again and Dyer turned and left, closing the doors.

Spenner relaxed again into the back of the chair and began to smoke. The tobacco was strong but it intoxicated his nostrils and senses and he closed his eyes. He felt contented once more, soothed and calmed, and he thought it would be easy to remain here and to dream. If only Lester were not . . . but his thoughts were surprised when Lester moved. The boy left his chair and dropped to the footstool at the side of Spenner's chair. Spenner opened his eyes and looked at him. Lester was gazing upon him like a new and curious object. Spenner sensed an adoration in the boy's wide and direct eyes, blue in color, so much like those of the woman above. Was the boy sentimental, Spenner wondered, for there was a tenderness in his eyes also.

"Dad," he asked, "whatever happened to you . . . all that time?"

48

Spenner puffed on the pipe and his throat became hot and burning. He coughed and took a deep breath, thinking over the lines he must recite again. "I had amnesia, after the war." He paused. "Did Anton tell you anything over the telephone?"

"Just that you had come back and he did say that you had had amnesia. He also said you had been at Grant Deakins' office and told him you were in Tegner all those years until a strange man recognized you."

"That is right, Lester. I had been there some time. Until the man approached me, I never knew who I was for all that time. I became quite ill when I discovered my identity, but I will tell you about that later." He saw Lester's face become serious with a look of agony in his eyes and his head moved slightly to the side. "Yes, Lester, I was very ill. Quite so." Spenner coughed and then raised his hand to his chest as if to stifle any additional coughs. "The war . . . you were just a baby then and I was stricken with amnesia. That part of my life I cannot remember. I know nothing about it."

Lester was silent, staring at Spenner and the agony in his eyes took on a wondrous look that made his eyes brilliant. His lips parted slightly and he whispered, "It sounds awful, Dad. You were hurt?"

"I guess so. That is what brought on the amnesia."

"I cannot believe not knowing a whole part of your life."

"It can happen, Lester. All I knew was that I was in the town of Tegner and my name was James Spenner."

Lester blinked but his eyes were wide and disbelieving. "How did you get that name?"

"I cannot say except that it is a name I just . . . used."

"Gosh," Lester said softly. "Your story is unbelievable and you have suffered so much." He bowed his head on the arm of the chair. Spenner was relieved that he could no longer see the boy's eyes, his vacuous, suffering look; but he stared at the blond head, the hair thick and shiny as a child's. He reached over and patted Lester's head and the hair was soft and clung together like a skein.

"It is unbelievable, Lester, but, oh, the grief I feel now is greater. All the years I have missed with you and Lee and your mother. I had no part in your growing up." Spenner glanced upward over the fireplace at the portrait. The woman's gaze was steady and penetrating upon him. He gasped as he said, "And, Gessie, dear sweet soul, ill

49

and dying and I was far away and not knowing anything. I cannot bring back any of that."

Quickly, Lester raised his head. "Take it easy, Dad. I am certain it was all that you say. Such grief for you, but you are back now and we can start together again."

Spenner turned and looked at the boy. Were his blue eyes filled with tears? Lester's eyes were moist and he looked so troubled. Spenner grabbed the boy's hand and he felt it trembling. "Lester," he said, "everything will be fine now." He smiled and then asked in a light voice, "Now tell me about yourself. You are at school, you said. What are you studying there?"

"Archaeology."

"Archaeology?"

"Yes, beginning third year."

"But why study that, Lester? It is about old ruins and cultures, is it not?"

"In a sense," Lester replied, "but one learns from those things also. I enjoy studying the past. It is fascinating. There are excavations being done all over the world and my dream is to be a part of them. Museums and specific foundations support such projects and I am hoping I can work for one of them."

"It is all so . . . old, Lester. These things that you wish to dig up tell of the past, to be sure, but also man's follies—the graves that were failures. I think it is just a repeated experience of death."

"But we must learn about that, Dad."

Spenner smiled. "So you dig up these ancient relics or whatever and then what do you do with them?" Spenner laughed slightly. "You say you learn so you lock them up in glass cages and display them, show them off. Right?"

Lester smiled at him. "Oh, Dad, I don't know. They are studied and, well, it is what I want to do."

"Well, I wish you success, Lester. If that is your dream, your wish, I hope it comes to you." Spenner paused and then asked, "How about Lee? Does he go to school, too?"

"No," Lester replied. "He will be getting married soon to Karin Brantford and he wants to go into business for himself."

Spenner became thoughtful as he heard about Lee. "Married?" he questioned first. "Her name is Karin Brantford?"

Lester nodded. "Their engagement is an understanding now but the formal announcement party will be in a few weeks."

"And the business?" Spenner asked cautiously, "what kind of business is Lee planning?"

"He does not say specifically. He is planning some projects but he is waiting until he receives his money."

Spenner's body stiffened and he turned to look into the fire. The wood crackled as the consuming fire lashed around it. Lester rose to shake the log and the flames spurted and rose higher. Spenner decided to say nothing about the money, to show complete indifference to the statement.

"Is he like you, Lester?" he asked.

"Well, we are twins, but I guess we are different, too. You'll see."

Spenner leaned back in the chair and closed his eyes.

"You are tired, Dad."

Spenner opened his eyes quickly and they focused on the painting of Gessie Whitmore. Again, Spenner felt haunted by the steady gaze of her eyes. "You are Gessie," he said in a whisper. Then Lester's face appeared between them and he looked into the soft blue eyes of the boy. Lester took the pipe and laid it aside. "Maybe you would like to retire, Dad? It must have been one hectic day for you."

"Oh, it has, Lester. It has been hectic. Perhaps I will go to my room."

"I will go with you," Lester said and helped Spenner to his feet. The two of them moved out of the library and along the corridor to the stairway. Spenner was surprised that his body was shaking and he held tightly to Lester's arm. They trudged up the stairs, following their shadows cast before them, to the landing and then turned right to the second level. They went to the room at the end of the passageway and Lester pushed the door open. A lamp on a night table sent a small, bidding light across the floor.

"Oh," Spenner whispered softly, looking into the room.

"Not much different, Dad," said Lester. "Can you manage?"

"Oh, yes. Yes."

"Sleep well. We will begin many things . . . starting tomorrow." Lester took Spenner's arms and shook him as he had done when they first met. He said nothing more but he smiled and then left.

Spenner stepped into the room and closed the door. The tiny

light made the room shadowy and without depth. He waited for a moment until his eyes could focus, then he looked around and could see a bed, several tables and a desk in one corner. He moved toward the lamp and turned it up. Now he could see that the room was magnificent and the tables and desk and the bed posts were highly polished. He noticed his small, cheap valise atop a hard wood table at the foot of the bed. The room was cold as if a window had been opened recently, yet a musty odor remained and mingled with the oil scent of furniture polish.

Spenner walked slowly around the room, appraising everything but touching nothing. I am here, he thought, in the middle of it all . . . of everything! It had been a trying day, a hectic day as Lester said, and it seemed to be so much theatre—performing, acting, trying to make things believable and real. Yet, it had gone well. Oh, yes, it had gone well. He knew he was tired, he was aware of the strain and he felt tense and nervous, yet his spirit was high for he felt sure of himself. He had regained his confidence. He was not exhilerated but he sensed success. Success, is it? Why should he think of a word like success? It had been easy to do *this thing:* people accepted so much without question. He had convinced Grant Deakins and Anton Dyer and Lester. Yet, by every measure, Deakins would certainly check him out, every facet of his story. And poor old Anton Dyer had been overwhelmed and his sentimental enthusiasm seemed genuine, but he must not forget that Dyer knew Collis Whitmore longer than anyone. Maybe the butler was old but sometimes the elderly have uncanny memories, especially of years long ago. Anton Dyer was also a part of the household and capable of watching every move Spenner made. He must be careful of Dyer.

Spenner walked to a large easy chair by the window and sat down. He closed his eyes and his face relaxed for he thought about Lester. He had been the easiest to deceive. The boy had accepted him in an almost worshipful manner. A strange howl sounded in his throat as if he were about to cry out but he did not. Lester . . . what about the boy? Spenner thought about those eyes, his mother's eyes in color, but so much more pained and sensitive. Lester had seemed appalled by his suffering. Ha! Spenner thought, *my suffering!* The boy believed and accepted it all. It is what I wanted, but how infuriating that a lad who calls himself a scholar can be so naive. So young and knowing so little. He does not understand pain and suffering at all. Ha! He wants to study the past; the boy wants to dig up old ruins. Perhaps that is an escape for him because maybe he is afraid, afraid of the future. He is, nevertheless, an agreeable lad and overly eager to be so, yet archaic and frightened. The howl sounded again in his throat and it sounded as a laugh. Spenner was laughing. Lester, you are . . . my son! A boy like you for me? To believe that I could have such a one as you! Oh, my boy!

Spenner rose and once again walked around the room. He was tense and tired and he knew he could not sleep but, perhaps, he should lie in bed. It would soothe him and ease his thoughts. He took off his clothes, all those tight new ones that Thurston had bought for him. Immediately, he felt his body swell out and sag and he sighed with relief. He opened his valise to get an old pair of pajamas which were loose about his body. The bed was high but his body succumed to the soft mattress and he relaxed in its deep folds. The quilt which covered him was lightweight but he could feel the warmth of it spreading over him. Physically, he was lethargic and prepared for sleep yet his eyes could not close and he stared into the darkness.

Time passed and there was a stillness all about him. It seemed so long and did he really sleep? It did not seem possible, yet the stillness did not change, until his thoughts were startled by a sudden, whirling noise from outside. The sound began softly in the distance but Spenner heard it coming closer. It was the sound of a motor with an even, throbbing rhythm. It grew louder as it came nearer and passed under his window; then it became quiet as it faded away and stopped. Spenner got out of bed and hurried to the window. A light-colored sports car had pulled into the driveway before the garage. A man got out and seemed to sway as he braced himself by the car. He moved along the side of the car as if to support himself for he walked unsteadily. The light over the garage shone on him and revealed the yellow color of his hair. He moved away from the car, standing uneasily, for his tall and thin body was moving to one side and then the other.

"Lee!" Spenner whispered as he caught the resemblance to Lester. Spenner watched as the boy crossed the lawn toward the house. His coat was open and he hurried, which was unwise, for he stumbled and did not walk evenly. Spenner heard a faint noise from below, in the house, and guessed that it was the door, opening and closing, to admit the boy; then the house was silent. Spenner remained by the

53

window, straining to hear a noise or footstep on the stairs or along the corridor but he heard nothing.

After a while, he made his way back to bed but a floor board creaked beneath him and he jerked as if afraid. He continued on tiptoe and soon was back in bed. He did not relax now, he lay stiff and straight, glancing around—for what—in the darkness? Everything was quiet, it was dark, as the night should be.

Chapter Four

He imagined that he slept in short intervals and in a fitful manner, but when he awakened the following morning, he felt as if he had been in a deep slumber. He came around slowly, his body was sluggish, and his senses were groggy and he strained to function. He struggled to sit upright in the middle of the huge bed and tried to bring his body strengths together. The events of yesterday had been unnerving and the little sleep of the night had made him feel ill instead of refreshed. He was dizzy and his head ached but he blinked his eyes as he looked again at the luxurious surroundings. The dizzy feeling made the room waver in his gaze and the brightness stunned him. Sunlight shone through the windows, indicating that the day was advanced, and its luster cast a glow over the furniture and floor and made them more gleaming than before. He thought it might be late but he could not estimate the time.

He left the bed and dressed as fast as he could. He also put on his hat and short overcoat. He opened the door and listened carefully for any sounds from the hallway or the corridor below. The house was silent, so Spenner stepped out and walked quickly along the hallway and made a cowardly descent down the stairs. He crouched close to the railing, peering over the side to the corridor below, listening again for any sounds and measuring each step to the next stair to avoid any noise or creaking boards. He reached the first level and the corridor to the door was clear. He wanted to step out unseen. He started toward the door when he heard footsteps coming from behind the stairway.

"Good morning, sir." It was Anton Dyer.

Spenner halted immediately and turned to look at him. Dyer had come upon him as noiselessly as a cat. Had Dyer heard him or was it coincidence that he left the servants' quarters just at this time? Dyer was smiling and the sentiment was gone from his face but there was concern on his countenance. His forehead wrinkled in surprise as he looked over Spenner, fully dressed for the outdoors, yet his first question was, "Did you rest, sir? Mister Lester gave explicit instructions that you were to sleep and rest as long as you wished."

"I slept well enough," Spenner replied, trying not to reveal his anxiety and irritation. He knew he was not alert; he was tired and listless. "Is it late, Anton?" he asked.

"It is almost noon, sir."

"Almost noon?" Spenner said with surprise and tried to smile. "Then I did sleep well!" He was trying to be amusing, making an excuse, so as not to explain his feelings to Anton Dyer. He just wished that he had not met him.

"You are all right, sir?" Dyer asked.

"Oh, yes. Yes, Anton," Spenner replied quickly. He felt more irritation as if Dyer understood his thoughts. Dyer's heavy eyelids gave the impression he was looking downward, yet his eyes would roll along the lids and focus directly on Spenner. But the sincerity of his concern was there and Spenner could only try to be cheerful and he talked softly. "I am fine, Anton, but is Lester about?"

"He went to his classes," Dyer answered.

Spenner nodded his head. "That is good. I want him to continue. I mean I want everything to continue. I do not wish to disrupt a thing. You do keep the schedule, Anton?"

Dyer replied in the affirmative and Spenner went on, "And Lee? Is he in today?"

"He is riding, sir."

"Oh," said Spenner, surprised once more. "I have not met him yet, Anton, and I am anxious to see him."

"There will be a dinner party this evening, sir. Mister Lee left the instructions this morning and his fiancée, Miss Brantford, and her mother will be guests."

Spenner felt tense and the irritation was becoming overpowering. He mumbled words about "fulfill your duties, whatever is asked," and he turned away.

Anton Dyer stepped around him. "Are you going out, sir?"

Spenner smiled at him. "I would like to walk, Anton, and get some air. I was going to stroll about outside, just to . . . look around."

Dyer bowed slightly. "Very well, sir, but would you like company? I would be happy to go with you."

Spenner continued to smile but his attitude became firm. He

shook his head. "Thank you, Anton, but I want to go alone . . . to see things." He tried to be reassuring. "Do not worry. I can manage. I will walk for a while and I will not be long."

The soft tenderness returned to Dyer's face and the concern increased. Spenner turned quickly away for he could not look upon that worrisome face any longer. Yet, he was aware that Dyer was watching him closely as he opened the door and stepped outside.

Immediately, he felt relaxed to be away and by himself and the cold air whipped at his drowsy body. The sun was bright but the atmosphere was chilly and, high above, thick clouds rolled tediously through a pale blue sky. Spenner followed a path that went around to the back of the house. The house was large and the grounds were vast also, spreading away toward outlying forests. Spenner tried to walk briskly because of the cold, but he still felt a weariness in his limbs. His head still ached and the cold air increased his pain. He winced and walked slower but he had to bend forward to feel comfortable.

A sandy path led off toward a wooded area and Spenner turned with it. Reed grass grew tall and golden along the short path and soon Spenner moved into the forest. It was thick with conifers, those seasonless trees which seem to grow everlastingly, and their prickly branches spread in all directions. The fragrance of the pines was overwhelming and pleasant and the forest was in a calm sate, quiet and primitive. Spenner felt an added chill in the dense atmosphere and he bent over further with the cold.

Ahead, he saw a definite rise in the land. It was a man-made clearing and it had been tended for a square of the land was outlined by an ornate, iron fence. The place was a cemetery plot and the tombstones stood like stalagmites within the area. The ground itself was a fading green and barren except for the scattered evergreen bushes that hugged against the grave markers.

Spenner approached the gate and pushed it open. The gravel path spread like a creeping vine to each gravesite. Spenner walked along and then stopped before a tall stone of pink granite marble in the center of the plot. The name on the stone, in single block letters, was GESSIE WHITMORE and the dates of birth and death. A single, four-petal flower was carved in one corner and the leaves turned down one side of the headstone.

Spenner stared at the marker and he thought of the portrait in the library. So the woman with the frail body but steadfast look was resting here, had been for sixteen years. His mood dwelled on the picture of that delicate face and smooth skin, and his body shook although he knew it was not another chill. The dizzy feeling increased and he tried to steady himself but was forced to grab onto the headstone. He held it tightly and then, without reason, from his chilled body and aching head, he called out, "Gessie!" He knew he was alone but he looked around as if there was anyone there to hear him. The forest was still and calm but he felt uneasy. Ah, he thought, am I ill? Why should I say the name of this dead woman? Am I distraught? He took his hand and covered his face. There was no perspiration but his skin was firm and cold like ice. He turned as if frightened and started back along the path. He locked the gate and looked no more at the markers. He returned through the forest and he tried to hurry when, at last, he saw the spacious clearing near the estate. The area was bright for the autumn sun had once again pierced through the clouds and covered the area with radiance but not warmth.

Spenner was crossing the area when he heard a heavy, beating sound behind him. He turned to see a horse and rider coming at an easy gallop and fast approaching him. Spenner halted for he knew he would be overtaken and it would be foolish to walk on. In the sunlight, the hair on the head of the rider shown as brightly as it did in the artificial light over the garage the night before. The rider was Lee and, dressed in sand colored riding suit and sitting atop a palomino horse, he looked like a specter striding in the bright sunlight.

The horse and rider slowed when they came near Spenner and then continued in a trot until they were beside him. Lee looked directly at Spenner and his glance was coming closer and steadier like the probing lens of a camera. Lee's stare was impersonal as well for it was cold and arrogant. Spenner did not move but he looked him over, avoiding the stare. Lee looked like Lester, to be sure, and there was no mistaking them as twins, but Lee possessed the hauteur for he sat straight in the saddle and looked commanding. There was no indication of the stumbling, wavering figure of last night.

Lee did not dismount and he kept his hand tight on the reins rather than offer a handshake. After a moment, his countenance changed. His eyes flickered with curiosity and he tried to smile. The corners of his mouth turned upward but his lips were insolent and the forced smile was mocking and malicious. He leaned forward in the saddle as if to scrutinize Spenner more closely, then he laughed, loud and deriding. "I cannot believe it! After all these years . . . a father! You *are* my father?"

Spenner smiled at him and nodded his head. "Lee," he uttered but his voice was trembling and the name was said so softly that it was almost lost.

"So you are my father!" Lee retorted and then laughed again.

"Lee," Spenner said once more but his voice remained soft and uneven. "I know I am a shock . . ."

Lee interrupted. "You are indeed a shock."

A real chill gripped Spenner and went through his entire body so he almost wavered. "I want to tell you . . ."

"I want to hear," Lee interrupted again. "You must have *some* story to tell."

"Yes," Spenner replied. "I am grateful," his voice stumbled and once more the words were almost gone. "I am grateful," he began again, "to be back with you and Lester."

Lee was smiling, with a sneer, and all the while gazing intently at Spenner. "Double gratitude, no doubt."

"It does mean much to me," Spenner went on. "It has been so many years and I will tell you."

"Sure you will tell," Lee answered and tugged at the reins so the horse's head jerked from side to side. "But I cannot listen to any of your explanations now. I am meeting Karin on the trail."

Spenner smiled at Lee. "I have heard that she is your fiancée."

Lee nodded. "I have invited her and her mother to dinner to-night."

"Anton told me."

Lee nodded his head again. "We are going to the theater but I thought we would have dinner here first. Guess why? Just to meet you." He turned the horse quickly and Spenner fell back, almost falling to the ground. He caught himself but his trembling body was more shaky as he wobbled on his feet. Lee laughed and looked back once, with a contemptuous grin on his face and then he rode away in a quick gallop. He rode directly into the sun and Spenner squinted his eyes to look after him. His gaze began to flicker and they looked like two riders and two horses bounding over the turf. Spenner's cold face perspired now for moisture drops rolled down along his temples. I am perspiring, he thought, when I am so cold. He closed his eyes and when he opened them, the vision had vanished for the horse and rider had entered the woods and disappeared.

Spenner stood alone in the center of the wide, clear field. Now a strange feeling came over him. He felt embarrassed and it gave him a troubled feeling about himself. Such an encounter! He had been helpless in his meeting with Lee. He had hardly spoken and, when he did, he was rudely interrupted and any words he uttered were whispered and mocked. Spenner knew he had not reacted properly to Lee. Oh, if only he had not had such a restless night! He was weary and dull and the cold and the chill had numbed him too much. The visit to the cemetery plot had not done him good either for it upset him, renewed his dizzy feeling and made him feel that he was losing control of himself. Oh, that Lee was brash and arrogant, talking and acting as he did and arranging a dinner, too, without any consideration or questioning beforehand. Just telling Spenner to be there, to be inspected by his guests. Spenner shivered for he was quite cold but now he was angry as well. He was angry that he had made no response, no objection, no idea to these insolent directives of Lee.

Spenner walked back to the house. He was near a side door so he pushed it and it opened onto the corridor. He entered and heard voices at the far end. He stepped around to see Anton Dyer standing squarely in the doorway with his stocky body blocking anyone from entering. His voice was firm and peremptory and directed to someone on the other side.

"He is not in at the moment," Dyer stated. A male voice answered beyond but the words were not distinct and Dyer answered quickly, "I am unable to say. I have no idea where he is or when he will return." With that, Dyer closed the door and locked it.

"Anton?" Spenner asked curiously, coming along the corridor. Dyer turned immediately and was alarmed when he saw Spenner.

"A Mr. Kirkland, sir, of the *Review*," Dyer answered hurriedly but his voice became level and courteous. "He requested an interview for his newspaper."

Spenner was startled. "An interview?"

"Yes, sir."

"Why?" Spenner asked, still surprised. "Whatever for . . ." He paused and considered, "not with me?"

"Yes, sir," Dyer repeated. "It is about your return. They want a story, as they say."

The newspapers! An interview! How soon they have discovered me, Spenner thought, and now to tell everyone. His planned story, for anyone to read! His return had not been secret for long. How did they find out so readily?

"I could not," he stammered. "Now now, Anton. I could not."

"I thought so, sir, and I told Mr. Kirkland accordingly. The man is persistent, however, and said he would call again."

"I don't want anything like that," Spenner stammered on in a whisper.

"I understand, sir," Dyer answered softly. "Do not distress your-self. I will try to see that you are not bothered any more."

Spenner shifted his glance away from Dyer and moved toward the staircase. Dyer stepped before him. His eyes were clear but became small in size as he looked at Spenner.

"If you feel well, sir," Dyer asked, "perhaps you would like to meet the staff? I have explained to them about your return."

The staff, Spenner said to himself as he paused, was little to worry about since all of them were hired within the last few years and none would *know him*. He nodded to Dyer who went to the servant's quarters and reappeared with the staff. There was Mrs. Roland, the cook, and a housekeeper and laundress whom Spenner recognized as the harried woman who had aided Dyer in serving last evening's meal. There was a gardener who looked like the house-keeper-laundress and Spenner was not surprised when told they were brother and sister. Two men worked in the stables, one of whom carried out delivery chores and was chauffeur also. All of the staff were speechless and looked polite when introduced to Spenner, but there was an obvious curiosity in their eyes and in the expression on their faces. Spenner suspected that, in their quarters, they talked wildly and at length about him—the master who had appeared like some ghost. Spenner glanced them over and stumbled over the phrase, "pleased to meet you," and thanked them for their service. They smiled and Dyer dismissed them but they were silent as they went back to their quarters.

Dyer remained and turned to Spenner. "Did you enjoy your walk?"

Spenner nodded. "Yes. I walked through the forest and when I returned, I met Lee while he was riding. We could not talk for long because he was to meet his fiancée. He told me about the dinner tonight."

"Yes, sir," Dyer replied. "The dinner will be at seven o'clock. Those were Mister Lee's instructions."

"Whatever he wishes," Spenner said and hesitated. He shifted his body so he did not look at Dyer. "My sons are grown and I have missed so much of their lives."

"I am certain you will make up for that, sir."

Spenner hesitated once more and then he said, "I went to the grave where Mrs. Whitmore is buried. Is it really sixteen years since she is gone?"

Dyer's eyes widened briefly. "She was ill for several years. She was not strong and had been confined to bed."

"What was her illness, Anton?" Spenner asked. "I hope she did not suffer."

"Well," Dyer began, "she had consumption. She had not been well for several years, and I believe that particular night was bad for her. She was out of bed, trying to leave her room, when she fell and hit her head against the table. I believe that her weakened condition made her fall and killed her quickly without any suffering."

"Was no one there with her?"

"It was late, sir. She was sleeping and the nurse had left for the night."

Spenner stood rigid and silent for a moment, then slowly he said, "Thank you for telling me, Anton."

Spenner went to his room and fell into the chair by the window. He did not want to admit to Anton Dyer that he felt ill although he was certain that Dyer, and perhaps the staff, thought he did not look well. He was still chilled and he sat numbed, unable to close his eyes, and he stared out into the distance. The sun was bright but he knew it was cold. He moved back into the chair so the cushions would close about him and his body would warm. When I am warm, he said to himself, perhaps I can sleep a little and then this ill feeling will leave me. I can remember that the sun was warm even in the cold places outdoors. Spenner's head inclined against the back of the chair. Now he closed his eyes and the sun was blotted out but a warmth, near and close, slowly was coming over him.

He awoke suddenly and looked around. The room was silent but he noted that fresh linens were on the bed. Anton Dyer must have come in, he thought, and it reassured him that he had slept so well that he had not been aroused by anyone entering. The linens, placed on the bed, however, reminded him of the dinner that evening. He cleaned himself and dressed in Thurston's new clothes and then descended to the library. The fire was going and the room was warm and cozy. He sat in the leather chair and occasionally glanced upward at the painting of Gessie Whitmore. The portrait was provocative and he could not look at it for long. Her gaze was spellbinding and forceful and it seemed to accuse him—but of what? Certainly, no specific look could be in her eyes unless he imagined it. He thought of her resting place under that pink marble stone and how easily he had found it in his walk. A disconcerted feeling came over him and all of a sudden, as it happened at the cemetery plot, he blurted out her name, "Gessie!"

The doors opened and Spenner sat upright, looking quickly over his shoulder. In the doorway stood Lee. He stared at Spenner, then stepped inside and closed the doors behind him.

"I have been looking for you," Lee said. "You were not in your room."

"I came down early," Spenner said uneasily. He studied Lee's face, wondering if he had heard him utter the name of Gessie. If Lee had, he said nothing and there was no curiosity on his countenance.

"I thought you looked ill when I saw you earlier," said Lee. He possessed the same arrogance. His lips were petulant, he would not smile and the hauteur was still in his glance. He swaggered slightly as he came forward and stood by the fireplace. He stood as straight as he rode. He looked elegant in a black velvet jacket and his hair was brushed sleek and shining close to his head.

"I am all right. I slept." Spenner answered. He motioned toward the opposite chair. "Sit down, Lee."

Lee shrugged his shoulders and shook his head. "I prefer standing." He was looking downward at Spenner; his look was unflinching and appraising and then suddenly, he laughed, the same mocking laughter. "You need new clothes. You ought to go to Thornburgs right away and order some."

Spenner was completely surprised. He had been aware of the elegance of Lee's attire but he had not thought of his own appearance by contrast. Now he recoiled in the cheap and nondescript trousers and shirt. He wore no coat and he sensed that he obviously was not suitably dressed for a dinner party with guests.

"I know you have not had time for shopping," Lee went on, "but I advise you to do it as soon as possible. I suggest some dress suits, a tuxedo, silk shirts, but you know . . . you must have had such a wardrobe before." His tone changed and became solemn. "You can afford it now, you know."

Spenner's body stiffened but he decided to ignore the comment. He nodded his head slowly and replied, "I'll go to Thornburgs soon."

Lee's expression still was serious. "Of course, you would not know the store as Thornburgs. In your day, it was Woodbridge. Remember?"

Spenner's glance flickered and he looked away from Lee. Thornburgs? Woodbridge? How would he know?

"In your day, as mayor, I understood you did a great deal of business with Woodbridge." Lee continued. "Thornburgs took over several years ago."

"I had forgotten," Spenner stammered. "I had forgotten about Woodbridge." He tried to laugh. "You see, that is my problem . . ." He looked at Lee but he was not smiling so Spenner went on, "Can't you sit down, Lee? We were to talk, were we not, and I want to tell you about the things that happened."

Again, Lee refused to be seated but he said to Spenner, "Go on, tell me."

At that, Spenner began to recount the story again but he spoke almost by rote, without emotion, for he sensed that his audience was not receptive. Lee was quiet and asked nothing, he showed neither interest or incredulity. He allowed Spenner to ramble on and then he said simply, "So now you are back to take charge of everything?"

"Oh, no," Spenner replied hastily.

"Then what are you going to do? Mother is dead, Lester and I are grown. I am going to be married. The estate? What will you do with it?"

"Well, I . . ." Spenner began. "I . . ." he tried to begin again but stopped.

At that moment, Anton Dyer stepped in to announce that Mrs. Brantford and her daughter had arrived. Lee immediately rushed for the door and Spenner heard excited voices in the hallway. Spenner got to his feet as Lee reappeared with a slender and very beautiful girl on his arm. She had dark hair and wore a coral colored dress that looked vivid in the firelight and cast a blushing tint onto her face. She looked to be a lively, impudent girl with sparkling eyes. She was laughing, then whispering, close to Lee's ear.

"The characters are mixed up," Spenner heard her say. "No one knows who is who and everyone is somebody else!" She laughed at Lee but stopped when she looked forward and cast a long, unsmiling gaze upon Spenner. She said nothing but tossed her head back and returned her attention, laughing and whispering as it were, to Lee.

A woman followed them into the room and she was an identifying, older replica of the girl. The girl's mother, of course, and she was tall, which gave a slenderness to her body; and her hair was dark, too, but short and scuptured close to her head in large waves. She was dressed in black and wore pearls and also a strange-looking jeweled ornament in her hair situated between two deep waves.

"Mrs. Brantford," Lee said, casting a glance at her, "this is my . . . father." He deliberately hesitated and stumbled over the introduction and then he laughed. "I cannot get used to *father*." Turning to the girl, he swung her forward. "And this is Karin." Lee's arrogance had not dimished but a look of warmth and happiness had spread over his face when he looked at the two women. He was smiling, full attention upon Karin, but she tossed her head again and looked once more upon Spenner. Her eyes gleamed with curiosity, but her first glance, long and unsmiling, was repeated. Her lips were painted a bright coral color like her dress and they twitched slightly. It was the kind of mouth that could say much without words.

"Such a surprise!" she said carelessly.

"Hello," Spenner said softly. His throat seemed dry and he did not know what to say, yet he stared at her and sensed a response to her youthful beauty. He wanted to hold her attention and he went on speaking. "I heard you mention characters, everyone being someone else . . ."

"Oh!" she interrupted in a spirited voice, "It is the play! We are going to see it this evening. One of those French style plots where everyone masquerades as somebody else. Each performer has two characters."

"It sounds interesting," Spenner replied, his voice still soft.

"It is a comedy. A farce. Very funny, they say. I was telling Lee about the reviews." She turned to him and laughed and whispered to him.

"It may be funny," Lee said as he drew his head away for her laughter tickled his ear, "but I doubt if it is believable. People must be idiots to be fooled like that." He looked at Spenner and asked. "Don't you think so?"

"What?" Spenner replied deliberately as if he had not heard what Lee was asking.

"Impossible," Lee went on, answering his own question. "No one can pass for another, not for long."

"We shall see," Karin said teasingly as she tugged at Lee's arm.

Spenner had been entranced by Karin's beauty but not so much that he had not been aware of her haughtiness, so similar to that of Lee's. His demeanor was serious and seemed menacing, while her insolence was playful and teasing yet possessive and forceful for she could dance around him with a tittering amusement and he succumbed easily.

Spenner was aware that Mrs. Brantford had stood quietly back after she entered the room and had been studying him earnestly. He looked directly at her, so she stepped around the laughing duo and made straight for him. She offered her hand and said, "How do you do, Mr. Whitmore? Your coming back is very much of a surprise for all of us."

Spenner saw the cold sparkle of diamond rings on her fingers and when he grasped her hand, he was surprised that the flesh was cold also. She withdrew her hand quickly and clasped it in her other as if to try to warm them both.

"I know I have surprised many. It is awkward," Spenner said to her.

Mrs. Brantford was self assured and stood very straight, almost regal, with her chin in and her eyes cast directly upon Spenner. Spenner was once again acutely aware of his appearance as he sensed that, like Lee, her appraisal of his looks and clothes was complete disapproval. Spenner stepped back and he hit the chair but it braced him.

"But are you well?" Mrs. Brantford went on. "Lee thought you were ill when he met you."

"Yes," Spenner replied, his voice very low. "Yes, I am well."

She tilted her head slightly. "How fine, really, that you are well, after being ill for so many years."

"I was not ill," Spenner answered quickly, "not truly. Amnesia."

Mrs. Brantford did not answer for Karin spoke up and said, "That is the surprise, mother. Years and years of amnesia."

Spenner turned to her and tried to smile.

She did not look at him but her eyes blinked in mockery. "Such a surprise!"

Anton Dyer entered the room with a tray of cocktails and the three of them followed him to the table for the drinks. They looked at Spenner but he shook his head and declined to join them. He stood still, supported by the chair, and watched them. They remained at the table and talked amongst themselves. Spenner did not care to hear what they were saying and not once did they look back at him. He resented them. He suspected hostility in each and he sensed that they did not like him.

"Where is Lester?" he spoke up and forced himself to speak loudly to break them apart. "Will he be here?"

Lee turned and answered, "He will be late. He has some project at school. But we will not wait. No need to keep dinner just for him and make us late for the theater."

They went to the dining room and Spenner felt uneasy at being at the table with them. He did not know what to say to them and he wondered why he had to do this . . .

This time, the dinner was fish, which was covered with a cream sauce and looked like a yellowish puddle on Spenner's plate. Spenner stared at the food, the aroma was oil heavy and scented with herbs, but he felt no appetite. He picked at the fish and a large white flake broke from the puddle. He tasted it and was surprised for the fish was delicious and succulent, the sauce a bit too rich, but he wished he were inclined to eat more. He poked another flake loose and stared at it mournfully but he did not eat it. He moved the flake to the side of the plate. If he could get it away from the sauce . . .

"Mr. Whitmore."

He heard the name but he did not respond.

"Mr. Whitmore."

The name was repeated and Spenner only said, "Hmm," when he paused and looked up, startled. He realized it was Mrs. Brantford who was speaking to him.

"Mr. Whitmore," she repeated a third time and now her gaze was holding his attention. "You have returned at the correct time."

Spenner blinked and looked at her with curiosity. She continued as though she did not expect a reply or would wait for one. "The correct time for the engagement party for Karin and Lee. It will be at our home within three weeks."

Three weeks, thought Spenner, that would be about the time for *the plan* to be completed . . .

"The invitations have been posted and it is too late to have them properly worded," Mrs. Brantford was saying. "But who could guess that Lee's father would return? Of course, you must come, although the circumstances are exceptional."

Spenner continued to stare at her. Mrs. Brantford was soignée, a very neat, very precise person and she looked and acted incredibly perfect. Her hair ornament gleamed like a star in the candlelight, making flickering lights around her head. She sat straight and regal, her head tilted slightly forward as she ate, and what delicate manners of eating! The knife hardly was used and the fork was reversed and tiny bits of food were picked with its tines and lifted upwards to her mouth. In between, she sipped little draughts of wine without getting her lips wet.

"An engagement party?" Spenner repeated softly, not knowing what else to say. He looked at Karin and Lee who had glanced at him at the first mention of the party. Their looks were steady, not cheerful, and seemed to convey the message of Mrs. Brantford that his appearance had to be accepted.

Mrs. Brantford smiled at them and then turned again to Spenner and replied, "The formal announcement will be made at that time."

"I have already told him," Lee said, nodding toward Spenner, "to buy a tuxedo."

"How nice, Lee," Mrs. Brantford smiled again. "It will be such a surprise to introduce your father." Spenner heard Karin and Lee laugh lightly but Mrs. Brantford overlooked the laughter and went on speaking. "Very unexpected, you understand, but I guess it can be explained. It must be explained." She paused. "For now, Mr. Whitmore, perhaps you can explain what happened, in your own way. Briefly, of course."

What happened? Tell them, *briefly*, what happened. Spenner wished that he could laugh or that he could invent a story for them which would be hilarious and exaggerated. That would suit them; they would be surprised and aghast, not knowing if they should laugh, laugh, laugh as they are doing now. He would like to see their faces as he imagined: Mrs. Brantford with her mouth open, speechless, her fork dangling food in front of the gap. Karin's face would be frozen like an idol with her large eyes staring in disbelief and, devoid of impudence, would make her entire countenance vacant and expressionless. Lee . . . well, Lee must be like her, an idol face with eyes wide with amazement but they would most certainly contain that look of contempt.

Spenner lowered his head as if afraid they might read his mind and, despite his thoughts, he answered simply and quietly, "As I said before, I had amnesia."

"But how?" Mrs. Brantford asked. "Can you explain how it happened?"

"I was hurt," Spenner stammered. "I was hit . . . it was during the war."

"And it made you a different person? For twenty years?"

Spenner frowned and moved uneasily in his chair. "I cannot explain it. It happened."

Mrs. Brantford raised her head high. "It does not sound comprehensible. The complete disbelief of it all."

"Mother!" Karin spoke up but there was a snicker in her voice. "What is the disbelief? You have heard of amnesia?"

"Of course, I have heard of it, dear," Mrs. Brantford replied and cast a sly glance at her daughter, "but I have never been able to understand it and I am trying to get an explanation for amnesia."

"But only doctors or psychiatrists can do that," Karin answered.

Spenner glanced at Karin and smiled. "I believe she is right. I am not able to explain the condition."

Mrs. Brantford shook her head. "Then can doctors or psychiatrists explain how one can become a completely different person?"

Karin did not reply. Apparently the discussion had gone as far as she could carry it. She shrugged her shoulders and cast a helpless glance at Lee. He smiled at her but said nothing.

Mrs. Brantford turned again to Spenner. He imitated Karin, he shrugged his shoulders and mumbled. "I do not know. It is true, nevertheless, in my case."

Mrs. Brantford's head still was held high but she shook it slightly and then asked, "You lived those years in . . . Tegner?"

"Yes. I lived in Tegner."

Lee interrupted. "He does not remember how he got to Tegner. Just fell there, from out of the sky, no doubt." Karin giggled and Mrs. Brantford smiled slightly at both of them.

"You do remember your life there, do you not?" she asked Spenner.

Spenner nodded. "I do. I had the name of James Spenner."

"But you do not remember your life, your family, before that?"

"No."

"That is what I wish could be explained by any doctor, or psychiatrist, if you wish. How one can get hurt and then become and function easily as another person in another place."

"I never saw a doctor or a psychiatrist," Spenner answered. "I do not know what they would say about the situation. I only know I was there, I called myself by what I thought was my name. I worked at odd jobs."

"Fascinating!" Karin spoke up and her voice was lively, "but not like being a mayor, I am sure."

"Then a stranger approached . . . my father," Lee had paused again at the word and then laughed at his own remark. "This stranger spoke his true name and, *presto*, he came back to our time and our lives." Karin joined in the laughter and the two young people were becoming silly as well as sarcastic. They were making merry of Spenner's story just as he had wanted to tell a ludicrous story to them. Lee continued, "After all, what is in a name? That is the question, is it not?" He looked up as the door opened. "Well, here comes the scholar."

Lester entered the room. He was breathing fast and his face was flushed, obviously from rushing about. He wore no tie and was straightening his shirt collar over a plaid coat. He looked quite informal and he paused by Spenner's chair and patted his shoulder. "Hello, Dad," he said.

Spenner smiled at him but Lee continued to speak, "So you have come," he said and his voice was as irritable as his look as he watched Lester greet Karin and Mrs. Brantford and turn around the table to his place. "Since you are late, you could have taken additional time to dress."

"So sorry," Lester replied easily. He glanced around the table so that his apology included everyone. "I had an experiment to complete at the Harding Museum. I could have dressed, but I did not want to take more time from your dinner party, Lee. I am glad you did not wait."

Lee shook his head at him. "It is not appropriate because you know better." He looked at Karin and her mother. "We did not wait dinner as we are going to the theater later." His voice became lower as he said, "Those studies! Nothing takes priority, does it?"

Karin giggled to the angered Lee. "I am happy you are not so serious, but if Lester wishes to be a bookworm, why not?" Once again, she shrugged her shoulders and then plopped a large black olive into her mouth. "Why not?" she repeated. All of a sudden, her eyes rolled upward and her thoughts took another direction. "The plot!" she exclaimed. "Just think of that plot! Everyone is somebody else!"

"What is that?" Lester asked in surprise.

"The play, Lester," she replied emphatically. "The play we are going to see later."

Spenner's glance settled on the two boys while their attention was diverted to the excited Karin. Seen together, the likeness of their appearance was compelling. Each was tall and had a thin body and flaxen hair. Yet, the facial expression of each displayed a personality noticeably unlike the other. The bone structure of each face outlined an almost duplicate of the other, but the eyes and mouth of Lee were stern and tense while Lester's were soft and relaxed. Spenner sensed a tension and strain between them and was aware of a provoking influence in Karin Brantford. She could tease one and chide the other and believe that her fascination could excuse it all. He looked at her again. She still was savoring the olive and her eyes rolled upward once more and they shone with an intensity and something of a child's delight. The candlelight, like the firelight, gave her a glow. Suddenly, Spenner found himself talking to her. "You are a student . . ." he stumbled, as if aware that the question was wrong.

She grunted unexpectedly but her eyes rolled down as she looked at Spenner. "Oh, no," she replied. "I work."

"Work?"

Karin reached for another olive. "I am an artist," she stated evenly.

71

"Oh," said Spenner, very surprised.

"I am a commercial artist," she went on. "I work for the Willoughby Company."

Mrs. Brantford spoke quickly. "Karin is a commercial artist for the present. Hopefully, she can become independent and devote her time to original paintings. She is quite capable and has the talent."

"How wonderful to be an artist," Spenner said. "To be able to paint things just as they are."

"Or as I see them," Karin said.

"She must study abroad," Mrs. Brantford went on. Her head remained high and her eyes became dark and serious. "There is no substitute for that kind of training. Expertise is what she needs."

"That is one of our plans after we are married—to go abroad, live there for sometime so Karin can study," Lee said. "I want so much to do that for Karin." He looked at her and they both smiled, then they leaned toward each other as if in a mock caress but they did not touch. They laughed together as if there was some secret understanding between them.

Spenner turned to Mrs. Brantford. "Are you an artist, too, Mrs. Brantford?" he asked.

"Not a bone of me," she replied quickly. "No inclination whatsoever. I was a legal secretary, Mr. Whitmore."

"Oh," Spenner said softly as the word *legal* made him shiver.

"I should have been a lawyer," she continued, "but it was not so easy in my day. That is why conditions like your amnesia interests me so. The only experience I have had with it has been from a legal, rather than a medical, viewpoint."

"Well," Lester spoke up, looking first at Spenner and then at Mrs. Brantford, "it has to be a medical question because amnesia, like a sickness, can be diminished and cured, as Dad experienced."

"Mr. Whitmore was ill, mother," Karin said. "I do believe."

"Dear children," Mrs. Brantford said evenly, "how can anyone explain a person who forgets who he is and what he has done and, all of a sudden, recovers and returns to everything different and claims it as his own. The mind cannot be treated like a sore. The medical option does not satisfy me; I just wish to have a more definite explanation, that is all."

"I don't think I was ill," Spenner said but his voice was uneven as he stated his opinion.

"Then do you think amnesia is a legal question?" Mrs. Brantford asked. "What about your actions, Mr. Whitmore? Are you responsible as yourself or when you were, you said, James Spenner?"

Spenner shook his head. "I do not know," he replied.

"You are being too legal, mother," Karin said, her voice was light but its tone had become higher like the teasing pitch she enjoyed using. "Mother is always so legal."

Lester answered to Mrs. Brantford. "Amnesia has been recognized by both medical and legal professions."

"But how is it solved?" Mrs. Brantford asked. "Amnesia is a provocative situation and I think it is highly suspect."

Lee spoke up, nodding toward her. "I have suspicions about it, too, and I believe people can forget when it suits them."

Lester looked at him and there was a sternness in his glance and in his voice. "There are degrees of amnesia. A blow to the head can bring it on, or stress, fright, or unusual conditions." He turned to look at Spenner and smiled. Spenner nodded and smiled back at the boy.

Mrs. Brantford's eyes darkened again and they gleamed as she went on speaking. "But seldom is there any brain damage. In my experience in the legal profession, amnesia has been the most perverted cause I know. People suspected of having committed a crime often claim they 'blacked out' or do not remember their actions. I have seen that."

"There has been improvements on that score," Lester answered. "Examinations by psychiatrists or even drugs can be used to determine the truth in such cases."

"The medical position once again," Mrs. Brantford replied.

Lee made no comment to Lester but spoke directly to Mrs. Brantford. "Are you saying that amnesia can be used as an excuse," he asked, "for a crime?"

"Exactly," replied Mrs. Brantford with a smile, "because I have seen it used that way. In the legal profession, amnesia has been a sham. A patient, with a lawyer, can convince a jury of his misfortune and win a large sum of money. I remember cases whereby lawyers produced in court skull X-rays showing a fracture line, convinced juries of amnesia type injuries and gained settlements when actually the patients had no disabling symptoms."

"Schemes!" Karin cried out in her spirited voice. "The world is full of them!"

"Schemes?" Lester retorted. "That is sham and dishonesty. A genuinely ill person can be deprived of his compensation. It can work that way also."

"Then we do not know if one is sick or a criminal," Lee said, trying to imitate the light whisper of Karin. "How can we know?"

"It is reprehensible what people will do for money," Mrs. Brantford said flatly. "To get for themselves or deprive others and they attempt to make it honorable with such righteous backing as amnesia. To me, amnesia is only a trick and," she paused and smiled at her daughter, "yes, Karin, a scheme."

Karin sighed happily and finished her coffee, then took forth a cigarette. Immediately, Lee offered his lighter and she inhaled deeply and puffed smoke into the air. In smoking, she took on some of the regality of her mother. She looked sophisticated as her posture became straight and stiff, her arm was raised close to her body, and she held the cigarette delicately between her fingers. Her face relaxed and she seemed to concentrate on smoking—to do it right. Suddenly, she looked at Spenner. "Oh, Mr. Whitmore, I did not think about the smoke. Does it affect you?"

Spenner shook his head. "No," he answered but he knew she tried to tease him with the question for she smiled haughtily when she asked.

"Well, thank goodness. I don't want to *add* to any problems. Really." She turned to Lee. "We must be leaving soon. If we do not arrive at the beginning, we will be very confused. We will not know who is who."

Lee answered with a slight sneer. "Isn't that the point? Aren't we deliberately to be confused by who is who?"

Mrs. Brantford stood up, tall and straight, and surveyed the table. "Yes, we should leave," she said. She looked downward at Spenner and offered a short but necessary farewell to him. She looked long at him, then smiled as she turned to go. Spenner had not looked at her until she smiled. He had been acutely aware of her towering, dressed-in-black presence standing over him like a threat, but in her smile he saw the same teasing, disdainful guise that he had seen in her daughter. Karin and Lee rose obediently and followed her out of the room. Their voices were heard briefly in the hallway, then there was silence when the outer door closed.

Lester and Spenner sat alone at the table. Finally, Spenner spoke. "Lester, do you believe that amnesia is a scheme or a trick as Karin and Mrs. Brantford have said?"

Lester looked at him and shook his head. "They talk so much and doctors and lawyers can do whatever they wish about amnesia. You alone know what you have been through and how you felt. All that talk sounded so trying to me and it must have been the same for you."

Spenner smiled at him. "I must expect it, Lester. After all . . ."

"You should not have to explain constantly. It is not fair."

"People have questions and they do wonder. It is only reasonable, but I am certain it will subside after a while."

Lester was silent for a moment, then he asked. "Do you want a smoke, Dad? I will get your pipe or we could go to the library?"

Spenner shook his head. "I think not, Lester. I am not really tired, but I believe I will go to my room now, unless you wish to talk."

Lester did not answer immediately. He looked undecided and he was shifting restlessly in his chair. "No," he said at last. "I have lessons I can do."

"I will say good night then," Spenner said as he got up and stretched his tired legs. He went to his room and sat in the large chair before the window. He looked out at the dark night beyond and remembered that just that morning, when he awoke, this same window was bright and brilliant with sunshine. Strange, he thought. He had been tired and weary then, before all that brilliance, and now, with its darkness, he was wide awake, though fretful and anxious.

If he had not been alert, he may not have heard the sound. His hearing was sharpened and he turned his head quickly. He heard a footstep outside his door. He remained motionless and then, once again, he heard a muted noise, this time against the door. There was a push against its weight and a slight, scraping sound as the door opened. Spenner moved forward in the chair so he could face the door directly. The door opened further and a shadowy form passed into the room. The door was closed with the same, muted noise with which it had been opened.

"Dad," a voice said softly.

"Lester?" Spenner replied with surprise as the dark figure moved toward his voice.

"Yes, Dad," the voice repeated.

"Oh!" Spenner said. "I'll get a light on."

"No, don't," Lester replied hurriedly. "We can talk in the dark." He moved forward and halted as he came close to Spenner. "Can't you sleep, Dad?"

"Well, I have just been sitting here, Lester. I am not tired, but there is another chair along the wall. I can get it."

Lester interrupted. "Don't bother, Dad. I can use the footstool." Lester fumbled for the footstool and, at last, found it and swung it to the side of Spenner's chair.

Even in the dark, the shadows soon made forms and bright streaks of Lester's hair began to reflect in the dimness. "You cannot sleep either, Lester? Or study?" Spenner asked.

The light hair wavered as if shaking in the negative. "I tried both but I am wide awake and I cannot concentrate."

Spenner could not see Lester's face but he sensed an uneasiness in his voice. "Is anything wrong?"

"I want to talk to you, Dad."

Spenner sat back in the chair. "Certainly," he replied and his tone was even but low.

Lester did not speak immediately. His head wavered again as if he were trying to steady himself. The tenseness in his voice increased when he spoke. "Dad, I am so glad you have come back. Now I have someone to talk to, to tell things."

"Of course, Lester," Spenner said.

The boy continued. "What I want to talk about is something that happened quite a while ago."

"Oh." Spenner was startled but he became wary. Quite a while ago. Whatever could Lester mean?

Lester went on. "I have not said anything to anyone for a long time because there was no one I could talk to . . . until now."

"About what, Lester?"

The boy hesitated and now the bright head tilted upward. The tenseness was still in his voice but now he whispered, low and soft. "Dad, mother was murdered!"

Spenner's body felt as though something had been thrust into it and he bent over in pain. He felt like he wanted to fall forward but he gripped the arms of the chair as if to hold himself steady. Had he heard correctly? "Lester!" he uttered in amazement.

"It is true, Dad. Mother was murdered. I know—I saw it happen."

Still amazed, Spenner asked. "You saw it?"

Lester nodded and the light hair moved up and down like a dim light. "Yes. I saw it. I saw how mother died."

"She died of a fall," Spenner said quickly. "Anton told me so."

"That is what they all said. That was the verdict."

"The records must show that, Lester."

His head turned away as he said, "There may be records, but they are false."

Spenner was silent for a moment. He remained stunned and surprised by Lester's words. "That is serious, Lester, to talk that way."

Once again, the light head moved and now it bowed forward. "Mother was ill and she had to remain in bed, that much is true," the anguish returned to Lester's voice, "but that night . . . when she died . . . I heard noises coming from her room. I got up and was going to her but I got only as far as the landing on the stairway when her bedroom door opened. Mom was there, in the doorway, like she was trying to get out. The door opened wider and I saw a man behind her, holding her back. Dad, I just dropped down. I guess I was frightened, but I saw him hit her and I saw her fall."

Spenner was shocked and he stared at Lester, watching his bright colored head weave about as if the story he had just told was wrenched from his body. "You saw a man there . . . and he hit her?" Spenner asked, aghast.

"I did."

"What *kind* of man?" Spenner asked urgently. "Can you describe him?"

"I could not see him clearly. It was dark, except for the light in mother's room and he was behind her, but he was a *big* man."

"Big?" Spenner's voice was weakening and he felt as if he were suppressed.

"Yes," Lester continued. "He came after her and pulled mother back and hit her."

Spenner's voice was low and even. "What happened afterwards, Lester? Did he run? What?"

"I do not know. I saw mother fall. It was dark and I just ran. I was so frightened and I ran back to my room. Then I began to scream and everyone in the house came to me and I told them but no one believed me. The man was gone." Lester's voice faltered. "I should have gone to her." His head moved on the arm of the chair, closer to Spenner. Spenner reached out and rested his hand on Lester's head. The boy's hair was smooth and soft beneath his palm.

"Lester, how could you? What would you have done?"

"If I had gone to her and screamed then, the man might have been caught and, at least, I could have seen him. No one believed me the next day either."

Although the shock was still upon him, Spenner was beginning to reason over Lester's story. "Who did not believe you, Lester?"

"Everyone here and the police and they called Dr. Vargas and Mr. Hillberry. They did not believe either."

"Who is Mr. Hillberry?"

"The undertaker. He took mother's body after Dr. Vargas said it was an accidental death—that she had fallen. All kinds of officials swarmed around the house. I tried to tell, I really tried, but they told me I was upset and I should go off."

Spenner said quietly, "You were five years old then, Lester."

"That is why they did not believe me or listen to me. They said I was shaken by mother's death and that I was hysterical."

"But Anton Dyer? Didn't he believe you?"

The light head was shaking. "No, Dad, he was like the others."

"Lester, you said you have not said anything again through all these years?"

"Who would I talk to, Dad? I never said anymore, but I cannot forget it. If only I had done something then—it was like I was a coward and ran . . ."

Spenner stroked the boy's head. "Lester, Lester," he spoke softly, trying to be reassuring. "You say that now but at the time—*think!* You were so young. To talk about being a coward is to talk like a man. If a man was there, as you say, you might have been harmed, too."

"*If!*" Lester cried. "You sound like you do not believe me either."

Spenner gripped Lester's shoulder. "Lester, you have told me a shocking story, against the facts, and which happened many years ago. But that does not mean that I do not believe you. I was only chiding you for thinking you were a coward at that time—you were a five-year-old boy."

Lester's hand came up to touch Spenner's. "Dad, I knew I could tell you. I knew just as soon as you came back."

Spenner breathed heavily and his hand slipped away so he no longer touched the boy. "It happened so long ago," he said softly.

"I know," Lester answered and his voice became sad. "I guess there is nothing that can be done now, but I had to tell you—how Mom died."

There was a silence between them. After a moment, Lester lifted his head and he stirred as if turning around on the footstool. "Mother is gone and it happened long go, as you say. I guess it has to remain settled. I know you have troubles, Dad, and you have been through a lot, but I wanted to tell you because it is the truth."

Spenner was looking out into the dark night. As he stared, he began to distinguish slim forms of distant trees like pencil drawings. The branches formed patterns that changed and twisted and moved to design anything and everything. How it is, Spenner thought, how it all is! His voice, when he spoke, was a hoarse whisper. "I am glad, Lester, that you have told me."

Lester rose and Spenner heard the footstool scrape the floor. Lester moved away as he said, "I'll go, Dad."

Spenner let him go. He heard the door close with a brief noise, then he was alone again. Spenner closed his eyes. His thoughts were in a turmoil and now he felt exhausted. Yet, he knew he would not sleep for his mind was racing like a whirlwind over Lester's story. A murder! The boy's mother! In this house! If the story were true, then the stark reality, which he did not mention to Lester, was that someone had to be accountable for such a crime.

Should I be concerned? He wondered. After all these years and what am I? Just here for a short time to complete a plan. Outside, the tree branches were still moving and forming different patterns and, he wondered—how can that be when there does not seem to be any breeze or wind at all to stir them?

Chapter Five

Miss Martin did not see him immediately as he stood outside of the glass doors. He may have appeared at the moment she removed her spectacles to clean them and when she put them on again and looked up to check her vision, she saw him looking intently at her. She gasped for he was very good looking and the fact that he was gazing directly upon her made her face blush and she felt flustered.

When he entered, he was not smiling although the corners of his mouth did turn slightly upwards, but the amusement was in his eyes. He was handsome but he he was more intriguing because of a forcefulness in his personality. He was of average height and of average build but he walked with a determined gait, head high, and a look so even and direct, with that touch of humor, that he was unnerving to the beholder. His overcoat was slung over his arm and he wore a dark suit and a pale colored tie, yet his presence was overpowering, like a force contained, but with nothing aggressive about him.

Miss Martin felt even more nervous when he stood before her and she fell uneasily back into the chair. She blinked her eyes and cautiously looked up at him. Now he was smiling and his dark eyes brightened with a roguish pleasure.

"I'm to see Grant Deakins," he said and his voice was low and suggested the same control that dominated him. "I am Johnson Buell."

Miss Martin could not speak but shook her head as she verified the appointment. She looked at him and smiled as nicely as she could. She studied his face for a few additional moments, but her voice wavered when she told him he could go directly into Mr. Deakins' office.

Johnson Buell gave her one more smile and walked toward the office, but he was met at the door by Grant Deakins. Deakins puffed with excitement as if he had risen hurriedly from his desk, and he greeted Johnson Buell warmly and with a firm handshake. Johnson Buell did not reply; he only bowed his head slightly and followed the instructions to hang his coat and then take the big leather chair that Deakins indicated.

Buell's eyes never left Grant Deakins' face as he watched him close the door, return to his desk, and seat himself comfortably in his chair. Buell rested his elbows on the arms of the chair and clasped his hands up in front of his face. Over them, he stared at Deakins and interest joined the amused look in his eyes as he prepared to be the audience examining a performer.

Deakins began with a smile, aware of the keen gaze upon him, but his grey eyes were serious and his eyebrows raised with anticipation. "Mr. Buell," he began, "I am aware of your outstanding reputation as a private detective."

Johnson Buell nodded as if accustomed to such an approach.

"Our office has need of your services," Deakins continued, "and I am to employ you for a discreet but important piece of work."

Johnson Buell nodded once again. A slow smile crossed his lips but it was covered by his hands.

"You are available?" Deakins asked in an even tone.

Johnson Buell spoke to Deakins for the first time. "I am available," he said.

"Good," Deakins answered and he puffed himself up once more, then settled into his straight, professional posture. He opened a desk drawer and withdrew a large, heavy, clasp envelope which he placed before him. He did not open it but he continued speaking. "Two days ago, an unusual thing happened: a man literally returned from the grave. A man came to this office and said he was Collis Whitmore, who had been mayor here in Valiterra twenty years ago when the war was on. Now the mayor disappeared then and there was no trace of him, so he was presumed to be dead. Now this man who claims to be the former mayor said he had been a victim of amnesia all that time."

Deakins shifted his weight and his voice became softer and more subtle. "I did not dispute him and I admit that I thought he was Collis Whitmore when I first set eyes on him. He looked a little different, of course, but it had been twenty years and yet the resemblance struck me immediately." He paused and looked at Johnson Buell as if there should be some question but Buell remained silent.

"I went along with him," Deakins continued, "and I took him to his home, the former mayor's estate. There, the butler, Anton Dyer, reacted as I had done: he accepted the man right away and seemed convinced that he was the former mayor. The rest of the household were newer employees; and the mayor had twin sons but they were infants when he disappeared and would not know. The mother of the boys is dead. Now, the problem and why I have called you, is to prove that this man really is Collis Whitmore."

Johnson Buell did not answer for a moment. He appeared thoughtful and earnest, then he asked, "You believe that he might be an impostor?"

"I am not too certain," Deakins replied, "but I want the man investigated and traced to determine if he really is the mayor because in three weeks the Whitmore boys will be twenty-one years of age and the trust will become effective. Our firm, and I personally, always have handled the affairs of the estate and I feel responsible, especially for the two boys."

Grant Deakins knew of another's concern which he did not mention. It was a telephone call he received earlier from Mrs. Brantford. "Can it be true?" she had asked. Her voice was calm but he sensed that she was making an effort to keep it controlled and with an aspect of surprise. "It is so hard to believe," she went on, trying to speak in a light voice, "after all these years. You know how devastating this can be," and he remembered she added quickly, "to the boys, you understand? They are on the thresholds of their lives and this can have such an impact."

Deakins assured her that he was just as surprised but he spoke firmly when he said he intended to check—everything would be checked out.

"Really?" Mrs. Brantford had replied although the question was feigned. "I believe that is very wise, Mr. Deakins, very wise indeed, just to be certain. It should be proven that this man is the father of Lee and Lester. Those poor boys . . . after all these years. Of course, Karin and Lee plan to proceed with their marriage plans."

"Yes, indeed they should, Mrs. Brantford," he had told her.

"We merely are standing by, you understand?" Mrs. Brantford had said.

Deakins had acquiesced although he was not quite certain of the meaning of her words but she had halted the conversation with a request that she would be available for any assistance.

"How did he explain his return?" Johnson Buell was asking and Deakins blinked quickly and once again raised his eyebrows.

"When he was amnestic, he called himself James Spenner and he lived in Tegner. He came from there. He claims that a strange man approached him in a cafe, recognized him as the former mayor, and when the stranger spoke his name, his mind returned. He said he had a seizure afterwards, a terrible seizure, and he wanted to die. In fact," Deakins said with huff in his voice, "I thought he would have one here. He seemed well enough but . . . strange behavior."

"Did he say anything about the man who recognized him?"

Deakins shook his head. "Only that he wore dark clothes. He said the man irritated him and he tried to ignore him." Deakins picked up the envelope in front of him. "I have accumulated as much information as I could about the mayor and his life which is information, really, from twenty years back. I have included the new material that this man, James Spenner, came forth with. It is as complete a portfolio as I can offer if you decide to accept the assignment."

Johnson Buell did not reply nor did he reach for the envelope.

Deakins was aware of the hesitation. "Well," he asked, "can it be so difficult for a private detective to trace a living man?" Deakins' forehead relaxed and became smooth as he let himself go a bit and he laughed at his last question.

Johnson Buell's glance returned the merriment and he smiled. "I have done it," he answered curtly.

"Then I hope you will do it again, Mr. Buell," Deakins said, "for us. You see, my concern is for the Whitmore boys. Their mother died about sixteen years ago and she made some unusual provisions in her will. If Mr. Whitmore had not returned, the boys would have received all of the estate." Deakins stopped again. His forehead rose and creased with a deep wrinkle. "Mrs. Whitmore made an additional testamentary deposition many years ago when her husband's fate was unknown. She established that upon her death, the boys would receive her share *but* if Mr. Whitmore should return before the boys reached twenty-one years of age, the entire estate would revert to him. So, you understand, this man can claim a sizeable fortune."

Grant Deakins pushed the envelope across the desk, closer to

Buell. Johnson Buell glanced at it but did not pick it up. Deakins smiled, but his face did not relax. "So you see, too, that this man has overcome amnesia and returned at a fortunate time for him."

Johnson Buell nodded. "And you believe that he may be an impostor, returning for the money?"

"I only want to be certain that he is *not* an impostor," Deakins replied. "I cannot discredit him entirely. As I said, he impressed me from the first, but I want this check made on him." He hesitated and remembered the words spoken by Mrs. Brantford " . . . just to be certain." Thinking again of their conversation, he continued to use her words. "After all, the boys are on the threshold of their lives. They are planning. One is to be married and the other wants additional education, and I feel I must be absolutely sure—for their sakes."

Johnson Buell looked intently upon him and studied him carefully. In his low, even voice, he asked, "I can understand your suspicions about the timing of his return and the money involved, but tell me, Mr. Deakins, what else is it that makes you doubt this man?"

Grant Deakins thought for a moment. He settled back in his chair and looked around, not helplessly, but as if to consider his thoughts further. Finally, he began speaking, slowly and softly. "Well, I believe his appearance seemed so—*contrived*. The man just looked contrived to me. He had all new clothes, not the best, to be sure, but nevertheless new and he also carried a new, cheap valise with him. Everything, it seemed, to make an appearance. I do not know if it has any meaning or relevance, but it was a personal impression." Deakins stopped and then asked, "You will take this case, Mr. Buell?"

At last, Johnson Buell reached forward and took the portfolio.

A swift smile came over the face of Grant Deakins. He rose and came around the desk to shake Buell's hand. "I know there is not much time, only three weeks . . ."

"I have taken the case, Mr. Deakins," Buell interrupted as he, too, had risen and shook the hand offered to him. He said no more but gathered his coat and started toward the door.

"Thank you," Deakins said softly. "I am here for any assistance." Johnson Buell stood in the doorway and nodded, then left. Grant Deakins stood quietly and looked at the closed door. He had a notion that he had had his say and that now Johnson Buell would handle this affair in his own way.

Chapter Six

The following day was sunny and the cold had diminished slightly. The weather should have been vitalizing to Spenner, but instead he was upset and worried. Since he had come to the estate, he had been weary and tired. He had little sleep and his thoughts were agitated constantly. What had he come into? Over and over again, he thought about Lester's story and he tried to tell himself that it was fantastic, that it could not be true. Yet, the more he thought about the story, the more a strange picture was emerging in his mind and the picture was becoming clear and intense. He could really see the five-year-old boy crouching in the stairway, seeing his mother in her bedroom doorway, and the man who came from behind and hit her. As often as he thought about it, Spenner could visualize the entire story and the idea frightened him.

He shook himself this morning as if trying to throw away his thoughts. This should not be. It was too dangerous for *the plan!* He had expected to be a little nervous, but what he had experienced was terrifying.

He had left the house and began walking, not in a specific direction, but he headed across the driveway toward the wooded area. It was desolate there, it hedged the front of the property, but a road and a gate cut through it and it was a way out. He did not know why he wanted to follow that road, but it seemed that he could not help himself and he was driven to go outside for no apparent reason. He shook himself once more and stumbled along and while his steps were shaky, his mind was telling him that he should be alert and confident, he must think of *the plan* and nothing must interfere with that. Oh, Lester's story! Why had he told him? He wished that Lester had not spoken . . .

"Going someplace?" he heard someone ask and he turned quickly. Lee had driven up beside him in his white sports car. He was moving forward slowly and then stopped beside Spenner. Lee was not smiling, instead he looked aghast at Spenner for today Spenner had put on the ill-fitting handouts he had received from Maria Lundee. "Are you going anywhere?" Lee asked again in disbelief.

Spenner became keenly aware of his appearance and the disdain with which Lee looked upon him. "I was going to town," Spenner answered uneasily.

"To town?" replied Lee and his disbelief increase. "Any special reason?"

"To buy clothes," Spenner answered hurriedly, trying to sound convincing.

Now Lee gave him a sardonic smile. "Splendid! I should hope so. Did you call for a car?"

"No," Spenner answered slowly.

"Cars are available. You know that."

"I had forgotten," Spenner replied.

Lee looked at him for a moment and the smile left his face. "Get in. I'll take you." He leaned over and opened the car door.

Spenner tried to resist. "It is not necessary, Lee. I can go back and call for a car."

"I am going to town myself," Lee persisted. "I am on my way to the office."

Spenner blinked and bent forward as though he had not heard correctly. "Office?" he asked and added, "Now?" He was surprised for he thought it was late in the morning. It was sunny when he stepped out, but then he was not certain, he really did not know the time. He had been so absorbed in his thoughts.

Lee did not comment on the time. "I am an apprentice," he said. "I arrive at my convenience."

Spenner blinked again. "That is unusual," he said softly.

"Of course," Lee answered and he laughed slightly with a tone of derision. "It is unusual because I am going to be the owner and the boss. It is my own business that I am setting up."

"Oh," Spenner answered thoughtfully, "and what kind of business, may I ask?"

"I am going to deal in imports and exports," replied Lee and then his face became serious and surliness returned. "This is a sea coast city and such an enterprise should do well. I am buying a business and I have committed quite an investment to it."

Investment, Spenner reflected and wondered if Lee's commitment was based on the inheritance. Surely, he thought, it must be.

"Get in," Lee urged.

"I don't want you to go out of your way," Spenner said with a half-hearted protest.

"I am going right by Thornburgs," Lee said with determination.

Reluctantly, Spenner climbed in and Lee started off with a rapid acceleration. He turned from the driveway onto the road without slowing and increased speed when he entered the highway. His face was petulant but he sat resolutely at the wheel and did not look at Spenner. Spenner glanced at him occasionally but only by half turning his head, and he sat equally mute. He wanted to talk to Lee but he did not know how to do it. He thought about the theater. Perhaps he should ask about that. It would be a harmless beginning and Lee seemed happy about going there with Karin. Before he could say anything, however, he was startled to hear Lee blurt out, "Do you like Karin?"

Spenner looked hurriedly at Lee for he was surprised by the question. The petulance was not gone from Lee's face but a slight smile had broken through it. Oh, Spenner said to himself, the only thing to bring a happy smile to his face is the thought of that girl. "She is lovely," Spenner answered with truth. "You are fortunate, Lee."

"I know," Lee responded quickly. "Of course, she is a bit fascinated by that French cult, yet I want to take her to France to please her. She can study painting if she likes. I will have the business, so it should all work out."

Spenner nodded. "That will make her happy, I am sure."

Now Lee glanced at Spenner. "Money should not be a concern. I am counting on the inheritance. The estate is to be settled when Lester and I are twenty-one. You know when that is, don't you?"

Spenner's body became tense but his gaze looked straight ahead and he dared not turn to look at Lee. Yet he wondered what Lee's expression could be. Was he scruntinizing, testing or challenging Spenner's reaction? Spenner decided to answer forcefully. "Well, yes, Lee, I remember when you were born. The birthday is soon, is it not, in three weeks?"

Lee was silent for a moment, then he answered, "Right! That is the day the estate, the money, will be settled. You will have to be included now, but you know that, don't you?"

Spenner did not reply. He felt uneasy and apprehensive about the insinuations in Lee's remarks. He was grateful that Lee said nothing more for they had entered the center of town and Lee was twisting and turning the car as he drove through various congested streets. At last, he pulled up and stopped before Thornburgs store. "Old Woodbridge, remember?" he asked in a determined tone of voice as Spenner got out. He looked up and down at Spenner and shook his head. "Get some decent things and be sure to get a tuxedo. You will need it for the engagement party. You know, they might think that you are someone trying to pass yourself off as my father. If they do, have them call me at the office so I can verify your credit."

Spenner remained on the sidewalk, looking after Lee as he drove away. A tuxedo! Credit! Indeed! He sensed anger and resentment within him. To be so directed by this youngster! He had not thought of such things and he had not planned to come to Thornburgs. Lee had surprised him and he had responded to the unexpected meeting only to sound plausible. Spenner sensed also that he did not want any hostility which could work against *the plan*. Now he was here at Thornburgs and he had to go through with the visit because Lee would be waiting for a telephone call about credit!

Thornburgs store front looked small and unimpressive but Spenner pushed open the door and stepped into an interior of complete elegance. There was silence within, like a church, and chandeliers glittered from above. The carpet was so thick and heavy that Spenner walked through the foyer without a noisy footstep. The clothing was in show cases which were enclosed in glass with pink and yellow lights, like haloes, expertly surrounding the clothes.

A young man, with a haughty expression, but perfectly groomed and dressed in an ensemble like one of those in the show cases, approached Spenner. The look in the young man's eyes became distressed as he glanced over Spenner and he could not manage even a discreet half smile.

Spenner still was filled with resentment and his anger made him step squarely in front of the young man. Spenner raised his head and threw back his shoulders. In doing this, the large black jacket he wore fell more loosely from his shoulders and looked twice as ill-fitting as before. The jacket had a frayed collar and cuffs and the buttons did not match. Spenner had lost the original buttons and had replaced them with anything that fit. His hat was a matted fur piece which he held in front of him. He knew he presented himself as a vagrant; nevertheless he looked directly at the young man and said, "I would like a tuxedo."

The clerk's eyes changed to a look of horror. "A tuxedo?" he whispered softly in disbelief.

Spenner nodded and he felt a bit of sarcasm as he surveyed the young man. "Yes," and then he repeated, "a tuxedo, and a good one. I must look my best for my son's engagement party."

The clerk was shaken but he stood his ground and did not move. "Of course," he answered hesitatingly and his mouth remained slightly open as if he was uncertain as to what to say next.

Spenner smiled and hoped he looked a bit arrogant as he said, "I am Collis Whitmore."

The clerk looked aghast and could not disguise his disbelief. His mouth remained open and he still was unable to say a word.

Spenner felt a tinge of enjoyment at teasing the clerk and he smiled again and casually rolled his head to the side. "I want to look nice for my son Lee's engagement party. You understand, I am sure?"

The clerk was hesitant and off balance. He was definitely unsure but he tried to remain controlled and poised lest he say or do anything to offend a client. Slowly, he muttered, "You are Lee Whitmore's father?" He tried to sound casual as in an introduction. "I had no idea . . ."

"I have just returned," Spenner interrupted, "and you must call him, at his office, and he will verify my credit."

The clerk's eyes flickered with surprise but he began to regain his composure. "Yes, sir," he answered rigidly and even bowed a little. "The fitting rooms are this way." He turned and was off and Spenner followed dutifully. They passed other clerks who were molded in the same superciliousness and they stared wide-eyed at Spenner.

Spenner smiled at them. He acted proud and confident as he stepped along in front of them. He called out to the young clerk ahead of him. "A good tuxedo now! A good one!" He laughed as he saw the young man's shoulders tremble but the clerk did not turn around to look at him.

When Spenner left Thornburgs, he crossed the city square and walked several blocks in one direction. He stopped once to check a telephone book for the address of the Hillberry Funeral Home and he stopped one other time to ask a newspaper vendor if he was going in the right direction to reach Oak Street. The old vendor nodded while pointing with an outstretched arm, "Just keep going, about four more blocks."

Spenner continued until he came to Oak Street where he paused to decide which way to turn. He decided to turn left and walked slowly as he checked addresses on the buildings. At last, he stopped before a long, one-level brick building set back from the street. A large window, without curtains, faced him and there was a tall, gold statue, looking like some goddess in the center of the window. A sign along the walk identified the place as the Hillberry Funeral Home. Spenner approached and opened the door. The interior was like Thornburgs, quiet and with thick carpet, but it was extremely cold. A bell was on the front wall with a sign beneath it saying, "Please Ring." Spenner pressed the bell and heard its tinkling echo far in the back confines of the building. Soon, a door closed and soft footsteps approached, then a tall man dressed in a dark business suit and tie appeared. He smiled at Spenner and asked, "May I help you?" There was a fragrance about him as he came closer and Spenner suspected that it came from spray, used on his hair which was absolutely white but lay smoothly in place over his head.

Spenner removed his hat and held it with both hands before him. "I am Collis Whitmore," he said.

The man halted immediately and a surprised look came over his face and then it flushed quite red. "Mr. Whitmore!" he exclaimed. "You are . . . I heard, but I cannot believe!"

"I returned two days ago," Spenner said simply. "You are Mr. Hillberry?"

"Yes, yes," the man replied.

Spenner went on and his voice was soft, almost begging in tone. "Mr. Hillberry, I wonder if you have time for a short talk?"

"Certainly, certainly," Mr. Hillberry answered. Because of an instinct for handling bereaved people, he took Spenner by the arm and walked him toward his office. The office, however, was more like a living room and Spenner imagined that it was another consideration of Mr. Hillberry's concern for those who mourn. There was nothing businesslike about the room—no desk, bookcases, cabinets and such.

Instead it was fitted like a comfortable living room and it was warm. Spenner was led to a large sofa and settled amongst the cushions. There was an identical sofa opposite him and additional chairs were placed around the room, all large and high backed with double cushions and padded arm rests. The room was painted in soft, variegated, pale shades of blue, light, azure, robin's egg, and such, all restful and consoling colors. The pictures around the room were seascapes, redefining, through water, the color and the serenity of the room.

Mr. Hillberry seated himself on the sofa opposite Spenner and there was a low table between them. The table held a centerpiece of blue flowers and even a covered dish of mint candies, but the necessary telephone was placed as far to the end as possible and behind a mounted, ceramic mold of sea shells.

Mr. Hillberry switched on a lamp and then settled comfortably into the sofa pillows. His manner was gracious and he generated a trust and sympathy that added to all the consolation of sorrowful people. "Well, Mr. Whitmore, this is a surprise, a big surprise, I should say, to see you."

"I know," Spenner replied softly.

"Amnesia, was it? All those years?"

"Yes," Spenner answered with a nod. "For twenty years. I was in Tegner. I had no idea of my real identity at that time."

"My, my! Such a burden!" Mr. Hillberry said, then smiled. "But now you have your identity. It has all come back to you?"

Spenner noticed that Hillberry's voice was gentle and comforting but it seemed controlled, for without that pleasantness, it would have been sharp.

"The change was sudden," Spenner replied and he kept his own voice soft and passive.

"Amazing, amazing! Like a miracle." Hillberry hesitated after his words and Spenner was about to speak but he did not because Hillberry's expression suddenly changed. The self-possession remained but his eyes gleamed with a sudden thought, "Are you thinking of returning to politics, also?"

Spenner was completely surprised and he would have sat straight forward had not the sofa been so deep and soft. Politics? Such a subject had never entered his mind. He studied Hillberry trying to determine the reason for such an unusual question. Yet, Hillberry's attitude remained intact. His manner was poised and beneficent but his eyes glistened with intensity. "You could not win, you know?"

Spenner blinked and sank submissively into the sofa pillows like a man floundering. He shook his head and pretended to laugh. When he spoke, he stumbled on the words so he sounded clumsy. "Politics? Oh, no, no, nothing of the sort."

The glint remained in Hillberry's eyes and he did try to smile. "I was only asking. I know politicians and they never seem to lose that sense of the game. Just as well that you think differently for, truthfully, Mr. Whitmore, I don't think you have any chance of coming back. Our party has been *in* since the war. Dr. Vargas was our most influential leader and got us on the track, so to speak."

Dr. Vargas! Spenner's eyes blinked again as he remembered that Lester had said Dr. Vargas had treated his mother. Spenner said nothing as Hillberry continued. "We have managed coalitions over the past twenty years, taking advantage of changes, and we are stronger than ever. I believe it will be hard to 'break us' as your party is, well, feeble. I am not being prejudiced, you understand, but trying to give you a correct assessment."

A consumate man of "the game," thought Spenner. He recognized the challenge and saw the righteous vanity of Hillberry. Yet, Spenner laughed again and shook his head as if in complete agreement. "You must be right, Mr. Hillberry. I would not argue with you. I have been away too long. I cannot think. I have no interest in politics now. 'The game', as you call it, is over for me."

Hillberry went on as if finishing a speech and unmindful of Spenners' words. "Anyway, you could not possibly try to get back on your record. A record of war and defeat."

Spenner moaned.

"War and defeat," Hillberry repeated. "Your party has not been able to overcome and climb over that."

Spenner moaned once more and threw up his hands.

Hillberry had remained firm and precise but he hesitated now as he observed Spenner. "People remember," he said softly and in a soothing voice.

"People remember," Spenner repeated the words in a whisper. He bowed his head and took a deep breath, then he moaned for the third time.

There was silence between them. Spenner wondered if he should speak but instead he decided to moan one more time. Now he pulled his head down further so that his shoulders slumped.

"Mr. Whitmore, I hope I have not upset you?"

Spenner tried to raise his head. "Mr. Hillberry, you are interested in politics. I understand that but I have come here to you on an entirely different matter." He shifted himself and tried to straighten his shoulders. "I have come to ask about my wife."

Hillberry's face became confused and it turned red. "Your wife!" he said softly. "But she is dead!"

"I know. The saddest note of my return. I have come to you to ask about her death for I was told that you were there."

Hillberry's face remained flushed as he spoke, as if to himself. "I had no idea of that. I did not think about *that*."

Spenner pushed himself forward to the edge of the sofa. His eyes were bright as he looked at Hillberry and he spread his hands open before him as if in begging. "I have been told that Gessie died many years ago, but I would be grateful for any information about her. You think me a fool, perhaps. I am certain you do, but I am a sentimental older man now who needs memories."

Hillberry's face softened a bit and began to lose the embarrassing color. "I believe I understand, but what can I tell you? Mrs. Whitmore had pneumonia."

"Oh?" Spenner said. "I understand she had a fall."

"Yes," Hillberry answered quickly. "That is correct but she was ill before that."

"I see," Spenner said. "So who treated her?"

"Dr. Vargas," Hillberry replied.

"Oh, the man who got you on the track, politically," Spenner answered. "Then perhaps I should see him."

"He is dead, I am sorry to say. He has been gone for several years," Hillberry answered.

"Oh," Spenner said once more and his voice was soft with disappointment.

Hillberry went on, "Mrs. Whitmore did have a fall which killed her."

"Was that the coroner's verdict also?" Spenner asked. "I only wish to be certain."

"Of course," Hillberry replied and he spoke again as if to himself. "I am trying to recall exactly . . ."

Spenner spread his hands in the helpless fashion again. "Oh, if you could—anything about that night—when she fell."

Hillberry settled back into the sofa cushions and his face was thoughtful and serious. "My brother was called that night and I went because I was assisting him at the time. Dr. Vargas was there when we arrived." His forehead wrinkled in concentration. "Your wife was on the floor and she was dead. Dr. Vargas believed, and I think we all agreed, that she had a bad spell that night and had gotten out of her bed and was trying to leave the room. She got to the door but she was very weak and ill and she fell and hit her head on a table nearby."

Spenner shook his head and cried out softly, "My poor Gessie! Oh, her soul!" He paused and then asked. "You think the fall killed her then?"

Hillberry nodded. "Yes, that was the opinion of all of us."

Spenner cried out again and began to sputter. "You saw the blow on her head?"

"I saw the laceration on her skull where she struck the table." Hillberry's voice became lower as he said, "The side of her head was quite smashed."

Spenner's head hung forward. "Such remembrances! I must hear such remembrances! Oh, such grief and sorrow and yet I have asked and I am grateful to know, though I must bear it. Gessie's last . . . Do not spare me if you remember anything else, anything at all."

Hillberry thought a moment. "I do not remember anything else. No nothing else."

Spenner shook his head. "If only my mind had been straight. If I could have been there. I feel I deserted her."

"You must not feel guilty, Mr. Whitmore. It was an unfortunate accident." He hesitated and then said, "and you had an unfortunate accident also."

"I know, but if I had been there perhaps I could have pre-vented . . . the accident. I shall always feel that way."

Mr. Hillberry leaned forward. Dealing with sorrow had returned his professionalism and he looked at Spenner with sympathy and understanding. His voice was soft but determined. "But how could you have done anything when you did not know?" He tried to smile. "She was badly injured but we made nice arrangements for her, I assure you."

"I am certain of that," Spenner answered quickly. "I am not questioning that at all. I appreciate this talk we have had, Mr. Hillberry. Any word about Gessie, even after all these years means so much. I am grateful and it has helped me." Spenner pushed against the cushions and got up. "You see what I am, a broken man, trying to know a part of my past that was lost to me."

Hillberry stood too and he took Spenner's arm as before and walked him to the door. "I believe you will be able to adjust to everything in time," he said and shook hands with Spenner as he bid him goodbye.

Spenner wiped his eyes before he set his hat firmly on his head and then left. He turned at the edge of the sidewalk and saw that Hillberry had remained in the open door looking after him. Hillberry did not smile or nod his head but kept staring after Spenner until he was out of sight.

Spenner walked slowly back toward the city square. His mind was going over the conversation with Hillberry. He had tried to make Hillberry believe that he was aging, inept and sentimental. Yet, he had gained the additional information that Dr. Vargas, who had treated Gessie Whitmore, was dead but both he and Hillberry were political opponents of the mayor's party and both were present when she died. He wondered if there could be a political aspect . . .

All of a sudden, his thoughts were disrupted and he became very alert. When he left the funeral home, he was conscious of Hillberry staring after him, but now he was a way past the funeral home and out of sight and yet he sensed that he still was being watched. He stopped and turned around and pretended to sight directions when he knew for certain that he was being followed. The man was strolling along the street amongst others and he was dressed in a long black coat and a big black hat that covered most of his face. He had been standing on the walk in back of the funeral home and Spenner had glanced at him when he left but thought nothing of him except for the color and large size of his clothes.

The man stopped and looked downward when Spenner turned unexpectedly and looked at him. He moved again when Spenner continued onward. Spenner, however, did not look back until he reached the newstand. He asked the vendor about buses and was told of one that went along the highway close to the estate. While talking to the vendor, Spenner looked back and saw the man coming after him at a slow pace. Spenner started toward the bus station where he had to wait in line for the bus. He saw the man, still coming, but he halted and remained on the opposite side of the street at a safe distance but able to keep Spenner in view. Spenner studied the man, but he could make nothing of him. The hat brim hid his face and the man slouched or perhaps cowered in the large coat so it was hard to determine his height. If he stood straight, he could have been much taller. The black coat was loose and without a belt so Spenner could not determine the build of the man's body either.

At last, the bus arrived and Spenner boarded but the man did not. He remained at his distance but watched until the bus departed. Spenner could not relax; his thoughts were anxious and perplexed. He was aware of swiftly passing glimpses of territory he had passed through earlier with Lee and several days ago with Grant Deakins. The bus went through the center of town, along the river bank and onto the highway. He knew he was going in the right direction so his thoughts returned to his interview with Hillberry and, mostly, of the man who followed him. Whatever for? Who could he be? Spenner was so engrossed in his contemplations that he was unaware that the bus had stopped at his departure point. The passengers, as well as the driver had to coax him back to reality and urge him to leave the bus. "Oh!" he said in surprise when he became conscious of them and their prodding. He tried to smile, but he was embarrassed and quickly jumped out of the bus.

The bus left hurriedly and Spenner stood on the highway looking after it until it was far away. Then he turned to the special, deserted road that led to the estate. He walked along the iron fence and then he passed through the open gate and went forward on the paved road. The trees were tall along each side but were looking skimpy as they were losing their foliage to the autumn season. Occasionally, the branches moved and made a rasping sound and several times Spenner halted and looked back as if expecting the black-clad figure to be there—but Spenner was alone. Ahead, the road was clear and quiet and Spenner moved slowly along to the house.

He opened the door and peered inside. The corridor was empty and dark. He stepped in and closed the door. By the time he turned around, a light came on and he saw Anton Dyer entering the corridor from the kitchen. Apparently, there was some sort of silent alarm that signalled in the kitchen or Dyer's quarters when the door was opened.

Anton Dyer's eyelids drooped but there was a worried look on his face. "Good afternoon, sir," he said anxiously. "You have been out?"

"Yes," Spenner replied. "Oh, I should have told you, Anton, but I went into town to order clothes. Lee took me in but I returned on the bus."

"A bus?" Dyer said in disbelief.

"It went right to the highway and I walked from there."

Dyer's face changed to complete distress. "A car is available, sir."

"I know, Anton," Spenner said softly and he realized that he had not acted properly as a mayor, or former mayor, and the head of the estate. He was not expected to take highway buses or walk along lonely roads. Also, Spenner suspected that Dyer was upset because he was not informed of Spenner's movements. Obviously, he wanted to know, perhaps expected, to be told of the master's whereabouts. Spenner continued. "I know I could have a car. Lee reminded me, but I wanted to . . . see things. To see if I remembered."

Anton Dyer stared at him for a moment. The look of dismay and disappointment did not leave his face. Nevertheless, he said, "Yes, sir," without any understanding, "but you must take care. We are concerned."

Spenner did not reply but he nodded and inclined his head as if in agreement. He looked up at Dyer after a minute, blinked his eyes, and asked, "Anton, what kind of alarm system do we have—now?"

Dyers' eyes widened slightly but returned to their droopy, languished look almost immediately. "The new alarm system was installed after the war, sir, when Mrs. Whitmore decided to stay on. She requested it."

So Gessie Whitmore had the new alarm system put in, Spenner said to himself, but he asked another question, "Is it hooked to your quarters?"

"Yes, sir," Dyer replied. "It is an electronic system throughout the lower level. If the outer bell is rung, of course, it rings in my quarters as well. It will also ring in my quarters automatically if the door is opened whether or not the outer bell is rung."

Spenner was thinking that the alarm system was in place at the time of Gessie Whitmore's death and no one could have entered

97

through the door without Dyer's knowledge unless he was not in his quarters at the time.

"Thank you, Anton," Spenner said and started toward the stairway when he stopped as Dyer said, "Sir, there is a letter for you."

A letter? Spenner was stunned. Whoever would send him a letter? He was grateful that his back was to Dyer so he need not show him the surprise that overwhelmed him. "A letter?" he asked, this time aloud but in a soft tone of voice.

"On the table, sir."

Spenner looked and saw a square, beige envelope lying on the hall table. Surreptitiously, he stepped over to pick it up and the name *Mayor Collis Whitmore* was written on the envelope without any address, stamp or postmark. "How did it arrive?" he asked.

"I must apologize, sir. I do not know," Dyer answered. "The bell rang while I was in the supply cellar. When I got here, the envelope was on the floor near the door. Evidently, it had just been pushed under the door. Of course, the deliverer was gone. I did go out and look around, but I saw no one. I am sorry, sir."

Spenner held the letter, just looking at it, mystified by its appearance. Then he shrugged his shoulders and said, "Well, I guess I should open it, whatever it is."

Anton Dyer bowed his head as if in agreement but said nothing.

Still, Spenner hesitated. He had a deep feeling of foreboding and he was confused by this latest in the series of erratic happenings which had not been considered or thought about in *the plan*. There was Lester's story of murder, the man who followed him and now a mysterious letter. Whatever did any of it mean? He knew he was expected to surmount any unexpected obstacles and keep *the plan* moving successfully, but these events were unnerving and directed straight at him.

He stood quietly for a moment, still looking at the envelope, then he broke the seal and withdrew the letter. There was nothing on the page except a curious design like a emblem. It was circular with an edge of small flowers resembling roses and in the center was a descending dove with one large rose in its beak. Spenner stared at the picture, bewildered, then he showed it to Anton Dyer. "Anton, does this mean anything to you?"

Dyer studied the design, then shook his head. "No, sir."

"This is all that is in the envelope, nothing more. I have no idea what it means," Spenner said.

"It is odd, is it not?" Dyer replied and his drooping eyelids did not flutter.

Where did it come from and who brought it here? Spenner asked himself. He folded the letter, inserted it into the envelope, and put it away in his pocket. "I guess it is nothing to worry about," he said uneasily.

He tried to smile but as he stepped forward, he stumbled. Dyer immediately came to him and caught him. "Do you feel ill, sir?" he asked anxiously.

Spenner answered but he did not look at Dyer. "I am all right, Anton. I do not know why I stumbled. Perhaps I am only weary."

"You are upset, sir. That letter has upset you."

"Oh, no," Spenner replied quickly. "I am just tired; I believe it is that. I did a bit of walking and there is so much to think about."

Dyer answered politely but the anxiety remained in his voice. "That is understandable, sir. It is difficult for you."

"Gessie," Spenner said softly. "It is Gessie. She has been in my thoughts. Anton, can you tell me about her? Was she ill for a long time and did she suffer? Dear Gessie, if only I could know."

Dyer looked uncomfortable and a sadness came over him. He hesitated as if thinking for the proper words. He began to speak slowly. "Mrs. Whitmore was not well soon after the birth of the twins, sir. Yet, she traveled a great deal—restless traveling—if you will accept my personal opinion. She always took the boys with her everywhere. She came back here to the estate from time to time but only for a short while and then she would be off again. It was amazing, really, that she could travel so much while she was ill. Even at the times she was here, she was not well. On several occasions, she fainted away. Exhaustion, I am certain, atop her condition, but she insisted on going on. Finally, when the boys were almost five years old, she came back to stay. But I believe she had little choice at that time. I do not think she could go on any longer. She was very tired, her health was bad and she did not improve while she was here. She became a bed patient."

Spenner listened carefully to Dyer's words, then he shook his head. "Poor Gessie, to be so ill, to be so confined at the last."

"Dr. Vargas insisted upon it, sir. In fact, he insisted that she remain in bed."

"Oh," Spenner said but he shook his head once more and looked at Dyer. "But, Anton, she was found away from her bed; she fell at the doorway." Spenner thought to mention that Mr. Hillberry had told him so, but he did not say it.

Apparently, Dyer did not wonder at Spenner's statement for he was not surprised. Instead, he nodded his head in agreement. "Dr. Vargas believed that she had a particulary bad spell and was trying to leave her room. She was too weak, of course, and fell against a table. Earlier, sir, Mrs. Whitmore took a chill and went into a near coma. She was saying things and seeing things and then pneumonia set in. I do not believe she could fight off anything after that, sir."

Spenner moaned and shook his head again. "Poor Gessie! Poor dear soul! In a coma, you say? Saying things and seeing things . . ."

"She was not herself then, as I said," Dyer interrupted. "I am certain any irrationality was due to her condition." He paused. "Perhaps it is too painful, sir, for you to discuss her."

"No, Anton, no," Spenner answered quickly. "I want to know. It is necessary for me to know. If I know these things, perhaps I can surmise what I could have done had I been here."

"That is not good, sir," Dyer's voice became mournful, "to think in that direction; it only brings on guilt. You should not be burdened with that."

"I know but it is the little comfort I can have; to believe that if I had been here, things might have been different."

Dyer's eyelids fluttered and Spenner thought there were tears in his eyes. Gently, he placed his hand on the old servant's shoulder as if to comfort him. "Anton," he said, "you are helping me, you are the only one who can help me to know about Gessie. It means much to me."

"I understand, sir," Dyer replied but Spenner felt his shoulder tremble beneath his hand.

"Anton, had she tried to leave her room before? Did she have to be restrained?"

Dyer lowered his head and swept a finger across his cheek to clear the tears. "Mrs. Whitmore did not like to remain in bed and, occasionally, she had to be restrained. But that was not often, sir."

Spenner continued his questions. "Someone must have been with her to watch her. Was there no nurse?"

"There was a nurse here all the time when Mrs. Whitmore first took ill and during the coma. She remained when the pneumonia set in, during the critical stage. But then Mrs. Whitmore made an improvement and Dr. Vargas called off the continuous nursing care. The staff, all of us, then took care of her. I assure you that she received the utmost care."

"I know, Anton," Spenner responded quickly, "I only wondered if a nurse was with her when she died."

"Unfortunately, sir," Dyer's voice became low and sad, "there was no one with her then. But if she had a bad spell, there was a bell that she only needed to press and one of us would have been with her instantly."

Once again, Spenner had to place his hand on Dyer's shoulder. "I am sad, also, Anton. Yet, I mean no offense to anyone. The staff, as always, has been excellent. I know Gessie received the best of care. I am sorry for all the questions, but I only wish to know, that is all." He hesitated and saw that Dyer was bracing himself and his posture was becoming straight and firm. "I am certain that Dr. Vargas did everything he could also," Spenner continued, "but I did not know him and I wonder how he was selected for Gessie?"

"Grant Deakins recommended him, sir," Dyer replied.

Spenner was thoughtful for a moment. "And my boys, Anton, was it hard for them?"

"The traveling was most difficult for such young ones. It was hard for them to settle down and it may have brought on tensions, especially in Mister Lester. He constantly had nightmares."

Spenner was surprised but he was careful to remain still. "Lester had nightmares?"

Dyer replied, "He seemed to be afflicted with a particular hypertension. He was a most restless and nervous child and he was upset by his mother's illness. He cried for her constantly. He was a poor sleeper and the nightmares occurred frequently. Dr. Vargas looked after him at times, but the boy was so young he did not wish to prescribe for him except for an occasional tablet to quiet him. Mister Lee now was different; he was obedient and no problem whatsoever. I do not say that he was not aware or concerned about his

101

mother's illness, but he seemed more able to cope and accept it. A good boy."

"The night she died . . . how did it affect them?"

"As expected, sir. Mister Lester had a terrible nightmare and was very upset, but Mister Lee was as controlled as a child could be."

Spenner was thoughtful as he listened to Dyer's words about Lester and Lee. He did not reply to the comments, but he looked upward and around at the second level of rooms. After a moment, he said, "Anton, I should like to see Mrs. Whitmore's room."

Dyer studied Spenner and the concern deepened within his eyes once more, yet he answered simply, "Yes, sir."

They moved along the corridor and Spenner started up the stairway when he realized he had moved too hastily. He should have waited and let Dyer lead the way to the correct room, but he could not hesitate now. He had to move with the assurance that he knew where to go. He had noticed a closed door next to his room and, surely, that would be Gessie Whitmore's room. Spenner moved forward up the stairway, turned at the landing and went toward the door. Dyer followed slowly behind him. Spenner took a deep breath and pushed the door open. He stared. Horrified. *The room was empty! He had made a mistake!* The room had no furnishings and the atmosphere was stale and musty, a room long closed. Spenner was dumbfounded. A moment he had dreaded had come. He knew it could happen; it was a latent possibility from the time he first talked to Alec Thurston, and now here he was, making a wrong decision, trapped, and no where to go. Whatever would he say to Anton Dyer? Spenner could not move but he squirmed inwardly as he heard Dyer's footsteps approaching behind him. Spenner could not turn to meet him or to face him, he could not look at Dyer and be accused.

Dyer came along side him and stopped. "I am sorry, sir,"he said. "I should have told you. Mrs. Whitmore's room was changed to the one across the corridor. She requested it when she became ill. She claimed the other room had more light and was warmer."

Spenner gasped with relief but his throat felt dry and it began to ache. He had braced himself for questions and an inquiring appraisal by Dyer, but the moment had passed. Yet, he could not relax; he knew he was stunned and he must have looked afraid. He had not looked at Dyer but he wondered if the servant had sensed his fear.

"The room across the corridor, you say?" Spenner tried to sound casual but his voice was shaky.

"The last one on the corridor, sir, on the south." Dyer replied and he pointed to the door on the opposite side.

"Is it locked?" Spenner asked.

"No, sir."

"Then I can go alone, Anton. I need not take more of your time."

Dyer said nothing but turned and descended the stairway. Spenner watched after him and the light from the windows touched Dyer's partially bald head, but the old servant did not raise it or turn back to look at Spenner.

Spenner had to dismiss him for he did not wish to turn around and face Anton Dyer. He waited until Dyer was gone, watching after him. Then Spenner started down to the landing. He paused there and thought: here is where Lester would have been, crouching below the stairs. Spenner kneeled as if to imitate the boy; he looked up and, yes, the door to the last room south was clearly visible. Spenner continued upward to the corridor and toward the room. He opened the door, looked quickly around, and stepped inside. The room was smaller than the other and the furniture obviously was too large and abundant for the space so there was a feeling of crowdedness. Spenner stood still for a moment, and then he backed against the door as the cramped room seemed to overpower him. He glanced hurriedly about. There was a bed along the far wall facing the door and covered with a sheet. The chairs were covered also but all the table tops were bare. His attention went immediately to the small table next to the door frame. He touched it; it felt sturdy, standing on two massive legs and the wide, square top had sharp corners. An unbalanced fall against it could have been fatal.

Spenner crossed the room to the windows. There were two and they were large for the room and each had an iron trellis on the outside. Both windows opened and locked *from the inside*. Spenner looked about. How could anyone get into this room and, he thought further, get out again? Certainly not through the ironworks on the windows. If anyone came from the inside, from the lower level, how could they penetrate that alarm system downstairs? If anyone came from the inside, he would have to leave that way also. Yet Lester did not see anyone descending upon him from his mother's room. How could anyone have gotten into this room?

Spenner looked around the room again but there was no answer to his thought. He left and closed the door. He was about to turn away when he saw the small window at the end of the corridor. He approached it and noticed that there was no trellis on the outside. He pushed the window and it opened; it squeaked slightly but it was not locked. Surprised, Spenner pushed it again and it opened wider. He looked out on the front of the estate. Looking down, he saw a ledge below the window. But how could one get to the ledge? While asking the question, he was looking at the answer—a tree, old and huge, that stood at the side of the window and close to the building. Spenner surveyed the scene carefully and calculated possible moves. In his imagination, he saw how someone could have gotten to the estate unseen through all the trees at the front, then make a short dash over the driveway to reach this particular tree. It could be climbed to the ledge and then, with care, someone could have made it to the window and gotten into the corridor and then to Gessie Whitmore's room.

It could have been done. It was possible. A "big man," Lester had said. Could a "big man" have done it? But what was "big" to a child of five? Any adult? Any man? Lester, oh, Lester! Fussy, disturbing little boy who had nightmares. It had happened sixteen years ago and the story of his mother's death was written then, officially. Yet, the boy retained an obstinate memory of what he had seen. What could be changed or challenged now? How would I start and what would I do, Spenner asked himself, if I believe Lester . . . if I believe him.

Spenner was looking again through the open window at the tree and the ledge. Suddenly, a cold wind swirled about him and he shivered. Quickly, he closed the window and walked away.

Chapter Seven

This time Spenner called for a car and he requested that Anton Dyer call it for him. When Spenner met Dyer at the door, he asked another request of him: To contact the newspaper reporter, the man who was here the other day.

"Mr. Kirkland, sir, of *The Review*?" Dyer's eyelids became more narrow as he tilted his head backward and stared at Spenner.

"Yes," Spenner replied, "and if he still wants an interview, tell him I will be available this afternoon if he wishes to come out."

Dyer seemed nonplused but he nodded in consent to the instructions.

"One more request, Anton," Spenner continued, "please order a wreath of flowers to be ready the day after next."

"A wreath of flowers?" Dyer asked and his eyes flickered with more perplexity.

Again Spenner answered, "Yes. Just leave the address of the florist for me and I will pick up the wreath myself." Spenner opened the door, but before he stepped out, he turned to Dyer and said, "Now I am going to Thornburgs again." He smiled at the confused looking Dyer and then was out the door and off in a large, sleek looking car driven by the chauffeur. The ride into town was smooth and easy and the car remained in waiting in the special parking facilities of Thornburgs store. When Spenner left the car, however, he did not enter the store. Out of sight of the chauffeur, he turned in another direction until he came to a public telephone. He opened the seam of his coat and withdrew a slim paper. He dialed the number and soon he heard the familiar low voice answer him as he asked, "Thurston?"

"Spenner?"

Spenner went on. "Some unexpected things have happened."

"Unexpected?" Thurston's voice rose slightly. "Not with the deception?"

"No," Spenner replied quickly. "I pulled that off. All are decided on that score and I have been accepted as the mayor—that was."

"What then?" Thurston's voice remained high but it was soft and calculating.

Spenner had to cough for his throat was tight and dry, then he answered, "Mrs. Whitmore was murdered."

There was a pause, then Thurston's voice came over. "Murdered? Who said that?"

"The boy, Lester," Spenner replied and his throat was aching. "How . . ."

Spenner interrupted. "He told me so; he saw the murder committed."

"Spenner, am I hearing you? Mrs. Whitmore has been dead for sixteen years. It is closed."

"But she was murdered, Thurston. She did not die from a fall as they said."

"You say the boy told you? He was only . . ."

Again, Spenner interrupted. "Five."

Thurston's voice became higher. "You cannot believe . . ."

"The boy was awakened that night; he left his room and saw his mother killed."

"Nothing is on record of anything like that, Spenner."

"I know," Spenner said. "No one believed the boy."

"And you do?" Disbelief now was apparent in Thurston's voice.

Spenner hesitated and wondered if he should have called Alec Thurston. Yet, he had a partnership with this man and he wanted him to know. "It has bothered me, Thurston," he said slowly.

"Bothered you? Ah, how could it bother you?"

"I cannot say really, but I believe the boy." Spenner answered and paused for his throat felt tight but he went on. "Thurston, if you could have seen Lester when he told me. The boy—remembering that time all these years. He was pathetic, suffering, and trusting me. I believe him."

"But nobody else did!"

"I know."

Thurston's voice was becoming agitated. "Well, just what are you intending to do?"

"I am going to try to discover the truth in Lester's story."

"Spenner, how can you do such a thing? That happened years

ago. It would be dangerous to start digging around too much in the past. Can't you see that?"

"Perhaps," Spenner replied. "Yet, I feel I must try. She was a sickly woman with two small children. Why would anyone want to kill her?"

"That is the exact point, Spenner. Why would anyone do it? There is no sense."

"But she was also the mayor's wife."

There was a pause before Thurston spoke again. He still was agitated but he was trying to control his voice, speaking low and pleading. "Leave it alone, Spenner. It is less than three weeks to the reading of the will; then we will have the money. For heaven's sake, don't go upsetting things now!"

Spenner coughed. "Lester has lived with this for sixteen years. Is he going to have it for the rest of his life?"

"Don't go off playing sentimental. Tell the boy what everyone has told him—that he was dreaming or lying or that you just do not believe him. Spenner, let it be! *Let it be!*"

"No, Thurston," Spenner answered softly. "I am going to do whatever I can, for his sake . . ."

Now Thurston interrupted. "Listen, Spenner, *do not blow it now!* I have a stake here, too. I have planned this for too long and if it were not for me, you would not have a chance like this either. You are there to get that money. Now, just ride it out, Spenner."

Spenner could hear the demand in Thurston's words and he sensed a panic behind them. "I am going to do some investigating, Thurston."

"Investigating? For what?"

"For what I told you—the truth. I sense that something is not right, something that you could not know when you made *the plan*. I will be careful; I am mindful of our pact, but I want to try to find out what happened." He halted and then added, "That is all."

"Spenner, have you blown your mind? Don't go playing detective. You will stir up suspicions and that will be bad for both of us. Mrs. Whitmore's death was settled sixteen years ago. Just leave it that way, underplay your part, and go through with our plans exactly as we have decided. Don't mess it up!"

Spenner remained calm. "I just want to see what I can find."

Thurston's tone of voice changed, it became more demanding

107

and now it was filled with anger. "Don't try to find anything. You forget, Spenner, that I can blow the whistle on you any time. I can expose you."

Spenner's body became stiff and he gripped the telephone tightly. Now he had to tell himself to remain calm but he knew he was angry. He tried to subdue his anger by lowering his voice and speaking slowly. "I don't mind telling you, Thurston, that I do not like the position I am in. I agreed to it but I do not like it. For all I know, I might have been set up."

He heard Thurston gasp. "Set up? What does that mean?"

"Funny things have happened and I mean funny. First, the murder—"

"There is no murder," Thurston interrupted.

Spenner paid no heed and continued, "I am being followed, I know it. And yesterday I received a letter with a curious looking dove design on it. Now what does all that mean?"

Thurston still was gasping as Spenner spoke. "That all sounds not funny, but ludicrous! Whatever are you talking about?"

Ludicrous! Just the right word, thought Spenner, and he wanted to say it. Ludicrous is the correct word for all the happenings but it does not include the background. Ludicrous does not apply to the oppressive sensation of someone walking behind you, watching you and checking your movements. Or does it apply to the humiliation of political threats or the troubled bafflement at receiving a letter with a symbol of something you know nothing about? All these things have been directed against me personally. Ludicrous? You think that, Thurston?

This Spenner thought but to Thurston he said, "It all happened, Thurston, and why? Someone knew about my arrival almost from the time I got here although this deception was supposed to be a surprise. For a man missing twenty years, I am not so forgotten. That is why I think I am set up and how do I know that *that* was your plan."

"Spenner, you certainly cannot think that I . . . *The plan* is just what I presented to you. I mean it. How could it be otherwise? We have a stake in this together."

Spenner's voice became hoarse and his speech was rough. "Well, I am not accusing but I am suspicious of what I am involved in. You talked of exposing, you know, and you call yourself a compassionate man?"

"I am Spenner. I assure you."

"Then you are not going to keep me from trying to find some answers. After all, I am the one in the center of everything and I could be blown right out of it all. That is why I am going to try to do something about things that do not seem right. I know our pact depends on me; I will not forget that, but do not threaten me."

"Spenner, I was not threatening . . . "

Spenner continued quickly for his anger was steady. "Don't call me off, Thurston, with any exposing, because if you have any part in *anything* outside of our plan, I can expose you too."

"Believe me," Thurston replied and his voice had modulated but it was wavering. "No need to talk of exposing. Let us forget that. I can only repeat that I know nothing, absolutely nothing, about these things—happenings—that you talked about. You did make this call with a story that is beyond . . ."

"Then I will try not to call you again," Spenner replied. "I am going to try to solve this situation; then I will be ready to go."

"Remember, Spenner, that will be less than three weeks from now, then we will both be away."

"I will remember," Spenner answered easily and he hung the telephone before Thurston could say any more.

Well, thought Spenner, he had told Thurston and again he wondered if it had been a wise thing to do. Perhaps he only needed to challenge someone and Spenner was glad that he had contended with Thurston even though Thurston reacted by becoming angry and upset and threatening. Ah, he thought, the compassionate man! I tell him of murder and happenings against me and, instead of awareness or understanding or even help, Thurston thought only of the catch—the money that he intended to . . . Spenner paused, for the word that came to him was *steal*. Yes, steal the money for a hidden place somewhere.

Yet, Spenner knew that the intention was his also—to steal the money and then leave. But today Spenner felt positive and determined for he realized that he was on to something else. When he believed Lester and then experienced the forebodings against him, he began to think and to plan. In these few weeks, he resolved to try to find some answers to the questions surrounding the Whitmores, for Lester's sake. The feeling made Spenner feel vital and invigorated again but, he could not diminish the thought that Thurston was correct. In three weeks whatever will be done, will be done and then he, too, would be away from it all.

Spenner raised his arm and with a rough gesture, he pushed open the door of Thornburgs. He walked quickly over the heavy carpet and circled around until he saw the young clerk who had served him before. Spenner threw up his arms as a greeting and he exuded an unusual confidence and good will. "Ah, hello." he said to the clerk.

"Mr. Whitmore!" the clerk exclaimed, trying to equal Spenner's effusive greeting without the loudness or exaggerated gesture.

Spenner was aware that he was a bit more presentable in clothes that Thurston had purchased for him, so he advanced toward the clerk with confidence. "I am back!" he uttered and smiled with bravado. "I am back because I need other clothes."

"Of course," the clerk replied without hesitation and he even smiled slightly at Spenner, though he raised his shoulders and straightened his posture as if to retain his aplomb.

"I want summer clothes," Spenner stated.

"Summer clothes?"

Spenner nodded. "For the beach, for the resorts. I plan to go where the climate is warm." He paused and then added. "A trip, you understand?"

"Oh, yes, yes," the young clerk answered but there was a questionable look upon his face.

"After my son's engagement party, just a few weeks away."

"Yes, Mr. Whitmore," the clerk's posture sagged a little but his voice remained calm, "and you are fortunate because we are now ordering and establishing our newest line for next summer."

"Ah, it has to be done, to order one season in another. I knew I was fortunate! I knew it!" Spenner spoke loud and lustfully.

The clerk turned. "This way, Mr. Whitmore. We will arrange an order."

"I must have everything within the next few days," Spenner said. "If you could hurry . . ."

"We will arrange it, Mr. Whitmore. What we do not have in stock as yet, we will have rushed in."

"Good!" Good!" Spenner exclaimed as he followed the clerk to another part of the store.

"You will want slacks and shirts? The designs are casual but most elegant."

"That I want," Spenner answered eagerly. "Everything for a hot climate. Beach wear, too," he went on. "Bathing suits and all. I intend to spend time swimming and sun bathing where the sands and water are warm. My dream!"

The clerk spoke in a condescending tone. "I envy you. Now we will start with beach robes. The latest designs are in lightweight knit, as absorbent as cotton, and in bright colors."

"Just for me!" Spenner exclaimed like a boy. "Ah, bright colors!"

Inexhaustibly, they continued for an hour to assemble a wardrobe with Spenner going into high glee over each selection. Soon, the clerk's mood changed and he began to laugh with Spenner in his exuberance. But the clerk looked comical when he laughed for his eyes squinted, making the skin beneath puff out over his cheeks and his lower lip caught on his upper teeth so he sputtered in muffled sounds while trying to be humorous. Spenner was surprised and smitten by the clerk's silly looking face so he continued to buy things so the clerk would continue to laugh, and at last Spenner amassed more clothing than he ever thought he would own.

"I am happy," he said when finished and profusely thanked the clerk. The clerk continued to laugh and to show his lower lip on upper teeth so he could say nothing. Yet, his head nodded over and over again and he shook hands with Spenner.

"I am happy," Spenner repeated as he left the store. He used the same gesture as he did on his entrance: he raised his arm and roughly pushed the door open and stalked out to the waiting car where the chauffeur had fallen asleep.

Mr. Kirkland of *The Review* was waiting when Spenner returned to the estate. He was in the library and was prepared for the interview with notebook and pencil. Mr. Kirkland was short and stout and had a canny, direct gaze in his eyes. He greeted Spenner without cordiality and then seated himself opposite Spenner in one of the large leather chairs. He held the small notebook on his lap and the short pencil was hidden in his fat, puffy hand so it seemed he was moving his hand rather than writing. Spenner had the impression that Mr. Kirkland absorbed more than he wrote. Spenner felt no fear, yet he sensed that this reporter would not be easily fooled.

Thus, Spenner answered the inquiries about the amnesia and the past years of his life in Tegner in a light and serious manner but with a minimum of details. Above all, Spenner wanted to appear affirmative and confident and that he had adjusted to his return to his former life. He would look directly at Mr. Kirkland when he answered questions and even if he had to default an answer, his gaze would not waver as he said, "I cannot recall everything of those twenty years," and he would end on a positive note so he would remain assured, capable, and the past would not overshadow him.

Mr. Kirkland would nod and, finally, he asked about Spenner's future plans. Spenner quickly announced that he would not return to politics or public life. Then he made the point he wanted to make. "I have planned, however, for the day after tomorrow. I am going to Memorial Park and place a wreath at the Memorial Monument as a courtesy and in respect to those who served during the war." Spenner hesitated and then went on. "Many years have passed but I wish to do it for those who served while I was mayor."

Mr. Kirkland was moving his hand across the paper and Spenner waited so he could be certain to write all the facts.

"A convenient time," Spenner continued as he watched Mr. Kirkland write, "would be around noon. I would appreciate your including the time."

A few more irrelevant questions and the interview was complete. Spenner thanked Mr. Kirkland for "his interest in an old politician" and said he looked forward to seeing the article in tomorrow's newspaper.

Mr. Kirkland was sedate and less courteous but he thanked Spenner for the meeting and departed without smiling, although his saturnine temperament seemed satisfied with the interview.

The day was cold when Spenner was driven to Memorial Park. He stopped on the way to pick up the wreath of flowers and also Grant Deakins. Spenner had asked Deakins along as he thought the presence of the lawyer would make the ceremony more important and official.

The park was along the edge of the sea and the area became more open and desolate as they neared it. The landscape was without color in this late autumn season and the thin trees bowed in obeisance to the strong wind from the sea. The road followed the water's edge where large waves freely tossed their white caps onto the nearby sands. The car turned into the park but returned in a half circle drive to face the sea again. The Memorial Monument was a huge, bronze soldier statue that stood in an enclave close to the shoreline of the park. A circle of people already was standing around the monument and others were merging into the circle in insect fashion and they gathered close together because of the cold.

The car was driven as near to the statue as possible. Spenner got out and his first glance went over the crowd which seemed to be only a jumble of quilted faces. Spenner looked the other way at the people approaching on far-off pathways, but they walked easily and directly and folded into the expanding crowd. No one seemed unusual or acted erratically. Spenner looked again at the crowd around the statue. They looked back at him but their glances were level, curious, and expectant. No one seemed in any way out of the ordinary.

Spenner strode along the path toward the statue which looked dull in the grey atmosphere and the blank backdrop of sea and sky beyond. Spenner walked to the crowd, hurrying so as to be ahead of Grant Deakins who followed behind him. The crowd was mixed, young and old, men and women and a few children. Their faces were red and cold and their bodies were covered with heavy clothing. No one moved; they only swayed when individuals shifted their positions.

Spenner raised his head to walk boldly and he was aware that it added an arrogance to his appearance and that pleased him. He wanted to be antagonistic; he hoped there was *someone* in the crowd that he could provoke. Yet, no definite movement was visible; instead there was a sound, a clap of hands, and it stimulated a reaction for soon a few others did the same. The clapping was not loud but it was dull and steady. Spenner smiled and now they smiled, too, as if on cue, and Spenner thought that he approached the statue in triumph.

He glanced upward at the oversized soldier, rising erect and proud looking above him. An unidentified face, as intended, but Spenner did not care to move close to read the memory of letters and dates that were inscribed at the feet of the soldier. The cold air slapped Spenner's face and made his eyes tear. If anyone believed he was crying, that would be all right Spenner thought. He wiped his face, then took the floral circle of purple and white chrysanthemums from Grant Deakins and placed it at the bottom of the statue. He bowed and stood silent. The clapping had ceased and the silence was all around him as if the crowd had vanished. An aura of reverence and hesitation prevailed, but when Spenner broke his posture and turned, murmurs rose from the people like a humming benediction. Spenner remained vulnerable, standing alone. He gazed out over the crowd and thought is there not *someone* there? I have placed myself before you. I have come out in the open and I am standing here. This is my purpose for all this, for being here. I have announced this ceremony so someone can come forward and make some move against me. *Let me know!* But the crowd remained a rippling crest, muffled and uncomfortable. Then Spenner was beckoned by a movement in the far background. He looked up quickly and saw the black-clad figure standing there, away from the crowd. The figure was motionless and alone like another dark statue in the dreary landscape.

"Ah," Spenner said quietly and started toward the figure. He broke through the crowd and, in his concentration on the distant figure, he did not see the man who stepped directly in his path. Spenner was thrown back and he staggered before the grotesque creature in front of him. He was amazed at the apparition. The ghastly creature was thin and scrawny and his face was wild looking. His head was raised so he looked directly at Spenner. Spenner saw that the grotesqueness was caused by the man's uneven eyes, one was wider than the other and curved outward but the look was like that of a trapped animal. A sneer broke over the man's face and he shouted, "So it is you! It is you, Collis!"

Spenner stared at the man, unable to shift his gaze from the red and sore-looking and frenzied eyes. The man laughed, showing a mouth without teeth and now he looked like a lunatic.

"So you are back, Collis?" the man screamed again.

Spenner looked back at him. "Yes," he said slowly, "but I don't know . . ."

"It figures! It figures!" The man screamed. "Don't know Old Blinkey, do you? Like so many others, Old Blinkey was not worth a darn!"

"Old Blinkey?" Spenner said the name and his voice was perplexed.

"To be sure, but wasn't Old Blinkey until the war when I lost my eye." He laughed again but his tone was full of irony. "Maybe I should have come around and paid my respects sooner," he stopped and then said, "Do I still call you your honor?"

"No," Spenner shook his head. "Blinkey," he said hurriedly, "you must tell me . . ."

"Tell you!" the man's voice was loud and derisive. "Me? Tell

114

you? You had all the answers, Collis. You knew everything. You knew it all."

Spenner sensed that the man was desperate, yet he tried to retain control to make some contact with this man. "I would like to talk," he said.

The man became nervous and infuriated. "What for? What is there to talk about now? I came here today because I wanted you to see that Old Blinkey survived. Not in good condition, to be sure, but I survived. Yes, Collis, that I did and I wanted you to know."

"I want to talk," Spenner persisted. "Come around and talk."

"Come around?" The old man laughed again. "If you want to talk, you come around to me." He turned away but Spenner went after him. "Like I said," he spun about and faced Spenner, "you come around to me."

"Where?"

"Where? How about the old place, the old saluting place, as we called it. We old soldiers remember that and it is still there. So come around, Collis, come there."

"But where?" Spenner asked hurriedly. "I don't remember."

"You don't remember? Then *think* about it. Your brains have returned, haven't they? You said so."

Perhaps the man frightened the crowd for they began to move away and scatter. With a surprising quickness, Old Blinkey twisted himself and took off amongst the crowd. Spenner tried to keep him in sight but the old man disappeared and was hidden in the latticework of the crowd. Spenner strained himself, looking quickly in all directions, but Old Blinkey was gone. Spenner tried to move into the crowd after him but someone grabbed his arm and held him back. It was Grant Deakins and he looked worried and anxious. "Is anything wrong, Mr. Whitmore?"

"Old Blinkey was here," Spenner replied quickly.

"Who?" Deakins asked and his face became more anxious.

"He was here. He talked to me."

"I know of no one with such a name, but do you see him now?"

Spenner shook his head. He still was looking wildly about into the crowd where Old Blinkey disappeared, but he suddenly paused and stood still. He looked toward the edge of the crowd. The black-clad figure, too, had disappeared.

Grant Deakins tugged at his arm and Spenner allowed him to

115

lead him back to the car. By the time they were seated and ready to leave, the area around the Memorial Monument was almost empty. The crowd had dispersed and the soldier statue was left in its silence.

Spenner settled back into the car as they drove away. "Grant," he asked softly, "where is the old saluting place?"

Deakins looked at him quickly. "I have never heard of it, Mr. Whitmore," he answered.

"It is still there," Spenner said and his voice became rambling. "The old soldiers remember it."

"I am afraid I cannot help you. I know nothing about it, nothing at all."

Spenner said no more but he stared ahead of him, thinking of the black-clad figure, Old Blinkey, and the saluting place or whatever it was.

Grant Deakins looked at him questioningly. His face became sad and he shook his head. "I am sorry," he said and sighed, "but I do not believe this has been such a good day."

Part Two

Buell's Case

I

Chapter Eight

Johnson Buell arrived in Tegner early in the morning. The railway station was almost deserted with only minimal trainmen and porters completing their last hours as the night crew. The evening lights still were on but their brightness was being dimmed by the first grey patches of dawn that were breaking through.

Johnson Buell carried his own luggage because there were few porters available and he was in a hurry to reach a taxicab. But he had to wait outside the terminal for the taxicabs were equally few at this early hour. He glanced around at his surroundings. They were bleak; the railway terminal was old and was situated in a decaying part of Tegner. He saw wooden buildings idle and ancient in style and, apparently, few in use for any purpose, business or residential. There were signs on some building fronts, identifying a restaurant, a shoe repair, and a drug store, but these places had not opened as yet so they looked as forlorn and as useless as the other structures.

The dawn was spreading over the sky, but the night had not faded rapidly; instead it moved away slowly so that the atmosphere was the troubled time, a pause that was neither night or day. The air was cold and Buell tucked his muffler closer around his neck. His entire body was beginning to feel the chill when at last a taxicab approached and stopped before him. Johnson Buell gave the driver the name of a hotel and they were off in a desolate, lonely run to the downtown of the city. Here the area was improved, it was modern and clean which made it seem properous.

When he got to his room, he unpacked slowly and then sank into one of the comfortable chairs near the window. He looked out over the part of Tegner before him. Nothing had stirred on the streets except for an occasional vehicle, a car or a van. He watched until the traffic began to increase and the street lamps went off. Other lights began to come on in various buildings and then the city people emerged, beginning the pulse beat of coming and going, coming and going along the thoroughfare and into the shops and stores.

Johnson Buell was thinking of the answers he had to find in this place. He could have come to Tegner a day sooner but he had delayed because he had gone to Memorial Park in Valiterra to see and study this man who said he was Collis Whitmore. Johnson Buell wanted to see how he looked, apart from the photograph, how he moved, and the expressions on his face. He saw Collis Whitmore tense and worried, almost frightened, as he constantly surveyed the crowd. He witnessed the shock of Collis Whitmore at the meeting with the old man who shouted at him. These things were not included in the portfolio given to him by his client, Grant Deakins. Buell had studied thoroughly the report given to him with all information possible on Collis Whitmore. He particularly remembered the last known report on the mayor twenty years ago. An emergency meeting of all officials was called as Valiterra was falling. The enemy was on the outskirts of the city and pressing toward the center. The officials were to meet at the mayor's office, but the records showed that at the time scheduled for the meeting, the building was already demolished. Rubble and ruin were all about along with smoldering fire. As the mayor had called for the meeting from his office, it was assumed that he must have been there, in his office, when it was hit and he was destroyed along with the building. No trace of him, of course, but now it seems he had escaped, was hurt perhaps, got amnesia and ended up in this place. Now it was his mission, Johnson Buell thought, to discover how that had happened.

Johnson Buell did not sleep or nap and he was more refreshed after the train ride by bathing and putting on clean clothes. He had breakfast at the hotel, and, while eating, he studied a local map of the city he had picked up at the desk.

It was now mid-morning when he stepped out into the street. He walked to the nearest place for car rentals and hired the least expensive automobile available. He adjusted easily to the car and soon he was driving smoothly in a westward direction. He pulled up before a tall, narrow, boarding house for men only in a section of Tegner that looked as old as the area around the railway station. Buell checked the number on the building; it agreed with the one listed in the report as the last address of Collis Whitmore or here the name was James Spenner. Johnson Buell mounted the short steps and rang the bell. Soon the door was opened by a squat, white-haired man with pale blue, watery eyes. He blinked at Johnson Buell and then his eyes became wide with anticipation.

"Are you the brother?" the man asked.

Johnson Buell was surprised by the question. "What?" he asked, leaning closer to the man.

"Pete's brother," the man answered.

Buell straightened himself and shook his head. "No," he replied.

"Well, a relative was suppose to come," the old man continued. "I thought it would be a sister."

Buell drew out his badge as he said, "I am Johnson Buell, private investigator, and I would like to talk to the landlord of this building."

The old man blinked once again. "Oh, well, that's me," he answered, "but I thought you came about Pete." He hesitated and his eyes became wide with fear as he looked at the badge in front of his face. "There was nothing wrong," he said hurriedly. "Pete died in his sleep, but there was no violence, no sir, no crime."

Johnson Buell stared at the old man who had lifted his gaze, pleadingly, upon him. "I am not here about any crime or anything to do with Pete. You say you are the landlord, then I want to talk to you about another matter. May I come in?"

The old man was still frightened and he looked doubtful, but he stepped aside and held the door open. "Yes," he said in a whisper. "Come in."

Johnson Buell stepped into a hallway of pitted and cracked linoleum although it reeked of cleaning disinfectant. The stairway was immediate, leading upward to two levels. Buell heard a general commotion above of frenzied talk and doors opening and closing. He turned to the landlord and he made his voice gentle and soft, trying to put the old man at ease. "I am here," he said, "to ask about a former tenant—James Spenner."

The doubt had not vanished from the old man's face and he did not reply but nodded his head.

"James Spenner was a tenant here, was he not?" Buell asked more emphatically.

"Yes," the old man finally answered, "but he left."

"When was that?" Buell asked.

"Oh, maybe a week ago," was the reply.

The answer was close enough so Buell went on with another question, answer already known. "Do you know where he went?"

The old man shook his head. "He did not say; he just left. He paid me though." The old man hesitated as a thought came to him. "There is no trouble, is there?" he asked.

Johnson Buell did not answer, but he shook his head quickly and went on. "How long did he live here?"

The old man became thoughtful as if debating with himself and, at last, he said, "Maybe five years."

Buell nodded to show his acceptance of the answer. "Do you know where he came from before he arrived here?"

"No. James Spenner never said," the old man replied and when his watery eyes blinked, tears rolled down his cheeks.

Johnson Buell suspected that the old man felt slightly intimidated and had not dared ask why he was here, asking questions about a former tenant. "Is his room occupied? If not, I would like to see it."

"Nobody took it yet," the landlord answered. "I'll take you up; it is on the top."

The top would be the third floor and as they started up the stairway, the hubbub suddenly became hushed, but a fetid odor became stronger as they neared the second level. Buell could hear running footfalls and the quick rasp of doors opening and closing. When they reached the second level, there was silence, but Buell could see several doors opening slightly and eyes beyond that looked quizzically upon him. They passed one closed door as they turned and the landlord said, "Pete's in there," as he pointed to the door. He hurried past and started up the stairs to the third level. As they were ascending, Buell heard muted whispers behind him. He turned quickly and saw a group had emerged, men with unclean and unshaven faces, startled and surprised, looking after them.

On the third level, the old man stopped before one door and opened it. He went in as he said, "This was Spenner's room."

Johnson Buell stepped into the bleak looking room. The floor was bare, without carpet, and the windows, facing front, were closed so the air was heavy and odorous. There was a bed in one corner and against the opposite wall was a desk with lamp and a bureau. A large, high backed chair stood facing the windows and the grenadine curtains, supposedly a light color, were limp with dust.

Johnson Buell was looking carefully about the room but he spoke to the landlord who had backed away into the doorway. "Was Mr. Spenner a good tenant?"

"Oh, yes. No trouble; kept to himself. He did not bother anyone."

"Did he go out much?"

"You know, I asked him that one time because it seemed that he didn't," the old man said nervously, "but he only said he went to the park."

"He had visitors then?"

"No, no," the landlord answered hurriedly. "I never saw anyone come here."

Buell went on, "He worked, did he? He had a job?"

The landlord hesitated. "Well, I cannot say there was anything steady. I think he worked at different jobs and sometimes he did not work at all."

"You have no idea where he worked, when he did?"

The old man shook his head. "No, as I said, I think he worked at many different places." He turned suddenly in the doorway for there was a commotion from downstairs. He looked around quickly, first toward the lower levels and then back at Johnson Buell. "He always paid his rent though. I believe he may not have had much else, but he paid me—all the time." He was becoming agitated as the noise from below increased. "Excuse me," he said, "but I think they have come about Pete."

Johnson Buell nodded. "You go ahead and take care of it. I will just look around a bit more."

The old man quickly disappeared. Through the open door, Buell could hear loud voices, sharp and demanding, and the trampling up the stairs; and all the sounds seemed to reverberate through the entire building.

"When did he die?" someone asked in a peremptory tone of voice.

"Well, his friend found him this morning," another voice answered. "They were going to sell newspapers today. At first, he thought Pete was still sleeping but then he. . . . " and the voice trailed off into a low murmur as they entered the dead man's room.

Above, Johnson Buell could hear the general noise and the movements, but he continued to survey Spenner's room. There were no linens on the bed, it was covered with only a faded quilt. The desk drawers were empty. He opened the closet and it was also empty. He glanced up and around and saw the cracked plaster and the holes in the ceiling and on the walls. He crossed to the murky window and pulled the curtain slightly so he could look out. Outside, on the street, was an ambulance van and two police cars and men in uniforms and plain clothes were talking amongst themselves, gesturing and describing with hands as they would enter and leave the building.

Johnson Buell released the curtain and looked around the room another time. He went over the meager furniture, the drawers, the closet. He checked along the floor for anything that might give him a clue to James Spenner but he found nothing. He was becoming colder and he sensed that there had not been heat in this room for some time, apparently since James Spenner left. Standing in the middle of the room, he thought, so Spenner lived here for five years as a recluse and near the edge of vagrancy, working just enough to keep this place.

Buell stepped out into the hallway and looked over the stair railing to see a stretcher with a covered body being carried by two husky medics to the first level. The other tenants assembled now without hesitation. They stood openly before their doorways and along the railing viewing the final exit of one of their own. There seemed to be little sadness, however; there was silence but like a tribute without sentiment.

Johnson Buell waited until the body was removed and then he descended the stairs. This time, when he entered their midst, the men did not scatter as before, as if they had forgotten about him in their absorption of the departure of Pete's body and he had caught them unawares. On the second level, standing next to Pete's door, Buell saw a skinny man with a wisp of a reddish beard. His head was bald and very white and looked like a skull. His eyes were glazed but there were no tears. Buell paused and then approached the man.

"You knew Pete well?" he asked.

The man was startled and he glanced furtively at Johnson Buell. Buell thought that the man believed him to be a part of the legal team that had handled the demise of Pete.

"We were going to sell papers today," the man replied and his voice was shaky.

"Did you ever sell papers with anyone else?" Buell asked.

The man nodded. "Sometimes."

"How about James Spenner?" Buell tilted his head toward the higher floor.

"Sometimes," the man answered again. "Spenner helped me sometimes."

"Where did you sell the papers?"

"Usually at the newstand two blocks away."

Buell hesitated for a moment and then asked, "Did James Spenner ever tell you where he came from?"

"Well, he was no talker and he did not mix," the man answered. "I never asked him where he came from." The man paused and lowered his eyes. "Around here, we don't ask questions like that. A man is here and we accept it. What he tells, he tells on his own." The man hesitated once more. "Pete was different. He was a talker. He was a smart lawyer, or had been, until he took to drink and was forced out of the profession. Yet, he could take anything from the papers and give you ideas and the low down about the real meaning of all that stuff they print. He was good at the newstand, too, because he would talk to anyone there the same way. A real speaker he was, and a good one."

"Did James Spenner ever talk to anyone at the newstand?"

The man shook his head. "Never did. He did his job, don't get me wrong, and he was honest, but he never got to talking with customers. That is why I preferred to work with Pete. He was more open and friendly but he always had that drink. He was that way most of the time, even when working. Drunk on the job but it did not keep the customers away. They seemed to like to talk to him."

Johnson Buell turned away, thanking the man who accepted with mutterings through his red beard. Buell halted when he reached the entrance and looked outside. On the steps, looking after the ambulance van, was the landlord and a chic looking young woman. Johnson Buell stepped around, still looking at her. She wore a black coat with a fur collar high around her neck and a tight fitting red cloche on her head. The small hat accented her oval face which was lovely with dark eyes and a full red mouth. Her countenance was serious and solemn and made her good looks static and true, like a picture. Buell

125

approached the landlord to thank him but his eyes remained on the woman as the landlord whispered, "Pete's sister."

Johnson Buell smiled lightly but turned away. The contrast was upsetting. Pete living here in these conditions, most likely the family black sheep, and yet he had family, at least one anyway, who apparently was successful, well dressed, smart looking and very lovely.

Buell drove up to the newstand that was supposed to be serviced today by Pete and the red-whiskered man. The stand was closed; there was no substitute vendor about and no newspapers. A few passerby stopped, viewed the closed stand and then moved on. Parked alongside the stand, Buell asked several passerby if they knew the vendors. Several shook their heads and muttered, "No, I only buy the paper." Others said, "There are different men here, no regulars." A few mentioned Pete. "One fellow could talk a blue streak." "I came just to talk to him." "Smart man, but I wondered why he had to do this for a living." When Buell asked if they could describe any of the other vendors, he received a terse reply. "Most of them looked like they could use a good meal."

Buell tried to describe James Spenner to them. "Do you recall a middle aged man, about fifty-five? He had dark brown hair, but quite gray, and a crooked nose? He worked, I believe with . . . " he hesitated and took a chance with "Red, the man with red whiskers." They remembered Red but one man mentioned Spenner. "Yes, I have seen him here, he has worked with Red, but he never said anything. He was quiet all the time. I asked him once if he remembered the war. I don't know why I asked except that he just looked like a veteran to me."

"What did he say?" Buell asked quickly.

"He just said 'yes' and that was all, no more. He looked pained and hurt by the question, so I never asked anything more."

Johnson Buell did not linger longer at the newstand because he was on his way to city hall. There, he inquired if there was any list or any information about refugees who came to Tegner during the war. The clerk looked disconcerted. "That is old," he said. "We put those records in the basement."

Buell felt a surge of optimism. Records! "May I see them?" he asked enthusiastically.

The clerk remained perturbed and he seemed put out. "Well, it would be a job to go down and find them."

Johnson Buell insisted. He said he needed information and finally he flashed his detective identification in front of the clerk. With reluctance, the clerk left his desk and headed toward a stairway. All the while, on the way to the basement, he made excuses, saying the records were old, never were complete, and nobody was interested in them any more. Besides, most of the records were of those who needed medical attention at that time, could not keep record of everyone because too much havoc then and too many people.

Johnson Buell replied that he particularly wanted to see medical records so the clerk said no more but sighed deeply. The basement was musty and dark. The clerk turned on lights as he went along, around stacked furniture and shelves of boxes and crates. He began reading labels on the boxes and after following a labyrinth of a date trail, he came to a shelf with a sealed box. "Here," he said, pointing to it.

Together, they lifted the box to a table. The clerk hastily swept away dust with his hand and then brushed his clothes as if the effort had dirtied him without reason. Johnson Buell said he was grateful and could look on his own, and politely told the clerk he could return to his regular duties. The clerk was relieved; he smiled and left hurriedly.

The box was dated twenty years previously and beneath were the words REFUGEE FILE. Buell broke the sealed tape and looked inside. The books were stacked neatly but they reeked from enclosure in stale air. They were medical records but they reflected a hasty keeping. A name was given with the malady and the name of a doctor. At times, either the malady or the doctor's name was omitted. Many had the additional word "Died" listed after the entry. Buell studied every page, looking for the name of either James Spenner or Collis Whitmore. He found none. He especially scrutinized any listing of an amnesiac, but nothing would fit to either name. He told himself that the records were not complete, as the clerk had said, but he packed the books carefully and sealed the box. He told himself that he had used the remainder of the day. He went upstairs to thank the clerk but he had already gone home.

In his hotel room that evening, Johnson Buell opened the portfolio and began his first report on pursuing the identity of Collis Whitmore. He remembered carefully the happenings of the day, the visits to the boarding house and the newstand and the study of the refugee file at city hall. Yet, a nagging vision kept coming to his mind and that was the thought of Pete's sister. He saw her over and over again, the dark eyes and brows, the red mouth, the wisps of dark hair around the small hat and fur piece that made her face so feminine and appealing. He had seen the sadness on her face also and he knew why he had turned away so quickly when he saw her. She reminded him of Randi Papin and he was surprised that he could still be piqued, in an agonizing way, by this resurrected memory of her. It had been his first case and his first love.

He was called, late at night, to the Papin home where a man had been shot. Buell was on the police force and had received his first promotion to detective. He was assigned to nightwatch and his precinct got the call. "J. B., you better hurry," he was told. "A shooting."

The sergeant in charge that night drove Johnson Buell to the Papin home. A policeman met him and asked, in a serious tone, "Are you the lucky one?" which meant that the situation was messy, tricky and volatile.

"What happened?" Buell asked.

The elder policeman answered, almost nonchalantly, "A man is dead; he was shot, over there in the garden. I understand he was a bridegroom. Was to be married tomorrow."

Johnson Buell nodded but his face became firm and determined. He made his way across the lawn toward an orbit of light. Other policemen were there, turning spotlights onto the ground with a variety of lamps, poles, and transformers. The scene unit photographers were there also, snapping more light circles like signaling stars. In the center of all the illumination was the lifeless body of a man lying on the gravel path. He was on his back, his knees doubled up slightly, but his arms were outstretched and his face was turned full front with eyes opened in a fixed stare. He was young and nice looking with clear skin and blond hair. He was wearing a dark-colored dress suit which was now covered with blood.

Johnson Buell approached the officer in charge to get the details. "A maid heard the shot," the officer began. "She was cleaning the room in there," and he gestured toward a well-lighted room with French doors just beyond a wide, brick patio. "She came out and saw him lying here with blood spilling out all over."

128

"His name?" Buell asked.

"Ralph Barnes," the officer replied. "He was going to marry the Papin girl."

Buell asked another question. "Any idea of what happened?"

"Nothing. We do have a gun, a funny looking object, which was found a little way down the path."

Johnson Buell went down the path to where the gun was found. It had been picked up and placed in a plastic bag. The gun was indeed a funny looking object for it was an ancient dueling pistol. The barrel was long and slim while the foresight was ivory and the butt was carved in an intricate, swirling pattern. Buell was told that it was taken from the gun collection of Harvey Papin.

The laboratory men still were at work, moving around in the light like nocturnal animals, searching for anything that might be important. The area was roped off all the way beyond the patio to the house. Buell strode slowly around the area with the men, his eyes to the ground, and, like the others, he was looking for anything, for any reason, to connect to the death of the young man. Buell trusted the men, but he was in charge now. It was his case and it was something he had to do—to see and know as much as possible for himself. But he was not dismayed for they had the gun, that odd looking dueling pistol, which he felt would not make the case too difficult.

After a while, he went inside to see the Papin family. He could enter from the garden through the French doors which opened into a living room. The room, however, was not orderly; it showed the remains of a party. There were cups and saucers and glasses on various tables along with rumpled napkins and crumbs of food. The room itself was so spacious that Johnson Buell did not see the entire family with one look. They were scattered about, oddly distancing themselves from one another rather than hugging close together. A heavy-set man with dark chestnut hair and moustache rose from a velvet covered chair to meet Buell. The man was healthy and virile looking and his brown eyes looked directly at Buell.

"I am Harvey Papin," he said and his tone of voice was deep and precise. "The man," he leaned his head toward the garden, "was Ralph Barnes, a salesman for my company. I own the Papin Machine and Forge company." He paused and his voice shook slightly. "To-morrow he was to marry my daughter."

Johnson Buell nodded, giving him an understanding look, and

began to ask his questions. He found out from Harvey Papin that Ralph Barnes was staying at the guest house across the garden until the wedding. Ralph Barnes had participated in the wedding rehearsal earlier and the dinner party which followed. After dinner, coffee and drinks had been served here but the guests had not stayed late, as Harvey Papin said, because of "the big day tomorrow." The maid was in the living room to remove dishes and clean up when she heard the noise from the garden. The patio light and the string lights along part of the path still were on, and she hesitated for a moment, uncertain about the sound. She saw no one, but stepped out, and followed the gravel path until she saw Ralph Barnes, lying there and covered with blood. She experienced the initial spasm of horror, then she was overcome by fear and raced back to the living room, screaming all the way.

The first person she encountered was Harvey Papin, who had heard the shot also and then her frightened, hysterical screams. He had been out in front of the house, bidding farewell to the last of the guests, and he hurried back to the living room. He listened to the frenzied outburst of the maid, went quickly to the garden to verify her description, and then called the police. By that time, the commotion had brought the other members of the Papin family to the living room.

Johnson Buell turned to the one seated on the couch as Harvey Papin said, "My wife, Donna."

"Oh!" she cried in a tearful voice. She was sniffling into a lace-trimmed handkerchief and she appeared flustered. She was surrounded and propped up by many pillows, but Buell could see that she was a small woman, pretty and fragile, with black hair and dark blue eyes. Her eyes glanced constantly around the room, as if afraid, but Buell thought this restless action made her look absent-minded.

"Oh!" she cried again as her gaze swept past Buell. "How dreadful, dreadful, with the wedding. . . "

Johnson Buell did not have a chance to speak to her as Harvey Papin quickly patted her shoulder. "Now, now," he said in a soothing tone, but she covered her face with the lacy handkerchief and buried it in one of the pillows.

Harvey Papin asked Buell if he could talk to her later. Buell agreed and turned toward a young woman seated beyond the couch in a high-backed chair covered with a floral print. "This is my daughter, Gloria," Harvey Papin said. Gloria had very short hair which looked blond but was dull and streaked. She was sitting slouched in the big chair with her head reclining on the back. She looked like she may have been drowsing or resting for her eyes opened at the mention of her name. Her eyes were light blue but looked faded and small under heavy makeup.

Johnson Buell extended his sympathies to her but, surprisingly, she laughed. Her glance mocked him as she said, "He was not to be *my* husband; he was Randi's."

Harvey Papin spoke. "Randi," he said quickly, "was to marry Ralph Barnes. She is our adopted daughter." He went to the other side of the room and called softly. "Randi!"

Johnson Buell had not seen her. She must have entered unnoticed and remained aside in her grief. She was sitting silently in a straight chair set in the shadows next to a high bookcase near the doorway. She rose and stepped out as Harvey Papin approached her. He placed an arm around her and whispered her name, "Randi, my dear."

"Oh, poor child!" Mrs. Papin cried out as she raised her head and her glance caught them. "Poor child!" she repeated. "Just before the wedding!" Her handkerchief came to her eyes immediately to wipe the tears.

Randi Papin's dark brown eyes were misty and sadness was heavy upon her face. Johnson Buell stared at her because it was hard to believe that she was the adopted one. Randi Papin had the healthy look of Harvey Papin, a glow that made him virile and her, sensual. Her dark hair and eyes were an equal match for Donna Papin's. In fact, she was closer in physiography to the Papins than their own Gloria. At the time of her adoption, perhaps the severe and restricting matching requirements brought forth Randi with the closer coloring and body frame while Gloria, with her light hair and eyes, looked like the outsider.

None of the Papin women had changed their clothes. They still wore their party attire and they looked a bit sacrilegious in an atmosphere talking of death. They were posturing in rose-colored lace for Mrs. Papin, magenta chiffon for Gloria Papin and acquamarine silk for Randi Papin. Jewels glittered on their bodies, rings, bracelets, necklaces and earrings.

Yet, as Randi Papin came toward him, Buell saw only her dark eyes, gazing steadily upon him with an imploring look. He was held by that look and as he stared back at her, he found that her eyes had depths. They became more lucid and limpid and he experienced an overwhelming wish that he, alone, somehow, could dispel all the sorrow and sadness that was upon her.

That was the memory brought forth by Pete's sister. The dark eyes, the lovely face, and the sadness—how much the same.

Johnson Buell quickly sat up. It had become dark outside and he reached for another lamp. He began writing again and he had to conclude with the phrase that he found nothing and made no connection to Collis Whitmore.

Chapter Nine

"Do I remember the name she spoke?" Spenner was talking to himself. "I know she said advertising but what? What was the firm's name?" Spenner paced back and forth across the room, trying to improve his concentration. "It sounded like Willis, or Williams, but maybe . . . " He stopped and consulted the telephone book. He scanned the names listed under Advertising Agencies, and he paused at the name of Willoughby Company. It was the only title close to Willis or Williams and, well, perhaps that was it. He dialed their number and soon a courteous, feminine voice acknowledged him.

"Karin Brantford, please," Spenner stated carefully.

The operator repeated the name and paused, possibly to consult the firm directory, then she said, "I'll connect you."

Ah, thought Spenner, pleased with himself that he had discovered the right place. He heard another buzzing sound and then a different voice, masculine this time, answering, "Art department."

"May I speak with Karin Brantford, please?" Spenner asked.

"Hold on," the voice replied and then Spenner heard the voice, fainter and in the distance, call out, "Karin, it is for you."

Soon, her light, lilting voice answered, "Hello?"

Spenner hesitated only for a moment and then said, "Karin," he paused for her name had come so easily, "this is Lee's father."

He heard her slight gasp. "Oh!" and then silence before she said, "Yes?"

Spenner continued quickly. "I am sorry to disturb you at your work. I am certain you are very busy, but I wonder if you would have lunch with me today?"

She gasped again. "Oh!" and there was another silence.

"You have other plans?" Spenner asked.

"No," she answered slowly and he sensed that she was hesitating about accepting.

"I would like to talk to you about something in particular." Spenner tried to make his request sound urgent and important.

"Well, all right," she said and then her voice lifted slightly. "I guess I can meet you."

"Can I pick you up?" Spenner asked. "I can call for a car."

"I have my own car," she replied quickly.

"Then where shall we meet? Wherever you wish."

She thought for a moment and then answered. "I can meet you at Henri's, at one o'clock. Do you know where it is?"

"No, but I will find it."

She went on in a determined tone. "Henri's is down by the waterfront. You cannot miss it."

"Thank you," Spenner said and heard the telephone click as she hung up, but he already had started to say, "Thank you again," which she did not hear.

Spenner called for a car but this time he drove himself. He knew the way into downtown Valiterra; he crossed through and headed toward the waterfront. He had to drive further north along the shore line but Henri's restaurant was not difficult to find. It was a large, sprawling stone building with a scalloped facade that faced the sea, and the name was written in bold letters on a canopy that covered the entrance.

Inside, the elegance was stunning and luster was the only word to describe the polished wood, the glittering chandeliers, and the silver and crystal table settings. There were many tables and each was covered with an immaculate white cloth and in the center was a vase of fresh flowers.

Spenner requested a table near the windows where he could look out over the endless, shimmering sea. He could see the parking lot at the side of the restaurant also, and he was able to see Karin drive up in a small, red car. He watched her as she came toward the restaurant, but she did not see him. She had no hat against the cold, but the collar on her coat was pushed around her ears and her hair was tucked inside. She wore high boots, light in color, and a matching purse that hung over her shoulder.

She saw Spenner when she entered but dutifully followed the maitre d' across the room. Her skin was tinged with pink from the cold and it made her face as glowing as the candlelight had done. She looked querulously at Spenner; she sniffed but forced a smile and

134

seated herself easily in the wide, armed chair. She still did not speak as she unbuttoned her coat and let it fall back over the chair. She stroked her hair to arrange it for it was long and loose, then she opened her purse for a paper handkerchief that she daubed around her nose.

Spenner felt uneasy and decided to speak first. "I hope this is no inconvenience," he said with hesitation.

"Not at all," she answered as she wadded the paper handkerchief and threw it into her purse. "I have only an hour for lunch, but I am glad to get away for that. Such a job!"

Spenner was surprised. "You are unhappy with your work?"

"Just bored." She sighed as a petulant child. Before she closed her purse, she pulled out a cigarette case. Spenner was about to apologize for having no matches when she withdrew a matching lighter and lit her own cigarette.

After a few puffs on the cigarette, she seemed to relax and she settled back in the chair. She looked directly at Spenner and stated, "You will *never* guess what I am doing now."

Spenner shook his head. "No."

She tossed her shoulders as if in disgust. "I am designing shower curtains!" she answered bluntly and the petulant look settled on her once more.

Spenner had an instinctive desire to laugh. Yet, he sensed that she meant the statement to be ridiculous, but as sarcasm, not humor. He controlled himself and answered softly and seriously, making his tone one of disbelief. "You are designing shower curtains?"

"Yes," she replied and tossed her dark hair back as the cigarette smoke swirled around her. "I am painting flamingoes, fishes, sea shells, anything aquatic for the bath." Now she laughed but without sentiment. "It is so boring and repetitious and unimaginative."

At that moment, a waiter approached. "Shall we have champagne cocktails?" she asked.

Spenner was startled but he said softly, "If you wish."

"You don't care for any?"

Spenner shook his head. "No." He waited until she finished the instructions for she was describing exactly how she wished her cocktail. Spenner was silent until the waiter left, then he asked carefully, "If you are unhappy, why don't you paint what you wish? Have your own studio?"

She laughed again, in the same way, without humor. Her eyes leveled as she looked straight at him. "That takes money."

Spenner replied, "Not all artists have had money."

"Then it is sacrifice," she said bluntly.

Spenner shrugged his shoulders. "But if it takes sacrifice . . . to do what you want?"

"Me? A starving artist? That is not heroic nowadays. An artist should live in the highest standards, luxurious, I think. When they pass away, their paintings are worth a fortune. They should have some of that wealth while they live. Their talent merits it. Nothing wrong with that."

"Until the paintings are sold," Spenner asked, not knowing, "does it take so much?"

"Absolutely; to be on your own." She paused and said dreamily, looking into the circle of cigarette smoke. "I would love to study in Paris. That is where I would like to be, but I do not want to live in one of those garrets, come down with consumption, and all that. That might be fine for a romantic tale, but it is not for me."

Spenner said, "Lee will take you to Paris. He said so."

Her head lowered and she shook her hair again. When she looked up, there was a glint in her dark eyes. "I know," she said evenly.

The waiter appeared with her champagne cocktail and menus. When Spenner opened the menu, he stared unbelievingly for it was written in French.

"Oh!" he heard Karin exclaim with delight. *"Filet de boeuf Richelieu!"* but she scanned the menu further and uttered other acclamations in French. When she finished, she looked at Spenner and asked, "What do you wish?"

"Well, I don't know," he replied.

She laughed. "I did not think that you would not know French!"

"Then you will have to order for me," Spenner answered, remaining calm and knowing that he had to be polite. "Whatever you decide." He folded the menu and put it aside.

Her smile was mocking. "Let me see then . . . " She scanned the menu again. "Let us have *potage crème crissonière*." She turned from the waiter to Spenner. "That is cream of watercress soup."

Spenner gulped but said nothing. He merely nodded while she went down the line, stating this and that, delighting the waiter who spoke with her in French. Spenner thought he caught words like

136

"potato" and "sauce," but he was not certain and somethings were "petite" and "au vin." Finally, whatever she ordered was completed and the waiter bowed happily and moved off to summon the feast.

"Are you wondering why I asked you to lunch?" Spenner asked seriously.

Karin settled herself in the chair once again. The cigarette was out but now she started on the champagne cocktail. She tasted it slowly, licked her lips and smiled. She did not speak but pressed her lips together, signifying that the cocktail was good. The pink color, given by the outdoors, had gone from her face, but her eyes were bright and sparkling. "You said you wanted to talk about something in particular. I did wonder, of course. Quite a surprise."

Spenner went on. "I want to ask you about an artist."

"An artist?" she repeated in surprise.

"I.thought you might know . . . I mean you are the only one I know in this field."

Her eyes widened and the sparkle in them shone brighter as she accepted his statement as a compliment. "Who?" she asked with interest.

"Roger Manning," Spenner replied. "He painted Mrs. Whitmore's portrait, as you may know, and I am most interested to know if he still paints."

"Oh, yes, he still gets many assignments." She paused and then continued in a determined tone of voice. "Now *there* is a settled, modern artist and I envy him. He has his reputation and his identity as an artist *now*. He has his own studio. He accepts only the work he wants, and he is free to paint on his own anything he wishes. Ideal. I wish all that for myself."

Spenner shrugged his shoulders. "If that is the ideal nowadays." He looked at her and smiled.

She paid little attention to his comment. "Sometimes he teaches at the university, but I assure you, he must be prevailed upon to do so. I was fortunate enough to go for one semester when he was the instructor. An excellent teacher—knew his business, I must say."

"Oh," said Spenner lightly, "so you admire him as a teacher and as artist, but did you like him personally?"

A smile settled on her face and she cast her eyes upward. She sighed and said, "He is dark and dreamy. The French type, you know."

137

That again, thought Spencer, and he smiled at her once more.

The meal was served as the waiter came forward with a tray laden with sumptuous food with sweet aromas. Karin's attention went completely to the food placed before her. She ate with the delight of a child. Small gurgles of satisfaction would sound in her throat as she chewed and tasted the various dishes that were so foreign and surprising to Spenner. The growing child was within her also. At the times when she would toss her dark hair and roll her bright eyes over the pleasures of the feast, her expressions and manners reflected the aggressive and sensual response of the grown up.

Spenner sensed that she knew her attributes and did not deliberately imitate any style. She would not be the one to imitate anybody, Spenner thought, and she was fascinating because she was so pretty and that excused much of her follies. Basically, she still possessed the virtues and faults of a child. The faults were accepted but did not cause amusement. The virtues, based mostly upon appearance, could not cover the faults for her entire demeanor was dominated by irreverence.

"By the way you speak of Roger Manning," Spenner said, "he must still be in this area?"

Karin nodded. "His studio is just outside of town."

"Then you must tell me where he has his studio. You see, I should like to pay him a visit and thank him for the portrait of Mrs. Whitmore. I appreciate it so much and I wish to express my gratitude to Mr. Manning."

"You have to take the highway out of town to Route 2, turn left and you will drive right to the place. You cannot miss it—it is the only house you will see. He designed that, too by the way. The strata of windows and porches are a bit overpowering, but it is his own peculiar mansion."

Karin finished her lunch with a *gateaux*, she explained to Spenner, but he saw they were only cakes. Yet, she exclaimed with rapture over the confections and ate two of them without a pause. She was off then, a working girl, she stated and left Spenner alone at the cluttered and disarranged table.

Spenner left Henri's restaurant and drove back through town, then headed in the direction Karin had given. He found the country road, made the left turn, and quickly arrived at the artist's mansion. Her description of the place was accurate for it was indeed "peculiar."

What a sight! It was overwhelmingly different and astounding. The building seemed to balance on various levels of stone, wood and glass, yet it was set snugly into place amongst giant, protecting trees. There was no way to determine a level of the house for the "strata of porches and windows," as Karin said, were not set in a regular pattern or design.

Spenner parked at the side and walked toward the mansion. He could not help but look upward at a great slant of windows which formed on a hedge over the entranceway. He pressed the bell but heard nothing resound within; nevertheless, the door opened without any delay and a stern looking man eyed him closely.

"Is Mr. Manning in?" Spenner asked. "I am most anxious to see him."

Apparently, unexpected callers were not tolerated for the man said coldly, "Do you have an appointment?"

Spenner shook his head. "No, but I wish very much to see him."

"Mr. Manning is a busy man. He schedules all appointments in advance."

Spenner persisted. "I am aware that Mr. Manning is a busy man, but my request is important."

The man's eyebrows rose in surprise at the challenge and he said, "Oh?" with a cold challenge in his voice.

Spenner looked directly at him. "Convey to Mr. Manning that I am Collis Whitmore and that I wish to see him, if possible."

The man gave Spenner a harsh look but he nodded and closed the door.

Spenner remained motionless when the door closed, then he stepped back and began to pace across the brick patio. He had a curious instinct to look upward again at the large windows for he had a feeling that someone was behind those windows, looking at him. Casually, he turned and looked up and his move was quick enough to glimpse a figure shy away from the windows like a shadow. Spenner had seen only the blurred movement, dark and swift, not an actual form. He was looking upward still when the door was opened by the man whose stern expression had not changed. "Mr. Manning will see you," he said curtly and stood aside so Spenner could enter.

Spenner felt as though he had stepped into a museum for the place was huge and cavernous and cold, especially cold. The frozen atmosphere enveloped Spenner immediately and was so penetrating that he began to tremble. He shook himself and rubbed his hands together as he followed the man up a stairway. The stairway was not straight. They moved back and forth from one short stairway to another, but Spenner believed they were heading toward the front of the building which contained the large row of windows. They reached a landing and went along a short corridor. The man opened a door and the window room became all light, expansive and bright, in direct contrast to the dark and chilly foyer below.

Spenner made his way past a wall of paintings. There was a variety of scenes and sketches, objects of different sizes, land and sea scapes, florals, buildings, and many faces, each painting reflecting a color and style suitable for its own. Spenner surveyed the montage as he passed and felt that some of the paintings appealed to him although he did not know why. He did not intend to stop, but he did as his glance settled on a portrait that hung just above eye level. The portrait was of a middle-aged man with a rugged face, determined countenance, and thick grey hair. He wore a dark suit but his lapel and shoulder were adorned with medals. It was the medals which attracted Spenner for one was the sign of the dove, the circular emblem that appeared on the mysterious letter he had received. Spenner stared at the picture unbelievingly and for a long while until he was aware of a figure coming toward him from the other side of the room. Out of the corner of his eye, Spenner saw the same type of shadowy movement he had seen before from behind the curtain. Spenner turned to look at him. The man definitely was "dark and dreamy" with an appeal that was tantalizing and overwhelming as he came closer. He had a mane of wiry black hair that spread around his face and an equally thick beard that completed the dark frame around his chin. His eyes were black and flashing and extremely sensual. He was big, tall and stout enough to carry off the heavy hair and beard with assurance, almost arrogance. There was an elegance about him but not necessarily that of a gentleman for his seductiveness was too prominent and unrestrained.

"Mr. Manning," Spenner said and was surprised that he stepped back as the artist came closer upon him. "I am sorry to disturb you."

"You are Collis Whitmore?" the artist asked in an amazed tone of voice as his dark, pitiless eyes looked over Spenner. "How strange, after all these years. What a bewildering surprise!"

140

"I suffered from amnesia," Spenner sighed as he used the sentence again. "It is a difficult story to explain."

Spenner thought there was amusement on Manning's face but he saw neither a smile nor a hint of laughter. Manning still was amazed as he went on. "A ghost! A ghost come forward! Who would have thought . . . " he paused and then said, "No doubt it is difficult to explain, as you say."

Spenner changed the subject quickly. "You have quite a mansion and studio here, Mr. Manning, but, to me, it is extreme."

Manning's face was stoic. "For you, perhaps, but to an artist, nothing is extreme. We express, in any way, whatever we wish."

Spenner tried to laugh but he sounded like he groaned. "That sounds like too much freedom."

"Oh, no, no. We have the conscience and usually we, the artists, whether painter, poet or philosopher, are the first with that—the conscience. We cannot be judged by what we express but only how we express it." He stopped and moved closer to Spenner. "What is the matter, Mr. Whitmore?"

Spenner could not discuss expression and judgment or conscience with the artist, and he had turned his face back to the painting. "I have been looking at this," he said, pointing to the picture. "Who is this man?"

"I do not know," Manning replied curtly.

"You do not know?" Spenner turned in surprise and faced Manning. "But you painted this?"

"Is he familiar to you?" Manning asked with his own question.

"No, I am only curious," Spenner replied.

"I painted that from another picture at the request of the family. They said he was dead and they wanted a portrait, so they came with a photograph. I intensely dislike such work, but the family was so insistent and they paid well."

Spenner was intrigued, "But the picture, why is it here?"

Manning's voice sounded irritated and impatient. "That is the first sketch. Many pictures on this wall are the preliminary sketches."

Spenner went on with questions. "Can't you tell me anything about this man or his family?"

Roger Manning shook his head. "They told me nothing; they wanted it that way. A man brought the photograph and came to pick

141

up the picture when it was finished. Why, Mr. Whitmore," his voice was even and low, "are you so interested?"

"That medal. This one," he said and indicated the dove emblem, "interests me. Do you know its significance? What does it mean?"

Manning came forward to better scrutinize the medal. "No," he answered. "I do not know its meaning. I thought all of these medals to be war medals, but I cannot tell you what they represent."

Spenner was silent. War medals! "I have another question, Mr. Manning, if you do not mind. Have you ever heard of the 'old saluting place'? It sounds like it has a war meaning also."

Roger Manning blinked with surprise but his dark eyes became intense. "How silly! I know nothing about such a place." His gaze became curious. "Mr. Whitmore, you seemed occupied and possessed by trivial, unimportant things. Whatever goes on with you?"

Spenner felt embarrassed and apologized quickly, then he said, "I came here, Mr. Manning, to talk to you about Mrs. Whitmore."

Roger Manning still looked quizzically at Spenner. He said nothing but his eyes narrowed and his look was forbidding. He turned and went back to the wider room where he shifted his large frame into a wicker chair which creaked beneath him. He motioned Spenner to a similar chair. The chair was wide and comfortable but it creaked under Spenner also.

"I have seen your painting of Gessie in our library and I want to talk about her. I am curious, you understand?"

"Yes," Manning answered slowly. "You like the painting?"

"I do." Spenner nodded. "It is remarkable and I must express my thanks for the fine work. It is indeed beautiful and admired." He was aware that his voice was droning on, expressing an unprofessional evaluation of the artist's work.

Manning shrugged his shoulders and threw up his hands as if this kind of flattery did not affect him and was meaningless. "What then?"

Spenner shifted himself and leaned forward. "You had to be together, you and Gessie, to do the painting, so I wonder if you could tell me about her? How was she while you were working on the painting?"

Manning scrutinized Spenner for a moment, and his eyes became small and absorbing. Slowly, softly, he said, "I loved her."

Spenner was startled and looked so quickly at Manning that his gaze caught the direct and mocking look in the artist's eyes. There was a silence between them; a feeling of renewing positions. Finally, Spenner blinked when Manning laughed. His laugh was amazing for it was soft and melodious. Spenner's body slumped and he fell backward into the chair. Even while laughing, Manning's look did not waver and he repeated, "Yes, I loved her. Your wife."

Spenner's voice was a whisper, "You loved Gessie?"

Manning laughed once more. "I was first attracted to her because she was an artist's dream. A titian beauty, a delicate person so slim and frail, with such white skin. How often is an artist blessed with such a model? Such flattery about your wife should make you happy, does it not?"

Spenner did not move; he sat benumbed. He was uncertain and still surprised at such candor.

Manning shrugged and went on. "I am frank, of course, and I give you my honest opinions. I tell the truth. I was an artist who fell in love with my model. It happens; I loved Gessie Whitmore. Does that make you happy, feel good?"

Spenner stammered. "Well, I. . . ." he uttered but could say no more.

Again, Manning laughed and now Spenner felt taunted and he looked directly at the massive, haughty man. Manning's laughter had opened his mouth to reveal large teeth, white and even. Strangely his mouth made Manning seem more sinister to Spenner. Spenner tried to straighten himself as he asked, "Why did she have the picture painted?"

Manning stopped laughing; he thought for a moment, then replied, "Why I believe she knew she was dying. I was aware of it in her pose. She could sit so still; she had the complacancy of the ill, to remain quiet and unmoving for long periods of time."

Spenner closed his eyes. "I heard of her illness," he said and his voice was shaking. "But, Mr. Manning, what of her attitude? If she sensed her death, was she despondent or afraid?"

Manning shook his head. "Considering her condition, her spirits were good. She never complained. I admired her determination."

"I understand that the painting, the work, I mean, was done at the estate."

"Yes," Manning answered. "She wanted it that way. For her

health, of course, it was easier. I did not mind; I would have accommodated her in any way, any way she requested."

Another silence came between them and then the horrific mouth opened and Manning laughed but this time the softness was tinged with sarcasm. He thrust his body forward toward Spenner and his eyes were smoldering and contemptuous. "You fool of a man!" he said with scorn. "I have just told you that I loved your wife and you ask only about the painting and her death. Don't you feel anger or rage? Don't you think to ask me if she loved me? You don't care about that?"

The chair creaked under Spenner as he pushed himself down as if he had been struck. His mouth opened but he could not speak.

Manning's voice was disdainful, almost strident, as he continued. "I describe her beauty and appeal and you have no reaction to that? I spoke of her hair, her skin, and her body, and you, her husband, say nothing to that? Doesn't it mean anything to you? No jealousy? What kind of a husband were you to such as she?" He paused but his harsh gaze never left Spenner, then he continued in his tone of derision. "I said I'd tell you the truth so I will tell you, whether you care or not, that she would not have me. I tried to win her and I loved her deeply, but she rejected me completely. Now, have you ever heard of a confession like that from a man who was infatuated and wanted another man's wife? When I see you now, I wonder and I cannot believe that her rejection was because of you; whether you, alive or dead, could have been such a vital memory for her."

"She wasn't. . . ." Spenner's thoughts seemed to stop for all he could say to himself was that he was indeed a fool. A fool because he had been made to feel like a man betrayed. He realized that even in a deception, sensibilities could not be forgotten. He had not acted his part. What could he say? Feebly, he muttered, "I have been away—twenty years."

"Ah!" Manning exclaimed. "What is twenty years? What is that for love? My feelings have never diminished. All these years, yes. But the yearning never leaves me. I cannot forget the emotion; my love for Gessie Whitmore was the truest feeling I ever had. She was ill, but even if I could have had her for a brief time, it would have been enough for me. Forever. Evidently, you are incapable of feeling or understanding such love."

A small wrath rose in Spenner. He had been humiliated, but if he had talked only of her death, it was for a different reason than Manning supposed. This boastful man had been at the estate many times. He loved Gessie but he had been rejected. Provoked, Spenner blurted out, "If those were your feelings and she rejected you, did you kill her?"

Now Maninng looked appalled and the expression in his eyes changed to amazement and confusion. "What?" he asked with disbelief.

"Did you kill her?" Spenner repeated and he felt a slight pleasure that he had nicked Manning with his verbal question.

But the accusation was only a slight wound and Manning recovered quickly. "What do you mean—kill? She died from a fall."

Spenner tried to go on and he said recklessly. "Were you there?"

"What do you mean, there? And where did you get such an idea as kill?" Manning's voice was angry.

Spenner sputtered on. "Maybe Gessie did not fall; maybe somebody was there. That is why I ask you if you were there?"

"How could I be there. She was alone."

"Maybe not. You knew your way around the estate."

"I was away," Manning stated.

Spenner halted and stared at him. "You were away?"

"I was in Switzerland, teaching on a grant. I did not know Gessie was gone until I returned several months later and was told that she had fallen and died."

Spenner's eyes rolled upward and then he dropped his head and clasped it in his hands. He had asked the question incorrectly and in haste. Manning had been away at the time, not even here. "I am sorry," he groaned.

"You are muddled in your thinking, Whitmore," Manning said. "You need to be careful what you say, even if you had a problem."

Spenner nodded and swaggered as he rose. "I will not take any more of your time, Mr. Manning. I thank you for speaking with me—" he hesitated and then added, "so frankly."

Manning said nothing but lifted his body forward and followed Spenner toward the door. "Believe me," he said, "you are not well. I believe your ordeal, whatever it is, is still with you. You should get some medical help, Mr. Whitmore. You should."

Spenner was relieved to end his meeting with Roger Manning. He was shaken and upset, and he remained uneasy as he left the mansion and went to his car. He did not look up, but he had a trembling feeling that Roger Manning was at the window looking after him.

Although it was late in the afternoon, Spenner wanted to make another trip, this time to the university. The campus was large and he drove uncertainly around the maze of buildings. He passed a science hall and noticed that the Harding Museum was attached to it. He thought this might be the place to meet Lester, so he parked the car and began to roam about the grounds. The air was cold and damp, and he was shivering for he was upset and disturbed as well as chilled. Finally, he sat down on a bench beneath an old sycamore tree which had an immense spread of branches. There was little activity around the museum building and he sat quietly, feeling the cold penetrate deeper into his body. He waited a good while, but at a certain moment, the doors swung open and noisy, exuberant students began to emerge. Spenner rose to meet them but he waited on the sidelines as the clatter of humans and speech converged and passed before him. He looked above them and soon he saw Lester, his blond head tall and standing out amongst the others. Spenner moved toward him. "Lester!" he called.

Lester turned; he was startled when he saw Spenner, but he smiled and broke from the ranks of the other students. "Dad!"

"I was hoping to meet you, Lester," said Spenner.

"Is anything wrong?" Lester asked.

Apparently, the distress was too evident on Spenner's face and in his voice, but he shook his head. "I thought we might have a talk, somewhere around here." He pointed to the bench he had just left. "How about over there?"

"Sure, Dad," Lester replied.

The wind had become stronger, making the old sycamore rattle its branches, but the leaves, falling and skipping over the ground seemed to be rejoicing. Spenner glanced around; the campus was becoming deserted and quiet again as the noisy students were moving on. Spenner stared into the distance, not knowing how to begin to talk to Lester. At last, he spoke, beginning with some words. "How is school, Lester? Are you doing well?"

Lester smiled. "Oh, yes. We are going on a 'digging' in four weeks. The class, you know. We will be at an archeological site down on the lower peninsula. We will be excavating for skeletons and

146

artifacts. I am excited about it, Dad." The excitement showed on Lester's face and it was in his voice also. His eyes were shining; he was happy and anticipation covered his face.

Four weeks, thought Spenner. I shall be gone; all this will be over and I will be away, far away. He smiled, to accept Lester's joy, but his voice was flat and low as he said, "It sounds interesting."

Lester's enthusiasm continued. "A sighting has been made amongst the old oil fields—fossils of some sort. There is evidence of a fire and it has been predicted that an ancient burial ground is there. A team—students and teachers—are going there for study and I am going to be one of them."

Four weeks and there would be no more of this chill. There would be sand, hot and healing sand. "Hm'm," Spenner uttered at his thoughts. His tone still was low, but it did not interrupt Lester who went on enthusiastically.

"Just think, not too far from here we may be tied to antiquity. "I am—" he paused and his voice changed to alarm for he had looked directly at Spenner. "Dad, are you sure there is nothing wrong?"

"Hm'm," Spenner repeated and straightened himself quickly. He had not been aware that his head had lagged and he had slumped to one side. "Nothing is wrong," he answered hurriedly. Not knowing what to do, he made a comic gesture by thrusting his hands into the sleeves of his jacket. His hands felt warmer but he also felt his trembling bones.

"We can move, Dad, go inside."

"No, no," Spenner protested but he felt trussed and immovable. "I am really all right." He tried to smile as he saw Lester's face, full of concern. The enthusiasm had vanished so quickly. Spenner tried to dispel the anxiousness on the boy's face. "I am happy to hear of your trip, Lester. I know it is of interest to you. I am happy you can go. Enjoy it and learn."

"It is what I want to do and—" he stopped. "What is it, Dad?" he asked, the worry on his face becoming deeper.

Spenner was sighing and shaking his head. "I have had a trying day, Lester. I have been upset. I went to see Roger Manning, the artist who painted your mother's picture. You remember?"

Lester nodded. "Yes. I remember."

"Lester, he told me that he loved your mother. Can you accept

147

that, Lester? Does it shock you or surprise you or do you feel betrayed or disappointed? Anything?"

Lester's face became more passive. "No, I did not know that."

"But how does it make you feel?"

"Gosh, Dad, I can't say that I feel anything now. It was long ago, but I never felt, what did you say, betrayed, by mother."

Spenner nodded. "And you were so young then." He looked downward and went on. "She did not love him, Lester. Roger Manning admitted to that."

"I know that, Dad, so there is nothing to feel betrayed or disappointed about, is there?"

Spenner did not raise his head. He closed his eyes for a moment before he answered. "Lester, I did nothing when Roger Manning told me. I could not even get angry. It was as if I had no feelings, none whatsoever; that for those twenty years, I had no emotion, nothing to connect to, no one to commit to, like I had frozen."

"But, Dad, you cannot judge that because you did not know; you had amnesia. Yet, you did love mother, didn't you?"

Spenner started to speak but he could not. His lips had parted but no sound emerged, no words formed within him.

"Dad?" Lester asked, leaning toward him.

Spenner raised his head and looked at Lester. They stared at each other and then Lester's blue eyes seemed to fade, as if they were receding inward and his expression became blank and helpless.

"Lester," Spenner said slowly. "I could not defend it, could not say it—what my feelings were for your mother. I did not know what was within me, so what can I say to you now? If feelings were not instinctive or real, should I make them up, pretend? Are you hurt by that? Are you disappointed in me?"

Lester stared at Spenner. His eyes were steady and questioning, but he blinked and a look of pain came into those eyes. Spenner shivered and his body swayed toward Lester. He is hurt by me, Spenner thought. Lester was unmoved by the declaration of Manning's love, but he is hurt by my lack of it. Spenner withdrew one hand from his sleeve and clasped Lester's hand. "Do not be hurt: I know you loved your mother. Forgive me, Lester. . . .."

Lester interrupted. "It is all right, Dad. Really. I understand." He tried to smile but the corners of his mouth fell immediately and the sadness remained on his face. "Perhaps you should not think so much about it or think so much about mother."

Spenner shook his head. "It is all I have been able to think about, Lester. I have to think about your mother and what you told me. I went to Roger Manning to try to find out *things* about your mother's death. I thought Manning might be of some help, but I had only that frightful experience. Lester, he turned me back; he made me feel insignificant, like nothing."

"I did not like Roger Manning either, Dad," Lester said softly. "He was haughty and arrogant to us, too, when he came to the estate. Oh, I know he did not want to be bothered while he was painting; that is understandable. He threw a fit at me one time when I accidently ran into the sitting room when he was working. He ordered me out like a bossy teacher. Mother was upset but she had to go along. I was wrong, I knew, but I just forgot when I went into the sitting room. He did not understand that. I could not like Roger Manning." Lester paused. The apprehension on his face was giving way but the color was pale and his eyes still were vague and uncertain. "If you went to see him, Dad, to find out about mother, then you must believe what I told you about her death."

Spenner nodded. "Yes, Lester, I believe your story. I am trying to find out anything I can, but I am not too successful. I don't know how to go about it. I ask the wrong questions or I ask them incorrectly."

"It goes back a long time, but what is important to me is that you believe what I told you. I had to tell you so you would know what happened to mother."

"I do believe you, Lester, but I wish I could find something to prove that you are right. You know, I laid a wreath at Memorial Park. I did it for a reason. I did it to see if I could get some reaction from someone. I made it public; I deliberately publicized myself and put myself in view but no one . . . " Spenner hesitated as he thought of Old Blinkey but, no, he did not want to mention that to Lester any more than he wanted to mention the black clad figure or the letter with the dove emblem. Spenner wanted to keep these things to himself for he sensed that they were sinister. Strange, he thought, that I want to reassure Lester but I do not want to confide in him. "I did not get any reaction," he said at last. "Nothing."

"But, Dad, do you think mother's murder had something to do with you?"

Spenner closed his eyes and he shivered. "What else, Lester? Can you believe there is any reason for anyone to kill your mother?"

"Dad, you are only bringing grief upon yourself."

Spenner patted the boy's hand. "Only to try to know, Lester, only to try to know." His body had been shaking so he fell back on the bench. "Yet, I feel so inadequate; I do not know what to do." He sat silently for a moment, then he blurted out, "Dr. Vargas!"

"What, Dad?" Lester asked, leaning closer.

Spenner's voice became low. "He was your mother's doctor. Dr. Vargas. I have been told that he is dead, but I should like to have talked to him. Perhaps he could have remembered something. Strange that no one attended her that night, no one was about. Poor woman! Ill and acting so afraid, constantly traveling, moving about like a frantic little animal. She installed a new alarm system, changed her bedroom!"

"Dad!" Lester called out.

"I must find out somehow!"

"Dad!" Lester called out again. "You are rambling."

"Am I rambling?"

"Dad, what is it about?"

"Hm'm," Spenner muttered and he looked up suddenly at Lester. "Dr. Vargas," he repeated slowly. "He treated your mother, you know?"

"Yes, I know," Lester replied softly.

"He is dead, I was told. He died in a car accident, shortly after your mother died." Spenner's voice became softer but he looked away from Lester. "Did he treat anyone else, Lester? You or Lee?" He thought of the nightmares that Lester was supposed to have had.

"Sometimes he gave me medicine," Lester said without explanation, "when I was sick."

"Sick? What kind of sickness did you have, Lester?"

Lester shrugged. "I was sick. He said I had to be quiet—to quiet down."

"Was that often, Lester?"

Lester shook his head. "Not too much." His glance turned and he looked away in the direction Spenner was seeing. The wind re-

150

mained strong and it was scattering the leaves in a turmoil across the lawn, like a whirlwind being played before them.

The wind stung Spenner's eyes. His eyes became so moist that his vision was blurred, and he could not clearly see the mad dance of the leaves. He tried to smile at Lester but the moisture in his eyes had formed tears and rolled down his cheeks. He grabbed Lester's shoulder for the boy's face was full of anxiety. "Do not worry anymore about this, Lester," he said. "Let me do that. You just think about your classes and your studies and the trip. Think only of that, Lester."

"Dad," Lester said softly and now he smiled.

"I believe we should go home, Lester," Spenner said softly. "I have a car. Oh!" he exclaimed. He had not balanced himself, one arm was still bound in sleeve, and he fell back when he started to rise.

Lester put his hand under Spenner's arm and helped him up. They followed the path back to the car. The sun broke through at that moment with a brilliant flash, lighting the ground like a stage for the dancing leaves. And even the bark of the old sycamore, when lighted by brightness, had splendor.

II

Chapter Ten

Johnson Buell began his day by going to the unemployment office in Tegner. He was surprised to hear the merry tinkle of a bell overhead when he opened the door. Inside, there was no need for privacy, no need to be summoned from some hidden cove, for the several desks were on the open floor. Everyone looked up at him when he entered. He had to go to several people as he identified himself and asked to see the manager. At last, he was shown into what must have been an office with a waist high cardboard wall around a desk where a portly man in a light, checked jacket rose like a gallant to meet him.

"Mr. Buell," the man said warmly. "A private investigator. Come in." Buell had only a walk to a chair and he was "in," but the man had a wide and friendly smile and offered Buell a hearty and strong handshake.

Buell was aware of a heavy aura of spice about the man and was glad when he returned to his place behind a steel desk. The man relaxed, clasped his hands before him, and continued to smile as Buell explained his mission.

"I would like to check the records of work given to James Spenner. I assume it would be temporary or odd jobs," he said. "I do not believe he worked on a steady basis."

"I see," the man replied, more as a platitude of speech, and he went on, "A temporary or odd jobs employee? We do not keep records of them very long."

"But it would be recent," Buell said hurriedly. "I believe James Spenner lived here for at least the last five years and did not leave until about a week ago."

"I see," the man repeated and, on being challenged, a frown

settled on his forehead and his cheeks sagged when he was not smiling. He unclasped his hands. "We will try." In an accommodating manner, he raised his hand and pressed a switch on a machine and gave instructions to someone to bring in any information on James Spenner. "Do not look in the regular file," he cautioned, "any records would be in temporary jobs file."

Immediately, Buell could see an elderly lady moving toward a large cabinet across the room. He was heartened when he saw her extract an envelope, and soon she was "in" the office and placed the envelope on the desk in front of the manager. "Well, we have something," he said and his spirits perked up. He smiled again and his cheeks rounded out like rubber balls. He waved his arm over the papers after he opened the envelope. "They are here indeed; take a look," he exclaimed as he pushed the file toward Buell. The man seemed to enjoy gesturing with his hands which were smooth and polished.

Buell scanned the papers. There were limited jobs that James Spenner had taken. He had worked as a painter and had done some landscaping and yard work. He had hired out as a fruit and vegetable picker to adjacent farmers. Odd jobs, Johnson Buell thought, and nothing that required a certification, neither was there any previous work records or references. James Spenner had hired on only as a helper in all respects. Buell noted the information and thanked the manager. The manager was profuse in his farewell, grateful to help, and smiling and waving as he led Buell to the door. At the outer door, there was another merry tinkle of the bell when Buell opened it and the sound continued maddeningly until Buell closed it and was outside.

Johnson Buell followed first the lead to the fruit and vegetable farms which were short drives to the outskirts of Tegner. The land was quiet, long acres of stillness and flatness. There was no activity and Buell discovered that his trips were in vain for the field offices were closed as there was no produce to pick at this time of year.

Buell returned to Tegner and looked up the landscaping firm. Their office was open, but, again, because of the season, there was no business. A young girl was in charge and her eyes widened with admiration when she looked at Buell. She giggled when he asked after the owner and answered that the owner was away; he always took vacation at this time of year. Buell asked if she could supply information about employees, but she looked confused and said she was a temporary employee herself, just taking messages and accepting mail until the owner returned. She giggled again when she said she had no idea of work records or where they would be. The owner, she explained, took care of all those important matters. As he left, Buell gave her a smile and knew he would receive another giggle in response.

The possibility left was the painting firm. At least, the work was not seasonal and their office was busy. Buell talked with a yellow-haired woman at the desk and then, unexpectedly, the owner himself came out to the waiting room dressed in the white painter's uniform which was covered with varied colored smudges. He removed his cap, however, when he greeted Buell and the two of them moved to a couch in the waiting room.

Buell's first impression was to apologize. "Am I interrupting?" he asked.

"No," the owner replied. "I just returned from a job and I have not changed yet. I can talk to you, give you some time, if you don't mind my appearance."

"Not at all," Buell answered quickly and went on to ask about James Spenner.

The owner said he did take on extra help for big jobs and, lo and behold, he remembered James Spenner. "Yes, I hired him several times when we painted high interiors and tall buildings. My regular men were needed for the scaffolds, so I took on extras like James Spenner for the lower sections of the buildings."

Johnson Buell felt an eagerness, an excitement within him that, at last, he made a special connection with someone and James Spenner. Yet, when he spoke, his voice was calm and controlled. "Was he a good worker?" he asked first. "Did he get on well with the others?"

The owner nodded. "He did his work and I was satisfied. Otherwise, I would not have rehired him, even for temporary jobs. No trouble maker if that is what you mean by getting on with others. He was a quiet type, though, and never talked about himself. I asked him once if he had family but he said no. I believe he was what is called a loner."

At that moment, the yellow haired woman came forward with a tray bearing bottles, glasses, and some ice. The owner pushed aside the magazines on the low table and the woman placed the tray before them.

"I always have a drink. Only one I must say, when I come off a job. Will you join me?"

Buell declined, saying that he was on duty, but he waited while the owner measured his drink and took the first draught, which was a large one and made him relax and sigh with pleasure.

"Did James Spenner ever say where he came from or anything about his former life?" Buell asked after the moment.

"Never did. As I said, he was not a talker."

"But how about identification?" Buell persisted. "Surely, you must have asked that of people you hired."

"Not for temporary work," the owner replied. He smiled at people who passed by and then chuckled as he said, "I wonder if these customers realize that I am the owner, sitting here in the waiting room, dressed in a painter's uniform, drinking, and talking with a private detective." He chuckled again. Buell agreed, but he noted that the yellow-haired lady was serious and did not let on. She conducted business as usual in an unconcerned and diplomatic way.

"No, I never asked for credentials," the owner went on, "because those temporary jobs would make for more book work. James Spenner was no exception; but I will say one thing about him—he was different. I have hired people for a long time and I can pretty well size them up. Now James Spenner was a good worker and I had no complaints about the jobs he did for me. Give a man a can of paint and a brush and a flat wall—who can't do that? Yet, he was not the worker type. He had an edge about him that made him seem above that; he had just a little finesse that indicated to me that he was not a working type. Now I never mentioned that to him; I thought it no use and he was not a talker anyway. It was only my impression, but I could not shake it."

Buell was intrigued by the owner's observation but, again, he concealed any eagerness and asked calmly. "If he was not a worker type, could you guess what his type might be?"

"Something professional, I would say," the owner replied. "Maybe a teacher, but indoor work, a desk type, something like that."

"A politician?" Buell asked with caution.

The owner considered the question for a moment. "Well, maybe, if he had been a talker," then he snorted. "I think he was too subdued, too much to himself, I don't know."

Buell went on. "If James Spenner was not a worker type as you say, then why did you hire him?"

"I sensed a desperation in him, a desperation that told me he needed work badly, but he was not aggressive about it. That desperation, you know, was not negative to me. I saw it as a willingness to work, work hard, do what he was told, with no trouble and no questions asked. I hired him on that basis." Against his word, the owner prepared himself another drink. "What is all this about James Spenner anyway?" he asked. "To me, he was a sort of nothing, a passive guy with little going for him. Has he managed to stir up trouble? I wouldn't believe!"

Buell smiled and thought carefully. "He is applying for another job, you might say. I am merely scouting for his record, his recommendation, for the position for my client."

"Well, if you can use anything I have said about him as recommendation, you are free to use it." The owner's face began to flush. "But then I might as well tell you about the only time I saw James Spenner wary and taken by surprise. We were painting the interior of the city hall. Because of the work, we had a corridor blocked off and people were rerouted to another side of the building. A policeman, of all people, and a runt with pop-eyes at that, came into the corridor by mistake. Of course, we had to shout to get him out of there. He was peeved and the little guy gave us some nasty looks but he made no move to hurry because he was staring at James Spenner. They must have known or recognized each other to look like that. I asked Spenner about it, but he said nothing, yet I could see he was shaken. I was certain there was recognition there. The policeman was from Tully, about thirty miles north of here. He had come here to give evidence or information about a violation up there. It was quite funny, that James Spenner could be so disturbed by a pintsized policeman."

Buell was intrigued by the story. "You say that Tully is about thirty miles from here?"

"North," the owner replied.

When he left the painting firm, Johnson Buell headed for Tully. Thirty miles was not too far and he arrived within a half hour. Tully was a small town and he had no trouble finding the police station which was half a block off the main street. The station shared an old building of massive grey blocks with the fire department and the city hall.

Buell stepped inside and instantly felt the dampness and moldy atmosphere so common to old stone constructions. He walked briskly along the dim corridor until he came to a door marked police head-quarters. The glass was opaque so he could not see in, but he pushed the door open.

There were two men in the room. They wore the same type of blue uniform and were identified as policemen by the insignia on their sleeves. The man at the front desk was the most squat man Johnson Buell had ever seen. His neck was so thick that his head seemed to rest on his shoulders. He was completely bald and the face that raised to Buell was wrinkled and the eyes were furious, small and penetrating, and they bore into Buell from under a deep scowl.

The other man could be a limb of this one. He was so small he was lost behind the desk as he slumped over his work. One cheek was sunken but the other bulged with tobacco. The pouch in his cheek gave the only curve to his face except for his uncommonly protruding eyeballs. He was bald, too, on the top, but had a narrow fringe of light brown hair forming a semi-circle on his cranium.

Johnson Buell advanced and extended his hand to the big fellow. "I am Johnson Buell," he said. "Private investigator," and he showed his identification.

The big body rose, large and solid, and the hand that gripped Buell's was bone crushing. "I am Sergeant Spooney," he said. He waved his hand at the men at the back desk. "This is Sergeant Swack-hammer." The man looked up, blinked his eyes like a frog, and went back to work.

"Sit down," Sergeant Spooney went on. "Right here." He pointed to a chair beside his desk.

Buell quickly surveyed the room as he sat down. Large windows were at one side but the trees so shaded them that they could see nothing beyond. The floor and the furniture were wooden, making the room seem dreary and uncomfortable.

On the wall behind Sergeant Swackhammer's desk was the most noticeable feature in the room. It was a large picture hung by long wires stretching from the ceiling boards. A wide, dark frame hung about the figure of a man in the classic boxer pose of wide stance and arms raised with clenched fists. The man was stripped to the waist, revealing highly developed muscular arms and chest. The face was square and stern with more hair on the black handlebar mustache than on the head. The eyes were small and steadfast under a scowl. The lower half of the body was clad in long black tights and high topped leather shoes. A magnificent belt encrusted with jewels surrounded the thick waist.

So this bulldog of a man, Sergeant Spooney, is an ex-pugilist, Buell thought and smiled to himself.

The only condescension to glitter in the entire room was a brass spittoon which rested beneath Sergeant Spooney's picture. Buell saw it just as Sergeant Swackhammer raised his head and spat juicily into the gleaming vessel. Buell was startled and looked directly at the fellow, catching his sharp, uncompromising look. The bulging eyes did not flinch and he spat again. He resettled the tobacco cud in his cheek, lowered his head and returned to work.

"What can we do for you?" Sergeant Spooney asked in a loud voice.

Buell began slowly. "I am here to find out about any record you have of a James Spenner."

"Sergeant," Spooney spoke to Swackhammer, "can you find anything for the investigator here?"

Sergeant Swackhammer did not speak but rose from his desk and went into a side room. From there could be heard squeaking noises of drawers opening and closing and, at last, Sergeant Swackhammer returned, shaking his head. "Nothing," he said in a surprisingly deep bass voice.

Sergeant Spooney turned to Johnson Buell with a look of resignation upon his face that indicated nothing more would be done. He began to turn his head aside when Buell said, "But I believe Sergeant Swackhammer knows the man or knows of him." Both sergeants turned their direct looks upon Buell, both stares were surprised and questioning. Buell went on, "I believe Sergeant Swackhammer saw this man in Tegner; he was doing painting work at the city hall."

Sergeant Swackhammer came forward and stood at the desk. The look on his face still was quizzical but his eyes had enlarged and seemed ready to roll out of their sockets. "That one?" he asked. "That is the one you are asking about?"

"Yes," Buell replied.

"He was one of the men I remembered from the fight over at Farmer Cline's place."

"Fight?" Buell asked in surprise.

"That ruckus?" Sergeant Spooney asked.

Sergeant Swackhammer nodded to him. "You remember that we were called over there?"

"Yes," Sergeant Spooney answered slowly and the scowl on his face deepened.

"These two men were going at it," Sergeant Swackhammer continued, "knocking each other all over the field. Finally stopped it but both were pretty bloody."

Buell asked, "What were they fighting about?"

"One man, the one you are asking about, said the other called him 'a coward and a fraud'."

Sergeant Spooney added, "There is no record, you see, because neither one pressed charges. It was dropped."

"Nothing else?" Buell asked as he thought of the words "a coward and a fraud." Someone had called James Spenner that.

"Nothing else," Sergeant Spooney replied with the same words. "We broke up the fight, and when they cooled off and pressed no charges, no report was made. Farmer Cline said he would take no action either."

"Where is Farmer Cline's place?" Buell asked.

"Biggest place you will see when you leave town on county road five."

After a short pause, Buell, in a thoughtful mood, rose and said, "Thank you, Sergeant, for your help." He said it sweepingly, along with his goodbye, to include Sergeant Swackhammer who acknowledged by raising his head, taking aim from this greater distance, and spitting a direct hit of tobacco into the cuspidor.

Johnson Buell made the trip to the Cline farm. He talked to the grizzled old farmer who recalled the fight but could not give the names of the men. Both had been hired for one field picking. "The fight was a bit bloody," Farmer Cline said, "but nothing too harmful or serious." Neither man was at his farm now and he had not seen them since. He assumed they hired with others or went elsewhere.

"I am a large land farmer and I usually hire extra when I have

159

a good crop and that year I had a good crop of green beans. I got the workers through the County Hiring Practice."

"I am looking for information on a James Spenner," Buell said, "and I believe he was one of the men involved in the fight."

"Well, if you say that is who he was, then it must be," the farmer answered, "but I cannot tell you either name."

Johnson Buell shook his head and decided to leave.

"I can show you the book," Farmer Cline said, "if you think you can find the other name." Buell agreed instantly and they went into the kitchen of the farmhouse. Farmer Cline brought forth a large, old ledger. There were several pages of names, and James Spenner was listed as employed for one season only and that he had come from the town of Oldin.

Since it would be a time consuming, almost impossible task, to trace all the other men listed in Farmer Cline's ledger to find the one who fought with James Spenner when he did not know the identity of the man, Johnson Buell decided to proceed to the town of Oldin. He consulted the map and noted that he was moving northward along coastal towns on the peninsula.

Oldin was different from Tully in that it was an industrial town with the main commerce being a paper mill. The mill was close to the sea and the timber was brought in from the outlying lands and the mountains. Oldin was larger, too, and a more bustling community.

As before, Johnson Buell went first to the police headquarters and inquired if a James Spenner had any record. He had none. On a hunch and a suggestion, Buell called on a private detective. At police headquarters, they told him about "Old Man" Ross. "He is a detective, just like you," they said. "Around here he is an institution. He has snooped around quite a bit, knows a lot and has seen a lot. Try him."

Buell found Ross in an old fashioned office above a drug store but in the very center of Oldin and looking out over the sea. Ross had been sleeping when Buell knocked at the door. He opened the door slowly, blinked, and then yawned.

"Don't apologize," he told Buell. "I always have a nap about now. Come on in." He showed Buell a straw-bottomed chair while he returned to the swivel chair behind his desk. The swivel chair was tilted back, the better to snooze in, thought Buell, but Ross was not a somnambulistic person. He may have been sleeping, but, awakened, his face transformed into that of a fox, thin and keen, with pointed nose and piercing brown eyes. His complexion was very ruddy and his hair was thick and grey.

Buell told him more about James Spenner than he had to anyone else but he gave no reason for his inquiry except that he was tracing James Spenner for a client. To Ross, however, he showed both the photograph of Collis Whitmore and the picture sketch which Grant Deakins had made of James Spenner. "This is supposed to be the same man, twenty years apart. Do you recognize him?" Buell asked. "He was supposed to be here in Oldin about six years ago, perhaps before that, then he went on to Tully and then Tegner. I have counted him as being five years in Tegner and one year between here and Tully."

Ross studied the picture but said nothing. He took the photograph and studied it, but nothing showed on his face. Yet, he looked at it cautiously and for some time. "Six or more years ago, you say?" he asked at last.

"That is my guess," Buell answered.

"You say his name is James Spenner?"

"I believe he used that name here."

Ross shook his head slowly, but he did not take his eyes from the picture sketch when he looked at it again. "That name does not come through, but—," he hesitated, "there seems to be something about the face. Not quite, but close."

"Can you guess at anything?" Buell asked hurriedly.

"You say you have traced this man for six years. How far back do you want to go?"

"At least twenty years," Buell answered, "since the war."

"The war. Ah, yes, the war. On this side of the peninsula, we were neutral, but we did receive refugees from the eastern section."

"Well, he could have been one of those. Are there any records available on those refugees?"

Ross' eyes began to gleam. "Hospital, most likely. They received the bulk of the refugees. It was necessary because they were a sorry lot—impoverished, sick, alone, nothing with them. There were rogues, too, and I had a heavy duty then, trying to maintain order, track down undesirables and such. I have a good memory of many of them and this one," he hesitated and touched the picture, "seems to strike some kind of bell." Ross leaned back and closed his eyes.

"Quite a few men worked up at the logging camp in the mountains and many were refugees." He hesitated again. "No, he did not look quite like this, but there is something similar. . . ." He stopped and sat up straight in his chair. His eyes were glistening like obsidian beads.

"Forget the hospitals," he said firmly. "Go right to the logging camp. You get there by taking the first road just outside of town. I have a hunch that the man you are tracing was working there at one time. I believe that is where I saw him."

The first road just outside of Oldin was a clear cut, dirt road stretching high into the mountains. Johnson Buell drove until he came to a clearing where he saw a wooden building with a sign "Office" above its door. Buell was met inside the building by a young man, about twenty five years of age, who wore thick spectacles which enlarged his eyes to look like blue marbles. He smiled constantly from the time Buell entered, and he said he had been employed as office manager at the camp for six years. He was friendly and inclined to talk, as if he had to explain his position, and he went on to say that he got the job because he was a relative, the son of a second cousin of the president of the lumber company.

Buell nodded and believed him as he surveyed the weak eyes and thin body of the young man. Buell noticed, too, that he had a heavy shoe on one foot which caused him to walk unevenly. Yet, the young man was cheerful and talked easily to Buell. He admitted that many refugees had been hired to work at the camp.

"Just a minute!" he exclaimed after Buell mentioned the name of James Spenner. "Mr. Spenner worked out in the camp for a while. He did not stay long, however, because he applied for an office job here and got it. He worked himself up to manager."

"What happened to him?" Buell asked quickly.

"He left abruptly; gave a short notice and was gone, no reason given." The young man smiled. "In fact, that is why I got this job. They needed someone in a hurry to take Mr. Spenner's place. Odd how he left and he had been employed here for seven years, too."

Buell was surprised. "Seven years? Here?" he asked in astonishment. "And no reason for leaving?"

The young man nodded his head. "It was just very sudden, that is all. I came when he left. It was a surprise but, as I said, it was a break for me."

Buell asked one more question. "Since James Spenner worked here for seven years, where did he live? Can you tell me?"

The young man smiled and an agreeable look settled upon his face. "He had the same address for seven years, too, according to our records." He had obligingly looked up the information for Buell.

Johnson Buell went to the address and found it to be a large house and the landlady, a widow, rented rooms.

"I rent to loggers and people from the camp, mostly," she said.

Buell told her that he had come to ask about a former tenant named James Spenner. She looked surprised but nodded her head at the name and allowed Buell inside. She showed him into a small parlor with overstuffed furniture covered on the back and arms with crocheted doilies. There was an abundance of green and flowering plants in the room which attested to the prodigious light received from two broad windows which were not covered. Buell saw a large tawny cat asleep on the windowsill, obviously absorbing as much of the light and sun as the plants. The cat opened its eyes, two yellow lights, and watched Buell as he crossed the room and took an easy chair.

The landlady offered tea, which Buell declined, so she made her way to a rocking chair which had an Afghan cover over its back. The landlady had only part of her dentures in her mouth and when she smiled, her mouth caved inward and the thin lips disappeared.

"Yes, I remember James Spenner," she answered after Buell asked her to tell about him. She began to rock slowly as she talked. "He had a good job, was office manager, at the paper mill and rented from me for many years. He was quiet and kept to himself, and he was clean and no trouble. He had no visitors, at least, he did not bring any here," she stated when Buell asked if James Spenner had any friends.

"You said that Mr. Spenner had lived here for many years and had a good job at the paper mill. Tell me, was it always so? Was he successful when he came?"

She shook her head. "Oh, no. When he first knocked on my door, he was a sorry sight. His clothes were in bad shape, wrinkled and dirty and he was physically weak and exhausted. A blanket was wrapped around him, the only covering against the terrible cold. He was a pathetic sight, and I let him have a room although he could not pay. He gave me a promise that he would pay when he got work. I took him at his word and trusted him. He started at the logging camp and paid as he said. He stayed on, and I never had any problems with him."

"How was his mental attitude when he first arrived? Did he seem unusual in any way?"

"Not to me," she replied. "He seemed alert, just down on his luck, I would say."

At that moment, the tawny cat came between them. First, it sniffed around Buell's trouser legs and shoes and then, with a graceful leap, it jumped into the landlady's lap. The cat immediately settled back into the sleep posture, curling up and closing its eyes, as the landlady began to stroke its head and neck.

"I understand Mr. Spenner left Oldin quite suddenly," Buell went on. "Did he tell you why?"

"He did leave in a hurry," she nodded her head, "but he never said why. He paid me and left. Never said where he was going either."

"Didn't you think that was strange?"

The landlady nodded her head again. "Yes, I did because it was so unexpected and I did not think that he would act that way. Mr. Spenner had been here for a while and was treated well, I believe, and I just did not think he was the type to act hastily and without consideration." She paused and looked down at the cat who turned its head slightly as she scratched beneath its neck. "It was strange, too, that the day after Mr. Spenner left, a man came here looking for someone. I often wonder if there might have been a connection."

Buell's eyes became wider and he looked directly at her. She began to look as sleepy as the cat. Her rocking became rhythmical and soothing and her eyes appeared to close.

"Tell me about this man," Buell said loudly. "Did he ask for Mr. Spenner?"

She smiled once more, closing her mouth, but the eyes flickered. "Oh, no," she said slowly, "that is why I wonder if there was a connection because the man asked for somebody else."

"Could he have asked for a Collis Whitmore?"

The landlady was silent and thoughtful and Buell hoped she was not about to doze. "I am not certain," she replied and her eyes opened wide as if making an effort to stay awake. "He said the name only once and I cannot say after all these years."

Buell looked into her face, to catch her glance while her eyes were open. "Can you remember what the man looked like?"

"He did not look well. He was sick looking with a white face and dull eyes. The man never explained much except that he thought he knew—" she hesitated. "What name did you say?"

"Collis Whitmore?"

She shook her head. "No, I really cannot say that was it, but anyway, the stranger said he was inquiring because he thought he knew the man from Port Bold."

A sick-looking man from Port Bold might possibly have recognized James Spenner as Collis Whitmore. Johnson Buell wondered, as did the landlady, if there could be a link in this case of the two names though the name of Collis Whitmore could not be verified. Nevertheless, back in his hotel room after a lengthy day, Buell ended his report with that summary statement and then added that the next place to go would be to Port Bold.

Johnson Buell usually labeled his cases. Just as the current one became the "Case of the Two Names," the first was the "Case of the Papin Sisters." On the morning after the killing of Ralph Barnes, Johnson Buell dispatched two officers to interview the guests who remained for the dinner after the wedding rehearsal and he himself went early to the Papin home to review the scene and to continue his inquiries of the family, particularly the Papin women. He had asked very little of them the previous evening, in deference to a request by Harvey Papin to delay any discussions with them because of the overall horror and grief that had come upon them.

As Buell approached the house, he was sadly aware that this was to have been a day of celebration and happiness for the Papin family. The weather that June morning was sunny and warm, which would have been a perfect complement to surround the splendor and bliss of the day.

Yet, he stepped into a house that was silent and forlorn. The maid let him in and she still was shaken by her experience of the last evening. Her self-control was gone, she trembled and her body slumped, as if in fear, and her face was red and swollen from crying. Johnson Buell asked her, in a gentle tone, to notify the family that he was here. Meanwhile, he would look around on his own. The wedding of Randi Papin and Ralph Barnes was to have taken place in the Papin home which certainly was large enough for such an occasion. The marriage service itself was to be performed in a formal sitting room. Buell stepped into the room and saw that the arrangements still remained, though now for nought. The furniture was removed and replaced by chairs set in even rows with ribbons and a floral piece on each end seat. The mantel over the fireplace, the focal point or altar for the ceremony, was also decked with flowers and candles. Fronds and baskets of matching flowers and foliage were also placed about the room. The mirror above the mantel was framed in greenery and smaller flowers, and, to the side of the mantel, were five chairs and music stands for the musicians. The room had been ordered closed and so was overly laden with the fragrance of the blossoms. The room was warm, and, with the heavily perfumed atmosphere, made Buell feel dizzy as he walked about.

On the previous ending, he had spoken mostly with Harvey Papin. He learned from him that the wedding rehearsal had not gone well. Gloria Papin, maid of honor, had tripped and fallen into a row of chairs. The music was not coordinated with the entrance march of the bridal party and Mrs. Papin's pet dog, a black poodle, had been banished to the next room, a move which it most heartedly did not appreciate, and set up one continuous howl after another. Mrs. Papin was fretful at the time and did nothing to restrain the dog. The others, not wishing to make Mrs. Papin more upset, did not attempt any disciplining of the poodle with the result that the music and the minister's words were discordant and almost obliterated.

Still feeling dizzy, Johnson Buell opened one of the French doors and stepped out onto the terrace. Across the wide lawn he saw the tent which had been set up for the wedding reception. A red and white striped canvas covered the top and here, too, flowers and foliage were the adornments. Baskets of red and white blossoms were hanging from each supporting pole and around the bottom of each pole were boxes of evergreen shrubs. The side awnings were rolled up so, unlike the indoors, air could pass through to the plants inside. Buell could see the bare tables with folded chairs around them, enough for at least one hundred and fifty guests, and in the center of the tent was a circular dance floor. Today, the caterers would have completed the setting; the tables would be covered with cloths and fresh flowers, the chairs brushed, and the far, long table would be overflowing with a dazzling array of fine food and drink.

Yet, the pavilion stood empty and quiet, a skeletal monument to a feast and a merriment that would never be. Everything was halted because of the murder on the previous night. Such a night! The eve of a wedding, when the mood was festive, gay, exhilarating, and highly expectant. The emotions of everyone involved would be high and suited the mood. It began in the dusk with the rehearsal and the dinner and continued into the night, the night time which is a refreshment from weakness, the time when most creatures began to dull themselves and think of rest. Perhaps the participants did also. There was the influence of music and the scent of flowers, heavy aphrodisiacs both, adding to the intoxication of the occasion and to act upon and confuse the senses. There would be thoughts of the last night of innocence, but anticipation of fulfillment, wonder, and un-bounded happiness to come with the morning. Youth and beauty combined for a ceremony the law allows, becoming careless in their emotions. For some reason, the bridegroom, the beneficiary of it all, in full glory of life, was taken from it, ending downward in a puddle of blood.

Johnson Buell shook his thoughts and stepped back inside to find Gloria Papin waiting for him. She was seated on one of the chairs set up for the wedding service and her legs had taken over another, lying straight across the chair next to her. She was set for sleeping, she was relaxed and her eyes were closed as if the warm room and the overwhelming flower fragrance had lulled her into a somnambulistic state.

Buell left the door open when he entered. "Too early for you, Miss Papin?" he asked heartily.

Her eyelids flickered and her eyes opened, never wide, and a smile came upon her lips.

"Ho, ho!" she said, trying to answer in a hearty tone also but her voice was weak. "It is always early for me." her smile deepened and, being aroused, the half-sleep appearance made her seem lan-guorous. "But I am ready for your questions," she went on.

She had, he learned, interrupted a vacation in England to return for the wedding. While there, she had succumbed to an English hairdresser and had come back home, almost completely shorn, with a few hairs shaped like feather tips sticking up from her skull and tinted pink.

"In Liverpool, was it?" her mother had asked, her face aghast with grief as she surveyed the horrifying result of her child's independent action. Yet, Mrs. Papin was driven into even greater grief and surprise by Gloria's announcement that not only had she had her hair cut in England but that she had become engaged to the hairdresser as well and as soon as the "fabulous lad could cut the tapes," he would join her here.

"Oh! That English affair!" had become the moan and despair of Mrs. Papin all through the wedding rehearsal whenever she looked at Gloria. Gloria admitted that she had had several cocktails before the rehearsal but needed them, she said, as finally, in exasperation, she had turned on her mother but was off balance and fell into the row of chairs.

"I had washed the pink color out, too, but, of course, I could do nothing about the cut."

Gloria Papin laughed after she made the statement. Buell was looking at her, studying her, as he tried to imagine that pink color around her head but it seemed too unreal. She caught his glance. She blinked her eyes and it seemed like a wink, then she looked steadily at him and smiled once more. Buell looked away and asked her about Ralph Barnes. He noticed immediately that she hesitated to reply. He looked back at her. Her face became passive but the smile broke through again and her light blue eyes became starry and fixed, like the stare of an animal watching its prey. "I did not know Ralph Barnes until I got here," she replied softly and the smile deepened. "But he was handsome. Almost too much!"

She told him that after the dinner party Ralph Barnes had headed across the lawn toward the guest house.

The last one to see him alive? Buell asked the question almost nonchalantly for he thought the answer would be the affianced, Randi, as he imagined a last, romantic farewell between the bridal couple, but he was surprised to discover that Gloria was the last one to see him.

"I saw him last," she said with no demureness. "I wanted to accompany him. He declined at first, but we talked for a while on the patio and then decided that I would walk part way, a compromise, which I did and then I let him go."

"You walked with Ralph Barnes?" Buell asked slowly, still trying to cover his surprise. "Why did you do that?"

"Well, he was a guest and he knew the way, of course, but he was soon to be family and I wanted to be friendly and get a little better acquainted. That is all." She wore heavy eye makeup at this time of day and, though her eyes appeared small and shadowy, she once again stared directly at Buell until he was forced to look back at her. She held his gaze for a moment with an interested look, then she smiled.

"You walked only part of the way with Ralph Barnes, then returned to the house?"

"Yes."

"Did you return through the living room?"

"No, I went around to the back stairs. It was closer to my room."

She was teasing him but he asked seriously, "Did you see or hear anything else at the time, like someone following you?"

She laughed at that. "How silly! We went alone."

Buell had to ask. "What were your feelings about Ralph Barnes?"

She affected a pose of thinking, then she leaned forward, closer to him, and looked expectant, as if to offer a confidence. "Can you be discreet, Mr. Buell?" she asked.

Buell was taken aback, though he was aware of her teasing. "Why, yes," he replied hesitatingly.

She sat back and gazed at him, then she laughed again for her question had been a tease. "I have already told you. I thought he was lovely, just lovely."

"He appealed to you then?"

"Yes," she answered slowly.

"Did you tell him that?"

"Silly! I did not need to tell him. He knew."

"Did he respond to you?"

She paused and sighed. "No. I don't think so."

Buell went on. "Can you tell me what kind of mood Ralph Barnes was in?"

"Mood? Of a bridegroom?" She laughed. "Oh, Mr. Buell, what else but happy, happy, happy?"

"But he did not want you to walk with him. Was he not serious or firm, even angry, about that?"

She appeared to be reflecting. "Well, he was not really angry. How could he be—with me?"

Gloria Papin had explained about her hair, engagement, the wedding rehearsal, and Ralph Barnes in a light, teasing style. She

169

could not be serious and did not seem to understand that a killing, a death, was a very grave matter. Johnson Buell did not squabble with her for he did not wish to destroy that first expression, that first impulse of an uninhibited response. Now, however, he felt anger toward her and he admitted to himself that it was because of Randi Papin.

He spoke to her in a determined voice with a note of sternness. "How can you act so flippantly and brazenly toward your sister's fiancé? And you are engaged yourself." Now he leaned toward her. "A man is dead, Miss Papin. Doesn't that upset you or make you feel any sense of sorrow? Your replies of 'silly' are ridiculous. This is not a silly business."

She just shrugged her shoulders. "I have told you what I know and how I feel. Isn't that what this business is about also? No lies, no lies." Then she added quickly. "I am sorry for Randi, though," she said it with a sigh but her light tone did not change.

Buell controlled himself and suppressed his anger. "Did you argue with Ralph Barnes?" he asked. "You said you talked for a while on the patio and that he did not really wish to walk with you."

"Silly," she said deliberately, with the teasing back in her voice. "Of course, we did not argue. I did try to lead him, however. I grabbed his arm, if you want to know, but he shook me off and I guess that is when I lost my ring. . . ."

"Ring?" Buell interrupted.

She nodded. "The one I got from mother. I did not miss it until this morning." She gazed at Buell, noting his surprise, and then she chided him. "You did not find it? Tut, tut, Mr. Buell," she challenged.

Johnson Buell left Gloria Papin and returned to the patio and pathway where Ralph Barnes had taken his final steps. The crime scene still was roped off and several of the unit investigators were making a daylight scan of the area. Buell went over the area again, trying to visualize the setting, the dramatic action that had taken place the night before. He traveled along the pathway, pretending in his mind that he was walking with another, until he stopped where blood had splashed around on the gravel and made a red marker where the body of Ralph Barnes had fallen. He inquired of one of the unit officers if anything of evidence had been found. "I am looking, in particular, for a ring," he said.

A ring, indeed, had been discovered but it had been sent to the laboratory and included with the gun as evidence. "Just where was it located?" Buell asked although he knew the information would be included with the ring. But he wanted to see exactly where the ring was found. The officer led him to the place under a bush, and between the patio and the blood spot.

Johnson Buell paused and reflected, glancing over the pathway and imagining, once again Ralph Barnes and Gloria Papin meeting on the patio. Gloria was attracted to him but she was an obvious flirt and perhaps teased him into walking with her. They walked this distance to the bush; they had a skirmish. If he pushed her away or took her arm from his, he may have pulled the ring off her finger. They parted then, she to her room, but Ralph Barnes continued along until someone, someone with an old dueling pistol met him. At least, Buell summarized to himself, that was the story he received from Gloria Papin.

Buell was told that Mrs. Donna Papin was confined to her bed when he asked to speak with her. She agreed to see him, however, and he found her seated in bed but comfortable amongst many pillows and the black poodle across her lap. She was stroking the dog and uttering soft, meaningless, expressions to him for his ears flickered with her voice. Mrs. Papin's face, however, was anxious and drawn, and her dark blue eyes were misty and tearful. She dabbed them with a lace handkerchief as she had the night before and she looked frightened as she bade Johnson Buell to a nearby seat.

Buell had a keen sense, going back to his days as a policeman, of people who needed soothing and he felt this feeling now for Mrs. Papin. He began by asking after her health and if she felt like talking. His voice was quite soft and he looked at her with concern. She assured him she would do what she was able, but she had to have her tea first. Buell quickly did the honors of pouring for her and propping her pillows even more so she could enjoy her tea. He waited until she herself began to talk and found that she wanted to discuss her daughters.

"I wish Gloria would marry as well as Randi," she uttered in a shaking voice, but she stopped immediately and cast a guilty look at Johnson Buell. "Oh, I mean I wish Gloria would marry someone like Ralph Barnes. Oh, to think that he is dead and poor Randi! What are we to do?" The poodle whined at the peevish tone in her voice but then dropped his head back to the warm and soft position on the quilt over her lap.

"You do not approve of Gloria's engagement to this Englishman?" Buell asked although he knew his question was redundant but he hoped it would keep her talking.

"I have not met him, of course, but did you see her hair? He did that to her! And it was pink! To look like that for a wedding! A silly hairdresser and a foreigner, of all things. She should never have been allowed to travel alone, but I had no idea Gloria would do such a thing. She wanted to get away, she said—to be 'in the world' so we let her go and this is what happens. She returned, so different, and I just do not know what to think. She was my own, my joy and because I could not have any more children after her, we adopted Randi. Oh, Randi!" she cried after she said the name. "Poor child! Such a tragedy for her!"

Mrs. Papin settled down after wiping her eyes and taking a few sips of tea so Buell could ask, "Has Randi been what you expected?" He noticed a look of consternation and disappointment on Mrs. Papin's face.

"Yes," she said slowly. "Randi did so well and it was good to raise the girls together."

Johnson Buell detected a hint of envy in her voice, but she went on. "She got Ralph Barnes who was such a wonderful man; he had good looks, intelligence and ambition. Harvey said many times he was the best salesman he ever had. I do really wish that Gloria would look to that kind of man. Yet, Gloria was a bit wild, I must admit. But we thought it only juvenile exuberance. She did not do well in school, just lack of interest, I know."

Her eyes began to mist so Buell asked quickly, "Mrs. Papin, Gloria tells me you had a ring made for her?"

"Oh, both of them," she answered. "I had rings made for both Gloria and Randi from my best pearl and diamond earrings. They were to be graduation gifts, and I secretly hoped it might persuade Gloria to stay on in school, but unfortunately, it did not."

"The rings are identical then?" Buell asked.

"Oh, yes," she replied. "but not engraved because Gloria did not finish school and I did not want to do for one and not the other."

Buell nodded his head. "I understand," he said softly and he now felt confident enough to ask about the evening of the wedding rehearsal.

"Everyone was so happy and excited," Mrs. Papin said. "Such an occasion to look forward to." She sighed but seemed more controlled.

"Did you see Ralph Barnes leave the living room and go out toward the guest house?"

"Not really," she answered. "The guests had gone; Harvey saw the last ones out. The family was still in the living room when I left. I had to go to the kitchen, you see, to check on final setting arrangements for the reception. We had a few last-minute cancellations, that always happens, you know and I had to leave the changed instructions for the caterers. After that, I came directly up here to my room."

"From the kitchen?"

"Yes," she nodded and now the tears came. "Oh, this was to be the day! Ralph dead! Whatever could have happened?"

Johnson Buell rose quickly and took her hand. "Please, Mrs. Papin," he said, "that is why I am here—to find out why and how this tragedy happened."

She calmed herself after a while and began talking to the poodle. Buell did not think it wise to pursue further questioning at this time. He propped her pillows once more and asked if she was comfortable.

"Yes," she responded meekly, so he thanked her profusely and left the room.

When Johnson Buell wrote his report of his interview with Mrs. Papin, he wrote two of them. He often did this. One was the factual account for the official record and the other was for his own use, his personal diary. His account was a parable, a completely inverted parable, expressing his own thoughts and it went like this:

A certain woman had two daughters. And the natural one of them said to her mother, "Mother, I wish to be set free and go out into the world."

And not many days after, the natural daughter journeyed to a far country and there indulged herself in riotous living.

But the adopted daughter at home was preparing for marriage and asked the sister to return.

And the natural daughter arose and came to her mother, but the

173

mother saw her and did not have compassion for her, neither did she fall on her neck and kiss her.

And the natural one said to her, "Mother, I am independent now. You have done much for me, you have put a ring on my hand and sandals on my feet, but I have my own life now. Bring the fatted calf and left all of us eat and be merry!"

Now the adopted daughter had remained at home and said to her mother, "Lo, these many years I have been serving you; I never transgressed your commands at any time, and I am grateful now that you have given me a feast and a celebration for my wedding that I might make merry with my friends.

"But when your true daughter returned, your thoughts were upon her and you became envious of me."

And the mother said to her, "Though you were not my own, you did right and prospered and were always with me. But why should you have so much when my own does not?

"It was right that we should make merry and be glad for you but my own daughter has brought me grief, which is heavier to bear, and she is alienated in her own house."

The gun that killed Ralph Barnes came from Harvey Papin's antique collection. Johnson Buell had studied the weapon that had been brought back to the laboratory by the crime unit. How odd a weapon, he thought, an antique dueling pistol, one of two, but a weapon of precision and elaborate decoration. The pistol was a beautiful instrument of destruction even though the decorative pattern was all on the butt and would be covered by the holding hand, while the sleek tube was without embellishments because any reflection on this surface could blind either party. Its hair trigger, too, was so refined that even almost delicate pressure could trip the firing mechanism. Such a weapon belonged to and was part of a certain code and tradition. In times past, the dueling pistol was used to defend a lady's fair name or a gentleman's honor and now it had been used to blast the lungs of Ralph Barnes.

Harvey Papin invited Buell to meet him in what he called his game room, the room which contained the antique weapons along with coats of arms and coats of mail. The room was eerie for the ancient hauberks were standing in the corners, faceless metal suits that, nevertheless, looked threatening and inpenetrable. The shields, hanging on the walls, were painted in a variety of colors and designs of strips, crosses and fleurs-de-lis. Large long guns and muskets hung on the walls also while other weapons, smaller and perhaps more valuable, were enclosed in glass cases. One of these cases had been broken into and a dueling pistol removed.

Buell stood looking at the case. Dueling pistols always came in pairs and a pair had been there but now one remained, while there was only a recession in the velvet-lined case where its twin, along with the cartridge, had lain.

"Is it usual for anyone to touch or use any of these weapons?" Buell asked, knowing that he had received information that morning that no fingerprints were found on the gun now at the laboratory. Whoever had taken and used that gun had their hands covered.

"No one," Harvey Papin replied. "I forbid it. I am the only one to handle these guns, even to cleaning them."

"But obviously someone has used one of these guns," Buell persisted.

"They stole it," Harvey Papin said hurriedly. "Broke the case and took the gun."

"It is an antique weapon," Buell went on, "could anyone just load it and fire it?"

"Oh, yes. Dueling pistols were carefully designed and made," Harvey Papin said. "Evidently someone knew that or just thought a gun is a gun and used it."

"We might say it worked for them."

Harvey Papin nodded. "Yes, it worked. Old gun or new, it worked. It killed a man."

"Do you have any idea of why anyone would do that? To kill Ralph Barnes?"

"No," Papin answered. "I have no idea. I am absolutely stunned by it." Before he finished speaking, he had picked up a pipe and carefully began to smoke.

Harvey Papin was a hale and hearty looking man who seemed proper and perfect in the masculine setting of the game room. He was heavyset with dark chestnut hair and moustache. His brown eyes were stern, but direct, and his voice deep and forceful. Harvey Papin might say he was "stunned" but his stature was so powerful and he smoked the pipe with such ease and casualness that it belied his expression of himself. Buell found it hard to believe that Harvey Papin could be "stunned" by anything.

As he looked at him, Johnson Buell thought of the woman upstairs, frail and whiny, pretty but completely left behind in the vital, running persona of her husband. Donna Papin obviously was not side by side with her husband. Buell imagined, however, that the initial attraction may have been his, for Buell had known men of physical power like Harvey Papin to be immensely captivated by petite, doll-like women.

Harvey Papin crossed his legs and settled back in a large chair, head raised and puffing slowly on the pipe. He removed it to tell Buell that last evening he had escorted the last of their guests outside to their automobiles. He confirmed that his wife had gone to the kitchen just as they left, and he assumed that Randi and Gloria had gone upstairs to their rooms and Ralph Barnes had left for the guest house. He himself remained outside until the guests had departed, but he came back to the living room immediately when he heard the shot and the screams of the maid.

"No," he said to Buell's question. "I did not see anyone or see anything suspicious while I was outside."

Johnson Buell had heard such high praise for Ralph Barnes that he was surprised when Harvey Papin, like his daughter Gloria, hesitated when asked about him. Harvey Papin puffed on his pipe for several minutes and his eyes darkened in color and a grim expression came over his face.

"Well," he began, but continued to hesitate. "He was a good salesman, but he pulled a deal without my knowledge, and that I did not like."

Johnson Buell blinked in surprise at the statement but he said nothing.

"Ralph was in the field at the time," Harvey Papin went on, "and discovered the possible merger of a company who did parts for us—small ball bearings. Ralph went ahead on his own and committed my firm to buy the company before the merger could take place. Now, Ralph explained that the timing was critical and any delay would have cost us the deal. New owners, he said, would have raised both cost and price of the ball bearings to us. Now, he may have been right, but he did it behind my back, acting without my knowledge or permission."

176

"Did it influence your business?" Buell asked.

"In the long run, I admit, it will probably be beneficial to my company, but a large sum of money went with the commitment to purchase."

"And Ralph Barnes did this without your knowledge or permission?"

"Yes," Harvey Papin replied and the stern expression on his face turned to anger.

"I take it that you did not trust Ralph Barnes after that?"

"How could I? He was in the field, traveling around, and he had built up a good, far-reaching network of contacts. Who knows what that could have done to me or the company in the future?" He paused and smoked for a while: then his face relaxed and a sharp glint shone in his brown eyes. "Of course I had made a plan. Naturally, I did not tell Randi or my wife or any close associates about it; but after he married Randi, I planned to promote him to a job in my office where I could watch him. It is an old management trick."

Johnson Buell looked down at his notebook but he could not write.

"No matter," Harvey Papin continued. "It turned out to be no matter at all. I am sorry for Randi. She deserved a nice and appropriate wedding and I intended to see that she had it." The glint of his eyes turned to a yellow gleam, he smoked leisurely, and Harvey Papin seemed oddly contented.

Johnson Buell asked to talk to the maid and he was shown into the kitchen. She came to attention when he entered, but he immediately requested her to sit down. The nervousness still was upon her and she no longer cried, but her eyes were red and sore looking. Buell spoke kindly to her, telling her that he wanted to hear the story once more because she may remember some details that were not recollected when the horror of what happened was full upon her.

She nodded her understanding and began her story again, but any unremembered details, as Buell hoped, were not forthcoming. She had served dinner the previous evening and also coffee and drinks in the living room afterwards. She returned to the kitchen and remained there until she received the call that the guests had departed and she could clean up. She verified that Mrs. Papin came to the kitchen to talk with the cook just as she was leaving for the living room.

Buell began other questions and she affirmed that no one returned to the living room and she did not see anyone until after she saw the "horrible, bloody body of Mr. Barnes" and came running back to the living room where she met Mr. Papin. She did not see Gloria Papin and Ralph Barnes on the outside patio, but she admitted they could have been out of sight on the side of the patio.

Buell asked about the back stairs to the house and the maid told him that the stairway was beyond the kitchen and anyone could enter there and go to the second floor without being seen. Afterwards, Buell slipped outside the kitchen to check her statement and found it true. The back stairs, which Gloria Papin said she had taken, could indeed be entered from the outside and ascended to the second level of the house.

The person left to question was Randi Papin, and Johnson Buell was aware that he looked upon it with trepidation. He was surprised that he was not calm, that there was a trembling inside of him and an uneasiness. She met him, of all places, on the patio, almost the last place where her fiancé had trod.

It was cool on the patio and the sky was serene and cloudless. Johnson Buell was mindful that this would have been her wedding day. On this day, she would have belonged to that nice looking, blond man who was listed in Buell's notes as intelligent, capable, ambitious.

Randi Papin was seated in one of the white wicker chairs, gazing out over the lawn. She turned as he approached and her dark eyes were limpid but so sorrowful that Buell wondered if he should proceed to question her. This feeling, along with his inner turmoil, made him excuse himself, but she said quickly, "Please stay, Mr. Buell. I assure you that I can answer any questions." She was wearing a blue dress that was dark in color but light in texture and folded in soft plaits almost to the ground. Her dark hair, arranged for the wedding, was beautifully waved and curled. She looked helpless and sad, yet so appealing and attractive.

Johnson Buell took a seat opposite her and he could only look at her for a full moment. He felt hesitant and cautious, hoping not to hurt her more. When he began his questions, he talked gently to her and she responded in quiet, short tones and did not offer any additional information or insights. She had known Ralph Barnes for six months and met him because he was associated with her father's firm, but they had been engaged for one month. She said they were very much in love.

Buell felt a curious feeling that he could only characterize as resentment when she spoke of love. His feeling was uncalled for, he told himself, for she spoke of another, but nevertheless, the pique, the irritation, was there. His feeling was overcome by surprise when she turned to him and said, "I am glad you are here. I know you will help."

He looked directly at her and for a full moment there was silence as they looked upon each other. Then she turned away and sadness came to her voice, "I cannot understand why this should happen!"

"That is why I am here," he answered quickly, using her words to try to calm and soothe her. She regained herself and nodded her head. Buell decided to change his questions and he asked about her sister Gloria. How well did they get along?

"Gloria and I got along well," she said, "but we were different. She was not happy to settle down or be restrained. She wanted freedom, she said, and finally she was allowed to go and she was off to England. I do not criticize her at all. I am glad she is that way and more so, to have the conviction to do it. I myself could not do it, but I admire that in her. I was pleased, really, that she returned for the wedding," her voice became tight and lower, "and to be my maid of honor."

Johnson Buell stared at her. Her talk about her sister was the longest and the easiest that she made. His other questions had been answered very tersely and with an attitude of much effort on her part.

"I understand she upset your mother with her appearance, her hair to be exact, and with her engagement."

"Yes," she replied. "Mother was upset with Gloria. I felt distressed by that because the Papins have been good to me and now especially with the wedding, everything beautiful and elaborate. I am adopted and I could hardly believe that I deserved all this from them."

"Did Gloria know Mr. Barnes before she left for England?" Buell asked to check Gloria's own statement.

Randi Papin shook her head. "Not until she returned home. Ralph was staying here of course. He came a week ago and we were all together for the preparations and. . . " She did not finish: her voice was soft and weak and ended in a deep sigh.

Johnson Buell went on. "When the dinner party was over and

179

everyone went to their rooms, can you tell me if you heard anything or had any suspicious that something might be wrong?"

Her head was bowed but she said, "No. We had a wonderful dinner although the rehearsal went badly. Yet, that was no worry, really, because it is said that a bad rehearsal makes a perfect performance. I left the living room after everyone was gone. I came to my room but I was excited so I sat up for a while, just thinking—just thinking about the future for Ralph and me. I did hear him talking to Gloria because my room is just above the patio." She paused and Johnson Buell leaned forward to hear her words. "I did see them turn onto the path toward the guest house. I heard the shot. . . ."

Johnson Buell was surprised and interrupted her. "You heard the shot?"

"Yes," she replied. "then I heard the screams. I came down to the living room and Dad was there already, telephoning the police and he told me what happened."

He called her name before he realized it. "Randi, do you have any idea why anyone would kill Ralph Barnes?"

She could not look at him; she shook her head and that was all. He had leaned closer to her to hear her words and now he could not move back. He was so much aware of her presence, the beauty of her face and hair, the sad, pleading eyes and the languid, graceful movements of her hands and arms when she raised them to pull at the throat of her dress or lowered them to straighten the fold of her skirt. He had seen and was aware of the pearl and diamond ring on her finger but he declined to mention it.

The seduction was coming over him but he was stifled. There was no way to break through the sadness between them; it was a barrier that could not be overcome. She had loved and been betrothed to another; all lost, and he could not come forward with an entreating word to her. Her hand could not be taken, or could he hold her, for Randi Papin had to linger in all this sorrow for her own time.

Johnson Buell closed the report book hurriedly. An ache overcame him and he was upset that he could cause himself to contemplate, so long, on that first case that was now beyond him, however poignant and frustrating the memories. He must not take any more time in this thinking, he told himself sternly, for on the morrow he must prepare for the trip to Port Bold.

Chapter Eleven

Another day had passed and on the morning of the next, Spenner approached Anton Dyer in his room at the servants' quarters.

"Sorry to disturb you," Spenner said lightly, but he noticed the quick look of surprise in Dyer's eyes. Otherwise, the butler's assurance was calm and poised and he answered quickly. "Not at all, sir, not at all."

Spenner stepped into the room. It was a cumbersome room as it was small in size, yet furnished with two heavy cushioned chairs and a matching divan and accents of tall, brass lamps. The room was comfortable, no doubt, but it was not a masculine style except, perhaps, for an older man like Anton Dyer who wanted the ease of pillows and overstuffed upholstery.

Spenner circled an oval table in the center of the room and hesitated when he saw a pipestand alongside one of the big chairs. The pipes and tobacco were identical to those in the library. Spenner smiled to himself and wondered if Dyer had borrowed and used them here and then hastily returned them to the library the day he came back to the estate. Spenner still was smiling when he turned around to look at Dyer who had remained by the door. Anton Dyer stood straight and stiff, although his face was softened by his puzzlement. He stood as at attention, as someone awaiting orders, and he looked the part with his straightforward demeanor and with his clothes which were brushed and his shoes polished.

Spenner sensed that his visit was unusual. "Anton," he began, for he decided to explain his mission immediately, "you know that the estate will be read and settled soon," he paused but noted no change in Dyer's expression. "It will be important," he went on, "for all of us."

Anton Dyer nodded his head but said nothing.

"If you do not mind, Anton, I would like to see the work journals of the estate, only to see who has worked here and, perhaps, make certain that no one is overlooked at the reading of the estate. You understand, Anton?"

"Yes, sir," Dyer replied but a shadow fell on his face along with a look of doubt. He appeared dismayed, as if Spenner's request was a foolish one. Nevertheless, he said, "I understand," and proceeded to a cupboard which he unlocked. Several shelves were filled with ledgers, and Dyer surveyed them casually. "You wish to see all of them?" he asked.

Spenner hesitated as if to decide, then he replied, "Oh, I think I will begin with the last fifteen to twenty years."

Anton Dyer pulled forth several thick journals. "The information will be in these books, sir."

Spenner took the heavy books and thanked Anton Dyer. He started to leave, but paused and said, "Also, Anton, if you know or remember anyone, perhaps not listed, will you let me know?"

Dyer came straight across the room and looked at Spenner. The expression in his eyes had changed from surprise to sorrow. "There is someone, sir, who I hope you will remember if there is nothing in the provisions of the will. I believe he is practically destitute now, but he worked here a short while after the war."

After the war! Trying not to appear overly excited, Spenner replied easily, "Yes?"

"He is Jonas Shelby." Dyer pronounced the name slowly and distinctly, and he was studying Spenner carefully. His lips twisted as though he wanted to smile, but it was a questioning and meager smile.

Jonas Shelby! Spenner flinched and stood stiffly. He noted Dyer's steady gaze and curious smile and a thought came to him—should I know? Should I admit? Why did Dyer speak this name so readily? Spenner delayed by shifting the heavy books in his arms and then said softly, "Jonas Shelby." Carefully, he shook his head as if not remembering and went on, "You say he is destitute? Can you tell me more about him?"

There was silence for a moment before Dyer answered. "He is now at the Valiterra Convalescent Home."

"Oh," Spenner replied lightly, trying to calm himself. "I see. Thank you, Anton."

Spenner moved quickly and left the room, but Dyer followed him into the corridor. "Sir," Dyer called, almost aloud and Spenner stopped and turned to face him. Anton Dyer came forward slowly. His glance was even and still questioning; but the slight smile had disappeared and an overall look of disappointment was upon Dyer's face. "I said Jonas Shelby. You do not remember him, sir?"

Spenner stood firm, but his legs suddenly felt weak and heavy. He had to continue to pretend—to pretend to be thinking. A frown crossed his face, and he shook his head. "No, no, I cannot recall at this *time*," he paused after he emphasized the last word.

Dyer's voice was not condescending as he replied, "But, sir, Jonas Shelby was a member of your city council and one of your closest aides."

Spenner closed his eyes and he fumbled for words, afraid to commit himself. He surprised himself when he stuttered and said, "Oh, that one! Perhaps it will come to me; perhaps I shall recall." Spenner paused and felt able to look directly at Anton Dyer. "You said he worked *here*, at the estate?"

"After the war," Dyer answered hurriedly. "He worked for only a short time on the books and records."

"Tell me, Anton," Spenner asked casually. "was he employed here while Mrs. Whitmore was alive?"

"Yes," Dyer responded. "but he left shortly after Mrs. Whitmore passed away. It was a brief time and it may not be listed in those books, sir."

Spenner's thoughts were teeming about the situation with Jonas Shelby, but he did not wish to discuss it more with Anton Dyer. "He is now in a convalescent home, you say?"

"Yes, sir. The Valiterra Convalescent Home."

"Thank you, Anton. Thank you again," Spenner said lightly.

He turned quickly away but once again halted as Dyer called out, "Sir!"

Anton Dyer stepped before him and the stunned look upon his face could not be disguised. He looked pained and sorrowful. "Mayor Whitmore," he breathed very slowly, "it is—" but he halted and could not go on.

"Yes, Anton, what is it?"

Dyer began again. "It hurts me, sir, to see you confused."

Spenner threw his head back. Confused! Whatever was Anton Dyer saying? Spenner tried to laugh, to make light of the mood, but his voice was dry and when he tried to speak, his words had a rasping sound. "Confused, Anton? Really?"

Dyer continued to look at him with the sad expression in his eyes. "I understand your condition, sir, but it is sad you cannot recall old friends. Jonas Shelby was one of those closest to you, yet you cannot remember him?"

The weak and heavy feeling returned to Spenner's limbs and he began to tremble also. What to say? What to say? "Poor Mr. Shelby," he muttered. "If he is destitute, he will be helped. I will do something."

Anton Dyer blinked his eyes, causing a tear to roll forward and settle on his cheek.

Spenner went on but he was whispering. "All this time to adjust, to think, to try to remember. It comes slowly, Anton, things come back slowly. Do not become upset." He smiled at Dyer and patted his shoulder. "Anton, just accept, for this time? H'mm?"

Dyer merely nodded his head and turned to go away. He walked gradually back to his room and closed the door.

Spenner stared for a minute at the closed door. He felt the uneasiness still upon him and it remained as he returned to his room. He placed the work journals on the desk, but he did not open them. He sat down at the desk and stared out the window although he did not really look at anything. He seemed inert and suppressible, yet his mind was swarming with so many ideas. His forehead was moist with perspiration, but it felt like a piece of wood, hard and pressing into his thoughts. He had asked Anton Dyer what he believed to be a harmless question about previous employees, with the full and sincere idea of possible recompense, but also to allay any suspicions about his true request for these work journals—that he wanted to check on people who had worked at the estate at the time of the murder.

Instead, Dyer had replied quickly, very quickly, with the name of Jonas Shelby and furthermore, Dyer had to explain that this man had been a member of the city council and one of the mayor's closest and most dependable aides. Why had Anton Dyer done so? Was it truly a hint of destitute former employee or was it to test *him*, to see if he recalled and confirmed so close an associate? The name could hardly be common, it was not that simple to be confused or mistaken over it, yet Dyer had precisely and hurriedly said the name of Jonas Shelby.

Jonas Shelby! Anton Dyer expected the name to conjure up reminiscences, to be remembered and to have Spenner exclaim, "Oh, yes, Jonas Shelby!" Should he have taken on Dyer's sadness and cry, "He is destitute, you say, and confined to care? How sad for my old friend and associate. I will surely see that he is not overlooked. Believe me!" Should he have expressed himself that way, Spenner wondered, instead of explaining confusion, reacting in shock, sputtering words and holding back any knowledge?

Spenner closed his eyes and hung his head. He began to relax under the weight of his thoughts. He slumped in his chair and it seemed so restful with his eyes closed, the light blotted out, and the dimness which kept things away and he need not see, he need not search. Yet, one small thought would not diminish and it pricked through his mind like lightning flashes. Should he? Should he? The game—should he give it up now, acknowledge, admit, say *it*? The truth? Jonas Shelby!

Spenner rested awhile and then later, in the afternoon, he left the estate. He did not call for a car but went himself to the garage and selected the same automobile he had driven before. He drove away from the estate and down the narrow road toward the highway. He was driving slowly, but he stopped the car so suddenly that the machine bounced and he twisted back and forth in the driver's seat. Then he sat silent, staring at the figure approaching him. The man was in the center of the road and he came slowly as his right leg dragged wearily as though he had walked a long way. The head was held up and the burnt-skinned face was visible but unsmiling under the knit cap.

"Alec Thurston!" Spenner exclaimed as he came alongside the automobile.

Alex Thurston lowered his head and looked directly inside at Spenner then he said, "I have been waiting to see you, Spenner. I thought you must come out sometime. "His dark eyes were bright and steady with a look of determination.

"I had no idea," Spenner said and then, with a swift thought, he asked, "You were going to the estate?"

"Of course not," Thurston answered sharply. "I would never

contact you *there*," he indicated as he thrust his head in the direction of the estate.

"Well, yes, but what then?" Spenner asked.

Thurston did not reply but a sardonic smile crossed his face as he glanced over the big automobile. "Say," he said with bitterness, "this is nice, isn't it, Spenner, to be driving something like this? Living in a big house? Did you ever believe it could happen? Really?" He began to chuckle.

Spenner was becoming calm after the surprise of seeing Thurston and he answered coldly, "Yes, it is nice, but why are you here?"

Thurston continued to chuckle and he did not reply to the question. Instead, he said, "Doesn't it make you happy? To have all this, with more to come?"

Spenner ignored his question and asked again. "Why did you wish to see me, Thurston? It was your idea of no contact unless its an emergency."

Thurston stopped laughing but the bitter smile remained on his countenance. "I thought we should have a talk."

"Get in then," Spenner said quickly.

Thurston nodded and went to the other side of the car and climbed in. His deformity made it difficult and, once inside, the stiff right leg was pushed like a stick under the dashboard. He looked the same, Spenner thought as he observed him, his baked skin was coarse and dry and his thickset body was forceful and overpowering. The smile on his face was gone and his attitude became hostile and demanding. "True. I did not want to have contact with you, Spenner," he began, "until the *thing* is over and, fortunately, it will be soon. Ah, I am grateful. I thank my stars that it will soon be over."

Spenner asked, "Then why come now?"

Thurston looked directly at Spenner and answered, "Because I've been upset since your call."

Spenner shrugged and tried to reply in a light tone. "I was reporting what had happened. You know what I told you was unexpected; it was not in our plans, it was unknown."

Thurston nodded. "Unknown to me, too."

"I believe you," Spenner said. "That was why I called—to let you know."

"But that was not necessary," Thurston replied quickly. "You are

186

doing fine. You had fooled everyone. I want assurance that you have disregarded that talk about a murder. It does not figure in our plans."

Spenner sank back into the car seat and his head dropped slightly. "I cannot disregard it, Thurston," he said.

Thurston stared at him in silence. His dark eyes began to glisten as they became narrow. "I thought so. That is just why I had to come here now. I am worried, shall I say, about my investment. Spenner, I am telling you once more to forget about *anything* except what you are here to do. That was our agreement, and I expect you to stand by your word."

Spenner raised his hand but he did not look at Thurston. Slowly, he said, "I am tracking a murderer."

Thurston slumped against the car cushion in exasperation. "So, you are going to be a policeman? A detective? Something like that? Solving a sixteen-year-old case?" He threw up his hands. "I cannot make you see!" he said with anger.

"Perhaps I can make you see," Spenner retaliated. Thurston looked at him but said nothing, so Spenner continued. "I am on my way now."

"To what?" Thurston asked, still angry.

"You did not ask me where I was going, did you? Well, I am going to a place where I believe I will confront a murderer."

"Ah! What nonsense! Just a drive. How infernally ridiculous!"

Spenner continued to speak slowly. "I want you to come with me, Thurston."

"Ah!" Thurston repeated in dismay. "But where?"

Spenner started and car and as he began driving away, he answered. "To the Valiterra Convalenscent Home."

"A convalescent home!" Thurston exclaimed with surprise and perplexity, not knowing whether to be amused or angry. His head tossed from side to side in a negative fashion and then he said with a snicker. "So, you are going to show me a murderer in a convalescent home. You have solved the case, just like that!" He snapped his fingers and laughed. "A sleuth! Who would have thought—Spenner the sleuth!"

Spenner was tense and he sat rigidly, his hands tight on the wheel and he looked ahead only at the road. His voice was low and composed when he answered. "I have a lead which I think will solve the murder, whatever you believe, Thurston. I have to pursue this because sixteen years ago my son believed his mother was murdered though no one else did."

Thurston snickered again. "And why not, I wonder? Apparently, it would have been a simple thing to do if it was murder. You seem to have solved this thing without difficulty. What a chance for you!" he said with derision.

"Thurston," Spenner replied with calm, "the 'why not' is the total consideration in this matter. 'Why not' anyone saw Mrs. Whitmore's death as murder is because they did not care to investigate and just accepted the idea that she fell and hit her head."

"So the murderer, then, got away?"

"Yes," Spenner nodded his head, "because no one looked further and no one believed my son who actually saw the murder."

Thurston sighed with impatience. "All right, so how did it happen? You have all the details? How did you discover what you say the others overlooked? You must, you know, since you are on your way to capture this murderer. Tell me, Spenner, how did he do it?"

"He climbed a tree. . . . "

"Climbed a tree!" Thurston interrupted and sat upright in the seat.

Spenner went on. "Climbed a tree and got in and out through an unlocked window on the second floor. An alarm system was installed on the first floor at the estate and it was the only way to avoid it. Mrs. Whitmore tried to run from the room. He caught her at the door and hit her. This man was employed at the estate and left soon after her death."

"And now we must know *why* he did it. Tell that, Spenner."

Spenner's grip on the wheel became tighter. "That is what he will have to explain, but I know he was a close friend of Mayor Whitmore and served on his city council. The motive, I think, is somewhere in the political turmoil of twenty years ago."

"Don't you see, Spenner," Thurston said with excitement rising in his voice, "this is what I am trying to tell you. If you start asking questions, you are going to be asked questions also, as mayor. What will you do then? This whole plan of ours can go up in smoke. We would be—caught!"

A sudden nervousness came over Spenner and he lost control of the car. He was off the pavement and onto the dirt track alongside the road. The track was uneven and soft and the car twisted and turned from side to side. Spenner was driving slow enough, however, to keep the car from turning over and he was able to bring the automobile back to the road after several slides and jarring bounces.

"Ah!" cried Thurston as he sank back again into the cushioned seat. His eyes were wide and glistened with alarm. "Are you trying to kill us? Really?"

The nervous jolt that hit Spenner had come quickly. He thought of the murder when he asked Thurston to come with him, he wanted to prove to Thurston that he was right, and now he thought more about the *plan*. It had magnified and he realized a bigger picture, a wider scope, had been added to their *plan*. Unconsciously, perhaps, he wanted Thurston to know, he wanted Thurston to see. "Are you hurt, Thurston?" he asked.

"No," Thurston answered but his voice was weak, "but be careful."

"Thurston," Spenner said slowly, "I can understand your feelings and I know why you are upset, but I have got to follow through on my idea." He hesitated and then asked, "What is it, Thurston, that makes us believe?"

"Who knows?" Thurston replied. "I have had so many beliefs."

"And none have been true?"

Thurston nodded. "Most of them, all for nought."

"Well, I asked you to come with me to see that what I believe it true."

Spenner said no more as he drove around until he found the Valiterra Convalescent Home. The place was a fairly new brick building of one level. The lobby was small and quite warm, and Spenner and Thurston were required to stop at the information desk.

"We wish to visit Jonas Shelby," Spenner stated. They were issued passes and given directions to Jonas Shelby's room. They found their way along a heated corridor with overhead, gazing lamps. When they reached the correct door, they hesitated. Spenner had stopped and Thurston, walking behind him, had paused also. The door was partially open and, cautiously, Spenner opened it wider and stepped inside. The room was quiet and orderly with an overall medicinal odor. The bed was made, the chairs and floor were dusted and the walls were sparkling white. In a corner, alone in the room and seated in a chair, was a man gazing out the window. The chair was large and padded with a reclining back, but the man pressed a lever at the side of the chair and it swung around easily and he faced Thurston and Spenner, who stopped immediately. The three men stared at each other in the silent room. Thurston had halted so abruptly that his limp leg threw him off balance and he stumbled against Spenner. In a surprised voice, he whispered to Spenner. "This is a murderer? Look! He has no legs!"

Spenner had seen the missing limbs right away and the sight had caused him to pause. He stared at the bulging, bandaged kneecaps with nothing beneath them, but then he looked up and became obsessed with the rest of the man. He was a man of fifty years or more and age and mutilation had shrunken his remaining body and disillusionment clearly was visible upon his face. His upper frame was thin and looked weak, perhaps because he sat far back in the chair to balance himself for the lack of legs.

"Ah!" Thurston whispered again. "Ah!" Almighty! This man climbed trees?"

Spenner remained stunned and could only stare at the man. He felt the tug at his coat sleeve; it was Thurston, trying to pull him back.

"Let us leave; let us go!" Thurston was pleading; and Spenner sensed that he should run away, but he could not move.

The man did not look or pretend to hear Thurston for his eyes were on Spenner. The eyes were grey and melancholy and his eyelids fluttered when he said to Spenner, "Is it you, Collis? Is it really you?"

"Yes, Jonas," Spenner answered softly. He was thoughtful because there was no surprise apparent in Jonas Shelby, as if he knew of Spenner's coming and was waiting.

"You got away," Shelby said, "and now you are back."

Spenner asked, "You *knew* that I had come back?"

"I knew you had come back," Shelby replied without explanation. He looked Spenner over and a slight, sarcastic grin came over his face. "You have come back, I understand, out of the depths. Out of the depths of what, Collis? The place where all reprobates and deceivers fall? You are not quite the same, though. Your face," he hesitated, "has changed. Were you hurt, Collis? So slight, but is that the only wound?"

Spenner sensed that Shelby's question was intended as a jab, so he did not reply. He wondered if the expression on Jonas Shelby's face might change but it did not. Shelby's gaze was steadfast and disenchanted. "You are," Spenner began as he looked over the partial body of Shelby. "You have been, like this?"

"Yes," Shelby nodded, "for twenty years. But you can join me. Sit," he said as he motioned toward two vacant chairs on the other side of the bed.

Thurston moved past Spenner to a chair in the far corner. As he passed Spenner, he looked at him with disgust and said, "Eh!" He flung his hands upward to accent his dismay and then slipped into the chair near the wall.

Now Jonas Shelby glanced at him. "This is Alec Thurston," Spenner said and hesitated before adding, "Someone I met recently; someone who has helped me."

Jonas Shelby only nodded once to Thurston and turned back to look at Spenner. "From your days of forgetfulness?" he asked.

"No," Spenner answered softly, "after that."

"Eh!" Thurston uttered again and slid backward and downward into the chair.

Spenner felt weak and almost fell into his chair which he had pulled close to Shelby. As Spenner sat down, he could see the deeper signs of aging and suffering on Shelby's face. The sad eyes were sunken in their sockets and framed by many lines and deep wrinkles. The skin on the remainder of his face had appeared smooth but now Spenner saw that it was old skin, speckled with brown and red spots. His white hair did not cover any part of his face for it was cut short and brushed back at the top and sides. Spenner thought of his words, "for twenty years," the time which had brought all this devastation to Jonas Shelby.

"Twenty years," Spenner said softly.

"I have been in a wheel chair since the war. I did not escape like you," Shelby spoke harshly. "They cut me down by blasting off my legs." He paused but his gaze was directly upon Spenner. "Why are you here now? Why did you come to see me? What do you want?"

Spenner was startled and his body stiffened in his chair. He hesitated and then said slowly, "I came to see you, Jonas. You were my closest and most dependable aide on the council." His reply was stumbling and uncertain.

"Well, you see what I am. Old friends we were, Collis, but now I am an isolated man. The friends I had did not fall away from me; I shrank within and became what I wanted to be—without an outreach

191

to anyone. I heightened and took to heart every hurt and criticism so I could be driven deeper into myself. I never fought back, but only wanted to disentangle myself from everyone. I end up now with more lost than my legs, but the only comfort I have is being alone."

"Jonas, I am truly sorry."

Shelby looked straight at him. "I believe you should be."

Spenner felt uncomfortable and restless. He looked away and said, "I am sorry, Jonas. I must tell you that, but I came to ask about another matter."

Jonas Shelbys' eyes widened with surprise. "What then?"

"I came to ask about Mrs. Whitmore," Spenner answered slowly.

"Mrs. Whitmore?"

Spenner nodded.

Shelby was silent and studied Spenner. "I cannot believe," he said softly, "that you came here to ask about your wife. Whatever for?"

Spenner's voice was struggling to become firm. "I have heard, I have been told things about Mrs. Whitmore and I must know."

Shelby leaned forward. Spenner was afraid he might tumble from the chair, but he did not reach out to restrain him.

"What must you know, Collis, from me?"

Spenner answered bluntly. "Because you worked at the estate when she was there after the war."

"Certainly, I was there. Mrs. Whitmore was kind enough to let me live at the estate. I had nowhere else to go at the time. It was not complete charity. I did do work and I was paid. I must say I had no complaints about the pay from Mrs. Whitmore. To me, she was generous. I kept the books and records, all the journals. What other work could I do?"

"Jonas, why did you think Mrs. Whitmore was generous and kind to you? Did you think she had to be?"

Shelby stared at Spenner. He seemed perplexed but he shook his head. "No, there was no reason for that." He paused and his voice lowered. "I never told her the truth about you, Collis. I never did. Believe that."

"Eh!" An exclamation burst forth across the room. Spenner knew the cry came from Thurston, but an anguish was spreading through his own body. Shelby's words hung over him but he struggled to reply.

"She died," was all Spenner could whisper.

"One year I worked there," Shelby continued as if he had not heard Spenner.

"How did she die?"

Shelby went on. "I left the estate after she died."

"But how did she die? I am asking?"

The two men paused and silence came between them. At last, Shelby said, "It was strange."

Spenner's eyes blinked. "Strange? How was it strange?"

"It was a strange night. I must say that, Collis."

"Tell me," Spenner asked, his voice becoming tense. "Tell me everything. Why it was strange."

Shelby began. "Mrs. Whitmore was ill."

"That I know." Spenner waited for Shelby to continue and was surprised for Shelby said nothing more. Shelby sat still and tense. His body had moved erect and his eyes were staring straight ahead. Spenner's voice became urgent. "She was ill, Jonas. Yes, that I know—and she died. How did she die, Jonas?" Still, Jonas Shelby said nothing. Spenner blinked with disbelief and then stated. "I have been told she died from a fall." He leaned closer to Shelby and repeated, "I said, she died from a fall." He leaned closer to Shelby and repeated, "I said, she died from a fall." Yet, Shelby remained immobile as if he had become transfixed. Spenner stared at him as his disbelief became more profound. "She did not die from a fall then, did she? Did she, Jonas?"

The spell broke, and Shelby shook his head and muttered. "How can I say, Collis?"

"But you were there and you said it was a strange night. I want to know what happened."

"How can I say, Collis?" Shelby repeated. "My quarters were downstairs at the back. I thought I heard something outside that night. I wheeled myself out and I thought I saw someone running away toward the trees. I did not know for certain."

"The trees? You mean the trees at the front of the estate?"

"Yes, but I said I *thought* I saw someone running, running off into the darkness."

Spenner sat upright. "You told no one? You did not say anything to anyone?"

Shelby shook his head. "I said I was not certain. It was dark.

193

The trees, the branches, could have moved and looked like someone and how could I follow or run after? I could not verify anything."

"But Mrs. Whitmore died that night. Didn't you suspect or believe that these two happenings might have a connection?"

Shelby's eyes blinked and his face became stiff. "What are you saying, Collis?"

"I am saying that Mrs. Whitmore may have been murdered."

Shelby's face remained stiff. "But why?" he whispered. "Why would anyone do that? Mrs. Whitmore died from a fall. There was no reason to connect anything. The doctor, the coroner, all said she fell. I could not go up there and see."

"Lester, my boy, said he saw someone hit his mother. Could not that make you wonder, Jonas, enough to ask questions and to report what you saw?"

"What I thought I saw." Shelby shook his head vigorously. "I was not certain; I was not certain at all."

"Did you hear, though, what Lester said?"

"No," Shelby replied. "I paid no attention to what the boy said. I thought he was hysterical."

Spenner stared at him. His thoughts were in a turmoil, but he could not sense if he was truly angry or just anguished. He felt a trembling inside of him that could have been either. How dare Shelby! How dare he! How could he be so negligent? He did not back up Lester. He refused to even give the boy some measure of support, some credence. So Shelby was not certain that he saw anyone, or did he? Was it only a shadow, perhaps, or a swaying tree branch that deceived his senses within a few moments of time? Yet, the boy spoke and this man, Jonas Shelby, did not even utter the word *perhaps* for him. Oh, Jonas, you had the intuition that something was strange that night. You said so and I saw it on your face just now.

"You are a man of conscience, Jonas," Spenner said evenly. "Unfortunately, you must live with torment, and you confess that you are an isolated man. It is understandable."

Shelby's face became stern. "You tell me that I am tormented, Collis? How about you? Do you not have torment and isolation also?"

Spenner met his gaze. "What do you mean?"

"Collis, you came here, asking about your wife's death. You talk to me about the circumstances, even mentioning murder, and accuse me of laxity and wrongdoing, even withholding information of which I was extremely doubtful."

"But you should have spoken it, Jonas, even in doubt and uncertainty and allow others to confirm it or not."

Shelby grunted. "So, you can say such things, Collis, to accuse me of neglect in the death of one. I, Collis, can accuse you of true treachery in the death of many."

"What are you saying, Jonas?"

Again, Shelby grunted. "I have told you, Collis, that I have endured hurt and criticism and become a lonely, despairing man, which has been my will, but I will not accept from you any accusation that I did not act properly in the death of your wife."

"And I must accept your accusation that I had anything to do with the death of many? I want to know."

"You want to know? You, of all people, Collis?"

"Yes," Spenner answered.

"Then, we will go back to the time you talk about—the war."

"I had—I got amnesia," Spenner answered quickly. "I do not remember."

"Amnesia, you say," Shelby shrugged his shoulders and his eyelids fluttered over his sunken eyes. "That is as good an excuse as anything else."

"But it is not an excuse."

"You remember your betrayal, don't you, Collis? You surely remember *that?*"

"Betrayal?" Spenner repeated the word and his voice cracked.

"Almighty!" came a faint whisper from Thurston on the other side of the bed.

"Oh, you know what betrayal is?" Shelby went on. "Oh, you do, Collis, just as well as Paul Arlan and Charles Orcott and myself. We remember." Anger was rising in Shelby and his face became red.

"What?" Spenner asked feebly. "I do not understand who you are talking about."

"You still pretend amnesia?" Shelby's head shook. "Then I will tell you, Collis. That was a terrible thing, a terrible night for us. Orcott's units were completely wiped out. We expected, we counted on his units to hold this city. That was the plan, you knew that, your approved plan, and then you sold us out." He paused and his eyes seemed to roll as he thrust back his head. "I supported you, Collis, even after you rejected the peace plan I offered before that. I was willing to go to *them,* offer compromise and negotiations, but you turned me down and said you would fight. You called me a pacificist and a dreamer and I accepted that and gave you my support regardless. If you deceived, me, then why did you deceive your military too? You said you would fight, then sold that out as well, and the army that was to save and protect us was routed and destroyed. When General Orcott came crying out that all was lost and demanding you—you—to account; you were gone, Collis, disappeared. How did you manage to get away?" Shelby's half body thrust forward at Spenner.

Spenner was rigid; he sat like a wooden image, hearing words and accusations and yet thinking that he had heard nothing correctly. He stared back at the intense gaze of Shelby which was filled with bitter resentment. Spenner blinked his eyes, but the intensity of the gaze upon him did not vanish; then he saw the liquid sparkles in Shelby's eyes and realized that the resentment was based on a deep and unforgettable hurt.

"Collis, why did you do it?" Shelby asked firmly and with blame.

Spenner could only shake his head. "I do not know what you are saying, Jonas," he sputtered and he said what had been his only defense, "I had the amnesia."

"Are you certain the amnesia was not deliberate? One should be original in lies and deceits."

"Jonas, how could that be when I say I cannot remember?"

There was a groan and Spenner thought that it came from him. He wanted to mumble and cry, but he knew he could not do it. Why can't I, he asked himself, but there was indeed a cry, and he realized it came from Thurston. Thurston, sitting in the corner was groaning. "Eh!" he heard Thurston mutter, and then another "Eh?" followed by a deep murmur of despair. Why, Spenner thought, can't I, too, cry and groan in despair?

"So you cannot remember?" Shelby went on. "Well, Collis, there were some of us who kept our minds. We remember, always." Shelby's head had not moved; it was poised before Spenner like a viper, the half body to the chair, the sleek head, and the eyes glaring and wide. Anger, though forced, returned to Shelby's face. "Shall I tell you, Collis, since you do not remember? Shall I tell you about it?"

"No," Spenner protested quickly, sensing the anger. Shelby was hurt and angry, and Spenner felt that anger was an easier emotion to deal with. Anger could be confronted and even turned around. But hurt feelings were like wounds, they went deeper, remained longer, and were harder to heal. "Jonas," he said, speaking softly, "it would do no good."

Jonas Shelby did not listen. "You left, did you not, after sending me to the western entrance to draw the enemy there, giving you enough time to go down to the vault and get away? Paul Arlan knew about your deception, too, and I sent him after you, but you were gone. Charles Orcott found me and saved what was left of me. When he came, Collis, he came for you. He said that Valiterra was doomed. The city was overrun and would fall. He wanted you, for you knew how it all happened. He was crying out for you, Collis, saying, 'If I get only one, let it be him!' "

"No!" Spenner shouted but his words were hoarse. "You cannot say that! You cannot blame like that!" He felt a cold sweat between his shoulder blades. "Jonas!"

"Look at me and say I am not to blame or accuse you? Is that what you say, Collis?"

Spenner was trembling and, with the coldness of his body, wondered if he was going to be sick. "You were my closest and most dependable friend," he repeated, speaking by rote. "How could I . . . " but he could not finish the sentence.

"Yes," Shelby replied. "How could you?"

Spenner felt certain now that he was ill. To the cold and trembling of his body was added a feeling of nausea and dizziness. His head became light, and he imagined himself drifting and floating as if his senses were losing their strengths. Some inner reserve, like a last resort, rose within him to combat the flight of his mental faculties. It was anger, he knew, anger that he had tried to suppress. He did not want to return anger for anger against Jonas Shelby; he wanted to confront the anger with discussion and, as he believed, to turn it around and diminish it. Yet, he realized that the anger was too deep within Shelby and could not be persuaded.

"You," Spenner faltered, not yet in control of himself. "You advised me, Jonas. You advised me not to fight, not to defend. Peace! Peace! Peace! That is all you talked about; that is all you wanted."

197

"Yes. Yes, I did," Shelby answered. "But peace is honorable. It is not betrayal or selling out. That is not peace."

"But there is a price for peace also, Jonas. You were the pacificist, the peacemaker, who wanted no part of fighting or war. And I listened to that. Indeed, I did listen to you. I made decisions on your philosophy, what you told me, what you suggested. And now you talk so easily of blame."

A deep, uneasy cry and then a grumble came from across the bed. Spenner thought he heard words also but they were spoken so softly and swiftly that they were inaudible. Spenner groaned, too, as if in reply, but it was a wailing within himself.

"My life was only to serve you, Collis," Shelby said.

"What did you suggest, Jonas? You wanted peace, and I had to protect this city. Can't you understand that a leader is restricted as well? That was my responsibility, my *only* responsibility, if you will. I believed in your peace and I wanted that."

"It would not come by treachery."

"Then who was deceived about peace? You for preaching it along with your compromises and negotiations, or I, who tried to contract for it with a strong enemy? Don't you see, Jonas, that either way, we were doomed?"

"We both lost, but that was no reason to run from it, Collis."

"You want me to take all the blame? My guess is that your conscience is tormented also, isn't it, Jonas?"

Shelby replied softly. "Do you know nothing about retribution, Collis?"

"Ah, that it is. Retribution talks of a tormented soul. You are tormented, Jonas, because your belief has no basis. You cannot proclaim your peace in the name of anything; therefore you cannot justify it. You cry, 'Peace!' You make it only a word and believe the aura is sufficient, but it was isolated and that is why it failed. It must be attached, a part of something. Could you not say that you believed in peace for any reason, because it was righteous, sanctified, even God's Holy Design?"

"Peace is all that."

"Then why don't you say that? You cannot because then you commit your purpose to those things also. You say 'peace', but you do not say 'why peace'."

"Do you really believe that so many would have died then and

198

so many would have suffered if they were offered a peace without a base?"

"I do believe that, Jonas."

"Yet you brought on the death and suffering by betrayal."

"I took the path that I thought would avoid all that."

"And that was betrayal."

"Because I was wrong, Jonas? Your peace would have brought on the same result, yet you feel righteous because you can still say 'peace' and feel honorable."

"How simple!"

"Most judgments are."

Slowly, Shelby said, "See Charles Orcott."

"Charles Orcott?"

A half smile appeared on Shelby's face. "Yes. When you talk about judgment, go to him, see his measure. He is on the west side of town in the only building on the Old Road. Go, Collis, and see!"

The two men had spoken rapidly and harshly to each other, sitting tense and unwavering, staring at each other. There were a noise against the far wall as Thurston's body fell against it as if stunned. He groaned. "Eh!" came from his lips and then a louder screech. "Ah! Ah!"

Shelby's small body stiffened. "You have returned to your estate, to live in the grand manner, haven't you, Collis? With only a forgotten memory of all the rottenness that happened?"

"I will help you, Jonas. The estate will be read soon. I will see that you are remembered."

"I want nothing from you, Collis." Shelby's head shook in sadness.

"Oh, Jonas, if only you had fought!" Spenner's voice failed, as if tired and strained.

His head was shaking but he rose from the chair and turned away. Shelby's voice came after him. "You cannot be forgiven, Collis!"

A figure bolted past Spenner and fled out the door. It was Alex Thurston and his uncoordinated body seemed to be pitching wildly as though he was being thrown out of the room. He was waiting for Spenner at the end of the corridor. He was slumped into a corner and the light from the lamp cast a shadow across his face. Yet, his eyes were wide and burning with an intense gaze which seemed to become stronger as Spenner came near to him. They looked at each other in silence, then suddenly Thurston shuddered. An odd emotion, a coldness, an isolated feeling came between them. Thurston backed further into the corner, into the shadow. "No!" he exclaimed.

"Do not question me," Spenner said quickly. He felt a pain cross over his face, and his mouth and jaw twisted but he said, "Do you understand? You *see*, do you not? Can't you even guess?"

Thurston's body had begun to sag and he was sliding downward. A groan, horrible and deep, came from Thurston's throat, but he caught himself, bent over, and bolted forward as if charging someone. He swung out the door and was gone.

III

Chapter Twelve

An earthquake hit Port Bold the day before Johnson Buell arrived. The quake began in the northern tip of the peninsula and tore through the city, so Buell had to enter Port Bold from the east as the southern route was blocked by a road cave-in where the earthquake ended. The airport was on the east side of the city, and the first sight that Buell saw was vultures soaring overhead. The big birds had been attracted to the city since the earthquake and were stirred up by planes over the airstrip.

Thousands of survivors were fleeing the shambles of the city as the government ordered the evacuation for fear of contamination of the drinking water. The planes were landing without the aid of the control tower, which was not operating as a result of the earthquake. The planes were bringing in water along with blood, plasma, food, clothes, and other supplies and leaving with people evacuated to other parts of the peninsula.

Buell saw a convoy of army trucks rumbling along on the road which was the only open corridor to the city and which had been cleared for the transport of rescue and clean-up crews. As they passed, they slowed their pace and Buell asked if he could follow them into the city. They agreed but cautioned him to be careful, that they were demolition experts with over two thousand pounds of explosives to be used to demolish weakened buildings in danger of falling. On the road, they passed the refugees fleeing the city by cars, trucks or buses, making for the outlying countryside because the damage there was light. Many were walking, trying to buy, thumb, or bribe a ride and many of them carried chickens and pets and what few pieces of furniture they could manage. Several carried weapons, giving the procession the look of a defeated army.

Johnson Buell entered a city that was devastated. The twenty-six square block of the central business district was in rubble. Many buildings still standing were falling as the trucks and tanks rumbled past. Injured people, arms in slings, heads bandaged, were sitting stunned on curbstones or walking around in a daze. Others were attended to in makeshift hospitals set up in dusty parking lots or on dirty sidewalks. The city's inner hospital was only a pile of rock with crushed beds poking up at grotesque angles, and it was evident that the patients had perished with the beds. Many bodies still lay in the streets as rescuers worked tirelessly trying to identify the dead and then tossing them into large common graves.

Fires smoldered throughout the city but the firemen were ineffective because the water mains were broken and there was no electricity.

Johnson Buell went along to downtown Port Bold where the situation was becoming more stable and was the central location for the actions by the citizens. He made his way to the city hall, an identifiable building with the framework still standing but most of the roof and the walls blown out. One side was completely torn away and the bricks remaining were like jagged teeth around the hole. Buell made his way inside. Any office doors remaining were open and people were rushing about, all in a hurry, and clamorous conversations were called back and forth across the corridor.

Buell make his way through the crowd until he saw the mayor's name on one open door. He peered inside and saw a group of people in a half-circle around a desk, but he could not see the person seated beyond them. He moved in and to the side and then he saw the mayor, weary, but struggling with questions and answers and giving directions to the people before him. It all seemed chaotic for Buell heard talk of everything from medical aid, water discussions, shelter and emergency plans, help from another town, all spoken in a disorganized melting of babble.

Johnson Buell wondered, how do I begin in all this? He left the mayor's room and took a stairway down to the lower level where the situation was hectic but less so than the one upstairs. He looked into an open room which had the appearance and size of a large basement, but boxes were scattered all over the floor. A few men were moving the cartons about, setting them right, and stacking them in ordered piles. Buell approached one of the men. "How much damage did the quake do here?" he asked.

"Fortunately, not too much," the man replied. "These boxes were tumbled down and about, but they are sealed quite tightly."

"Are these valuable then? I notice you are placing them in a certain order."

"Old records mostly," the man answered, "and historical information, but we have to stack them to get to the rubble underneath."

"I do not wish to interfere," Buell said, "but would it be possible for me to look at certain of the records?"

"No," replied the man, "but they are not in order. They're all mixed up."

Johnson Buell began touring the room, moving amongst fallen plaster and wood, noting that the cartons were dated by years. He continued looking, avoiding the working men, until he saw one box dated twenty years ago. He went to another worker nearby and asked if he could take the box aside and look at it.

The worker seemed perplexed but shrugged his shoulders and said, "If you want to take the time." Buell pulled the box aside to a corner where other boxes were stacked and the working men were not around. He cut open the seal with a pocket knife and saw within a row of paper files and newspapers. They were musty and brittle with age and he carefully picked up the top newspaper which began with the first issue in January. He went through it, folding each page which was certain to tear if he handled it hastily. He went through several other newspapers still dated the month of January. He came to one on which the front page told of the unusual cold weather even for that time of the year, and then his eye caught a parallel story of a rescue ship that had brought refugees into Port Bold. The refugees were survivors from the ship *Bellmann* which had left Valiterra but had been sunk on the other side of the peninsula. On another page, a few names of the refugees were listed, but the story explained that the list was incomplete due to the suddenness of the tragedy. No Spenner or Whitmore was listed.

At the moment a man came rushing down the stairs. "Got to get out!" he shouted. "A gas line has broken and a fire has started! Evacuate immediately!"

Johnson Buell took a little more time to note the name of the reporter who wrote the story about the rescue ship. The name was on a fold of the newspaper and the letters had faded, but it looked like Herman. He folded the paper out, trying to see the name more clearly, and it looked like Sherman. A crashing sound came from the stairway and the acrid smell of smoke was filling the atmosphere. Quickly, Buell closed the box and dashed toward the stairway. He thought he was near the top of the stairway, but the smoke was thick and swirling and he could not see the upper corridor. Suddenly, he felt weak and dizzy and he gasped for air. He tried to go forward but stumbled. He could not get up and he was falling backwards. Then he felt someone at his arms. He was lifted up, grasped by heavy hands, and pulled forward. They were out of the building and Buell felt the tightness in his lungs give way and he began to breathe slowly and deeply. He glanced aside at the one who had helped him and he had to smile into the wrinkled, ruddy face of an old man with his coat over his head. The age of the man was deceptive for his body was strong and solid and his hands were as large as bear paws.

"Are you all right?" he asked Buell. "You took your time about coming up; you took a lot of smoke."

"I am all right," Buell answered but he gasped, "and thank you." He began breathing evenly and finally was able to say, "All for a bit of information I just had to have."

"Risky," the old man replied, "especially at a time like this. We cannot fight the fire because the water lines are broken."

Buell shook his head. He looked up at the city hall and saw the fire closing around the remaining remnant of the building.

"It is gone," the old man said. "It is gone."

Buell stared at the fire and sensed the loss expressed in the old man's words. "Much is gone and destroyed," he said to the old man in a soft voice. "Can you believe, though, that I was fortunate to come across, at this time, a newspaper that was twenty years old?"

The old man studied Buell with a surprised look on his face. "You mean, you were down there, taking a risk, for that?"

"Yes," Buell replied and then he looked quizzically at the old man. "You do not, by any chance, know of a newspaper reporter by the name of Herman or Sherman who used to work here about twenty years ago?"

The old man seemed amused. "You want him? Well, T. Sherman is still around. I was an active fireman in those days and T. Sherman would follow us around like a flea on a dog to every fire or disaster we were called to. I got along with him, but he certainly was aggressive and arrogant."

"Is he here then, in Port Bold?" Buell asked expectantly.

The old man nodded. "He is retired, too, and lives down by the port."

Buell thanked the old man once more and turned to leave.

"Say," the old man halted him, "are you going there? Do you think you can drive?"

"I am going to try," Buell replied. "I believe I can drive."

"Well, if you believe so, but be careful."

"I want very much to see and talk with T. Sherman."

The old man shook his head but said, "You will find him living right down along the sea." He waved as Buell made his way to the automobile.

Buell stumbled but he no longer felt weak or dizzy. As he drove away, he looked back and could see the old man still waving. And behind him, the city hall was enveloped in flames.

Buell made his way toward the seaport but he was driving through a maze. Many of the streets were torn apart, others were blocked off for any traffic.. He had to drive further northward and come around the city on its western side. He came to the coast line and here the road was bumpy and uneven, but he did manage to get through to the port. The sea was rough and the waters looked murky and churned about in dark eruptions. The earthquake made it chaotic here also. The boats looked a helpless sight, many were askew and lay at all angles while others were pulled from their moorings and were drifting on the water. The quake had caused a slight tidal pull and a few owners had been quick enough to take their boats and head out into the sea before the water in the port became too shallow and would have crushed the boats on the rocks. Several crafts had been wrecked in this way and their scattered splinters were strewn amongst the rocks.

Johnson Buell stopped where he was able to park his car and went down to the shore where he approached a group of men who were looking forlornly at the wrecked boats and trying to salvage any pieces. Buell came to them cautiously extending sympathy for their loss. He encouraged them to talk for a while, and when he felt they were at ease with him, he asked about the newspaper reporter. Readily, they told him where T. Sherman lived. They pointed to a house on a slight bluff overlooking the port and advised Buell that the reporter had aged and was not too well.

Indeed, T. Sherman was just that for he opened the door at Buell's knock and stood there, white-haired and wrinkled and plagued with arthritis for his knees were bent and shaking and a gnarled hand held on to a cane for support. His clothes were ill-fitting and rumpled and about the man was a stale odor that indicated that body and clothes had not often been cleaned. He led Buell slowly into the house and the place was ramshackled with overturned furniture, tilted pictures on walls, broken pottery and glass, and a blanket was stuffed into a large portion of window that had blown away. The place was cold, and T. Sherman picked up a chair, brushed off the dust, and invited Buell to sit.

When T. Sherman sat down, he took on a different appearance. The cane was placed aside, the body was not crooked or trembling and the white-haired head was raised high as he looked squarely at Buell. Buell was drawn immediately to the man's face, the wrinkles were there but the eyes were intense and sharp looking. Those eyes sparkled when Buell began, in a light vein, by acknowledging his reputation as a reporter but now, would he answer some questions?

"Of course, young man," Sherman answered in a gruff voice and he smiled. "Quite a rumble, wasn't it? I understand the center of town was hit hard."

"I just came from there," Buell said. "It suffered quite a bit of damage. Fire is of concern now as I heard the water pipes were broken. The city hall was burning when I left. It was quite disastrous."

"Might have to evacuate everyone then because of the water situation, especially if we get tremors and aftershocks, which will cause more damage."

"I assume you have seen and reported many disasters in your time, Mr. Sherman?"

Flickers of excitement appeared in his eyes and a tenseness settled on T. Sherman's face. "Did I!" he exclaimed. "I have seen them all, every type of calamity you can name, T. Sherman was there and got his story."

Buell would not hedge with this man, knew it would not be wise, and said he came to talk about the rescue ship that had made it to Port Bold twenty years ago. "You wrote the story," Buell went on, "and I wonder if you can remember and tell me about that night?"

"Of course, I remember," the reporter chuckled as if the question were an easy one. "I do not forget many of the stories I have written. I was on assignment that night. It was January and it was cold, so cold. We were neutral in the war and Port Bold was a safe port." T. Sherman paused and his mouth twisted in a comical smile. "That was some time ago. You want to know about it now?"

Buell nodded. "I am interested in that episode of the time because I am seeking information about someone who may have been involved. It is important for a client of mine. You see, I am a private investigator."

T. Sherman retained his odd smile. "I am glad to help if I can. Now the rescue ship came here with survivors of the *Bellmann* which had been torpedoed in one of the worse disasters of the war."

Buell had to interrupt. "The *Bellmann* had come from the city of Valiterra?"

"Yes," Sherman replied. "The refugees were brought here in the darkness of early morning. They were a pathetic lot, most of them in shock and crazed and needed immediate medical attention. They were taken to hospitals all over Port Bold—wherever beds and treatment were available."

Again, Buell interrupted with determination in his manner and voice. "But did you get any names or identities of any of these people?"

"We could get very few names," Sherman replied. "Everything was too chaotic and the medical help was the most important thing at the moment. We did get a partial list, a few names later from the hospitals of the survivors who could speak or remember their names. There was trauma all around."

"Can you recall any survivor with the name of Spenner or Whitmore?"

T. Sherman thought a moment. His eyes were gleaming but he shook his head. "No, I do not recall either name. I can tell you, though, that I did a number of follow-up stories about the rescue because, naturally, the shock of the disaster kept the interest high. I recall two of the most memorable stories I covered at the time. The most unusual story was from a refugee who actually wrote to me. He began writing to me after several of my articles about the disaster and rescue appeared in print. He was hospitalized and told me he thought my stories were real and had true understanding and he included a poem about the tragedy that he had composed himself. Imagine, a poet! Anyway, I printed the poem in my personal column and it was a big hit. That started his correspondence, and he wrote faithfully every week for about a year. The readers looked forward to his poems. If a week went by without his poem, I would get complaints from readers."

"What was his name?" Buell asked.

T. Sherman laughed. "You know, I never knew. I just called him The Poet. That was how he signed his correspondence and that was how he was known. It is a funny thing with a reporter, at least with me, that I felt the deepest commitment to protecting the man's identity, if that is what he wanted. He turned down my request to visit him in the hospital; said, no, he was too ill and preferred just to send me his poems.

"That was why I felt intrigued and puzzled when, many years later, he wrote and asked me to meet him. You see, he developed tuberculosis and was sent to a sanitarium on the outskirts of town. He told me that with his final poem. After that, I never heard from him until this letter asking me to meet him at the railroad depot. I was very much surprised because it had been so many years since I heard from him, but I was more surprised when he said that he was bringing in a political prisoner and I could get the entire story."

Buell's body became tense and he felt an excitement within him. "A political prisoner? That was what he said?"

"All he said; no more identity or facts. He just wanted me to meet him and take over the prisoner."

"What happened?" Buell asked urgently.

T. Sherman sighed. "Nothing. I waited and waited at that railroad depot and neither The Poet or anyone else ever showed up."

Buell felt the disappointment but he could not relax. "Do you know why?"

T. Sherman shook his head and the comical smile returned to his face. "That was where my reporter's good intentions failed me. By honoring The Poet's request for anonymity, I did not know his name or could I describe him. I went to the sanitarium, and all I could say was that he was a poet and I believed he had left the sanitarium with someone else. Naturally, my description was of no help. I had to wait until they checked all inmates to discover who was missing. This took time, of course, and when they finally came around, they asked, 'You are inquiring about two missing persons?'

" 'Yes,' I told them.

" 'Well, we have no one missing, but we have two who had gone without official leave. They have both returned and were placed in sick quarters, but one was very ill and passed away.'

" 'May I speak with the other one?' I asked.

"After consultation with several of the rulers, as I called them, I was permitted to see the second escapee. He was not The Poet, he told me right off. He said that The Poet had perished after the ordeal.

" 'What ordeal?' I asked him. Well, he told me quite a story, and I will try to tell you in his own words and in his own way:

" 'I was roommate with The Poet. You can call him that, but I never knew. He never said that he wrote poems. I just got to share the room with him and we were not acquainted enough to share confidences, so he never told me about himself. One day, he had been to a counseling session and returned to the room quite excited. He said the counselor's new helper was someone he recognized from way back and he was certain that he was a traitor who had escaped from Valiterra during the war.

" 'The Poet told me that he was going to contact a newspaper friend and bring the traitor to him. Escape, I said. That means escape! Of course, The Poet replied, and he asked my help. He could not do it himself. He said he was too sick and weak, but the two of us could manage it. We had only to get the traitor to the newspaperman at the railroad station in Port Bold.

" 'Well, we got out of our compound and found and threatened the counselor's assistant. The man was stunned when we overcame him and tied him up. He was taken by surprise; he could not speak at first. Then he began to talk, and he was begging to be released. He said he had been in a hospital, too. Not as a patient, but working there so he could study and become a counselor to sick people. His transfer to the sanitarium was his first major appointment and, please, he begged us give him this chance. The Poet was in charge and said no, so we tied up the hands of the man and taped his mouth then threw a blanket around him. We got out of the sanitarium by taking a service vehicle and going through that gate. We got to the depot and onto the train and headed for Port Bold. It was hard for The Poet and me, but I could see The Poet was determined. Yet, we had trouble. The man got loose and jumped the train. We saw and jumped after him, but a chase like that is too much for a tubercular, I'll say. We chased him through corn fields and clover. The man was making for the road beyond and we had to catch him before that. I think we would have caught him if we had not run into the hay patch. The hay was wet and the man set fire to it; it caused a large smoke screen, and The Poet and I were stymied. By the time we got around and it was clear enough, we could not see the prisoner at all. He was gone and we know not which way. If he got to the road, he probably got a ride, but it was the end of the chase for us.

" 'I think it did The Poet in. He collapsed and by the time I got around to getting help and getting us back here, it was too late for him. He never pulled through. I know he was disappointed that he could not bring the man in; it seemed to be important to him. If I ever leave this sanitarium, I will try to track him down; not for me, but for The Poet.' "

T. Sherman looked at Buell. His face was serious for a moment after the story ended, then he smiled and his eyes twinkled. "That is it, that's the story. I never followed up on this political prisoner because there was so little to go on. No name, description, or identity, and with The Poet gone, what was the story? A political prisoner? Who and from where? It also happened a few years after The Poet first wrote and his following was gone; the inquiries about him had faded and he was forgotten. You know, too, there was always other news and stories after that to occupy my column." T. Sherman paused. "I do not know if there is anything in all this for you. . . ."

"There is," Buell answered, "a great deal for me."

The statement brought another smile to the face of T. Sherman. "I said there were two memorable stories connected to the rescue ship from the *Bellmann*. The other was an interview with Miss Ida, a person one meets once in a lifetime. I met her a day or so after the refugees were brought in to the hospital, and I was allowed to interview her for a feature story. She seemed to have survived better than most of them and she was quite alert. In my story, I called her Miss Ida. The name stuck and everyone came to call her that. She still lives here on the bluff; the last house on the road. She is quite a woman, but . . . well, I do not want to tell her story. I am certain she will talk to you if you want an interview. She might be of help."

"I will see her," Buell said and rose immediately. He extended his hand to T. Sherman and thanked him.

"I would walk with you," T. Sherman said, "and, believe me, I would like to, but it is a slow and difficult process for me these days."

Buell said he understood and thanked T. Sherman profusely once again. He left T. Sherman's dwelling and walked to the last house on the road. A nurse opened the door. Buell identified himself as a private investigator and said he wished to talk with Miss Ida. He explained that T. Sherman had made the recommendation. The nurse was hesitant and a worried look appeared on her face. He heard her repeat his identity, "private investigator," in a whisper and then asked if there was any trouble. Buell assured her that there was no problem whatsoever, and his request was for personal reasons only. Although still hesitant, the nurse asked him to step inside. She told him that she was concerned because Miss Ida was under her nursing care as she was invalid and blind.

Johnson Buell was unprepared and surprised at this description of Miss Ida. He repeated his request for an interview but he added, "if possible." The nurse left him to check. She walked away and entered a side door a short distance from the entrance. Buell was left standing in an elaborate marble hallway with a mosaic tile floor. The decor was white and gold. Every accent of table, painting, mirror, vase, was perfectly attuned and looked like a picture where every piece was drawn in harmony and design. Yet, Buell noted that even so solid and heavy a structure was not exempt from the thrust of the earthquake for it contained cracks and tilted positions like an irregular line down through the perfect picture.

The nurse returned quickly and told Buell that Miss Ida would see him. He was shown into another elegant room, a sitting room as luxuriously furnished as the entrance but the room was dark. On the far side, he saw a lady seated in a small chair before a fireplace. The chair was covered with a velvet robe and she wore a heavy sweater. She was nice to look at, and Buell's gaze dwelt upon her. A certain refinement was her characteristic, and she sat poised and posture perfect. She was not young, but her skin was smooth and unblemished and her hair was lustrous, more gold than yellow, and was drawn back and rolled in so neat a chignon at the back of her neck that not a strand was misplaced. She placed a large book aside on a small table. Her face was immobile, not following her action.

"If you are wearing an overcoat, Mr. Buell," she spoke softly, "you had best keep it on. We have no heat or light; the earthquake has done that to us. Of course, I do not need light for reading." Her voice had risen into a slight laugh. She extended her hand forward and Buell moved closer to clasp it. Her hand was small and cold, and he noticed a pearl ring on her finger, an accessory matching the pearls in her ears.

"I am sorry to interrupt," Buell began but she laughed.

"Do not apologize," she answered. "Reading is the pleasure of my life, and I have more than ample time for it."

Buell advanced closer and sat by the fireside. It was warmer here and he unbuttoned his coat but did not remove it.

"May I ask what you are reading?" Buell still looked upon her, absorbed in the relaxed and serene beauty of her face. Her eyes were a luminous grey though blank and staring with a startled look.

She laughed again and explained. "I am reading Elizabethan verse. Braille edition, of course, and I also have several magazines in braille." She nodded her head to the side toward the table. Buell noted the stack of thin, brown-covered periodicals and on the top one could be seen a series of raised indentations that somehow were words.

Buell was surprised. "You like Elizabethan verse?"

"Very much," she replied. "That century of English literature was rich in harmony and quite expressive in detail. I find that their vision of life was very positive."

"I know little about it," Buell said. "I am sorry."

"Do not apologize again," she said lightly.

"Miss Ida," Buell began but paused. "May I call you that?"

"Of course, you may," she answered. "I proclaimed many years ago that I was to be called 'Miss Ida'." She hesitated. "You say you are a private investigator, Mr. Buell? I am happy to talk with you but why have you come? T. Sherman is an old and good friend, but if he could not tell you what you want to know," she paused once more to laugh, "well, I do not know how I can help."

"I did have a good talk with T. Sherman, but he referred me to you for additional information of 'your story' as he said." He hesitated as he heard her laugh, softly this time. "Miss Ida, you are from Valiterra, are you not?"

"Yes," she replied.

"Can you tell me why you came here and settled in Port Bold?"

"I came after the war," she said. 'Valiterra was defeated and lost. I managed to escape."

"Escape? How did you do that?"

"I had money to bribe myself out. I paid dearly, plus all the jewelry I had to get on the *Bellmann*."

Buell answered softly but evenly. "The *Bellmann* was sunk."

"Yes. It was disastrous in every way. I was a fortunate one who was thrown into the sea but managed to get onto a life raft and then picked up and brought here to Port Bold."

"Miss Ida, may I ask if your condition is a result of the *Bellmann* disaster? Were you injured then?"

She laughed heartily. "Heavens no! Then it was shock and exposure and a few broken bones, but what I am now is the result of something else, another disaster, may I say?" She paused. "Old T. did not tell you my story then?"

"No," Buell replied.

"My story is no secret. I have been crippled and blind for fifteen years. I was injured by a jealous man, a man I was to marry. He owned a lumber company here in Port Bold and was called The Colonel. He was older than I, but I did love him and prepared to make a good wife for him. Then Tim came along. He was my age and handsome, and tried to change my mind, but I would not. He was persistent and, of course, The Colonel found out about him and imagined the worst—that I was unfaithful to him. He plotted to kill Tim. He thought Tim was waiting for me at my place that night and killing him at such a rendezvous would just be murdering the other man, awaiting a tryst with his betrothed. Tim had never been to my place. As much as he pleaded, I would not have him. That night, my place was bombed and burned and only I, not Tim, was there. I was rescued and lived, miraculously, but left as I am today. The Colonel was unconsolable. I released him from the marriage promise, but he was so distraught and conscience stricken that his health deteriorated rapidly. He died weeping, and his only solace was to leave me his inheritance. I have never had concerns about money matters."

"You have quite a story, Miss Ida."

"Now T. Sherman might tell it differently," she said and laughed.

Buell reflected a moment and wondered how T. Sherman would tell her story. Yet, when he spoke, he said, "T. Sherman told me that he talked to you in the hospital after you were brought here by the rescue ship."

"I cannot forget that," she replied. "That gruff old man came up to me, a leer on his face and just stated that he wanted an interview. At first, I was taken back by his forwardness and arrogance, then I found myself accepting his boldness for I sensed a reliability in the man and that he was asking nothing for his personal vanity. We became good friends, and I have liked and respected T. Sherman ever since."

Buell decided to begin his real questions. "Miss Ida, do you remember Collis Whitmore? At one time, he was mayor of Valiterra."

"He was mayor at the time of the war," she answered quickly.

"Do you know what happened to him? I understand there was no trace of him when the war ended."

She began to tuck the robe closer around her. "Would you place another log on the fire, Mr. Buell?" she asked. "It seems to be getting colder."

Buell obliged as she began. "That is strange for we were picked up by the same rescue ship."

"The same rescue ship?" Buell asked, surprised. "You mean he was on the *Bellmann*?"

"Certainly. He was struggling in the water and I helped to pull him onto the life raft."

"You pulled him out of the water?" Buell asked, still surprised.

"I did," she answered in an even tone.

"Was he hurt or injured?"

"Not that I could see. Oh, he was dazed and shocked like all of us and he looked like a drowned animal but I do not think he had anything seriously wrong with him."

"Did you speak to him, Miss Ida?"

"I said only once, 'Mayor Whitmore'. He looked at me and seemed frightened but he said nothing."

"You called him by name and he responded?"

"Yes."

"What happened then? Was he taken to the hospital?"

She shook her head. "When we got into port, a large van came

214

to take us to a hospital, but mid-way, he made a stir. As I said, he seemed more frightened than anything. He rose up and fought off those that were helping us, and he jumped out of the van and disappeared."

Buell sat silent for a moment before he asked, "You never saw him after that?"

"No," she replied.

"And you are certain it was Mayor Collis Whitmore?"

"Yes. I am certain."

"Miss Ida, you say you never saw or heard about him after that?"

"No. I settled here in Port Bold. Soon, I met the Colonel . . ." she paused, "but I have told you that story."

"I know it has been many years, Miss Ida, but can you describe Collis Whitmore as you knew him?" While Buell asked he drew forth the picture sketch of James Spenner from his portfolio. He looked at it as he listened to her description and tried to imagine twenty years of physical change.

"The mayor was a young man then, about thirty-five. He was not a tall man, but neither was he stout. He slouched a bit, had dark brown hair and eyes—surprising eyes for they were set wide apart."

Before he left, Johnson Buell promised to send Miss Ida any books he could find on Elizabethan verse. Braille, of course.

To Johnson Buell, the knowledge unfolded like the petals of a flower; and when all was known, it was amazing that it was so simple. All the anguish and worry and despair seemed so overdone as the answer, once known, was so ordinary that Johnson Buell concluded that his suppressed attraction for Randi Papin had made him prolong the investigation and kept him from admitting the truth.

Yet, Johnson Buell could prove nothing. What he had uncovered could not convict anyone. Any lawyer could mock the evidence and make it all circumstantial. Buell needed a confession.

He went to see Randi Papin once more and, again, she met him on the patio. He had arrived first this time and had taken the same chair as he did before. He rose when she came out through the French doors. Her dark hair was perfectly dressed as if it always retained its wavy coiffure. She wore a dress of deep red, russet, in color, but it was cool looking with short sleeves, no collar, and a scalloped neckline. She was smiling as she approached him. Her gaze was full upon him, but she looked cautiously at him, studied his face earnestly, and then quietly looked away.

She did not sit down, instead, she suggested they walk. He agreed and they started down the gravel path. They said nothing, but walked silently along. The day was warm and the perfumed scent of flowers and lawn was carried over them by a soft breeze. Buell was thinking of the first time he walked here; it was night time and there was excitement and horror, and the body of Ralph Barnes, smeared with blood, lay across the pathway.

Johnson Buell had something to say but he struggled to begin. Finally, he spoke although his voice was low and the tone was wobbly. "Randi, why did you kill Ralph Barnes?"

They stopped suddenly. She did not look at him; her face bent downward. Her body had tensed but she did not tremble. In a little while, she began to walk once more and he followed but said nothing. Then she said, speaking softly and with surprising calm, "You can prove that?"

"Yes," he replied.

"Then an explanation is necessary," she stated.

He walked closer to her. "You are the only one who could have done it," he said. "The guests were gone, there was no prowler, no alarms were broken or sounded, so it had to be someone in this house. Your father was out front taking care of the last of the departing guests. Your mother had gone to the kitchen. Gloria was on the terrace with Mr. Barnes and walked with him a short way but left him when he did not want her company to the guest house."

"I was in my room," she said hurriedly. "I went there as soon as the party was over."

"No, Randi," he said softly, "you went first into the gun room, took the pistol and left by the door in that room. You confronted Ralph Barnes coming down the path," he hesitated as he was about to say, 'shot him', but uttered instead, "used the pistol on him and then returned the same way through the gun room and waited until the others were assembled in the living room and then you entered last."

They stopped once more. She said nothing but still did not look at him. She was able to stand very still. It was an uneasy quietness, however, not the kind that comes with relaxation or the strained excitement that accompanies concentration, but rather a stillness that closes in and isolates oneself.

"Randi?" he asked, awaiting her reply.

"Why would I kill the man I was to marry?" she asked.

"That I do not know; only you have that answer." He paused and then said evenly, "I note that you just said 'the man you were to marry' not 'the man I love'. There is a difference. To me, you have made an error and I let you know that I am aware of it."

"You need not consider my feelings," she said, "but you believe that what I said is a motive to kill someone?"

"No," he answered, not embarrassed to say it to her.

"And you can still accuse me?" All the while, she had not looked at him. She looked away into the distance not seeing anything directly.

"Because it is the only explanation. I thought carefully over the testimony each member of your family gave me and you are the only one who could have killed Ralph Barnes."

"Such a statement requires proof, you know."

"Yes," Buell replied slowly, "and it is found in the identical rings you and Gloria have."

"But you found hers here on this path."

Buell shook his head. "No, Randi, that was your ring. It came off either when you dropped the gun or, perhaps, Ralph Barnes pulled it off, trying to take the gun from you. You ran away and you did not have time to return to retrieve it in the dark or else you were not aware it was gone until later. Fortunately for you, the ring was not found until the next morning and, meanwhile, you took Gloria's ring and wore it as your own." He stepped closer. "You see, Randi, I saw Gloria's ring on her finger the very night of the murder. Gloria admitted that she had had several cocktails that evening and was upset with your mother and I believe she was unmindful about the ring. She actually could not recall having it on after the murder. She did not miss the ring until the following morning when she saw that it was gone. Our crime unit found the ring the next day and I, too, assumed it belonged to Gloria."

"You did not suspect her?"

"No," Buell answered. "Not when I went to the laboratory and saw the ring. I saw the same kind of ring on your finger the next day when I came to question you."

Her voice became softer. "You did not believe the ring I was wearing was mine?"

"No. It had to be Gloria's ring you were wearing. She was wearing the ring the night I came here right after the shooting. Therefore, the ring we found was yours."

"The rings are identical," she said and her voice became softer.

"I know what I saw, Randi," he replied.

"That does not sound like proof. It may be your theory, but it is really only one's word against another."

Johnson Buell nodded his head. "Yes. It is circumstantial evidence. Any good lawyer could free anyone on such charges. There would always be that 'reasonable doubt' and no jury, I think, could convict."

"Then what is your case? Do you want to arrest me?"

"All I can hope for is a confession." He wished that she would look at him. He wanted to look into her soft eyes and he knew he would even plead with her.

She refused to turn and look at him. Her scultured head remained taut and she continued to look away. At last, she spoke and her voice was lower and more even. "This is your first case, is it not?"

"Yes," he replied.

"You want to do well; it is important to you, to make the most of an opportunity."

"Yes," he said again.

"Should I make a confession, then? To please you and further your career?"

He was silent for a moment; her words startled him. He tried to answer with determination. "No, I never thought of that. I make my decision on the knowledge I have."

"Yet, you admit it cannot convict anyone?"

"That I do."

Silence came between them. The breeze had died away but the fragrance of the garden lingered. Buell was waiting for her to speak, but the silence continued, and he was aware that he was becoming nervous and agitated. A sound came at last but it was not speech; it was a harrowing cry overhead from birds in a tree. Buell looked up to see a large raven that had raided a nest and held a nestling in its beak. The cries came from the parent birds who could no nothing but protest. Soon many birds of different species flew into the tree

218

and began a continuous chirping against the murderer. It was a raucous clatter, but then, surprisingly, a song sparrow amongst them
began its song. The notes were clear and sweet and trembled in the
bird's little throat, but it did not cease its singing. The chorus changed
and other birds began singing, too, remembering, perhaps, that they
are singers of life, not death.

Randi Papin spoke then. "Allow me a short time to get ready,"
she said, "then you may arrest me." She said no more but turned
and walked away. She strode slowly back along the gravel path onto
the terrace and through the French doors. She closed them behind
her and disappeared, as if into a mist.

Harvey Papin used the entire legal department of his firm to
defend Randi. Their collective minds and tactics were impressive,
and soon they accumulated that smug arrogance that assured them
that their case was easy and they could not lose. They pressed for an
early trial, claiming that to be in the best interest of all.

The prosecution, however, was struggling and had a difficult
time. They sensed the circumstantial nature of the case and they had
no clear evidence against Randi Papin. They knew Johnson Buell's
testimony about the rings was tenuous at best. Buell urged the prosecution to delay the trial as long as possible because he hoped that
time, with its attendant partners of impatience, weariness and frustration, would force a confession from Randi Papin. Randi Papin,
however, remained firm and reliable. True to her defense, she did
not give in.

Above all, without a confession, the prosecution could not establish a motive. Finally, they settled on the motive of jealousy—jealousy
of Ralph Barnes' attraction to Randi's sister, Gloria. The idea was
made plausible by the erratic behavior of Gloria herself. She admitted
his attraction to her, her flirtation with him, and she was confused
by the identical rings. She could not definitely identify her own or
Randi's or could she corroborate Johnson Buell's story that she had
her ring on that night of the wedding party. She simply did not
remember.

However, Gloria's fiancé finally arrived from England to stand
by his fiancée and her family as he announced. Johnson Buell found
him to be a likeable chap, a very precise person, and unshakeable.
Buell got the notion that this English hairdresser could more than
handle the volatile Gloria. He openly defied any reporter asking about

the jealousy angle, and he would clamp his long arms around Gloria and they would parade about in a constant embrace of love and affection.

When Harvey Papin saw him, a blanched look came over his face. He seemed appalled, but he smiled and said, "Well, just so he does not go into selling ball bearings."

When the hairdresser saw Donna Papin, he treated her equally tempestuously. Donna Papin had a relapse after Randi was arrested. She wailed again about the "killing of a dear boy" and "now another heartache and burden for Randi!" She had several lace handkerchiefs by her bedside. "We were to have a wedding!" she would cry and fall back, prostrate, amongst a heap of soft pillows.

"Mother!" the fiancé hairdresser called out as he lifted her up, limp and shaking, from her pillows and gave her a swift slap on the back. "Face up!" he went on. "Be firm!" He had her sitting up and, if she began to fall back, he would slap her again. "Never give up!" She responded rapidly in kind. She automatically sat straight when she heard him coming and, in a short time, she left her bed for a chair. When he approached her, he had only to smile slightly with that "stiff upper lip" attitude and she would look rigidly at him without a tear in her eyes.

The trial went as Johnson Buell had thought. The Papin family was strong and united and firm in their support and protection of Randi. The defense firmly established the "beyond a shadow of a doubt" measure, and, if there had been any doubt, Randi Papin erased it when she took the stand.

On the day she testified, Johnson Buell entered the court and crept into a seat in the last row. He could not take his eyes from her. She never lost her self-control. She did not crack, but he sensed a winding down, a crumbling within her. To compensate, she became more and more stoic, tempering all movements like steel and taking inward every bit of reserve strength she had to keep her body and mind from breaking. Only her eyes reflected the change. They seemed to enlarge, to become more hollow, and to lose their glimmer and all hope of joy. At last, then, she was free.

Johnson Buell, the young detective, lost his first case. Long afterwards, he wondered if her appeal had made him err. He wondered how he had misjudged. Perhaps he should not have arrested her, knowing the evidence, but he was certain of her guilt. He had used feelings and emotions, and he had calculated and trusted that the basic human tenants of honesty and the belief that right would prevail would be forthcoming. He needed a confession from Randi Papin; he trusted for it, but it never came.

Randi Papin was beautiful, poised and soignée, yet what did he know of her beginnings? The adoption process erased her heritage and thrust her into the life of the Papin family. It was hers to accept, but could there have been something in her unknown past? Something from generations of humans, that was dark and evil and an undeniable part of her? Could that evil come forward, arouse resentment, and even turn her to kill?

Always, her quietness had absorbed him; he thought it part of a subdued femininity that made her alluring especially to him. Yet, could that quietness be that of an onlooker, one not really included in the game, so to speak, and the Papin life was one she subconsciously rejected or felt herself unworthy or unqualified for participation? With Ralph Barnes, she would have continued in the same lifestyle, but did she decide, at the last moment, to make a break rather than continue as an alien with Ralph Barnes in a way of life she deeply resented and hated?

After the trial, Randi left the Papins. She went on her own to another part of the country. She stated that she would take care of herself, find some employment and, regardless of what it was, it would sustain her. The case was turned over to other investigators and detectives, but there never was another suspect in the killing of Ralph Barnes.

Johnson Buell made his final entries into his report for Grant Deakins. He closed the file and tucked it away into his luggage for he was preparing to return to Valiterra. He made his last entry in his own personal records also, and he made them as follows:

> So they said to him, "What is your name and he said, "James Spenner."
> And they said to him, "Your name shall no longer be called James Spenner, but Collis Whitmore, for you have served as mayor and have struggled with God and men, and have not prevailed."

Chapter Thirteen

Collis Whitmore went straight to the Old Road. It was an odd road, one block in length. There were only two buildings on the block, a church and a small parsonage. He stopped at the corner and stared at the buildings. A church—he had not expected that. The church was neat looking, yellow brick with brown trim and a low hedge of evergreens on each side of the entrance. The parsonage was the same kind of picture, a small yellow brick building with the brown trim and the green hedge. Everything about was quiet; no one was seen and the entire vicinity was empty.

Whitmore left the car and walked up the pathway to the church door. He paused before the sign next to the door and read the words:

CHURCH OF CHRISTIAN WORSHIP
SERVICES 8:00 AND 10:30 AM
REVEREND CHARLES ORCOTT

Whitmore stepped back and stared unbelievingly at the words before him. A feeling of frustration came over him, as if he had started a journey but had not come to the place he planned. The frustration made him feel tired; he sensed a first edge of failure. Slowly, he sat down on the church step, the only place to which he could fall.

What was he doing? Chasing a possible murderer and what had he found? A crippled Jonas Shelby and now Charles Orcott, a minister. He was getting nowhere; he was going about this entire matter in the wrong way. His head began to ache, and he bent it forward to try to ease the pain, but it still throbbed and he covered his face with his hands.

All of a sudden, he heard the sound of a door being closed. It was not distant; in fact, it came from the parsonage next door. Whitmore looked up and stared, aghast, at the figure who stepped out. He was an unexpected sight in a long, black coat and a large hat.

Whitmore quickly saw the man as he had seen him before, outside the Hillberry Funeral Home and on the outskirts of the crowd at Memorial Park. The man was coming toward him as easily and as quietly as he had moved before.

Whitmore rose as the man came closer. He stared at the face under the black hat. The eyes were dark and keen with a steadfast look, yet the whole face appeared benign for the cheeks were puffed from a closed smile. The expression did not change as the man came closer.

Collis Whitmore looked back at him, just as steadily, and then he whispered, "Charles Orcott? But it is Reverend Orcott, is it not?"

The man bowed his head and then extended his hand. "It is," he replied in a deep resonant voice, "and, Collis, how are you? I saw you approach."

"I have seen Jonas Shelby," Whitmore said slowly. "I found you through him."

"Poor Jonas," Orcott replied. "I call on him many times and have through these years."

"He said you saved him."

"Yes, but, unfortunately not as he should be."

"He has not forgiven."

Orcott nodded and his smile waned. "I know. He possesses much bitterness. My efforts to overcome that have not been successful, but I cannot give up." The eyes looked directly upon Whitmore but the smile returned as he spoke. "Come," he said, "we will go inside and talk." He took a key from a large chain dangling at his waist and unlocked the church door. The interior was cold and the rows of dark pews were empty, but there was not a sense of stillness or quietude. Whitmore had a feeling of some movement, some life, as he followed Charles Orcott down the aisle. Their shadows were wavering and Whitmore glanced upward and wondered if the delicate movements could be caused by the candle flickering high above in the sanctuary lamp. The flame was tiny, but it was bright orange and weaved against all sides of its glass holder.

"It is nearing the end of Pentecost," Orcott said as they passed the altar and pulpit adorned with green paraments. "It is a long season for the church, but it is the season of growth and life." Orcott's voice was so smooth and low that he almost sang the words. He turned around and waited for Whitmore to join him. A glow had entered

Orcott's eyes and they sparkled. His smile become wider and his cheeks swelled more like a light dough and became tinged with a pink color.

"Green for so long," Orcott went on waving his arm at the paraments, "but then we go to Advent and the purple color. Purple is for repentance, but I must say that I love that color." He cast a glance at Whitmore. "Perhaps it is because I love repentance also. Collis, we have purple on the altar and pulpit and a hanging Advent wreath right overhead," he pointed upward, "with three purple candles and one pink. A beautiful period, beautiful for the church."

Whitmore could not grasp the satisfaction or the gladness that had come over Charles Orcott. In fact, Whitmore stepped back. He surveyed the area Orcott was describing; he saw the richness of the cloths but they covered flat pieces with straight angles and hung limp at the corners. Green, purple—he could not imagine an aesthetic change. He looked upward as Orcott was telling of the wreath but he saw only a hook high in the ceiling which probably held the wreath.

Orcott raised his hand to bid Whitmore to continue to follow him. "My office is here to the side." They moved out of the sanctuary and into a small hallway. Orcott opened another door and led the way into a pleasant room. A large desk occupied most of the room but there was adequate space for a black leather couch and two chairs. What caught Whitmore's eye, however, were books. Books lined every space on shelves around the room. They stood straight and even to the edge in perfect standing order. Their bindings were a mirage of colors in red, blue, green, and brown, each color assigned a different shelf and Whitmore's first thought was that it all reflected a military inclination.

Whitmore sat down in one of the chairs, just across from the desk, and looked at Orcott as he removed his hat and coat. Orcott's hair was white and thick, and his body was heavier than it seemed under the dark coat. He still was dressed in black, the color of his suit, but it could not disguise a figure just beginning to slide into overweight. There was a softness about his body, a padded lining that was not yet fat except for a slight pouch over his stomach and hands that were as plump as his cheeks.

"So, Charles, you have become a minister?" Whitmore spoke.

Orcott seated himself but did not reply instantly. He looked at

Whitmore; it was a careful look and the sparkle remained in his eyes. He nodded his head and then answered, "Yes."

Whitmore hesitated before he spoke again. "You followed me."

Orcott nodded again. "I could not believe it was you, Collis. I was merely verifying the truth."

"Why didn't you just pay a call? Come to the estate?"

The two men looked upon each other. Orcott's gaze remained careful and his keen stare was direct but hesitant. "I would never come to you, Collis, unless, of course, there was a change."

"A change?" Whitmore repeated. "What does that mean? A change in me? Do you consider that I have been gone for twenty years?"

"I know," Orcott replied, "and you look well enough for all that."

Whitmore had a sudden thought, but he asked cautiously, "And why would you not come to the estate? Is there any reason that keeps you away?"

Orcott shook his head and laughed lightly. "There would be no reason to come there unless, as I said, there was a change."

"I asked what kind of change? Were you thinking of change as a religious man?"

"Perhaps so," Orcott responded, "but that involves things like forgetting, forgiving, and, above all, repentance. In a sense, they all go together."

"And you would not come to see me because of these *things*?" Whitmore asked and his voice was brittle.

Orcott smiled at him and laughed again. "No, because I had no way of knowing. How could I? You see, Collis, you have it wrong. These changes were an unknown in you; therefore, they would have to be within me, if I wished to approach you. See?"

Whitmore blinked his eyes. "I do not understand religious stuff."

Orcott shook his head. "The changes that I speak of are not in you, Collis, but in me. It is I who must be possessed with forgetting, forgiving, and repentance."

"Towards me?" Whitmore asked furtively.

"Yes," Orcott replied, "towards you."

Whitmore stared at Orcott but he could not return the smile. "Does that mean you have not forgotten or forgiven?"

"No. I did that a long time ago, Collis. I forgave you. You were gone then. Away. And perhaps that made my confession easy. Now you are back, you have returned here, and I had to actually see you and look upon you to know if my forgiveness was genuine. I had to know if my thoughts and feelings would change."

"And?" Whitmore asked softly.

Orcott smiled and the sparkle gleamed in his eyes. "The feelings did not change, Collis."

Somehow, Whitmore dared not attempt a querrying look at Orcott and he hung his head. Uneasiness came over him, and he had to speak slowly when he said, "I came here to see you, Charles, and I will confess it—that I thought you might be a murderer. When you began by telling me that you would not come to the estate. . . ."

"Murderer?" Orcott interrupted and his eyes opened wide with surprise.

Whitmore answered quickly. "But that was before I knew you were this, a minister, in a church. I had no idea of that."

"But murderer?" Orcott asked again, still in surprise.

Whitmore nodded, but he could not look at Orcott. "You see, I thought you might have killed Gessie."

"Gessie? However did you come to think that?"

"I believe Gessie was murdered. Lester told me so."

"Gessie died long ago. Lester was just a boy, so young."

"I know," Whitmore replied and he still answered quickly and sharply, "but I believe him. He saw a man in the house that night, in Gessie's room, and Lester saw the man strike her. Everyone believed that Gessie fell and struck her head. I believe my boy."

Orcott's face became puzzled. "Well, that I never knew about the man."

His gaze was steady as he went on. "You believe that I was the man, Collis? You said so."

Whitmore said nothing.

Orcott went on, "I was away at the time of Gessie's death. I was doing mission work abroad. . . ."

Whitmore heard his words, "doing mission work abroad."

"I was gone for several years," Orcott still was speaking. "I heard of Gessie's death when I returned but there was no talk or opinion that someone had killed her. Collis, how did you think that I . . .

"I know now that could not be. Yet, I am trying to find out if I can. I am connecting her murder with me. I believe she was killed because of me, because of what I had done. There were three who knew what happened that night that Valiterra was lost—Jonas Shelby, Paul Arlan, and you. I thought it would be one of you. I have seen you and I have seen Jonas Shelby and I know that such a thing was not possible for either of you."

"That leaves Paul Arlan. Do you really think that of him, Collis?"

"I do not know, but I must talk to him."

Orcott shook his head. "I cannot help you because I have lost contact with him. I know nothing about him, and I have no idea where he would be." Orcott leaned forward. "Collis, can you possibly prove anything, after all this time?"

"I have to try," Whitmore replied.

"Should you find anything, Collis," Orcott asked slowly, "what would you do?"

Whitmore hesitated and his shoulders shrugged as he pondered the question. "Well," he said and hesitated again. "I guess there would be some kind of judgment, a reckoning would have to be made."

Charles Orcott leaned back in his chair. Oddly, this position made his stomach and waist protrude in a half-moon bulge of flesh. He crossed his arms before him and they lay relaxed and solemn like resting on a soft pillow. He closed his eyes and his face settled into a serious look of meditation. He looked contented, like an idol.

"Collis," he said at last, "I believe you are foolish to pursue this matter. I discovered many years ago that it is worthless to seek retribution. I should say it is worthless for man to seek retribution. Leave that to a power that knows and judges differently than we do. There is compensation in this life, Collis, but, perhaps, not always as we would have it. The judgments may be incomprehensible to us, but we must believe and accept them."

"That is easy for you to say, Charles—now that you are a minister. You are spiritual."

"But it was not easy to become that; it was the most difficult road I could have chosen. I stepped into it and I wanted to be a minister, but I was a great distance from being a dedicated servant. Often, it is a long process and can even be painful. It was thus for me. I made a quick vow but conversion is not that simple or easy. It takes a long time, Collis, for some men to have any resemblance of feeling that they are right with God. I began with the deletion of my possessions. I gave up everything, little though it was. And I thought that would

227

place me in high esteem. I thought I could be doubly blessed to give up all and follow Him, but He knows what He seeks in each man. I, being deprived and poor, was only a framework; I was deprived and poor within myself. Yet, I was caught now; I was committed to Him, but I could not find Him.

"I became tormented by visions and dreams. I *saw* Him in those visions and dreams, but, you know, I never saw His face. His back was to me, yet I knew it was Him. Always, He was walking away from me, but I had a clear sense that He bade me follow Him, that I was to go along after Him.

"But I began to think that I could never catch Him or walk beside Him. I began to believe that I was rejected, that I was not wanted or worthy. Sometimes, your very soul has to be ripped away, for you know what happened to me at that time? I became intolerant. I blasted away at every unrighteousness of others. I clamped down on sinners. I berated unbelievers. Once again, I thought I would be blessed but that assurance still did not come to me. I was really struggling with evil. The evil one always takes on one man, never ten or a thousand. He takes the soul he desires to tempt into a desert or a lonely place and, there, strives to take him apart. Yet, there was a sense, a small cord of strength within, that this temptation was a heavenly appointment. I believed that because I was seeking so desparately for something that I knew was *there*, something that He wanted of me, but I could not obtain it. I prostrated myself, begging for the mode, the way, to what I could not see or understand. Regeneration became a complete mystery.

"Then I decided not to seek but to accept. I would accept whatever was given and within my heart say, 'thank you' to Him for that, even if it meant seeing ever after only the back of Him. I accepted that He conforms all men as He wishes to fulfill His purpose. The will is His, not mine."

Orcott paused as his deep voice quivered. "Only then did I become filled with a deep feeling of security and trust. I knew that I was stronger than ever before. My denials and self-righteousness were meaningless. The struggle and the abominations I had collected were over and gone. Something, some feeling, was sustaining me, and I had a sense that I was moving in the right direction. It took time, Collis, to become a believer."

Whitmore had remained silent, listening, as Charles Orcott

poured out his testimony in his deep and resonant voice. It was compelling to hear Orcott speak, but Whitmore felt troubled inside of himself. His body was tense and he backed as far as he was able into the chair."I am amazed, Charles," he said at last and his voice sounded hollow, "to see you in these surroundings and to hear your story. I never thought of you as a minister. You were a military man, completely. In fact, the best I had. If it was so difficult, why did you become this?"

"I tried to serve you well, Collis," Orcott replied. He thought for a moment, then answered carefully. "That is a profound question, you know—to ask why a man becomes a minister. Yet, I might answer that *you* made the decision for me."

"Me?" Whitmore asked and risked a quick look at Orcott. "You mean because of what I did?" he added slowly.

Orcott did not answer directly but began by saying, "The night Valiterra fell, Collis. That was it. Many years ago.—"

"Twenty," Whitmore interrupted, not knowing if he spoke just to say something or if he advertently wished to halt the words of Orcott.

Orcott went on and repeated in agreement. "Twenty years ago, but it is as vivid to me now as the time it occurred."

"The defeat?" Whitmore asked hurriedly. The troubled feeling brought on a heavy beating inside of him, on his left side, under his heart.

"Yes, it was the defeat," Orcott answered solemnly. "I saw so much death and suffering the likes of which I, then a military man, had not seen–or hope ever to see again. I called them 'my men' for they were of utmost concern to me. I knew their capabilities, I knew their courage; they were men of great fortitude. It mattered not that we were less in numbers than the enemy, for I believed one of 'my men' was equal to five of theirs—if we were given a *chance*, a fair chance.

"I had the entire western flank of Valiterra defended. We were entrenched in those mountains and even the horrible winter weather was a help to us, but every outpost and entrenchment was given away. I know we could have held out and then driven them back, but we were given over by deception. They knew just where to find us, they wasted nothing, and they dug us out or burned us and I saw 'my men' slaughtered and roasted.

229

"I had to call retreat but even then they were valiant; 'my men' did not go berserk. They held themselves and retreated in good order. They tried to dig other trenches in the frozen ground as they backed away. They used stakes, pieces of weaponry, stones and boulders, any defense was permissable, but they could not hold. The enemy came after us as if in a trance. They were running and stumbling but they came on relentlessly, shouting for massacre. They came out of the snow storm like a specter, coming on us like a pack of wild dogs. We still made an effort; we made for garrison headquarters where equipment was kept. If we could have gotten that equipment, and especially ammunition, we still may have been able to turn the tide, but you know what we found, Collis? The place was locked, securely locked! It was deserted! A strategic area and no one was there! It was not planned that way. I know, for I made those military plans. That place was *never* to be evacuated or closed.

"After that, we could only run. The only direction left was toward the river, over the bridge, and into the city. We hoped to make some kind of a stand to try to save Valiterra. But even there, on the bridge, 'my men' were cut off because the exit tower had been taken and they were trapped. The bridge could not hold the weight of the men, and when it collapsed, the river was filled with drowning men, many dying in the icy waters. Still, in the face of the enemy and death itself, 'my men' went down *singing*. Can you believe that, Collis, singing and shouting our anthem? They were brave but doomed because they were betrayed. Yet they went down declaring 'Pro Patria'!"

Orcott's voice choked and he was stilled. He shook his head vigorously as if in disbelief. "That, as you asked, Collis, is what made me a minister. It was then I made a promise that I would serve Him forever if I survived. Do you know what it is, Collis, to lose everything? To see all things gone before your very eyes, and all that is left within you is one cry of 'I will, if He will'!"

"Charles," Whitmore whispered but he said no more.

Orcott began to speak again. "So I became like Jephthah, that shrewd warrior of the Old Testament, but in reverse. He was proud to lead his people, but he was pushed into a rash vow. Jephthah had success but it cost him a burnt offering. My vow was for myself. I have had no regrets about my decision, believe me. It has given me the strength to accept all the terms of life."

Whitmore felt the tenseness within him once again and the heavy feeling pressed harder under his heart. "How can anyone come to terms with life? For some, there cannot be reconciliation."

"No, Collis, it can be for everyone and I have found it."

"In this way?" Whitmore asked. "The church?"

"Not necessarily," replied Orcott.

Collis Whitmore lowered his head. He was not crying, but his eyes were soft with hurt and humiliation. He shook his head as if trying to discount some thoughts or words that came to him. He tried to raise his head, to look at Charles Orcott, but he could not. In a whisper, he said, "I sold out, you know?"

Orcott sat motionless; he did not waver. There was silence for the moment, then he replied, "I know. I knew twenty years ago."

"I gave away your positions on the mountains. I gave orders to close the garrison headquarters. I pushed your retreat."

"I tried to find you, Collis. I went to your compound but found only Jonas Shelby and Paul Arlan there. I told them of your betrayal and we tried to hunt you down. Jonas was shot at one entrance where the enemy was breaking through. He could not run for his legs were shot nearly off. I could only pull him away and we were able to drag ourselves to safety. Paul Arlan went to the other entrance underground trying to find you there.

"I did escape through the underground entrance," Whitmore said softly. "I guess I was just ahead of Paul Arlan. When I got up to the street, the people were there crowded as a mob and I stepped in and moved with them. We got to the port and onto the ship *Bellmann*. It was sunk, you know, but once again," Whitmore paused and his voice shook, "I was saved and was taken with other refugees to Port Bold. I lived there and in several places these past years."

Orcott's eyes blinked and he asked, "Why did you do it, Collis?"

Whitmore fell back in the leather chair and it crunched from his weight. He was trembling again and he rested his head on his hand. "Why did I do it, you ask? For the very reason that it all failed. I thought I could save the people, the city, your army, Charles. I gave away all our protection; I surrendered it for mercy or what I thought would be mercy. I made the error that after I gave my pledge, I found that I did not fully comprehend theirs. They demanded the ultimate—everything—and I had nothing left to bargain with, not even the very least of a moral request that justice be upheld. I gave up even that. You see, Charles, I should have known that there is a quality within some which cannot and will not be destroyed. I had forgotten, quite simply, that there will always be fighters."

Whitmore wished that he could raise his head and look beyond Charles Orcott once more at the mirage of red and blue and green that was the backdrop of the book shelves. He wanted to see the colors floating before his eyes even though the books they identified were immovable, straight and firm. But he could not look up. His hand held his head but it could not lift it. "What do you think of me now?"

"What can I think, Collis? You are not the only one who ever did what you did, but you were of our time."

"All the things you told me today, yet in none of your words did you condemn me."

"I said I forgave."

"For yourself, Charles, you can speak, but not for the thousands of others can you say 'I forgive'."

"Then I cannot condemn you for them either."

"I came here because I believe I have a mission," Whitmore said and shook his head. "I still must try to find the truth about Gessie. I cannot give it up, Charles. I believe I have a duty, a responsibility, and for Lester's sake."

"That is your road, then, Collis, and if you continue to follow it, you must accept all the bricks and stones upon which you trample."

"It is only one death that I seek to know about."

"Collis, have you not understood that what I have told you concerns one death also and that is the death of Christus? He had to die to give a very simple message of forgiveness and charity."

Whitmore shook his head once again. "I cannot, Charles," he whispered and put both his hands against the chair to push himself up.

"Can I help you?" Orcott asked as he rose too.

"No, no," Whitmore replied but he struggled and, at last, caught the desk top and stood straight. He reached across the desk to shake Orcott's hand. "Thank you," he said.

"Will you come to see me again?" Orcott asked.

"I do not know because I do not know what is ahead of me."

They walked out of the office and into the church, following the passage they made when entering. They strode softly and lightly down the aisle in the complete silence of the sanctuary. They stopped beneath the sanctuary lamp and Whitmore knew that Charles Orcott would go no further with him.

"It has been a long journey for me, Collis," Orcott said softly, "just as it may be for you. I wish for you the strength that has come to me. Today, Collis, I could stand on any bridge and cry out, 'Veni Iesu'!"*

Whitmore turned away and continued along the aisle of the church. He turned at the door and nodded to Charles Orcott, but he opened the door quickly and was gone.

*O Jesus, Come!

Chapter Fourteen

Whitmore did not eat his breakfast. The food was good and savory, he knew; but it did not interest him. He sat at the long table alone, staring down its length at the spread of untouched dishes before him. He was quiet and still, and his gaze was fixed and expressionless. His meetings with Jonas Shelby and Charles Orcott had numbed him. He was overpowered with grief by the appearance of Shelby and the confessions of Orcott. It made him chastise himself, asking himself why he had agreed to do this thing. Why had he agreed to this proposal, to return to his estate, get his money, and depart again forever? When Alec Thurston explained the plan he made it seem so easy and unencumbered, but Whitmore remembered how he had laughed to himself when he heard the plan. If Alec Thurston only knew that he was making arrangements with the true mayor! Whitmore remembered, too, how he had agreed to Thurston's idea because what problem could there possibly be for him? He did not have to pretend, he did not have to memorize names and places and other trivial data. He knew it all and the amnesia story was just an excuse, a subterfuge, to cover his return and gain, deservedly or not, what belonged to him. There was only a short time of wondering if he really wanted to come back. Yet, here he sat at his own table, completely dismayed, disturbed in thought and feeling trapped in circumstances that he never thought could occur.

He had been shocked by Gessie's murder, not her death but her murder for he believed that she was killed because of his treachery. Someone had killed her for what he had done twenty years ago. He believed it, and he had come back to that.

There were three men close to him who could have known what he had done that cold night so many years ago and he suspected them immediately. He had seen two of them, Jonas Shelby and Charles Orcott, and both were innocent. The surprise in each man was what he had become. The sensitive Shelby, unforgiving and without legs.

And the tough, military man Orcott had become forgiving and turned into a man of grace. There was the third man, Paul Arlan, who, he was told, had chased after him through the underground passage. If he could find Paul Arlan. . . .

Whitmore's thoughts were interrupted as he heard a movement behind his chair. He turned quickly to see Anton Dyer approaching.

Dyer looked over the table and then at Whitmore. "Sir," he asked anxiously. "You have not eaten? Is there something else you would prefer?"

Whitmore shook his head and answered, "I am just not hungry, Anton."

Silently, Dyer began to clear the table of the cold and untouched food.

"I have seen some old friends, Anton," Whitmore said as if to somehow placate Anton Dyer. "I feel a bit upset, especially after seeing Jonas Shelby."

Anton Dyer looked at Whitmore and he smiled. "It was good of you to see him, sir."

"It was sad, Anton, for I remembered him as an active, energetic man."

Anton Dyer nodded. "It was a tragic misfortune for him."

"I also saw Charles Orcott," Whitmore continued. "Did you know that he has become a minister?"

"I did know that," Dyer replied, "although I have not seen him since he entered the ministry." Dyer paused but he continued to look at Whitmore. "I believe it is good, sir, that you recall old friends and wish to contact them."

Whitmore looked at Dyer as he said, "There is another old friend I would like to find—Paul Arlan. He was on my council, quite a brilliant counselor. I should like to see him too, if possible. You would not know about him, would you, Anton? Where he might be?"

Anton Dyer thought for a moment, then shook his head. "No, sir, I am sorry but I know nothing about Mr. Arlan." Dyer turned and continued his work to clear the table. After a few moments of silence, he said, "There is another letter, sir, on the table in the corridor."

Whitmore sat quietly. Another letter! He waited, wondering, then he rose slowly and left the room. On the table was the letter in the same type of beige envelope and addressed to Collis Whitmore.

Whitmore opened the letter and it contained the identical mysterious crest that he had received before. Yet, he stared as he had done from the beginning at the descending dove with the rose in its beak. It was a jumble of signs that must have some meaning, a sense, to someone. Whitmore took the letter upstairs to his room and laid it open on his desk. He continued to stare at the design and then, in the next instant, he was writing a letter. The letter was to Mr. Kirkland of *The Review*, and Whitmore enclosed the picture of the crest. He asked a favor of Mr. Kirkland. He asked him if he would publish the picture of the crest in his newspaper and ask if it could be identified. He, Collis Whitmore, would be most grateful for any replies received.

Whitmore walked to the end of the road to post the letter immediately. On his return from the post box, he entered the corridor toward the stairway when he heard a sound in the library. It was a moan, soft and low, followed by laughter which was also low in tone but deep and strong. The door was open and as Whitmore approached, he heard the sounds continue in a mumble of human talk. He looked inside to see Lee stretched across one of the leather chairs and talking on the telephone. Lee looked up and then waved his arm in a signal to Whitmore to enter as he went on talking into the telephone. Whitmore advanced to the fireplace where he stood with his back to Lee, but he could hear Lee's laughter and rambling conversation. At last, Lee finished. He set the telephone aside but he remained sprawled across the chair.

"Talking to Karin," he said and the joy was still in his voice, "about the engagement party. I had to take the day off to do some errands for her. I still have to check with the caterers and the musicians group. The preparations! I had no idea!" He laughed again in the low, strong voice, but he wriggled in the chair and smiled with pleasure.

Whitmore turned to look at him and, glad to see Lee happy, he smiled at him and spoke lightly. "There are ceremonies and such, I guess, for engagements. The fuss and preparation, I imagine, is especially enjoyable for the ladies."

Lee was smiling still, so Whitmore was encouraged to go on. "Your mother and I had no parties, but I guess it was different then. We just got engaged and announced it at a dinner with her family. We told them just before the grace was spoken and her father included a blessing for us. After that, everyone ate and seemed more interested in the food."

Lee shook his head as if the story was unbelievable and funny, and then he became quiet. He studied Whitmore for a moment and then said, "I understand you had lunch with Karin?"

"Oh, yes," Whitmore replied, trying to retain the light mood. "I wanted to become better acquainted, of course," and then he thought he might as well admit his true intentions. "And I wanted to find out about the artist who painted your mother's portrait. I thought Karin would be of help."

Lee nodded. "She told me so, but why?"

"I just wanted to know about the artist so I could thank him. Karin did identify the whereabouts of Roger Manning for me and I am grateful. It is a beautiful portrait." Now he did not wish to admit his true intentions—that Roger Manning might have been a suspect.

Lee cast a swift glance at the portrait. "I suppose," he said and shrugged his shoulders. His face became serious and Whitmore sensed the gay spirit Lee experienced while talking to Karin was wearing off.

"Lee," Whitmore said quickly. "I think about your mother. I missed so many years with her and with you and Lester. I know you were young, but do you remember if she ever talked about me, said anything while I was away?"

Lee shrugged his shoulders again. His face remained serious and his lower lip drooped. "I don't know really; I cannot remember a lot of words or things she said, but I know that nothing was hateful. She never talked that way."

"Did you ever think about me or ask about me?" Whitmore went on.

"I guess I did or it may have been Lester. I do not know. When she answered, she may have been talking to both of us at the same time." Lee hesitated and Whitmore noted that his eyes had glanced swiftly at him. "I do remember that she had a picture she showed us. I recall that because Lester and I laughed at it. I believe it was your wedding picture, but both of you were dressed so funny. She had on a big hat and a flowered dress, and you were standing beside her in a shirt collar that covered your neck and looked as if it was choking you. You had an enormous flower in your coat lapel and the most awful shoes with pointed toes and curved heels." Lee paused and snickered. "I guess you were right about not making a fuss over a wedding."

Whitmore glanced up at Gessie's portrait. Yes, he thought, it was not much fuss that day. But she was more beautiful than anyone could imagine. She fixed her hair differently, just because of the hat. The waves were hidden and she had set curls all around her neck. The hat was white straw and made pretty mesh shadows across her face. There was a pink flower on the brim which could not be seen in the picture, but which I saw, standing over her. It was the same kind of flower I wore in my lapel.

"Gessie!" Whitmore whispered suddenly without reason.

Lee leaned forward. "What?" he asked for he heard only the whispered breath.

"I failed!" Again, Whitmore whispered the words.

"What?" Lee asked one more, and his face became perplexed.

"I failed," Whitmore repeated. "I failed her and I failed you and Lester."

Lee lifted his head and snorted. "How could you fail? You had amnesia; you did not know anything."

Whitmore turned around toward the fireplace, his back to Lee. He wanted so much to say to Lee 'Ah! But I did know! I tell you I failed because in *that* hour, many years ago, I thought of many more because I had to. I thought I could save you with everyone else. I did not guess that the safety I bargained for would not be safety for others.' Whitmore wished he could say these words to Lee but he could not. "I am responsible," was all he could utter.

Lee snorted again. "Well, if you think so," he replied halfheartedly. "It was long ago, though."

"I am anxious, Lee," Whitmore began and he shifted his body uneasily, "about your mother. I have been told that she fell. That that was how she died."

"That is right," Lee answered.

"How did you and Lester take her death? Do you remember?"

Lee thought for a moment. "Lester was excited and upset; he babbled and cried. There was a lot of confusion and people around here. I think Lester was sick, and Anton Dyer kept both of us away until everything calmed down."

Whitmore turned to face Lee. "Did you ever think that your mother might have been murdered?"

Lee stared at him. "Murdered?" He turned on his side and rested his head on one arm of the chair and scrutinized Whitmore. "How? How could anything like that happen? What an idea!"

"I know," Whitmore replied carefully. "Perhaps it is an idea but did you ever wonder why Lester was crying and babbling that night?"

Lee laughed with disgust. "Oh, I see. Of course, I do not know what he was crying about. How was I to understand his silly noises? He has always been going on about everything, talking and imagining all kinds of things. Look at him now. He has crazy ideas with his books and all this old stuff he wants to go digging for. Sometimes I wonder how we can be brothers, let alone be twins."

"I thought there might be something in what Lester said," Whitmore said softly.

"Silly," Lee answered as he swung his long legs over the chair and stood up. He shook his head at Whitmore. "You are a riddle, you know. You come out of nowhere and say you are my father. Now you talk about mother being murdered. All of it is ridiculous to me." Lee's eyes became stern. He closed and opened them but the uncompromising look did not change. "I guess when it comes down to cases, I just find it hard to accept you." He turned and made for the door. "I have to be on my way and get the errands done for Karin." As he went out, he began to whistle.

A few days later, Whitmore received a telephone call from Mr. Kirkland of *The Review*.

"Mr. Whitmore?" the reporter asked. "Is this Mr. Whitmore?"

"Yes," Whitmore replied. "Yes, Mr. Kirkland."

"I have received some responses on your picture," Mr. Kirkland began and then he laughed. "I must say there is quite a variety."

"I welcome anything," Whitmore said, aware that his voice was full of expectations. "I am glad to hear any bit of news."

"Well, one sounded like a crank, one of those perfectionists who can readily spot an error or a fault. He does not know what the picture signifies, but he says he is a bird fancier and the dove in that picture is all wrong."

"Oh," said Whitmore seriously, "how so?"

Kirkland continued. "It is flawed, he says, for it shows the dove's foot with four claws in front and one in back, but a dove has only three claws in front and one in back." Kirkland laughed again. "Is that meaningful to you?"

"No," Whitmore replied.

"Here is another answer," Kirkland went on. "Says the picture is a religious symbol; a downward dove is the descending spirit. . . ." Kirkland paused. "Would you like to hear the rest?"

"I would rather hear any other replies," Whitmore said quickly.

"Very well. Another caller believes he saw the design in an old hotel window when he was traveling, but he cannot name the place. A lady said she is certain it is a quilt pattern her mother used. Someone else believes it is a part of a family crest. . . ."

"I get the idea," Whitmore interrupted. "Actually the responses are a collection of ideas and guesses. They make no sense to me."

"That is what I thought also," Kirkland replied.

"Well, I thank you for your time and help, Mr. Kirkland," Whitmore stated.

"Not at all," Kirkland replied in a businesslike manner and the conversation was ended.

Whitmore thought over the conversation with Mr. Kirkland. The calls about the crest were certainly a motley and unbelievable collection of explanations, but he thought particularly about the bird fancier who said the dove was flawed. How curious to design a crest that was in error, a picture that was not perfect.

Later that day, Mr. Kirkland telephoned again. "I just received another call about the picture and thought you might like the information."

"Of course," replied Whitmore, expecting another casual and innocuous response.

"A man called," Kirkland went on, "and said that the picture was a symbol of a peace group."

"A peace group?" Whitmore repeated and his attention heightened immediately.

"Yes," Kirkland replied. "A group formed after the war."

Whitmore felt the tension within him and he kept himself rigid. "Did the man give his name?" he asked.

"No, he was reluctant to do that although he said 'find Arlan and he would tell all'."

Whitmore became more tense and rigid. "Arlan?"he said in a whisper.

"Yes, Arlan."

"What else?" Whitmore asked quickly. "Where and how?"

"He gave only one more bit of information. 'Arlan', he said, 'is at Temple'. After that, he hung up and I have no more to tell you."

Whitmore could not answer immediately. He sighed heavily and managed to say, "Thank you again, Mr. Kirkland."

"Mr. Whitmore," Kirkland said quickly, perhaps sensing the uneasiness and tenseness in Whitmore's voice, "if there is a story in this, you will get in touch with me?"

"Yes, yes," Whitmore answered in a hurry, "and thank you again."

Whitmore pushed the telephone away. Arlan! Paul Arlan! The man he wanted to see. No one knew about him, but now a telephone call to say that Paul Arlan could tell all about the mysterious crest, a symbol of a peace group. Arlan at Temple, he was told. Whatever could that mean? It was a clue, but whatever did it mean?

Still puzzled, Whitmore went to the quarters of Anton Dyer. When Whitmore stepped into the room, he was aware of a heavy scent of tobacco. The old servant was in his shirtsleeves and he was polishing a silver decanter. On a small table, a can of polish and a pipe were lying side by side. Dyer quickly took the items from the table and began to reach for his coat.

"No, no, Anton," Whitmore begged him, "just stay as you are. I wish to ask you something." Whitmore noticed that Dyer stood to an angle as if to hide the burning pipe he had put aside. Whitmore smiled and looked the other way as if he had not noticed.

"Anton," he began, "does the name Temple mean anything to you?"

Anton Dyer hesitated, still trying to compose himself. "Why yes, sir. It is a school."

Whitmore was surprised at the answer. "A school?" he repeated.

Dyer nodded. "A school."

"Where, Anton? Do you know where it is?"

Dyer hesitated once more but his answer was direct. "It is out of town, sir. It is a long trip to get there."

"I never knew or heard. . . ." Whitmore stopped and then said, "I should like to visit the school, Anton. I will drive there and," he paused, "I should like you to go with me."

Dyer's face was bewildered and uncertain. "When, sir?" he asked, still speaking with hesitation.

"We leave immediately, Anton."

241

Anton Dyer did not move. There was a questioning flicker in his eyes and he closed them quickly. When he opened them, his gaze was more calm but the eyelids drooped and he looked sad. "Very well, sir," he replied softly and in a low voice.

"You see, Anton," Whitmore said reassuringly. "I believe Paul Arlan will be there. I said I should like to see him and talk to him. You know the way to the school; you can direct me there."

When the car was brought around, Anton Dyer emerged from the back entrance. He was dressed very warmly in a heavy overcoat, a hat, scarf and gloves. His countenance remained perturbed, and he did not look at Whitmore as he entered the car.

"Which way?" Whitmore asked.

"Take the highway south, sir," Dyer replied.

With that, they set off. They left Valiterra by the highway, traveling south for quite a while, until Dyer directed Whitmore to turn off onto a smaller roadway with nothing but a vast expanse of country fields on either side. The road was well paved and they could drive at a reasonable pace through the flat, dull colored and barren country. They drove for quite a while, and then, far ahead, they saw a protrusion in the landscape as they approached a plateau of buildings. As they drew nearer, they saw a fence around the group of buildings and, on the farther side, a line of tall trees.

Whitmore stopped before the gate. "This is the school?" he asked.

"Yes, sir," Dyer replied and then he said evenly. "Temple is a military school."

"You did not say so, Anton," Whitmore was startled and he glanced quickly at Dyer.

"I was worried, sir," Dyer answered. "I do not know why, but I thought it might worry you to mention that Temple was a military school."

Whitmore wondered why Dyer would think that a worry, but he decided not to say more and he drove silently into the compound. The drive was lengthy. They passed several buildings, all the same and one the duplicate of the other. They were of grey stone, austere, and plain. The roads and the walks were swept clean, and the grounds were meticulous with each tree and bush trimmed to rigid and defined proportions.

Whitmore drove into the parking compound of the Administration Building. After he parked the car, he sat for a while staring at the long, low building before him. It was late afternoon now and dusk arrived early in the shortened daytime. There was no light or shadows cast on the building, and the gloom seemed to settle down like a soft cloud.

Anton Dyer had remained silent, but at last, he spoke. "Do you wish me to go in with you, sir?"

"Yes, I think so, Anton," Whitmore replied and then they finally left the car.

They entered the lobby of the building where they were confronted by a bronze statue in the center. The statue was an oversized soldier, erect and determined, confident looking in the metallic cast. Beneath was a plaque that identified the monument as General Temple, in whose honor the school was named.

Whitmore went toward the desk while Dyer followed behind. Dyer looked around, from right to left, as if he were out of place and it made him uncomfortable and embarrassed.

A young man, neat and clean, and dressed in a dark blue uniform, had entered from a side door and was waiting for them. He stood straight and his eyes looked directly at Whitmore without flinching.

"I am looking for Paul Arlan," Whitmore said to him.

"Mr. Arlan is a teacher," the young man replied without hesitation.

"Oh," Whitmore said with a smile and looked eagerly at the young man." I would like to see him, if I could. I realize he must have a schedule of classes, but if it were possible?"

The young man did not smile in return but turned to an index machine and flipped through the cards.

"Mr. Arlan is at field three at this hour."

"Field three? Can I go there?" Whitmore asked, still eagerly and with a smile.

"Yes. Follow the main drive east to Building Three; the field is directly behind it."

Whitmore thanked the young man and turned quickly to leave while Anton Dyer trailed faithfully behind him.

The field behind Building Three was a firing range. At this hour it was covered with artificial light and the sounds of popping firearms could be heard as Whitmore and Dyer grew near. They had to park the car a distance from the field and approach on foot. A line of grey clad cadets was shooting at targets placed on the opposite side of the field. A tall, thin man, dressed in a grey uniform walked behind the row of cadets, stopping at certain individuals to correct their gun sights or their aim, or offer advice, often pointing and gesturing toward the targets.

"Is that him, sir?" Dyer asked. Both had stopped, and Whitmore was staring at the man.

"Yes," he replied and looked at the man for a long while. Finally, he said, "I guess I will have to disturb him, at least for a while."

Dyer asked another question. "Is it possible, do you think, to disturb him?"

"I shall try," Whitmore answered.

They walked closer toward the field and the bullet sounds became louder. Now the voices of the cadets could also be heard. The words were indistinguishable for they muttered aloud, sometimes shouting and sometimes laughing, all interspersed with the gunfire. Whitmore and Dyer went toward the tall, thin man who was walking away as he had not seen them. They could hear his voice, too, but it was clear and precise as his instructions hovered over each cadet.

"Paul!" Whitmore called out.

The man stopped and turned quickly. He faced Whitmore and Dyer squarely, but the visor on his cap was low and shaded his face so his expression or reaction could not be seen except for the mouth which opened slightly and then curved into a smile. He did not move as Whitmore and Dyer came closer.

"Paul," Whitmore said again. "Paul Arlan."

The tall man answered and his voice was as clear and precise as when he gave instructions to the cadets. "Collis Whitmore," he said and still smiled.

"Can I disturb you?" Whitmore asked.

"Why not?" Paul Arlan answered. "This is just practice for night firing." He turned to one of the cadets and gave him instructions and the cadet stepped out immediately and stood in Arlan's place.

Paul Arlan walked toward a small grove of trees with benches underneath. Whitmore and Dyer followed, but Dyer discreetly stopped by a lone bench. "I will wait for you here, sir," he said. Whitmore nodded and went on to the next bench and sat down beside Paul Arlan.

"Anton Dyer is the butler at my estate," Whitmore stated, nodding toward the bench where Dyer sat. "Do you know him?"

"No," Arlan replied. He leaned back on the bench and crossed his arms in front of him. He looked directly at Whitmore and smiled again. "So, you finally took up my invitation, Collis. I had to send several of them. It took a while to contact a colleague and have them delivered at appropriate times."

"An invitation?" Whitmore asked in surprise. "How was I to know? I did not understand the meaning of your invitation, and there was no name or identification."

"I know that," Arlan retorted. "I did it deliberately to tease you, to make you wonder—and maybe to make you worry. When you went public, your request in the newspaper was sent to me. Then I decided to call *The Review* and practically declare myself."

The surprise could not leave Whitmore. "You wished to tease me?" he asked.

"And to make you wonder and to make you worry," Arlan replied.

"With that picture?" Whitmore went on. "Because it was a symbol of a peace group? That I did not understand either."

Paul Arlan laughed. "Yes. How would you know the significance of the crest?"

"It was flawed, you know," Whitmore said quickly to indicate that he did know something about the crest. "A dove does not have five claws."

"Correct," Arlan answered. "What else did you see, Collis?"

Whitmore hesitated and then replied cautiously, "There was a flower. . . ." but he could not go on.

"A dove and a flower," Arlan stated. "Do you know what they represent? They represent peace. At least, the symbols of peace."

"But I said . . . the design is flawed."

"Which is wrong, is it not?" Arlan was speaking deliberately and strictly as a teacher. With his arms still folded before him and the smile on his lips, he seemed condescending. "So that is peace, then. It is flawed and the crest depicted it perfectly."

"Paul," Whitmore began and he was astonished. "You said that crest was the symbol of a peace group. You mean there was a group who accepted that idea and believed it?"

"The crest meant something more, something that goes along with peace, like vengeance."

Whitmore had to look directly at Paul Arlan and he realized that he was staring at Arlan's face. Arlan's face was irregular and it was because of his eyes. One eye was larger than the other and the eyelid did not close over it. It gave Arlan a queer expression of constant surprise and a threatening, hypnotic stare.

"Vengeance!" Whitmore said softly.

"Vengeance, Collis, against everything that was not honorable for and about the war." Arlan paused and then he laughed. "But the group is finished now; we have disbanded. Only, occasionally something will 'pop up' from the past."

"Like me?" Whitmore asked.

"We deal with it," Arlan said simply.

"How do you deal with it, Paul? Send out those invitations, as you called them, to tease? I do not understand that or your purpose or whatever you believe."

Arlan's face became thoughtful. "All things must be decided on their own, of course, but we insist on, what shall we say, payment? Yes, payment in some kind." He paused and then continued. "We were a small group but dedicated. We met and made our decisions at the old saluting place."

Whitmore straightened his body. *Saluting place!* "I do not know about that, either," he said as he shook his head.

"Well, it was the old barracks where troops were billeted and the only one standing after the war. We saluted it for its stand, and it became our meeting place. But, as I said, the group is not active anymore; I mean consciously active."

"This group judged and punished, then, as they believed? How did they decide that?"

Arlan's face turned aside and he looked across the field. "Collis," he began, "we lost the war. You know that. We were defeated militarily, our army was routed, we were overcome and held in bondage; all because we were the losers. In a situation like that, Collis, many become traitors. Traitors, by the way, before, during, and after the war. Our peace group sought out these people to condemn them, persecute or punish them. We did it according to our own beliefs and our honesty as human beings." Arlan turned to look at Whitmore and his expression still was thoughtful but the queer eyes looked sinister. "You are a 'big fish', Collis."

"Now that I have been drawn here, am I to be told the payment?"

Arlan's face twisted into a slight smile and the serious look was gone. "So you have asked about payment? I have talked about payment but what is it really? Eye for an eye, tooth for a tooth, or is payment something that works out in its own way? I have seen and been aware of both. Eye for an eye, literally, can be a simple method, straight up and down, one and two, and it is over. Swift. Yet, I have come to consider and appreciate another dimension of payment which I call the second alternative. It is subtle. Sometimes it takes a while, but it always seems to work out. It works within the problem or the person himself. So my philosophy has become to push aside the 'yes' or 'no' and wait for the second alternative."

"It sounds like you are talking about conscience, Paul."

Arlan smiled again. "Perhaps conscience can be a second alternative, Collis, but payment will come to you in its own way and in its own time. I will do nothing to you."

Whitmore stared at the man beside him. Arlan was sitting straight and stiff, his body held exactly in place without slumping.

"You had me come here to tell me that?" Whitmore asked.

"Yes," Arlan replied. "I admit my own curiosity also. I really wanted to see you."

Now Whitmore turned away and looked across the field, a stage of artificial light and mock action. Men shooting, targets falling, the chatter and noise of destruction but all simulated and pretentious.

"Paul," Whitmore spoke at last. "You were my chief adviser, the best counselor I could have hoped for. You were that and I also remember you as a fastidious, very neat person."

"Now you are talking," Arlan replied and he smiled again. "I was just that, wasn't I? A fastidious and very neat person. Showers and clean clothes twice a day and did you ever see my private room in the council chambers?"

Whitmore shook his head."

Arlan went on. "Paraphernalia like you never dreamed. Everything to keep my body in order, you might say. I worried about my hair in those days. I had scalp vibrators, brushes, special ointments and shampoos. All that, but look at me now." He removed his cap and he was almost bald, only a fringe of grey hair grew around his head. "I faded fast, didn't I?"

"You were blond," Whitmore said slowly.

"No more. What is left is grey and I do not worry about it any more. I do not bother about shaving either when I can get away with it. So I am not as fastidious and neat as I used to be. Here at Temple, of course, they want us to be precise. It gives me pleasure, though, to present myself in a classroom, unkempt where all these bright young cadets have to be groomed and clean, and they have to sit there and look and listen to me. Oh, I have gotten by with it because I always know the inspection days. The cadets have never reported me because I suspect there is an understanding, an honor, amongst them not to report on me."

"You are not an example then?"

"No. In fact, I do not care to be. I ceased to care after the eye surgery. The hair and the good appearance could not make up for the eyes. I had a growth on my lower eyelid that had to be removed. It was a rather large growth and it was malignant. After it was cut away, the gap in the eyelid had to be filled by grafting skin from the upper eyelid. My head was bandaged for three months, the eyelids sewn together. The result you see—one eye larger than the other. The cadets call me 'cock-eyed'. I know it and I hear it, but it does not make me angry because it is true."

Whitmore said softly, "Appearances are not so much."

Arlan did not answer but the smile was gone. Whitmore sensed a certain sadness about Arlan and wondered if the restrained smiles and harsh posture were practiced and controlled responses that Arlan had adopted.

Whitmore had a thought but he hesitated to speak. He looked at Arlan and wondered if he should say his mind. Arlan was silent and still and his face was somber. Whitmore decided that he would speak, to say what he wanted. "I have seen Jonas Shelby and Charles Orcott," were his words. "They knew what happened; they knew what I had done," he paused and then added, "and so did you, Paul."

Arlan nodded. "I knew what happened, Collis," he said. His voice was crisp but he spoke slowly and softly. "I knew what you had done. That day will stay in my mind forever. I will tell you about it, Collis. It began about nine o'clock that morning. It began snowing, but Lillian, my dear Lillian had gone to church as usual. I heard the church bells ringing at just that time, and I said an *Amen* for her. Then the airplanes and the bombardment began and lasted for hours. I believe it ended only because the storm increased and the snow became thicker and heavier. The airplanes were replaced by tanks

248

and heavy armor and then the soldiers. They were sighted advancing like ants toward us. I wanted to get to Lillian and find her. It was havoc to try to cross the city. The storm was enough but we had to contend with eluding the enemy and the gunfire as well. I got to the church; I mean what had been the church, for it was bombed out completely. But I found Lillian, amongst the statuary—just as broken and dead. I left frantically, hoping for some kind of help and got back to the council building. I came back to see Jonas Shelby shot and torn and to hear Charles Orcott tell of your betrayal. I took off after you, but I never found you or saw you."

Whitmore raised his head. "Your wife," he said slowly but his voice faded away.

Arlan continued as if he had not heard Whitmore speak. "I was captured and thrown into a filthy camp with nothing but stench and disease all about. There I got the cancer that effected my eyes and skin." Arlan looked across the fields again. His posture remained rigid. He said something under his breath, but the words were not clear. Whitmore leaned closer to hear but Arlan turned at that moment and faced him. "Why did you do it, Collis. What were *they* to you that you would do such a thing? I wanted you to come here so you could give me an answer."

Whitmore winced and looked away at the field and heard the battle noises. When he spoke, he stumbled over his words. "I wanted to try to save everything," he said.

"Ha!" Arlan scoffed. "Such an answer. You saved nothing."

"Paul, I believed *them* for mercy."

Arlan looked at Whitmore and his uneven eyes twitched in a curious fashion. "Perhaps you were right. If you had not done anything, you may have had the same results. We would have lost, our city surrendered, and all we possessed and treasured given up. But Collis, you denied us the chance to fight for these things."

"Paul, is it better to die than to kill?"

"How can you ask that? You did not die; you escaped, you ran from it."

"I knew my belief, but I could not act on it." Whitmore shook his head against the sadness which was overcoming him. "If blood was to be shed, let it be on another's hands, not ours."

"You think you have no blood on your hands? You really believe that? Blood spills; it covers the knife as well as the wound."

249

Whitmore shook his head once more, and he shifted his body in order to sit more upright. "Paul," he said softly, but his voice was even. "I do not know exactly how to say this. But to me, you were, how shall I say it—you were—perverse. I had trouble with you in the council. I could not count on you. I knew your abilities; you were as sharp and precise in your thinking as in your appearance. Yet, I could never rely on you. I believed you thought one way; but when the votes were put forth, you were the opposite. I could never count on you, Paul."

.   "Oh, you are right," Arlan answered quickly. "I am perverse! That is the word for me. I knew you could never believe in me, and I wanted it that way. I never wanted to be 'counted in' by anybody. I did it deliberately and, you know, I am still that way. Do you know what I do here at Temple besides conduct firing practice? I teach history, and do you know why?"

Whitmore shook his head.

"I teach history because of the wars. I find that fascinating. I can become completely absorbed in the planning, the tactics, the *thinking* of the leaders and the prophets of war. The devious thinking, the exalted rational of military maneuvers, excites me like nothing else. I lay it on thick for the cadets when I declaim the glories of war and the brilliance of the master generals and the directors of unbelievable stratagems." Arlan paused and laughed lightly. "It is not perverse, Collis, it is precise."

"Perhaps they go together," Whitmore answered softly.

"I am only keeping up with the prophets who tell of war."

"I do not understand it," Whitmore said. "You belonged to a peace group, yet, here you are teaching boys how to shoot and proclaiming admiration for all the battles of mankind."

"Oh, yes, Collis, because then things are lined up and spelled out and you know the direction toward the enemy. In the peace group, there was no mercy. There we could revenge—the real onslaughts, the payments that I was talking about. You yourself believed in peace and mercy but they do not go together."

"I shudder at your words, Paul, for I see no brilliance about war."

"You think my nature is perverse because I preach war. But you have been responsible for more deaths that I could ever realize."

Whitmore was silent and he stared at the ground. At last, Arlan looked at him. "What is the matter, Collis? Are you shocked by what I said?"

"Perhaps, in a way," Whitmore replied, then he asked quietly. "Paul, do you blame me for Lillian's death?"

Arlan did not reply immediately. He hung his head and his face was serious. "I should say 'no' but when it happened as it did, there should be a reason, a responsibility on someone. If there had not been that attack. . . . " Arlan halted and shook his head, but he did not raise it.

"Paul, has the peace group ever taken payment against an innocent one or an outsider who may have been close to what they named as a traitor?"

Arlan shook his head. "Not to my knowledge. The rule we followed was payment against the guilty only."

"Paul, I ask because if you blame me for Lillian's death, did you, in return, kill Gessie?"

Arlan's eyes widened in a ludicrous fashion. "What?" he asked in surprise.

Whitmore went on. "I believe that Gessie was murdered. I discovered that when I returned, but I cannot prove anything. I believe that she might have been murdered because of me, because of what I had done. You knew what I had done so I thought. . . . "

"That makes me angry, that you should say that!"

"Could anyone in that peace group. . . . "

Arlan interrupted again. "I said we acted only against the guilty, but I have confessed that I would do nothing against you. So why, then, would I harm your wife? I have been here at Temple since the war, and I have returned to Valiterra only briefly to meet with the peace group. I cannot stay there; I have never had a wish to do so. Memories—" He hesitated and said no more.

Whitmore got to his feet but dropped his hat as he rose. Arlan bowed from the waist and picked it up. He smiled sadly and handed the hat to Whitmore. They did not shake hands or look at each other again.

"Will you ever come back here again?" Arlan asked.

Whitmore shook his head. "No, I do not believe so."

"So be it, and I think it is just as well."

Whitmore turned away and walked toward Anton Dyer. Together, they walked silently to the car, but, in the back of them, they heard renewed charges of gunfire and the piercing, quick commands of Paul Arlan.

Whitmore and Dyer were silent as they drove back to the estate. Dyer, in particular, sat in a dazed kind of stupor. His eyes stared ahead with a blank, vaporous look that was glazed and eerie.

"Anton," Whitmore finally asked, "what is the matter?"

In response, Dyer blurted out, "Mrs. Whitmore was murdered?"

Whitmore realized that Dyer had overheard the conversation with Paul Arlan.

"I believe so, Anton," Whitmore answered softly.

"In the house?" Dyer asked, still astonished.

"Lester told me so. He was awakened by noise that night and was going to his mother's room, but he stopped on the stairway landing when he saw his mother in the open doorway and a man behind her who hit her and knocked her down."

"Lester saw that?"

"He said so, but no one believed him."

Dyer was silent for a moment. His face was solemn, as if thinking. "The boy did say something, but he was so little and he always had bad dreams and nightmares. Sir, it could not be possible!"

"Anton, I cannot help myself. I believe him."

"There was no evidence to that, sir. The doctor was there, the coronor; they surveyed everything. There was nothing to indicate that there was a crime."

"I mean no accusation, Anton. I mean that it is possible that it could have happened as Lester saw it."

"But in the house. . . . " Dyer said softly, "in my care." He closed his eyes and his head shook.

Whitmore could not see if Dyer was crying, but he heard soft mumblings coming low and deep from his throat. "Oh, I had a fore-boding about going to that military school."

"Anton," Whitmore said quickly, "do not reprove yourself. You have been everything to my home and my family that I have not. I was not there, but you cared for the estate. You have looked after my sons and raised them, you shared the grief at the death of my wife. Even you, Anton, expressed both the joy and the sorrow of my return."

Anton Dyer did not speak. He continued to mumble in whispers to himself.

Whitmore thought to himself. And now, Anton, you, along with Jonas Shelby, Charles Orcott, and Paul Arlan, know of my betrayal. Surely, he overheard that also.

They drove on saying no more and it was dark and late when they returned to the estate.

Chapter Fifteen

The day arrived when Lee and Lester Whitmore became twenty-one. Collis Whitmore had prepared for this day for his sons. He purchased gold wrist watches for them at Thornburgs, and there was to be a buffet luncheon with guests in celebration. Later, in the afternoon, Grant Deakins was to read and settle the will of the estate.

Despite the plans and preparations, Whitmore was totally apprehensive. He did the tasks, but the expected joy was not there to overcome a sense of dread within him. It was the time of culmination of his plan with Alec Thurston. The boys would receive their part of the trust, and he would receive his share to divide as agreed with Thurston. If he kept to the plan, Whitmore told himself, he could leave as early as tomorrow, with the money in tow, settle with Thurston, and then head for the land of sunshine and sand. He would be far away from this place and people. This was the important day of the plan. How wonderful and easy it had sounded when first discussed by Thurston, but it had gone afoul. He had returned to the rawest emotions possible—hostility, suspicions, hatred, love, and all entwined with a hint of murder. He had been stunned by the manner of Gessie's death, and he had been shocked and ashamed by his meetings with Shelby, Orcott, and Arlan. He knew that what they had told him caused this apprehension and grief within him that would not go away.

He had not anticipated such a situation. Then he said to himself, did I really believe that I could come back to my home, see my sons and others I knew, and expect to stand amongst them like an invisible statue and receive no reaction? Were they simply to carry on and move around in their lives as before? He misjudged it all and he fooled himself. Yet, there was one nagging idea that cut a fine thought through all the heaviness of feeling. He could not dismiss a deep belief within him that, somehow, *this*, his coming back, was the best possible thing he could have done.

Anton Dyer had seen to the arrangements for the special lunch in the dining room. Yet, Whitmore noted that he, too, seemed to go about his duties with an unusual air of solemnity. He looked thoughtful and serious, as if troubling thoughts were on his mind. He tried to smile but the effort vanished quickly, and his eyelids were more drooped than ever. He moved quietly about placing vases of red carnations on the tables, shifting some flowers. He set the birthday cake in one place, then moved it to another. It seemed trivial but as if he was showing an attempt to make things perfect and right.

Gifts were put on the table around the places of Lee and Lester and included presents from the staff of the estate as well as from the friends of the boys. Telegrams and cards had arrived and were placed with the gift packages. The wrist watches were in small, elegantly wrapped boxes, and Whitmore tried to place them unobtrusively amongst the pile of packages and papers.

The guests were mostly young people although Grant Deakins and Mrs. Brantford were included. Whitmore noticed that these two were huddled together, off to one side of the room. Their conversation seemed intense and extremely serious. Mrs. Brantford shook her head several times and Grant Deakins gesticulated with hands and facial movements most unusual for his deportment.

The door opened and Lee and Lester entered together. For the first time since Whitmore had seen them, they were dressed alike in dark suits with a red carnation in their lapels. Immediately, shouts of acclaim went up and the Happy Birthday song was sung in a raucous and unharmonious manner ending in laughter and great jokes. Karin rushed forward to kiss Lee to another swell of laughter and jokes. Without hesitation, Lee took over and directed the party atmosphere with an obsessive delight and a celebrating mood. He stood in the center of the room and reacted to the acclaim with a song of his own, and his audience approved with applause and shouts of joy. Lee touched and slapped those who joined in his wit and repartee. He had brought champagne and soon toasts began for everyone. The mood of the party became lighter and a little more frenzied.

In his surprising mood, Lee stopped Anton Dyer. "Bring in the staff," Lee said with spirit, "they, too, should be included in this special day. Bring them in, Anton!" This act of magnanimity was greeted by the others with a shout of approval of "Yes! Yes!" and this time Lee was touched and slapped with congratulations by the guests.

He embraced and kissed Karin again, which brought forth another resounding "Yes!" from the guests and everyone was coming together in loud and prolonged merriment.

The guests finally settled into circles of amusing and fluctuating talk underscored with the clinking of glasses when the staff stepped into the room. They stood in a line, and they seemed embarrassed, but the feeling soon vanished as they were greeted with cheer and applause. They faces were red, but they glanced at each other with wide smiles and sparkling eyes. Lee went forward to meet them and he carried a champagne bottle. "Glasses, Anton," he said swiftly, and then raised a toast to them as if reading a proclamation. He complimented them on their service, their loyalty. Then he mentioned the food, the table setting, the party, their gifts, and soon he began to stammer and look around for other things to pay them tribute. At last they drank a toast to it all.

Whitmore looked at Lester. He seemed happy, too, but more subdued. He joined in the champagne toasts and he smiled and thanked everyone—but quietly, and he stayed behind Lee all the while. Soon he turned and came over to Whitmore. He carried his glass of champagne with him. "Dad," he said, "it is great, isn't it?"

Whitmore nodded and smiled at Lester. "It is a wonderful day for you and Lee."

"Twenty-one. That is the official age, is it not?" Lester said and then took a drink of champagne. He had taken a large sip, and his eyes widened immediately and his nose wrinkled. He shook his head as if to throw off a sudden, light sensation and then he laughed. "Oh!" he cried and set down the glass. "I have had too much! Powerful!"

"Champagne is deceptive, Lester," Whitmore said. "It looks so light and clear, the bubbles make it look cheerful, but its strength creeps up on you and knocks you over before you know it."

"I *know!*" Lester answered quickly.

"Lee is happy," Whitmore went on.

"That is for certain," Lester replied. "In fact, unusually so."

"Well, it is his birthday as well as yours, and the official age, as you said." Whitmore looked around and noticed that he and Lester were by themselves. The staff had departed, and the guests formed their own groups and lingered around the buffet table, discoursing loudly and to their own. Even Mrs. Brantford and Grank Deakins resumed their talk which had been interrupted by the entrance of

Lee and Lester and the introduction of songs and jests and toasts to everyone.

Whitmore turned to Lester and quietly asked, "Do you like your brother, Lester?"

Lester blinked as if the effect of the champagne was still upon him. "What?" he asked as though he had not heard correctly.

"Do you like Lee?" Whitmore repeated.

Lester was hesitant, but then replied softly, "He is my brother." His face flushed red as if embarrassed. "In that respect," he hesitated, "I like him, I guess. There is a tie between us."

"Yes," Whitmore agreed, "just being a family is a tie that is unchangeable. Like us, father and son."

Lester smiled but the embarrassment was in his smile also. "It is there. Nothing can change that, but why ask such things?"

"Well," Whitmore replied, "I was wondering about you and Lee and how you felt about each other. You are different."

"I know," answered Lester. "Lee and I are not close; we are really not alike."

"That happens in families. They belong to each other, the tie is there. But it can be strained, and members of a family can be varied and at odds with each other."

"Odds? Did I hear the word 'odds'?" Grant Deakins had ambled over and surprised them as he stepped beside Lester. His posture was straight as usual, but he seemed forced to control his stance. He constantly arched his back so his shoulders would stay in line. His eyes twinkled with joy and good will as, apparently, the party mood had overtaken him. Immediately, Whitmore looked around for Mrs. Brantford and noticed that she had joined Karin and Lee. Unlike Grant Deakins, however, her stature was poised and straight and her countenance far less jovial and not particularly happy.

"We are speaking of families," Whitmore explained to Grant Deakins, "so varied in personality that they can be at odds with each other."

"Oh, precisely," Deakins said quickly and then his gaze went from Whitmore to Lester. Whitmore noted that the twinkling eyes of Grank Deakins were not to be taken lightly for the alertness and sharp intelligence still were there. "But not in this family, I hope," Deakens went on and his gaze returned to Whitmore when he spoke.

Whitmore remained silent for a moment, then he said carefully,

"I guess we should not think of odds. Today is an important day for the Whitmores."

"It is our day, for all of us," Lester said. "At least, Lee and I are now legal. Is that the word?"

Deakins smiled slightly. "I guess legal could be the word."

Whitmore looked away. Grank Deakins, he thought, expressed his own situation exactly. For him, everything would be legal also.

"Collis," Deakins remarked, "you overcame your amnesia at a most fortunate time." His voice tried to be light and humorous.

Whitmore looked quickly at Deakins and saw that the lawyer's twinkling eyes bore upon him like a light beam. Whitmore shifted and turned slightly, "I am. . . . " he paused for he was going to say 'fortunate' but then he would use Deakin's word, so he said instead, "grateful."

"How good for Dad," Lester said, "to come back now." Deakins turned to look at Lester, the expression in his eyes not changing. "Dad had it rough for twenty years. He does not need to live that way any more."

Deakins shook his head slowly. "No," he answered so quietly that it sounded like the coo of a dove.

Whitmore was beginning to feel tense and he tried to laugh. "Let us eat," he exclaimed. "This is a party, a birthday party. Let us enjoy it. Later, Grant, you will be able to read to us all about the inheritance. The *legal* part, as Lester said." With that, he took Lester's arm and he also grabbed Deakin's arm and moved them toward the table and into the guests who were well into the way of celebration.

That afternoon, the estate papers were to be read and settled. The time was delayed later than scheduled because the luncheon party did not end when expected. Several guests lingered and continued their innocuous banter since food and drink still were available. The result was drawn out farewells with additional tributes and satiated jokes until, at last, they were pushed gently out the door. Karin Brantford and her mother were asked by Lee to remain. They agreed willingly, and Grant Deakins approved saying, "they will soon be members of the Whitmore family."

Lee escorted them into the library after Grant Deakins followed by Lester and Whitmore. Anton Dyer was asked to attend on behalf of the household staff. A table was set up in the library and Deakins began to cover it with books and papers. The party atmosphere was not present in the somber and quiet library room. Like the change of rooms, the geniality had disappeared from Deakins' demeanor and he took his place behind the table with absolute seriousness and decorum. Because of the lateness of the afternoon, the library was barely light. Deakins asked Anton Dyer if a lamp could be moved to the table, and Dyer quickly took a lamp from a corner table to fulfill Deakins' request. The lamp shown a bright light upon the table, but cast up a ghostly illumination on the lower half of Deakins' face while the upper half was shadowy and his eyes looked like dark holes.

Deakins assumed the air of the barrister, and he began methodically and slowly to read a history of the estate. It was an excellent presentation of the legal and mathematical picture of all the property. It reflected the precision and detail of the way a man like Grant Deakins worked.

Whitmore sat quietly, listening to Deakins' speech, but he felt a stirring of uneasiness within him. Hearing the organized speech of Deakins, Whitmore sensed that here was a man who would be devoted to finding all the facts about any professional situation. Deakins was talking about the history of the last twenty years; everything checked and checked thoroughly and all things were ever in balance.

"The fortune is not what it was in the most prosperous days," Deakins was saying. "It has dwindled, but it is sufficient to ensure that the estate can be maintained reasonably in the future and that satisfactory income can be provided for such. If," he went on, "there is any wish or consensus to sell the property, a very good profit can be realized."

Lee shifted his position on the leather couch and settled down deeper into the cushions, laying his head back in almost a reclining position. He looked warm; his face was flushed and his eyes continually blinked and then expanded with a curious delight. A smile came over his lips and he turned to look at Karin. She smiled in return and twisted her shoulder in an eloquent shrug. Her dark hair was glossy but she messed its curls when she laid her head upon Lee's shoulder. Mrs. Brantford sat beside them, but she did not look at them. She looked regal, yet a little too tense. Whitmore noticed that her hands were moving as she clasped and unclasped them.

Whitmore was seated to the side with Lester in a chair beside him. Lester was toying with a piece of blue ribbon he had taken from one of the gifts. He would weave the ribbon through his fingers and

259

then pull it taut or loose so it would either fall apart or tighten his hands together. He seemed absorbed in this silly trick, and Whitmore wondered if he was mindful of the serious words spoken by Deakins.

Deakins had paused to slip additional sheets of paper in front of him, and he began another detailed report on the current condition of the buildings, the land, the stables, and then the tax standing including future duties and assessments. Carefully, he stated that there were no charges against the estate or requests for charities. At last, he came to the matter of personal income. First he read the bequests made to the staff. There was a particularly generous bequest to Anton Dyer. Dyer's face glowed at the announcement and a large smile spread across his face. He had been standing, but now he moved back toward his chair and sat down. All the while Deakins had been given his report, Anton Dyer had seemed anxious for he constantly rose from his chair, stood for a while, and then sat down. Now the anxiety was gone and he was flushed with assurance. "Thank you," he said aloud and bowed his head. "Thank you."

"Now for the future," Deakins went on, "the money can remain in trust and invested or it can be dispersed in a lump sum."

Lee began to laugh and he looked at Karin, but aloud he said, "One sum—that's for me. I am not for those little allowance deals. I like to do my own investing." Mrs. Brantford turned to look at him and she smiled. The smile lacked warmth, but it was a smile of agreement. She nodded her head and she smiled the same smile upon Karin and patted her daughter on the shoulder.

Grant Deakins did not look at them or pretend to hear Lee's words. When he looked up, he glanced at Whitmore. Deakins' look was inquisitive as if he were inviting or expecting some question from him, but Whitmore remained silent and said nothing.

Deakins looked down again at the papers before him. He thumbed through a few papers, but he returned to the page before him and began again to speak. "The trust, of course, was established at the time Lee and Lester were born. Besides the bequests revealed, the remainder of the estate's assets would go to the Whitmore family. Mr. Whitmore is first and sole inheritor but, upon his death, two-thirds possession was to be given to his wife and the remaining one-third to be divided among the children at the age of twenty-one. Mrs. Whitmore's share was to go to the children but only if her death followed that of her husband's. If her death preceded that of her

260

husband, her share reverts back to him rather than the children." He paused and then continued. "In other words, if Mr. Whitmore had not returned, the boys would have received all of the estate. But Mrs. Whitmore made an additional testamentary deposition many years ago. She requested that upon her death, if the first inheritor. . . ." he paused again, "which would be Mr. Whitmore, should return before the boys reach the age of twenty-one, the entire estate would revert back to him."

Lee's head jerked up. A deeper flush came over his face. "Why did she do that?"

"Mrs. Whitmore never knew if her husband was dead or alive. She wanted that provision made and to remain open if by any chance he were still alive. She was ill; you boys were small, and she believed she would pass away before the children matured. If Mr. Whitmore were to be found in the meantime, he was then to make any provisions as he wished. Otherwise, our offices were to provide for the estate and the children."

Whitmore leaned forward in his chair. His mind was in a turmoil but he had the overwhelming thought that he had it all! More than he believed, more than he hoped for! Everything belonged to him! Still, he had to speak, as if to confirm it. "Then I," he said slowly, "as first inheritor, receive the entire estate?"

Deakins nodded. "Precisely."

Whitmore wondered if the words were spoken loudly or if they sounded that way because of the silence in the room. A sudden pall had fallen over it. There was not a sound or movement, and the stillness seemed forever—that it would never be broken. Then Whitmore heard the words, "Well, I'll be!" and he thought it was Lee. He glanced at Lee, but he was aware that pairs of eyes were turning to look at him. He saw the stares of Lee, Karin, and Mrs. Brantford directed at him. Their gazes were straight and incredulous, and the three of them sat stilted in a pose as if they were frozen and unable to move.

Finally, a sound stirred in the room and it was Anton Dyer rising from his chair. Satisfaction still covered his face and he stood stiffly for a moment. Then he straightened his coat, pulling at his lapels, and left the room.

Whitmore looked quickly toward Lester. Lester was sitting quietly, his head bent down. The blue ribbon had fallen to the floor and he did not reach down to pick it up. Lester looked downward at the ribbon and stared at it, but he left it at his feet.

Grant Deakins closed the portfolio before him. He began to gather together the other papers and soon the table was cleared. There was a creaking sound from the leather couch as Lee shifted his body forward and stood up. His body trembled, but his face was rigid and angry. His lips moved but the words were inaudible. He turned to leave so he could meet Grant Deakins at the doorway. They stopped and looked at each other for a moment and then Deakins said, "Be careful, Lee." Deakins turned and left as Karin and Mrs. Brantford came to Lee. They said nothing but the three of them stepped into the corridor and were gone.

Whitmore looked again at Lester who still was gazing downward at the floor. "Lester," he said gently, "are you disappointed?"

Lester did not raise his head but moved it from side to side. "No," he replied.

Whitmore went behind Lester's chair as he prepared to leave, but he did not touch the boy. Whitmore paused at the doorway to look back at Lester. Lester had raised his head, and his gaze had followed Whitmore. They looked at each other silently. Lester's eyes were shining and wide as if the effect of the champagne was still upon him. His eyes became liquid, as if close to tears. But he said nothing and smiled at Whitmore.

Whitmore went down the corridor, passing the dining room. He heard a commotion in the room and stopped to look in. Lee had returned to the table and was pouring champagne into a glass. The glass filled quickly for he poured the champagne rapidly and then drank it just as fast. He sputtered out some words and swayed against the table as he made a feeble attempt to raise high the empty glass. He was stopped by Karin who took hold of his arm. "Lee!" she said with determination. Whitmore saw that she came from a corner of the room where her mother stood; it was almost the same spot where Mrs. Brantford had stood earlier talking to Grant Deakins. Whitmore could not see Mrs. Brantford's face for her back was to him, but her posture was rigid and her head held very high and thrust back to that the black waves of her hair touched her neck.

Karin's face was serious as she approached Lee and her red mouth was tense. "Lee," she repeated, but she stopped when she saw Whitmore in the doorway. A surprised expression came over her face and she murmured softly, "Oh!" The look on her face and her exclamation made Lee turn around to face Whitmore. Lee leaned against Karin but he again raised the empty glass. "Father!" he said with a smirk. His face was firm but his eyes were glittering. "My long lost father, returning at the most opportune moment to claim his portion. Will you join me in a toast to such a worthy providence?"

He began to pour champagne into two glasses but Whitmore shook his head and said, "No, Lee."

Another smirk crossed Lee's face. "All right. Whatever you say. You are in charge, totally." He paused and laughed sardonically. "Your will," he began but his body swayed and Karin had to steady him.

Suddenly, Mrs. Brantford turned and came toward him. "Lee," she said and her voice was surprisingly moderate. "Do not be so harsh with your father. After all, the provisions were made by your mother and I am certain she intended them for the good of all."

"It was her money anyway," Lee said cynically. "She was the one who had wealth; he did not have much. . . . "

"Lee," Mrs. Brantford interrupted and then turned to Whitmore. Her dark eyes looked directly at him and she tried to smile. "Lee is upset," she said gently.

Whitmore nodded but his glance returned to Lee. Whitmore felt stunned and helpless; he felt that there was an empty, shallow place, a part torn loose, somewhere inside of him.

"I understand," he said quietly to Mrs. Brantford.

Mrs. Brantford smiled again. "What could you have done? I assume it was hard for your wife, not knowing anything about you for all those years, not knowing if you were alive or dead."

Whitmore studied her face. She looked pretty for she was very calm and she spoke with gentleness. Yet, there was a tenseness about her as if she controlled both the calm and the gentleness, forcing them to be upon her.

"I believe Lee will see it that way, too," she went on. Her eyes were direct and, unlike her outer appearance, were uncertain.

Lee looked at her and his eyes were glazed. "But you did not finish," he began but again she interrupted him.

"For this time, Lee. For now," she said and motioned to Karin to lead him toward a chair. Karin placed an arm around Lee and they went together. She tried to control his walk; but they both weaved from side to side, and the chair almost toppled over when she seated him.

"Is that not right, Mr. Whitmore?" Mrs. Brantford asked. "What has been done is best for now?"

"For now!" Lee cried out. "Do you realize that 'for now' I have nothing?"

Karin quickly placed her arms about Lee. "Lee," she whispered soothingly, "don't carry on so."

"There has been much champagne," Mrs. Brantford said.

Whitmore nodded. "I know."

Yet, Lee cried out again. "Ha! Such a birthday present! Who do I thank? Ha!"

Mrs. Brantford remained calm and gracious as she stepped toward the doorway. "Perhaps, Mr. Whitmore, another time would be better to discuss things with Lee?"

"Yes," Whitmore replied. "It is good that you and Karin look after him." He turned away, but looked back once to see Mrs. Brantford still in the doorway. She smiled when he looked at her, but then she closed the door.

Whitmore went back down the corridor and soon he heard laughter coming from the back of the stairway. The door to the servants' quarters was opened, and he heard the chatter and laughter coming from there. The staff was having a good time. The merriment was high when the singing began. He thought it was Anton Dyer leading the singing for his voice was stronger than the rest. It was not melodious singing or a particular song, but just happy singing to blend with the laughter. Whitmore thought for a moment that he would like to join them, but changed his mind and went back to the stairway and up to his room.

The following day, Whitmore went to the offices of Norman, Benchley and Sundahl. For a moment, he stood outside the glass doors and looked in upon Miss Martin who was busy sorting papers at her desk. She looked up immediately when Whitmore opened the door. Her eyes blinked behind her spectacles, and then she lowered her head and raised her eyes to scrutinize him over the top of the spectacles. Her large eyes brightened with surprise and her lips turned into a smile as if she was pleased by Whitmore's appearance in good, well tailored clothes for she said, "You are looking very well, Mr. Whitmore."

"Thank you, Miss Martin," Whitmore replied and asked to see Grant Deakins.

Without hesitation, she sent the message through the electronics system, and Whitmore was told, with another smile from her, that he could "go right in."

Grant Deakins did not come out to meet him but waited at the door of his office. As usual, he was immaculate in dress and appearance, but his face was serious and weary and he stood like a cardboard poster in the door frame. His eyes brightened also as he observed Whitmore's dress and poise, and he greeted him with a quick handshake and led him into the room.

"Sit down, Collis," he said eagerly and Whitmore took the same chair he had when he came into the office about three weeks ago. The chair was comfortable and Whitmore remembered how to sit easily into the soft leather folds. Grant Deakins moved to his place behind the desk and began to gather together some papers which were before him.

"Am I disturbing you?" Whitmore asked. "I know I have no appointment."

"Oh, no, not at all. I am glad you came, Collis," Deakins answered hurriedly. He smiled but the expression on his face and in his eyes remained serious and steady. He placed the papers in a neat stack on the side of the desk so the space before him was smooth and uncluttered.

Whitmore began to talk on the level of the cleared desk, gradually raising his eyes to Deakins' earnest face. "I came to see you," Whitmore began, "because there are certain matters to be straightened," he paused before he finished, "after yesterday."

Deakins said nothing, but Whitmore noticed that his eyes flickered.

"First," Whitmore went on, "there are two things." He shifted his position in the chair and a lump of cushion hit him in the back. It felt awkward and he shifted again. "The first thing is about the will. Gessie made some unusual provisions, I know, but I think I understand why she did it."

Again Deakins said nothing but nodded his head.

"But I can change things, can't I?" Whitmore asked quickly.

Deakins' look was steady, studying Whitmore; but his voice was casual when he responded. "You are the sole inheritor, Collis. You may make any provisions or changes as you wish."

"Well, I thought about my sons," Whitmore continued. "They are twenty-one now. They want to be on their own and have their own lives."

Deakins moved and arched his back. His head raised but his eyes were closed. "That is is understandable," he replied and there was a gasp, reflecting pain, in his voice.

Whitmore did not respond for he himself felt uncomfortable as he leaned deeper into the chair cushion to avoid the irritating bulge that rubbed against him. "The second thing is that I am concerned about their lives. I did nothing, I was not able to do anything for them while they were growing. I had no influence but now I can, or should I say, I am in a position to do something about their future."

"Yes," Deakins answered simply.

Whitmore's throat felt dry and he began to cough. His voice was rasping as he continued. "Lee and Lester had plans. I know. I could just give them money to do what they want; at least, what they thought they would receive if I had not returned." He paused to cough, then looked directly at Deakins. "But I won't do that," he said evenly.

Deakins' eyelids moved and his eyes closed briefly but he remained composed.

"I won't do that," Whitmore repeated. "Yet, I will make provisions or changes, as I said. Lee wishes to start a business of his own. I would like to give him that start, but only that. You will set up a fund for that business only, no allowances or extra funds for anything else, only the business. He will have to work and make his own success in the business he wants. You understand, Grant?"

Deakins nodded his head slowly. "Yes, I understand."

"I wish you to consult with firms about the business that Lee wants to establish. Get the costs then let me know the figures and I will set the amount." Whitmore stopped for he saw Deakins arch his back again and a swift look of pain came over Deakins' face. "Are you all right, Grant?" Whitmore asked.

"Yes, yes," Deakins answered quickly. "My back has been giving me a bit of pain lately. Not constantly, just every now and then it acts up; nothing to worry about." He hesitated and then laughed. "At least, for now."

Whitmore studied his face but observed that the pain did not disappear quickly from Deakins' face. He said no more about it, however, but stated, "You know then what I am asking you to do about Lee?"

"I understand," Deakins replied, "and Lester?"

"Lester," Whitmore whispered softly and his head drooped. "The dear boy; he wants to be an archaeologist and go off digging in all kinds of places."

"That is his interest, Collis."

"Yes, and if that is what he wishes to do, his education should be completed. I want that; a fund must be set aside for that. For him, also, I want no extras, no money 'just given'. When he finishes his education, he must take care and support himself."

Now, silently, Deakins leaned forward and reached aside for papers and a pen. "And the remaining?" he asked solemnly as he began to write. "Any other dispositions, Collis?"

Whitmore had a strange feeling of relief; he relaxed and began to pull himself upward from the folds of the soft chair. "The estate can be sold," he said evenly. "Whatever accrues, I believe, will be added to my portion. The servants and the staff, as you know, have been provided for."

Deakins did not look at him but continued to write. "Any plans for yourself, Collis?"

"Well," Whitmore answered, "I believe we are getting on, Grant; we are beginning to feel our aches and pains."

"Yes," Deakins agreed.

"I do get this cough now and then. And if it continues," Whitmore coughed again as he spoke, "I may go to a sunny and warm climate. Winter is coming on, you know, and I am not certain that I wish to stay around."

There was silence between them and Whitmore stared at Deakins, not willing to interrupt the writing, his instructions, that Deakins was putting down on paper. Deakins paused and then Whitmore spoke. "Do you think me hard or cruel that I give so little to my sons?"

Deakins continued to look downward. "That is not for me to say, Collis. Everything is yours to do with as you decide."

"The boys are provided for," Whitmore said quietly. "I had to do that for them." He paused and repeated, "Of course, I did not give them what they would have had if I had not returned." He glanced at Deakins who continued writing as if he had not heard. "About my return," Whitmore repeated in a louder voice. "Has anybody said anything unusual about my return?"

Grank Deakins stopped his work and looked directly at Whitmore.

"Collis, you know there were many things *said* about your return. Unusual? Perhaps, because it was so unexpected, a complete surprise to everyone. Surely, you understand such a reaction?"

Whitmore leaned closer and he almost touched the desk. "Yes, that I know, but there may be something else."

"Something else?" Deakins asked slowly.

"I thought perhaps you were contacted," Whitmore answered, still straining his body forward.

"Contacted, Collis? By whom and about what?" A strange look of surprise and distress came over Deakins' face.

"I am asking if you were contacted about me—about what I did before I came back? Somebody?"

Deakins tilted his head back which gave an arrogance to his appearance because he did not smile, and his lowered eyelids seemed harsh and scrutinizing. "It might be time, Collis," he said and his voice was firm and steady, "to be very frank about what you call 'your return'. It is on your mind and now you are asking me if I have been 'contacted'. That seems strange that anyone should contact me. Why? No one did, but I will tell you that I did some contacting about you. Yes, I checked on you. It was the right thing to do and, of course, my duty as far as the estate was concerned. After all, twenty years and not knowing if you were alive or dead." Deakins stopped and grabbed his back as, once more, the pain crossed his face. He waited a moment and then went on. "When I saw you here in my office, I was surprised. Very much so, and why not? To see you after all that time! Collis Whitmore, standing there, so subdued, so silent and uncertain, that, indeed, you seemed like a ghost. You looked older, a change to be expected. But to come back just when the estate was about to be settled. I had to wonder if you could be an impostor and when you explained 'amnesia', I thought how logical. A perfect arrangement. Do you blame me, Collis, for being suspicious?" Deakins paused again and lowered his head slightly. "So I had to check you out and discover if your story, so to speak, were true. I had to look at you as a stranger amongst us, until I got my report and I knew."

Whitmore nodded his head. Of course, he said to himself, you would do that. I knew, Grant Deakins, that you would do that. I knew it was necessary for you to do that.

"You were on the ship *Bellmann*," Deakins went on. "It was sunk but you were one of the fortunate ones to survive. You were taken as a refugee to Port Bold."

Whitmore looked up quickly as he heard Deakins' words and he began to feel perspiration breaking out on his body.

"Do you remember that, Collis?" Deakins asked quietly.

Whitmore did not answer. The perspiration around his body seemed to become heavier, and he was aware that his face was wet around his upper lip and on his forehead. So the question was asked: 'Do you remember that?' His answer—he halted in his thinking and wondered, should I admit all now?

Deakins began talking again. "After several years, Collis, you ended up in Tegner and went under the name of James Spenner, but you never had amnesia, did you?"

He could trace all that, Whitmore thought, the physical things, where I went and my name, but he could never know my mind. "No," he replied softly, "I never had amnesia. The name of James Spenner was one I just made up and used for myself."

"Collis!" Deakins whispered. "All those years! And why now? Why did you return now?"

Should I admit it now, he asked himself once more. He sighed heavily and said slowly, "I came back for the money, my part of the estate. It is rightfully mine, and it is legal. Everything seemed in good order for I trusted an unbelievable piece of good luck that came to me. Out of nowhere, a stranger approached me and told me about the estate to be settled. It seemed so easy to do, and the amnesia story was just the reason I needed to cover my return. That is why I came back. Think what you wish, Grant; I am not asking to be excused on any terms."

"You are proud and serious, Collis," Deakins said at last.

"I have shocked you, Grant?" Whitmore asked.

"Yes, Collis, you have."

"And I have been shocked, too. For I have discovered betrayal done unto me."

Deakins' eyes widened and he stared at Whitmore. "Betrayal?" He repeated the work in a whisper.

"Betrayal done to Gessie," Whitmore replied. "You must tell me how you heard about her death, Grant."

Deakins remained surprised and he seemed uncertain about his response. The stare in his eyes became fixed. "I heard about Mrs. Whitmore's death while I was away at a legal conference. I was called there, and I returned as quickly as I could." He hesitated. "How can you say there was any betrayal in her death? What kind of betrayal do you mean?"

Whitmore shook his head as he heard the explanation of Grant Deakins. He struggled to go on. "You recommended her doctor, Doctor Vargas, did you not?"

Deakins nodded. "He was a specialist and Mrs. Whitmore agreed to see him."

"He was called when she died?"

"Yes, he was called and arrived shortly after I did." Deakins replied, but his voice was shaking with astonishment. "Collis, why these questions? I do not understand."

Whitmore was silent for a moment, then he pushed himself out of the chair. He stood in front of the desk and looked down at Grant Deakins. "Grant, I am not mocking you, but I will say no more about this."

"Collis, what is it?" Deakins asked and his voice was anxious.

Whitmore shook his head. "I cannot say more. I do not wish to upset you, Grant, for you have been good to my family, serving us all through the years." He glanced down at the one piece of paper on the desk in front of Grant Deakins. He tried to smile as he said, "I know you will handle properly all the things that I have asked."

Chapter Sixteen

The weather turned cold for the Brantford engagement party. The guests quickly left their cars and scurried up the short stairway where the door was opened immediately so they could enter the warm and dry vestibule without any wait. Nevertheless, most of them shook themselves as if shivering and rubbed their hands together all the while exclaiming such topical expressions "Such a drop in temperature!" "That wind, so raw and penetrating!" and "Whew it is bad out there!" Then they would remove their heavy coats and parkas and fur lined boots and gloves.

After they shed their wraps, the guests stepped into an adjoining room, and soon a glow came over them as they began to appraise the dress and appearance of others and sort out their companions and escorts. Their enthusiasm was heightened more by the sight of tables filled with food and drink, particularly one table which contained a bowl of hot, spicy punch. The aromatic vapors of the punch were overpowering and hung heavy over the table. The punch was dark red in color, indicating the wine choice and contained raisins and almonds as well as cloves, orange rinds, and cinnamon sticks. The potency was in the warmth of the punch and the guests were warned, jokingly, to take very little for it would "take the chill out of every bone in the body!"

On the food table, appetizers were arranged and decorated like a flower garden and almost as fragrant. There were hot and cold meats, cheeses, tidbits of breads, and raw vegetables and fruits, and small pancakes set aflame in thin, delicate sauces. The tone became convivial as the guests crowded both tables, laughing and talking; and no longer did anyone mention the weather, it was entirely forgotten.

Whitmore and Lester came together. They entered the lively room at the same time but Lester went forward alone to the food table. Whitmore hung back in the doorway, to scan the crowd. He was dressed in his new tuxedo and that, at least, made him equal with the other men. The crowd, as expected, was mostly young people. He saw many who had been guests at the birthday luncheon. He saw Roger Manning and Grant Deakins standing apart, like himself, but smiling upon the young people.

Mrs. Brantford approached from another entrance and when she saw Whitmore, she moved across the room toward him. Her movements were relaxed and assured and she paused to greet Lester and say a few words to nearby guests. When she reached Whitmore, she looked at him directly but a stiffness had come over her. She tried to smile out of courtesy, but her lips parted only slightly and her eyes were firm. Her greeting was brusque and very short as if she realized that she could not hide an unfriendly feeling toward him. She stood before him, elegant and commanding in appearance. Her dress was white, of a shimmering material, and she wore a jeweled ornament in her hair. Whitmore bowed to her greeting and he was able to smile at her.

"Have something to eat and drink," Mrs. Brantford said curtly, turning slightly toward the tables. "Dinner will be later." With that, she turned completely and engaged a young couple in quick conversation.

Whitmore still smiled to himself and made his way toward the tables. As he came near them, he saw Lee and Karin standing in a circle of laughing people. Karin had a glass to her lips and her head tilted backwards so Whitmore could not discern her expression, but Lee was boisterous, laughing, talking briefly, and then laughing again. When Karin lowered her glass, she saw Whitmore and stared at him as he approached. She smiled as briefly as her mother had done, then raised her glass to him and drank again. Her hair was arranged on top of her head and the straps of her vivid blue gown were low on her shoulders so that her neck was pink and smooth when she thrust her head back.

After Karin raised her glass, the gesture made Lee turn around and his face flushed deep red when he saw Whitmore. He gazed steadily at Whitmore but then he laughed and the laugh was embarrassed also as he pulled Whitmore into the circle of guests. He introduced his "Dad" in a light manner, trying to laugh but his voice was brittle. Whitmore stood stiffly and looked around at those who looked at him. He bowed his head to the guests, but he noticed that Lee's levity did not extend to them for their faces had a perplexity

272

about what to do. They glanced at each other and Whitmore heard a whispered "Dad?" as a question and a few surveyed him outright with curiosity. Whitmore guessed that Lee had told his friends very little or nothing about him, but a vacuous young lady giggled and said, "Oh, you?" Fortunately, the rest did not question, and Whitmore bowed out and moved away. He looked back and saw that they shrugged their shoulders and returned to their own talk and, apparently, they became disinterested in him quickly.

He went into a second room where small tables had been set up with cloths and flowers and were occupied by those who had carried in their laden plates and glasses. Music was supplied by a group of three men in formal dress who played softly and in moderate tempo. Despite that, the room was as noisy with laughter and talk as the first.

Whitmore glanced around the room, but this time he looked at the walls for they were covered with paintings. They were nondescript except that there were so many of them. Whitmore moved closer and saw that they were Karin's paintings. To see a few was to see them all for there was nothing life-like or realistic about them, although the subjects varied from faces and animals to flowers and landscapes. Color was there in each painting, but the general range of all of them was flat and uninspiring.

"Waste!"

Whitemore turned quickly as he heard the word spoken beside him. He did not see anyone for the voice came from behind a large frond of a fern plant. Whitmore carefully parted the fronds and identified the presence of a slim, blond, young man who wobbled unsteadily on his feet.

"Waste!" he said again as he blinked at Whitmore.

"Waste?" Whitmore repeated the word and he saw the young man place an empty flask in the planter.

The fellow's head bobbed like a cork when he nodded. "Waste of everything! Everything is wasted!"

"You don't like the party?" Whitmore asked.

The fellow stepped out from behind the plant and swayed toward him. Whitmore became aware of the alcoholic smell of him and he could see that the young man's shirt was damp and warm. "I am one who would like to blow it all up!" he stated in a wavering, uneasy voice. "All that gluttony! Everybody overdoes it! Blow it up!"

"You are a friend?" asked Whitmore, hoping that the fellow would give his name.

The young man interrupted. "I know them all, but I see things differently than they do."

'It is waste, you say?"

He nodded again. "Saturnalia! Only they cannot see it. They think it so much fun, so enjoyable! They want so much!" He was silent for a moment and then concluded with a hiccup.

To Whitmore's surprise, the young fellow stepped out onto the floor. There was no dancing for the music was intended as soothing background for the guests at the tables. Nevertheless, the young man began to sway and turn his motions into a solo number. He mimicked the music by snapping his fingers and began to tap his feet on the slick floor until it sounded like exploding firecrackers. The musicians looked grim but continued to play. Whitmore heard excited gasps from the guests at the tables. They were momentarily rigid with surprise as they looked at the swaying fellow. Soon, many of them grinned in amusement and one called out, "Keep going, Harry!"

Harry's eyes widened with glee after the shout of encouragement, and he increased his swaggering tempo and he hopped around more wildly, swinging his arms and shaking his head, altogether in an imperfect rhythm. "Blow it up!" he exclaimed. "Blow it up!" but the guests laughed now and applauded his dumb comic performance.

At the sound of the commotion, Mrs. Brantford appeared at the entrance. She gasped and her eyebrows raised slightly at the sight of Harry. She smiled weakly as she looked around at the guests, but her smile at him was derogatory and condescending. Harry, in turn, exaggerated her smile and tossed his blond head wildly and gave her a salute with a wave of his arm. She turned quickly and signaled the orchestra to cease playing. She announced that dinner was ready and she swept away toward the dining area.

Whitmore held back, remaining on the periphery of the clusters of guests, noting their scramble to group together and to find partners. Harry had stumbled into a chair where he almost collapsed but was picked up by a tall girl with red hair. She took his arm and lifted him and finally steadied him on his feet. He smiled broadly at her, pleased, not only by her obliging assistance, but what he probably thought to be pretty looks. Her head came almost under his nose, and when his head swayed toward her, his face became buried in her mass of tight curls, most likely natural, and tied in place by a green ribbon which matched her dress. Delight shown upon Harry as he did another dance step and instructed her in a few more dance struts. They made their entrance into the dining hall with a kick and a leap.

Whitmore saw Roger Manning approaching from the vestibule. They sighted each other at the same time, so Whitmore had to wait as Roger Manning was coming toward him. There was a sensual, easy smile on Mannings' lips.

"So, Mr. Whitmore, you have come?"

Whitmore was uncertain about the greeting but he replied, "And why not? This is my son's engagement party."

"I thought you might be on a spree of some sort," Manning went on, "as I understand, you are a very rich man now."

Still uncertain, Whitmore answered softly, "Yes."

"How good for you," Manning said and laughed lightly. "How nice to have wealth and all that goes with it. But you know what I envy about you?" He paused and his black eyes glistened at Whitmore.

Whitmore looked at him curiously and replied, "No, I have no idea."

Manning continued. "I envy the amnesia."

"Amnesia?"

Manning nodded. "How wonderful to forget. Yes, to forget. A blessing, I would say, to forget oneself and be somebody else. To blot out all reproof and have no pricks of conscience."

"Amnesia is an illness," Whitmore said quickly.

"If so, then it is a blessing without suffering, is it not?"

Whitmore answered slowly. "I do not know about amnesia."

"The results!" Manning continued. "The results! Look at them! Twenty years you can be someone else, not knowing, not caring about your real person, then come back, accept your wealth and live, as they say, happily every after. Remarkable, don't you think?"

Whitmore shook his head. "I cannot say."

"Ah but to me it is. To become a different person for a time, to act and think in another zone entirely."

Whitmore stared at Manning. The artist's eyes were glistening with pleasure; his voice was low and soft, and he seemed believable for what he spoke. Looking at him, Whitmore laughed. "Perhaps you have a point," he teased. "Amnesia might be remarkable if one wishes

275

to forget something for a period of time, but it all hinges on control. The fantasy can be appealing, as you suggest, but I do not believe that amnesia is a thing to be put on and off as a matter of conscience."

"Is it a dream then?" Manning asked and shrugged his shoulders. "For you, it was a dream?"

Whitmore turned away. "I guess we should follow the others. We are last." Manning shrugged his shoulders again in an insolent gesture and stepped ahead of Whitmore and walked into the other room.

The tables were well set and attractive. They were covered with ecru lace clothes made in a circular pattern and with scalloped edges. A winter bouquet of chrysanthemums and evergreens was placed in the center of each table and was flanked by two tall white candles. White napkins were placed upright before the dinner plates which had a scenic design of a horse and sleigh in a snowy setting. The glasses and silver were highly polished and each had a vine pattern curling up the stem. It all made an eye-catching scene for there was much to look at; a conglomerate of patterns and designs, all different and not so simple, an acceptable blend but not reflecting a precise and exact taste.

Whitmore was seated across from Harry and the red-haired girl, both still engaged in pleasant, laughing banter. Mrs. Brantford had taken her place at the first table and she sat tall and straight, facing everyone with dignity and haughtiness. Karin and Lee were seated beside her. Their expressions were strained and bewildered, and they made no attempt to smile. Whitmore gazed at them for a long while and wondered. There was an unhappiness upon both of them. The gatherable joy that they always had when together was gone. Their party, Whitmore said to himself. Why are they not pleasant and happy and, at least, make a better show of it for their guests? Then he thought, perhaps they are too young to make a show of feelings when their mood was otherwise.

Would anyone else notice, Whitmore thought, as he looked around the room. Roger Manning and Grank Deakins were seated next to each other. Grant Deakins had a soft cushion against his back and occasionally a look of pain came over his face. Both men, however, were watching a threesome seated across from them. The trio consisted of a gaunt-looking man in a shrimp colored shirt and a girl on either side of him. Whitemore heard one say, "sisters," but it seemed unbelievable for they were so contrary in appearance—one blond and the other brunette, plump and thin, quiet and vivacious. The brunette was the thin and quiet one, and she sat obediently, but the blond girl had carried grapes with her from the fruit bowl in the other room and was plopping them into her mouth. The man gazed upon her and her chewing gave the appearance of talking to him. But in fact, all were silent.

Whitmore looked for Lester and saw him seated next to a very pretty woman, delicate looking, with small features, and beside her was a man with an intense look on his face, extremely composed and stiff. Lester was especially absorbed in the woman, looking directly at her with a rapturous look on his face. She seemed flattered and smiled at him, shaking and nodding her head.

Then the dinner began. There was a variety of wines to go with meat and fowl as well as breads, several vegetables with sauces, and an odd salad with sardines. The guests seemed satisfied and happy for their laughter and talk became increasingly clamorous as they consumed the food and drink.

Whitmore enjoyed the meal, too—what little he ate of it for he was more interested in the conversations around him. His attention was piqued when he first heard Karin remark, "Paris is out," which was followed by "talented daughter" from Mrs. Brantford. Whitmore cast a glimpse toward them and he thought he saw them looking at him, but their glances were averted so rapidly that he was not sure. Mrs. Brantford, especially, had turned her supercilious glare on Harry and the red-haired girl. Indeed, the two of them were obviously reveling in each other's company for their laughter was never ending, one giggling and then the other continuing when one stopped, then they would join in chorus and laugh together so their mirth was perpetual. It disturbed Mrs. Brantford for her look upon them was caustic and her smile, when she tried to smile out of toleration as hostess, was irreverent. She no doubt thought them boorish and disrespectful, and thus, demeaned her party and the other guests.

Whitmore laughed to himself, partly to see the displeasure of Mrs. Brantford, and because he truly thought Harry and the girl were delighted in each other. Whitmore was amused at the sight of these two young people bound in a joy that seemed nonsensical. Their first reaction to one another was an exuberance, a blithe feeling that resulted in their exaggerated display of laughter and giggling combined with loud voices and silly chatter. A show-off performance, to be sure, that set them aside in their own world of perspiring faces, glazed eyes, and smiles so locked in place that it seemed a wonder if the mouths should ever close again. Ah! thought Whitmore, it is a court-ship ritual and a joy if only to be accepted for the two people involved.

Once, Harry caught the look of Mrs. Brantford upon him. Of course, he mistook its intent and he believed he had enthralled her. In reply, Harry raised himself from his chair and toasted her from his section of the table. Mrs. Brantford looked away immediately and frowned. Karin and Lee had looked at Harry also and Karin had seen her mother's displeasure, yet, the two of them seemed unperturbed, bound by that odd sense of disharmony between them.

Poor Harry misjudged it all, thinking he was particularly enter-taining and had gained the approbation of the givers of the party. So, after his toast to Mrs. Brantford, he announced, "I shall tell a joke!" The red-haired girl screamed with delight and clapped her hands. The other guests turned toward Harry. Some were stiff like an au-dience waiting for reaction, others were amused, and Mrs. Brantford's face, for the first time, changed color as a flush crept around her cheeks and forehead.

"There was a man," Harry began, "a well-do-do man who lived in a big house and had many possessions, but he was not a happy man for he was much put upon by others. One day, he bought a new pair of trousers but the legs were about three inches too long. To save a few pennies, like all wealthy people do, he took the trousers home and asked the maid to take three inches from them. 'I have no time,' she replied. 'This is the canning season. I have too many jars of this and that to put up and the mistress would dismiss me if I did not do this task'.

"The man sighed and went to his wife. 'Shorten your trousers?' she exclaimed.

"'Only three inches', he replied meekly.

" 'How can you ask?' the wife announced. 'This is the week of the Charity Bazaar. Really, I am too busy'.

"The man nodded and with the trousers over his arm, he ap-proached his daughter. 'My dear, can you shorten these trousers, only three inches, for your father? I would be so grateful'.

"She began to wail. 'Oh, Daddy, not at a time like this! I am

278

going to the Musicians Dance and I must have the last fitting for my new gown!'

"Well, the man, so put upon, just shook his head and walked away. He put the trousers back in the box and left it on the hallway table so he could return to the store the next day and have the adjustment made. 'I will have to pay the price,' he said with regret as though it would be his last coins.

"But the maid had finished her canning task and the kitchen had all been cleaned. She thought about the master and told herself that she should have altered his trousers. Yes, she should do that for the master. She tiptoed into the hallway, took the box back into the kitchen and cut three inches proper from each trouser leg.

"That evening, the wife returned from her meeting. Passing through the hallway, she saw the box with her husband's trousers. 'I should, really,' she said to herself. 'I should really do that for him'. So she took the box to her room, altered the trousers three inches, and happily returned the box to the hallway.

"Later that evening, the daughter returned from the dance. She was happy because she had been popular and had partners for every dance. Still joyous and wide-eyed, she spotted the box on the table. 'Daddy', she sighed, still in the glow of her triumph. 'How little to ask. I shall do it for him. I cannot sleep anyway. Only three inches to cut off.' She took the trousers and did likewise.

"The next day, the man returned the trousers to the store and requested that they shorten the trouser legs. Afterwards, he put the trousers on and, before a horrified clerk, he stood there in trouser legs as high as his knees."

The guests responded to Harry's joke with abandoned laughter, perhaps more for his arrogance and foolishness than the joke itself. The redhead, of course, was sincere and clapped her hands and laughed with a gaiety to be wondered at.

"Flood pants!" someone called out raucously. "The man was ready for the flood."

Whitmore laughed, too, not heartily, but at the genuine spell of mirth which had been created. He should his head and looked at the first table for the response he suspected from there. Some undercurrent laughter had trickled down that way, but it ended with Mrs. Brantford who now was visibly angry at Harry and his friend. She glared at them, trying to be outwardly calm, but she was breathing heavily as her chest was heaving. Whitmore could hear her mutter "the loud-mouth" and "inconsiderate" as she droned on in anger. At last, she rose and stood straight as a beam before her guests. She surveyed them with a haughty look as if to quiet them, but she regained enough dignity to announce that coffee would be served informally in the room just off the entrance. It was obvious that she wished to break up the table arrangements and scatter the guests to overcome the embarrassment created by the rowdy Harry.

Whitmore noticed that Grant Deakins was one of the first to rise from his chair. He rose slowly, and he did not look well, but he seemed eager to escape from the gaunt-looking man and the two sisters. Roger Manning, however, did not move so rapidly as he seemed enchanted by the girls. He moved around the table toward them, and Whitmore concluded that he intended to take one of the maidens off the young man's hands. The blond girl, who had eaten grapes, had risen as she saw Roger Manning approaching. She smiled and turned her gaze fully to him. A look of impudence came over her face and she twisted her shoulders and tossed her blond tresses around with the movement. The gaunt-looking man was up. He looked at her and his face became as shrimp colored as his shirt; and he looked uncomfortable and upset. It is well, Whitmore thought, that Manning take the girl from him, but his eyes opened in wonderment as Manning went instead to her sister. Manning leaned over her chair and addressed her directly. She turned slightly and the look of her dark eyes went to him as straight as an arrow. Then she smiled just to him. Manning held her chair, and she rose easily and gave him her hand. They walked slowly away and, oddly, the gaunt man now became more flustered as the blond girl turned on him. Her flirtatious air had vanished. She was agitated and pouted and shook her curls as in a fit of temper.

Whitmore saw Lester coming toward him. The boy was overjoyed and excited as he grabbed Whitmore's arm.

"Dad," he panted, "you will never guess! You will never guess who that is!"

"No," Whitmore replied, trying to be mild. "I will never guess, but who are you talking about?"

"Those people I sat with!"

"Oh," Whitmore said softly for he had noted Lester's absorption in them during the entire dinner.

"That is Maggie Tucker!" Lester went on, pronouncing her name with deliberation, "and I cannot believe what she does!"

Whitmore's forehead went up. "No?"

"She is an archaeologist, Dad, and a world wide traveler. She has been everywhere—to the remotest ruins of ancient cities. The things she told me . . . oh, Dad, I want to do the same. Go to the places she has been and see and dig in those sites!"

"How did she get here?" Whitmore asked.

"She is just passing through. She is a distant relative of Mrs. Brantford's sister, I understand."

"Oh," Whitmore replied, but he did not feel impressed.

"Anyway, she has just been digging into ancient ruins northeast of the city that was Babylon and she discovered several tablets she believes to be part of the writings of the age before the Flood."

"Lester," Whitmore interrupted, trying to control Lester's enthusiasm. But the boy went on.

"She was so ecstatic over her findings that she took no precautions and allowed herself to be captured by bandits."

"My, my," Whitmore remarked, but still Lester would not halt.

"She was held for almost a month. International strings were pulled," Lester finally paused to laugh. "She said 'twisted', but she was released to her husband."

"That him?" Whitmore asked with a nod toward the intense looking man.

"Yes," Lester replied. "Both had to leave the country, and she was barred from searching for any more Flood writings."

Whitmore looked at Maggie Tucker with surprise. She was pretty and fragile looking with small features and a trim body. She did not seem physically attuned to archaeological work, but the appearance may have been deceiving. Her husband was tall and composed beside her. He hovered around her and placed his arm on her shoulders when she moved.

"What happened to them?" Whitmore asked.

"Well," Lester went on, "there was so much ado about the capture of Maggie Tucker because everyone suspected something deeper."

"Something deeper?" Whitmore stared at Lester. "You mean deeper than the stones of Babylon?"

Lester nodded. "There were rumors that *he* is a secret agent, maybe a spy. That is why she was captured; she was suspected of collusion."

Whitmore continued to stare at Lester. The boy's face was shining with enthusiasm. Cautiously, Whitmore said, "Lester, do not commit yourself or get carried away by things you do not understand."

But Lester went on. "Dad, she has asked me to join her next party. They are going into the most primitive jungle on earth."

"You want to do that, Lester?" Whitmore asked quietly.

"I would, Dad, I would." Lester replied as he shook his head vigorously. He was off quickly as he saw Maggie Tucker and her husband leave the room and he followed behind them.

The room where the guests had gathered before dinner had been straightened and cleaned with new cloths on the tables. A heavy aroma of coffee permeated the room. The musicians had arrived, but they were another group, also. They were dressed in a current mode of light trousers and garish shirts. There was to be dancing now, and the music was amplified and began on a loud beat that, once begun, did not seem able to diminish. The music bothered Whitmore for it was too loud and too fast, although it amused him to watch the young people move easily into the rhythm and keep up to the frenzied beat of the music. It became a bobbing and waving and arm raising dance as an abandoned spirit seemed to catch the dancers as they swung about in reckless ecstasy.

Whitmore moved out of the room and back into the entrance foyer. It was empty now and Whitmore breathed a sigh of relief as he spotted a comfortable looking, high-wing chair in a corner. He settled easily into the chair and leaned back against the heavy upholstery. He closed his eyes, not to sleep, but to allow the furious sounds of music and dancing from the next room overcome and numb him into a kind of unaffected lethargy. He continued to hear sounds, however, sounds other than music. They were close to him and he was startled when he realized that the sounds were voices from a half-partitioned room behind the chair.

"But, Karin, we are still going to marry?" It was Lee's voice, anxious and trembling.

There was a hesitation, then the soft, subtle answer from her. "Perhaps."

"Then go ahead with the announcement. Isn't that what this party is all about? To announce our engagement?"

The soft, subtle answer came again. "This party was mother's idea. She wants to do things so splendidly."

There was a pause, then Lee asked, "Didn't you want this party?"

"I guess so, to make mother happy."

"Then why not go ahead with the announcement?"

"Well, I am not certain that mother is so happy anymore."

"Karin, why do you say that?"

"Plans change, you know. Mother thought things were all settled for us. . . ." Karin's voice broke off.

There was another pause before Lee spoke. "You mean about the estate?"

"Well," Karin hesitated and her voice became softer. "I only mean that your father appeared at the right time, did he not?"

"You know that I have always thought his return to be an inconvenient and disgusting surprise."

"He took from you, Lee," Karin's voice had regained a bit of firmness. "I do not like him."

"How do you think I feel about him? I do not even know him; he does not mean anything to me. Of course he is just taking away from Lester and me."

"Of course," she repeated.

"But, Karin, you said your mother was unhappy. I understand that but, surely, you are not going to call off our plans? Surely not?"

There was a silence and no answer. Then Lee continued, but his voice was unsure and pleading. "I can invest what I do get, Karin. I will talk to Grant Deakins about it."

"Invest!" she replied quickly. "Such time with investments! You will never receive what is lost now. I thought we were going to Paris right away. I made plans too, you know. Now I am not so certain anymore."

"We can go to Paris. . . ."

"Ha!" she laughed. "When? After all your investments come through? I won't be able to paint a stroke by then. It would be useless for me to wait that time."

"Karin!"

Whitmore heard a light footstep moving away, then heavier steps following after. Whitmore sat rigid, still listening, but there were no longer the voices from the room beyond. He sat for a while, making certain that no one discovered him. Slowly he moved, easing himself away from the chair and creeping along the shadows of the wall until he came to the entrance of the lively dance room. The dance was continuing in bravado fashion, taking on a heightened excitement and revelry. The ballroom had darkened and colored spotlights flashed like stars over the heads of the dancers. Whitmore could not see the dancers unless the circling lights touched them. One couple he saw was Roger Manning and the dark-haired girl. When the spotlight caught them, she was looking upward at him, not smiling, but holding his gaze with determination. He was looking at her with equal determination and he was holding her tightly. They spun around and came before Whitmore when the lights came on and the colored spotlights and the music stopped.

"Oh, hello," said Manning, almost bumping into Whitmore. "Looking for a dance?"

"No," replied Whitmore swiftly.

"Looking for someone then?" Manning asked, noting Whitmore's gaze around the room.

"No," Whitmore said once more, then turning to Manning, he asked, "Would you mind if I talk to you for a moment?"

Manning seemed dismayed to be asked a professional question at this time, and he looked helplessly at the girl hanging on his arm. "What is it, Mr. Whitmore?" he asked brusquely.

Whitmore glanced around the room once more. "These pictures," he began, "were done by Karin Brantford. What kind of an artist is she?"

Manning shrugged his shoulders. "I would say not much. She is adequate and has painted some nice things, but she does not have the *sense* of what makes an outstanding painting. She cannot paint a kind of life or meaning into a picture."

Whitmore pondered the words he had just heard from Roger Manning—adequate, nice—with which he evaluated her artistic work. Certainly, they were bland words suggesting a mediocrity that Whitmore had felt before.

"I doubt that she would ever get any pictures hung," Manning went on and ended his critique with, "I mean in a museum or gallery." At that point, the girl tugged at his arm for the music had started again and the two of them moved off into the crowd.

On the far side of the dance floor, Whitmore saw Grant Deakins approach Mrs. Brantford. They spoke earnestly to each other and Deakins appeared perplexed and defensive. Whitmore made his way to join them, but he had to make a wide circle around the crowded floor. The music had swelled once again, and it seemed to echo louder along the wall. Whitmore backed away and to the side and then he saw Lester with Maggie Tucker and her husband.

"Dad," Lester said as he came to meet him. "Can you come and meet Maggie Tucker?"

Whitmore glanced quickly at the renowned archaeologist and her husband who were standing close together, looking after Lester.

Whitmore caught Lester's arm. "Lester," he said, "I would like to very much, but not just now. Can I see them a little later?"

"Dad," Lester said softly and his voice was pleading, "she is famous and they both are busy people."

"Later," Whitmore answered and turned aside before Lester could reply. But Whitmore had noticed the startled and chagrined looks on the faces of the delicate Maggie Tucker and her secret agent, or spy, husband. Whitmore was looking for Mrs. Brantford. He saw her at the entrance of the foyer without Grant Deakins, but Karin and Lee stood before her. Karin was agitated, and Lee was speaking rapidly to her mother. They all became stilled when Whitmore approached.

"Where is Grant Deakins?" Whitmore asked.

"He went home," Mrs. Brantford replied with a toss of her head. "He was not feeling well; his back was bothering him. He just said his goodbye and left."

Karin looked at Whitmore and then tossed her head like her mother. She looked sulky and irritated and stepped away when Lee came close to her.

"I see," Whitmore said to Mrs. Brantford. "I wonder, perhaps, if Mr. Deakins discussed anything with you?"

The supercilious demeanor had returned to Mrs. Brantford, and she was thoroughly stately and determined in her manner. "Mr. Whitmore," she replied, "how can you ask? Of course, Mr. Deakins and I have conversed; he was a guest."

"Karin!"

The call came from Lee who had moved toward Karin, but Mrs. Brantford stepped before him.

"I insist on the announcement, Mrs. Brantford," Lee said and his voice was shaking.

"There will be no announcement," she answered firmly.

A sob came from Karin and Whitmore heard an anguished gasp from Lee. "Mrs. Brantford!" he said pathetically, then he tried to turn again to Karin. "Karin," he called again, "we must talk this out!" Beside her mother, Karin gained the same composure. She tossed her head at him and looked at him, straight and direct. Her eyes were moist and the wetness remained under her lower lids, but her glance did not falter. "Mother says there will be no announcement, no engagement."

"But you?" Lee asked hopelessly.

"I have decided the same, and I will not change my mind." Her voice faltered with a sob.

"Go upstairs, Karin," Mrs. Brantford said quickly. Karin said no more but went quickly away, pushing through the couples on the dance floor. Once more, Lee started after her and was stopped by Mrs. Brantford.

Whitmore spoke up. "Mrs. Brantford," he said, "my son deserves an explanation."

He was interrupted by Lee, whose anguish gave way to anger. "You have caused enough," he cried, "for all of us!"

"I want to talk to Mrs. Brantford," Whitmore said with persistence.

"There is nothing to talk about," she answered. "It is settled."

A loud groan came from Lee and he fell against the wall and slid to the floor where he sat, benumbed and dazed, his head bowed before him. Mrs. Brantford glanced casually at him. "I know the truth, Mr. Whitmore, all the truth about you."

"What truth?" Whitmore asked.

At that moment, a body fell into the pots of ferns and both the body and ferns were overturned and spilled onto the floor.

"It is all blowing up!" came a cry from the rubble and immediately the red haired girl appeared, parting frantically over the fern leaves.

"Harry!" she called as she extracted him from the verdure and dirt. Harry was in a deplorable condition; his clothes were messed and dirty, his hair disarranged and wet and one eye was blackened. "Harry!" the girl called again, almost crying. "You and your ideas!

You should not argue!" She cried again at the sight of him and tried to hold him on his feet. "You must tell!"

"Tell what?" Harry's words were slurred.

"Tell what happened."

"Tell nothing," came his reply.

"Harry, you must describe the person who hit you."

"That is what I was doing when he hit me!" replied Harry. "The old horseradish!"

"Disgraceful!" Mrs. Brantford exclaimed. The dancing and the music had halted. A few guests tried to move around and swept the plants and their soil to the side. "There will be no fighting on my premises. Young lady," she said to the red-haired girl who was looking out under the arm of Harry as she supported him, "he should be taken home and put right to bed."

"Right to bed!" Harry shouted. "Dressed? Damnation!"

"Oh," said Mrs. Brantford in desperation. "Whatever kind of friends do young people have these days? Strangers must come. . . ." she shook her head at the guests around here. "Please, do not bother; it will be cleaned. Oh, this disastrous affair! Would that I had canceled it even with invitations and expenses and all! Please, I will summon help." She swung away quickly and left the room.

"Blow it up!" Harry began to sing. "Blow it up!" He and the red haired girl started away. "Blow! Blow!" Harry kept singing until they were out of the door.

"Dad, what happened?"

Whitmore heard the words from behind him. He was startled for a moment for he had stood silently and observed the events which had occurred so quickly and spontaneously.

"Lester," he said at last, turning to the boy. "Just an accident, unexpected." Together they stared at the dirt-laden floor, the plants sprawled forth from their containers, and Lee sitting sullenly against the wall.

"We better help Lee," Lester said and went toward his brother.

Lee threw up his hands in front of him in a combination of anxiety and irritation. "Leave me alone! Go away and leave me alone!"

Lester stepped back. He looked at Whitmore and there was sadness and hurt on his face.

Whitmore took his arm. "We will go now, Lester," he said.

Lester said nothing and he did not move.

"Is Maggie Tucker still here?" Whitmore asked quietly.

Lester shook his head. "No," he replied. "She has left."

"Then we will go, too." Whitmore walked away and stopped once to look back and wait. Slowly, Lester turned and came after him.

Chapter Seventeen

When Whitmore entered Lester's room, the short winter afternoon was beginning to fade. The draperies at the windows still were open, but dusk was settling in the room, matching the twilight on the outside. Lester had been waiting for him, very anxious and worried. Whitmore had seen the shocked look on the boy's face earlier that day when the policemen had come. Whitmore had been ready to leave. He was standing in the hallway; his suitcases, including the cardboard valise, were beside him, and he was waiting for Lester who was coming down the stairway to say goodbye to him. The arrogant and assured policemen had appeared at the door. They knocked loudly and when they entered, they flashed some badges and papers in front of Whitmore. Then, before the horrified look of Lester, they forced Whitmore into the library and shut the door.

They remained there several hours and now, at the approach of evening, they released Whitmore and he went to Lester's room. The boy was standing by the window, looking out into the gloomy space. When he turned around, his face looked more worried than before.

"Dad," he said simply but could say no more.

Whitmore came forward and took Lester by the arm. "Sit down, Lester," he said and walked with him to the small couch. They sat silently together for a long while.

"Lester," Whitmore began. "You are sad and worried. I do not mean that you should be this way. I know I disappointed you by not meeting Maggie Tucker, but I would like you to be as happy and excited as you were about her and her way of living."

Lester shook himself. "I just got carried away, Dad. I have calmed down. Meeting her and hearing about her seemed such a dream. I thought I could get caught up in it, travel anywhere, moving constantly. But really, no. I cannot do it that way. It was all a dream, a joke somehow."

Whitmore sighed. "Yes, Lester, that it was. That entire engagement party was like a dream, dreams that many of us wanted, yet it was a joke with the unreality of it all."

"Many things are unreal, Dad," Lester cried, "like those men that came today. What is it all about? I don't understand."

Whitmore looked at the boy's upturned face. In the dimness, his face was colorless and his eyes cloudy and pale. The eyes were sunken, set back in their sockets, making Lester look more depressed and melancholy.

"They were policemen, Lester. We talked together for quite a while, but they had their instructions to carry out." Whitmore paused and sighed. "It is a long story and, Lester, I am going to have to answer."

"It is true then?"

Whitmore nodded. "It is true. When I was mayor here twenty years ago, I betrayed this city and all its people when the war was on."

A sob sounded in Lester's throat.

Whitmore continued as though he had not heard the sob from Lester. "And then I ran away, took another name, and, Lester, I never did have amnesia. I was called out by a stranger who, unbelievingly, came to me and asked me to be myself. He called me to be Collis Whitmore. Can you believe that? Out of many, he chose me and asked that I be who I really am. Of course, he did not know for he asked me to be an impostor. Such irony! Yet, his purpose was money. You see, he knew about you and Lee and the inheritance, and he wanted me to come back to get my share and divide it with him."

"Dad, why didn't you just come back as yourself? Why did you do it that way?"

Whitmore was quiet. When he replied, his voice was low and shaking. "I was afraid, because of all those years. I was really hiding myself. Then, when the stranger came along, I got caught up in his scheme. To *pretend* to be myself! How could it fail? I saw it as a chance to come back, covered by a false statement of amnesia, get my money and then go away and stay away forever." Whitmore hesitated before he said, "But it did not happen that way. What I thought would be simple and clear has not been so. I deceived myself when I thought I could deceive others."

"Because. . . . " Lester spoke and his voice was choked. He took a breath and then went on, "because of the war and what happened?"

Whitmore nodded. "I will stand trial for it. Those policemen came," his voice was trembling. "I have been reported by Mrs. Brantford."

Another groan came through in Lester's voice. "I cannot believe that Mrs. Brantford would do such a thing."

"She must have her reason, Lester," Whitmore replied. "She reported me as a traitor. She obtained a petition against me. I thought I could get away but now I cannot go anywhere. Such a woman! She wanted so much for her daughter and herself. She feels that I have done another betrayal to them."

The day after the engagement party, Whitmore was called to the office of Grant Deakins. There, again, he gazed through the glass doors to wonder what would happen beyond. He approached Miss Martin to have her look at him through the same round spectacles, her glance now curious and uncertain. He went unescorted into the office of Grant Deakins and only then did he see Deakins as he was rising from his desk chair. Deakin's back was arched over, the first time Whitmore had seen the less than straight posture of the lawyer. Quickly, Whitmore became aware of a third presence in the room. Over the top of the leather chair, he saw the outline of dark, wavy hair. He approached to greet Mrs. Brantford who nodded slightly but did not turn her face to him.

Whitmore felt a new sense of uneasiness. His legs trembled but he went forward to another chair. When seated, he caught his breath and looked again at Mrs. Brantford. Her face was adamant, yet possessed of a sorrow he had never seen and aware that she was trying to overcome the sorrow with anger.

"I have asked you to come, Collis," Deakins began, taking time to reseat himself. He moved around until he was comfortable and could breathe a sigh of relief, "as Mrs. Brantford has a petition which I feel you should see because of the charges."

"Charges?" Whitmore asked quietly, but he did not stir in his chair.

Deakins hesitated but cleared his voice to speak evenly. "For betrayal of trust as a public official." His hand shook as he handed a paper to Whitmore.

Whitmore took the petition, staring at it, but unwilling to read all the words, only understanding their import. He looked again at Mrs. Brantford. Her face remained stiff and unpleasant but resolute.

"Public petition," Deakins went on. "It cannot be denied."

"Mrs. Brantford," Whitmore asked, "why?"

"You have been traced," she spoke defiantly. "You betrayed your public trust."

Grant Deakins stirred in his chair. "Yes, yes," he said quickly. "So be it, Mrs. Brantford, so be it." He turned to Whitmore. "This petition must still be approved, you understand, Collis?"

"There is proof, much proof, of your guilt," Mrs. Brantford went on, "and I feel these facts must be made known."

"Grant," Whitmore asked, looking directly at him, "did you?"

Deakins stirred again and a troubled look came over his face. "I only mentioned that I had a report that you left on the *Bellmann*."

"Making it a clear case of desertion in a time of crisis," Mrs. Brantford stated. "I feel I should do whatever is necessary to see that all information is made known."

Whitmore returned the paper to Deakins. "What then?" he asked.

"If the petition is approved by the court, then, Collis, you will have to stand trial."

Whitmore looked once more at Mrs. Brantford. "You want me to go, don't you? Just as if I never came? But whatever happens, you know it is not possible to stop now and put everything back to where it was, as if I never returned, as if I never existed?"

"Of course I understand that," Mrs. Brantford replied curtly.

"Then are you doing this to me because I arranged that Lee would not get the money you thought he would get?"

"Collis!" Deakins called out.

Mrs. Brantford's face remained stern. "Certainly not, Mr. Whitmore, although I admit that your arrangement, as you call it, influenced our change of plans."

"Change of plans?" Whitmore asked.

Grant Deakins spoke up. "I know you must sell your property, Mrs. Brantford."

Whitmore was surprised. "You are moving away?"

Mrs. Brantford's face flushed. "Yes, we are moving. Karin and I are going to stay with my sister for a while," she hesitated, then

292

added quickly, "but only for a while. Mr. Deakins, you cannot insinuate we are going because of the property."

"There is a heavy tax lien," Deakins answered slowly, "also your accounts. . . . "

"Are overdrawn," she interrupted. "I know, but that is only for the recent expenses of the engagement party."

"It seems heavy," Deakins went on.

"Please," she stated. "That has nothing to do with it. Karin is very upset, rightly so, after all the poor dear has been through, and we are leaving for a necessary change."

"Her marriage to Lee then, with what was left for him, would not have been enough?" Whitmore asked her directly.

Mrs. Brantford became defiant. "Mr. Whitmore, you cannot suggest that Karin was going to marry Lee for money. The engagement was broken, not because of money, but over the *name*. How could my daughter marry a man with the discredited name of a traitor? Whitmore could never be attached to the Brantford name!"

Whitmore answered quickly. "But Lee had nothing to do with that, Mrs. Brantford."

"Karin made her own decision," Mrs. Brantford replied. She tossed her head and her voice quavered. "Oh, my poor child. She so wanted so many decorations from life. And how sorry I am, as only a mother can be, that she cannot have them. Poor dear, she is now saying she must take some kind of examination, my talented one, you understand, must be tested to be admitted to an art school! My little one, who planned to go abroad for name experience and then have her own studio. To think her talent will have to be delayed!"

Whitmore sat back in his chair. Mrs. Brantford's outburst on her daughter was not loud or overly emotional, rather it came from disappointment and a maternal defense expressed in anger. "Mrs. Brantford," he said gently, "your daughter is a lovely girl, but she is not an artist. I have spoken with her and all her talk in French and of the French style was pretentious and juvenile. She has no depth for any of these things, and now I can only believe that those were her feelings also for my son."

"Really?"

"I am sorry we could not be friends," Whitmore said.

"What is that to you, Mr. Whitmore?" she asked. "What is that to you?"

"Your reward for turning me in will be very small," Whitmore stated.

"Really, now," Grant Deakins put in hurriedly. "Perhaps we should say no more. I wanted only to make this petition known." He turned to look at Whitmore and his gray eyes were sad. "I have to do this, Collis, although I am sorry to have to do this against the Whitmores." He sighed and his face relaxed. "Perhaps it will be the last of their affairs that I will attend to, and then I shall take a rest. It is time for that, I am sure, and my health is beginning to confirm it."

Whitmore told the story to Lester. "Mrs. Brantford," he continued, "was quite disturbed. Maybe a choice, or a combination, of losses, money or name, was too much for her and Karin. They had plans, too, but I believe it was best for Lee that he know about them now."

Lester nodded. "Poor Lee."

Quietly, Whitmore asked, "How is Lee?"

"He is," Lester began, "well, he is very down; he is depressed. He kept to his room, and I believe his moods have varied. I went to him, and I could see that, sometimes, he is very angry, then he feels sorrow and loss. When his moods come together, he seems to become hard and a determination sets within him. 'Lee,' I said to him, 'I know it is hard for you, but you have to make an adjustment if you are to go on'.

" 'Oh, I will', he told me and that is when his face becomes fixed and determined. 'I will adjust. I will do what Father directed. I will start a business, and I will become successful because I will believe only in myself. I will do it all my way, and I will never trust or have faith in anyone again, ever'.

"Lee, that is wrong. Just because Karin. . . . "

" 'Karin', he cried out at her name. 'Curse that proud beauty! She could not take my name, she said, because it was dishonored! Oh, but not by me, and for that I could whip her one hundred lashes!' Then Lee broke down and cried, 'No, I could not do that! Oh, that lamb, she could desert me, but never could I harm her in any way! If ever I struck her, I would give her a thousand caresses for every blow!' He cried out again. 'But I never want to love again! Never!

" 'Lee,' I said as gently as I could, 'about our inheritance. Do you think she counted on that?'

"Lee looked at me a long while and his eyes darkened with grief, but I think I hurt him with my question for he said to me, 'Lester, if that is so, if any attraction to me is for money, then I am more certain than ever that I will never, never rely on my feelings again. If Karin wanted only money. . . .' he could not go on and he shook his head. 'I wanted to give her everything she asked. . . .' but, once more, he could not finish the sentence.

"I asked him if he was angry at you about the inheritance. He was for I could see the anger on his face before he spoke. 'How can I not be? If he had not come back! He changed everything, spoiled everything! Lester, we both would have had more. We could do the things we planned, the things we counted on. Why did he do it!' "

Lester stopped talking and his head bowed. Whitmore turned to him and then he reached out and gently patted the boy's head. "I am sorry about Lee, and I am distressed by his bitterness. Are you disappointed in me, too, Lester, about the inheritance? Your mother made the provisions, and I could and did change them."

"No, Dad," Lester answered, but he looked downward. "I do not think like Lee."

"I thought you might think me unfair," Whitmore said, "but I could not give you the full portion and deny Lee. I gave only the minimum to both of you because," Whitmore hesitated and shook his head, "forgive me, but I wanted more for myself. Why? Why? I do not know."

"Dad, it was your decision to make," Lester replied and Whitmore thought he heard a trembling in the boy's voice. "You have given me enough. I can finish school and be on my own. I can go with the classes on digs and, after, perhaps I can get a job with a museum or an archaeological group. What else would there be?" Lester paused. "Dad, do not feel that you have been unfair for if you say that, then you might think so, but I do not. I am happy that you came back, just that. And I do not care about anything else."

Whitmore sat silently for a moment. He glanced toward the window and saw that the dusk was becoming deeper. "I never reckoned on a lot of things by coming back, but the most heartbreaking was to find out about your mother and what happened to her. I believe you, Lester, what you told me about her death. I believe you when you said she was murdered."

"Dad!"

"And I wanted to prove that, Lester. It was sixteen years ago, but I tried to find out why it happened and who did it. I suspected that she was killed because of me, for what I had done. There were three men who knew of my betrayal. They would have motive for revenge and I suspected them right away. I found them, Lester, but I also found that none of them did it. I also suspected Roger Manning, Mr. Hillberry, Dr. Vargas, but without an inkling of evidence. I am not a detective and I do not know their methods, so maybe I did not go about it correctly. There were no clues, no proofs, or indications that I could attach to the happenings of that night. Perhaps there was someone unknown. There were many citizens and soldiers, known not to me, but my family known to them. One of them could have come in the night to take revenge or outrage against your mother."

Lester cried and looked up at Whitmore. "Dad, you believed!"

"That is all I can do," Whitmore replied. "I think it would have been a miracle if I could have done more."

"Dad, can't you see that belief is a miracle in itself? It means everything that you believe me when no one else did. For sixteen years I carried the anguish of mother's death and you alone have taken that away."

"To be replaced now by mine?" Whitmore grasped Lester's head and pulled the boy to him. "Oh, dear son, you must know that if I have any reward in all of this, it is you. I ask only that you do not take my burden upon you as you did your mother's. Lester, do not grieve!"

There was silence in the room. Whitmore looked again straight out into the darkness. Lester looked out, too, his head resting on his father's shoulder. Their faces were blurred and dim in the twilight and, even close together, they could not see each other's face. Only sound, their voices, speaking softly to each other, came through.

"Dad, I must know. Will you be charged?"

"It is a certainty. Grant Deakins has told me there will be a special hearing to set the bond."

"You will have a trial?"

"It is the law and I must go through it."

"What will you say to them, when they ask you why you did it?"

"I think I shall say that I did it to try to prevent the horrors of war."

"Do you think, Dad, that they will send you away?"

"I do not know, Lester, I do not know."

Epilogue

The prison is situated outside the city of Valiterra, in a large enclave between the foot of the mountain and a bend in the river. The nearest building must be a church although it cannot be seen because it is on the other side of the river bend. Yet, every Sunday morning, precisely at ten o'clock, Collis Whitmore could hear the chimes of the bell. There would be five chimes, light and appealing and extremely clear. And for several months now, since he was confined, he would stand very still at that moment and count off each chime.

During his time in prison, Whitmore changed into a man locked within himself, transfixed, hypnotized, incapable of change and dead to any growth. He was resigned from all things and became an isolated man. The isolation was within himself and not without. The bareness and crudeness of the prison did not affect him. Of these conditions he did not complain or wince or indulge in fretful remarks. On the contrary, he never spoke a word about his surroundings or his treatment. He took it all without the slightest murmur. Only when the chimes would ring on Sunday morning would he appear attentive and aware of any stimulus.

It was himself that changed. He had become hardened, not to deprivation or insult, but to his own character. He was immune to his fate, he no longer belonged to himself. There was nothing within to touch or feel. This condition he brought to himself, to be tragically alone, to care for nothing and, thus, to end life within himself. Why then should he listen to chimes?

He had only one outburst before this characterization engulfed him. It occurred at the beginning of his confinement in prison. He awoke one night with a mournful cry and he heard that it was his own cry. He was coming out of a dream—in that state when sleep is leaving and wakefulness slowly takes its place. He heard the cry, deep in his throat, and his eyes opened immediately, but his head was twisting from side to side still in the controls of sleep. He sat up

298

and his body weaved to one side and he perspired heavily. He sat rigid for a minute, listening, but there was no outer reaction. No one was aroused.

In the quiet darkness, he thought about the dream that had made him cry out. He had been walking away from the estate. It was late evening, but back at the estate there was light from the overhanging fixtures on the garage and stables. He entered the sandy path that led into the wooded area. Although the illumination was gone, he knew the way. He stumbled a few times when he accidently stepped into the tall reed grass, and he knew he entered the forest when he perceived the dark, thick outlines of the conifer trees. He reached out on either side of him and he could touch the prickly branches. He began to ascend and he knew he reached the rise in the land. He went forward quickly until he reached the iron fence. The gate was to his side and he pushed it open. He felt the scuffle of gravel on the path beneath him and then he stopped. Ahead, he saw Lester digging in the ground, digging and digging and uncovering nothing but heaping only mounds of soil that grew higher and higher. Yet, Lester persisted; he would not give up. He spaded the earth, cutting deeper and deeper, and then suddenly Gessie appeared, rising out the excavation Lester had made. She literally flew upward and Whitmore saw her coming right at him. He fell down and cried, "Forgive me, Gessie, forgive me!" She did not stop; she weaved in flight toward him. A strange phosphorescent glow suddenly surrounded her and then the scream. At first, he thought it was Lester. But as he was shaken from his own sleep, he heard the cry within his own throat. He had no dreams after that. The unfeeling calmness took over and he became a stilted man.

One day he was told that he had a visitor. Outwardly, he showed no interest. Who would come to see him? He followed the guard like a sleepwalker, and as he moved toward the visitation room, he saw her standing just inside the entrance. Maria Lundee was waiting there, bracing herself against the door frame, her head cast downward so she did not see him immediately. At the movement of the doors, however, she looked up and her eyes flickered with amazement when she saw him. She tried to smile but faltered and her lips remained partly open as if in a limited, weak protest.

When Whitmore first saw her, a feeling of instinctive resentment passed over him. Yet, at the same time, he was surprised that something pierced his heart that saddened him. Her appearance, as always, racked his feelings and the first sight of her appalled him. She was "made up" today for her head was full of the round, golden curls and her lips were a crimson mark on her pale face. How ridiculous, he thought as he advanced toward her, that a grown woman should try to look like a doll and succeed only in making herself appear ludicrous and silly. Yet, her eyes brightened as she looked at him. She moved swiftly toward the visitor's chair. Whitmore sat opposite her and saw that she was not appealing because of her appearance only but because she was distraught and upset. As she studied him, she did not speak, as if she were trying to think of the correct words. Faltering, she smiled and the smile changed her face. It warmed her countenance and made the anxiety turn to sympathy. A simple smile, but for her it was of an enormous quality.

The red lips moved and repulsive as they were to him, he was more aware of her low, soft voice as she said, "James, I heard and I had to come and see you."

His head bowed with consternation as he thought, she calls me James!

"I am Collis Whitmore," he said, almost sternly.

She shook her head at her own mistake. "Oh, yes, I should be careful. But I have known you as James."

"Of course," he said, trying to be gentle, "but how did you hear?"

"I heard," she began. "I came to see you so I could tell," but she stopped and could not continue.

"Go on, Maria," he urged.

"I want to tell you," she started but again she stopped.

Whitmore studied her face which was becoming more and more troubled and her smile had gone. He sensed she was having difficulty trying to express herself. He decided to change their talk and ask about her son.

"How is your boy, Maria."

The troubled expression deepened and she shook her head. "Other treatments may be necessary; perhaps other doctors. At least, other opinions should be given. Oh, James, it is not good!"

She called him James again but her obvious grief and response about her son had her unaware of her error. This time, Whitmore did not correct her.

"Oh, it is a reason why I came," she blurted out.

"What reason?" he asked evenly.

"To tell you how I heard. I heard everything through Alec Thurston."

Whitmore was surprised. "Alec Thurston?"

She nodded her head and a few blond curls had loosened and fell out of place. "He came to see me at the restaurant. I remembered him for he had sat with you at dinner one evening."

Whitmore closed his eyes as he, too, remembered. "Go on, Maria," he said gently.

"He came to the restaurant to talk to me." She hesitated and withdrew a paper handkerchief from her purse. "Alec Thurston told me all about your plan," she went on and her voice was feeble, "and that it failed."

"Because of me? Did he say it failed because of me?"

Her eyes widened as she looked at him, and he saw the depths of bewilderment and disbelief. "I . . . yes, he did, but I could not believe you did . . . Oh, I am so sorry . . . he said you had been a mayor. . . ."

"I was. I was mayor of Valiterra during the war. If Alec Thurston told you everything, then you know of the plan, the scheme, we made together."

"Yes," she said softly.

"It failed and here I am, jailed. And Alec Thurston? Well, I do not know, but you said you saw him and talked to him. Tell me," he urged, "if you came here about that."

"He was a very sad and angry man when he came to the restaurant. He was sad and yet he seemed desperate, too. He complained about his luck. He said he never had any good fortune in his life. He was injured, you know. And he told me how it happened. Such a misfortune for the poor man! He came to Tegner after seeing you. He was a shattered man, he said, after meeting you. He could only cry, 'Deceit, deceit, always in my life!' He went on to tell me about his existence. He had taken residence in an old boarding house, but I do not know the place for the address was not familiar to me. He said he had one room, with only a bed; the light was dim and a faded curtain hung over the window. He told me that at night he heard strange things about the house—voices and soft footsteps. He heard his door rattle and he dared not sleep. And the filth! He described

301

the dirt, the stench of the place, and the vermin that crept over the walls and floor. Such a dreadful place for the poor, crippled man!"

"You felt sorry for him?" Whitmore asked needlessly.

She nodded and more curls became disarranged and hung lower on her neck. She wiped her nose and cheeks with the paper handkerchief. In so doing, she removed a bit of the red lipstick from her lips which made her lose some of the artificialness of her looks. Whitmore stared at her for the loosened strands of hair and the less color on her face improved her appearance to him.

"Perhaps he was only deceiving you, Maria," he said.

"Oh, I do not know; I do not know if he deceived me."

"It would have been deliberate for him to do so," Whitmore stated.

"I only know that he was despondent and said he would not have to endure all of this if you had not deceived him." She looked at Whitmore and her eyes were moist. "I could not believe that. I could not believe you to be deceitful. I told him so, but he said you were a war criminal, and had planned with him to gain your rightful inheritance, but you deceived him and he got nothing."

"Maria," Whitmore said softly, "what he has told you about his living conditions, I do not know. But what he said concerning me is true."

"James!" she said so quickly, so surprised, that again she spoke without thinking. He blinked at her use of his false name but, as before, he did not correct her.

She was breathing slowly. "You, a criminal?" She shook her head unbelievingly. "It is so hard to believe and," her head raised and looked about, "to see you here."

"It is true," he said quietly.

She bowed her head, and he suspected that she was wiping tears for she lifted the paper handkerchief to her face.

Whitmore looked at her but he could say nothing to console her. He only stared at the top of her head, seeing those round, yellow curls that aggravated him so much. Her head trembled with her crying and, suddenly, he felt the pierce to his heart that he experienced when he first saw her. Curiously, the anger at her appearance was subsiding. It did not affront him and he remembered her kindness to him, her concern. He admitted to himself that she was a gentle, thoughtful person, so much influenced by her heart.

"James," she said and raised her head.

"Collis," he replied quickly.

Her eyes were moist but she blinked and tried to smile. "Oh, yes, Collis. It is difficult to use another name."

"I know," Whitmore answered.

"Alec Thurston asked me something else," she went on. "He asked me to be a part of a plan, too."

"A plan?" Whitmore asked, amused but cautious. "Alec Thurston talked about a plan?"

Maria answered slowly. "A plan, he said, that would make all things right for him." She paused and a flush came over her face. "He said all things would be right for him and I could receive a great deal of money. An inheritance, really, if I came forward and said that my boy was yours. . . ."

Whitmore was stunned and he interrupted. "What?"

She looked up quickly for his voice was stern. Her eyes became vague and frightened. "That was his plan, truly. He wanted me to say that about you and then my son would receive an inheritance and he would get a share of the money."

So that was another of Thurston's plans! So frank and clumsy, yet so sly and sharp. The last attempt to gain something of the money for which he had schemed and gambled.

"But I would not do it!" Maria cried and her face remained stricken. "I told him I would absolutely not do such a thing! I came here to tell you, to let you know."

Whitmore stared at her. She almost cried again for her eyes were filled with tears. She looked broken hearted, and he sensed that never was there bitterness or resentment within her.

"Maria," he said gently, "do not be troubled. I know Alec Thurston, and he had a vision to become wealthy by any means possible."

"Oh, I was afraid for you, for anyone to think or believe such a lie. When I turned him down, I was afraid for him, too, for he changed so. If we had not been in the restaurant with others about, it is not certain what he would have done. He began to rave. Oh, not too loudly, but in a dreadful way. Just like someone talking angrily but trying to control himself. He said, 'I know his subterfuge. How slyly he invented the situations and placed me outside, knowing full well I was powerless to protest! He, oh, he thought I was defeated and disgraced. But was I? I, Alec Thurston, defeated and disgraced? Ha!

303

The truth has been revealed that *he* was the scoundrel.' He left then, poor, crippled man, angry and hurting. Oh, poor man!"

There was silence between them, but Whitmore's thoughts were obsessed. At last he said, "Maria, I am sorry for your anguish and all the grief you have been caused. But perhaps you can understand that I am defenseless."

"Oh, James," she stammered. "I mean, Collis. Forgive me, it is not easy to use your true name."

"I know," he answered.

"But we are all so much to be pitied!"

With that, she rose for their time together had ended. Her body was shaking but she grabbed the chair and steadied herself. He rose, too, and though he could not touch her through the glass partition between them, he put his hand before her where he would have touched her face. She smiled now, and she raised her hand and placed it just opposite of his.

"I am not likely to forget what you have told me as well as all your kindness to me."

She blinked and continued to smile. "It is hard to believe that this must be goodbye."

"It is the way."

She nodded an assent and hesitated for a moment. "Yes," she said, "it is the way, but I want to believe that there is yet another way. A way where all bitterness will pass away and there will be no more pain. We must believe that it can be so."

"Yes, he answered softly and, with that, he said farewell to Maria Lundee.

Later, after a time, he was to think more about her compassion. He had believed that he could not have love for others. But somehow, she seemed to represent that it could be so. He thought back to the time in Port Bold when he had trained to be a helper to the sick. Perhaps he could do so again, in time. But he really wanted a way to help Maria Lundee—to repay her charity to him. With that, he thought of the money, how he had wanted so much for himself. The reason, he never knew. It came to him and he arranged that his inheritance should be paid to her for the medical expenses for her son. "This, I believe," he said, "may help the bitterness and the pain to pass away."

There was one who got to the land of sunshine. Anton Dyer, the faithful steward, because of the generous endowment bestowed upon him, was able to go to a sunny land, warm and pleasant, and spend most of his days on a beach. Occasionally, he would visit a local tavern where he would expound on his days of serving a mayor and his household. He tended to become loud in his praise and many people heard him. But they did not object and listened to him without complaint.